Michael B Fletcher is a writer of adult and YA speculative fiction including fantasy, science fiction and horror. His first book *Kings of Under-Castle*, an anthology of humorous adventures featuring two rogues living under a medieval castle, was published by IFWG Publishing Australia in 2013.

Book 1 of his Masters of Scent fantasy trilogy was released in November 2022, with Books 2 and 3 to be released in 2023 and 2024 respectively.

Fletcher has also co-authored *Kat*, a YA science fiction with Paula Boer, which is to be published by IFWG Publishing in October 2023.

Fletcher has also published over ninety short stories, many with a 'dark' or fantasy bent, in magazines and anthologies in Australia, USA and the UK. An anthology *A Taste of Honey*, containing 43 of his stories was published by Double Dragon in late 2021.

He lives in Tasmania, Australia with his wife, Kim.

T0288789

Other Michael B Fletcher Titles by IFWG Publishing

Kings of Under-Castle (humorous short fiction collection)

Masters of Scent Trilogy: Volume 1

Masters of Scent

by
Michael B Fletcher

Masters of Scent

All Rights Reserved

ISBN-13: 978-1-922856-13-5

Copyright ©2022 Michael B Fletcher

Printed in Garamond and Iskoola Pota font types

IFWG Publishing International
Gold Coast

www.ifwgpublishing.com

Acknowledgements

I would like to thank the many people who have aided me in becoming an effective enough story-teller to have *Masters of Scent* published.

First and foremost is Kim, my companion who has had to bear most of the long apprenticeship writing process, warts and all. She has been my main editor and proof-reader throughout the years, sharing my failures and my successes. Without her I would never have achieved what I have.

Then there are the many people along my writing journey. I was fortunate to meet several of my long-term writing colleagues when I began Robyn Friend's novel writing class in 2005 where Masters of Scent began. My main writing companions of Shirley Patton and Paula Boer shared much of the journey, from commenting on the various chapters and drafts to being sympathetic but critical ears to all the processes that writing involves.

The vital area of the writing environment was greatly supported by a small, monthly writing group. Although the members of that group changed over time, other than Shirley and myself, many competent writers have passed through. So, thank you to them all.

Lastly, I'd like to thank Gerry Huntman of IFWG Publishing for his support and belief in my work. I look forward to working with him as each book of the trilogy sees the light of day.

LAND OF EAN
(NORTHERN & CENTRAL)

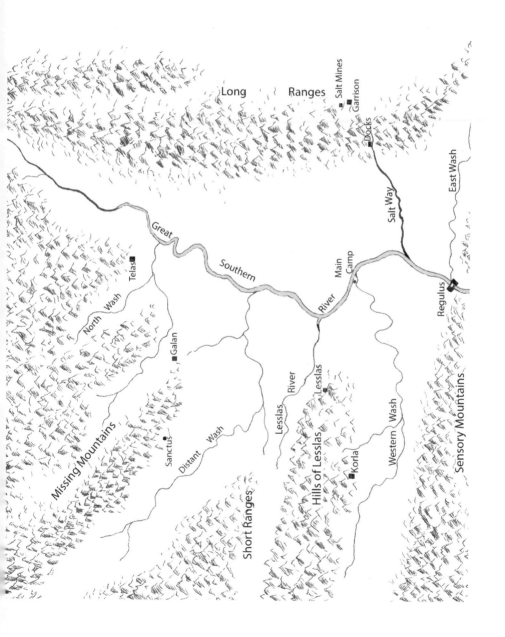

Land of Ean
(Central & Southern)

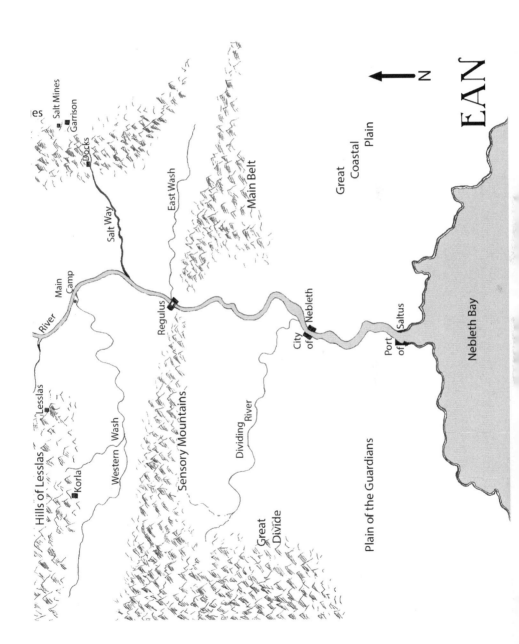

N

EAN

Salt Mines
Garrison
Docks
...es
Salt Way
East Wash
Main Belt
Great Coastal Plain
Main Camp
River
Hills of Lesslas
Lesslas
Korla
Western Wash
Sensory Mountains
Regulus
Dividing River
City of Nebleth
Port of Saltus
Nebleth Bay
Plain of the Guardians
Great Divide

Prologue

The breeze flowed down the hillside, carrying the resinous whiff of pine, an underlying sharpness of menthol, a faint gaminess of male animal, vanilla cut-grass odours, and vague floral hints mixed in with the fading notes of the recent rain. And something else, a scent that triggered a memory.

Frowning, he lifted his head and inhaled through his nose, then his mouth. After taking a few steps, he hesitated. The sun appeared brighter and colours bolder. A brooding greyness closed off his peripheral vision. Sunlight playing on the damp grass picked out slivers of mist that joined to form a faint, irregular line up the grassy slope, shifting as he moved closer.

He crouched and reached out through the mist to stroke the grass. The tantalising aroma tugged at his mind, giving the fleeting sense of something once desired, a memory attractive and compelling. He closed his eyes and inhaled, waiting for a spark of recognition, but nothing came. Disappointed, he opened his eyes and watched the mist rippling along its length, as if it were alive, to where it disappeared into the vegetation covering the brow of the hill.

He followed, his long strides zigzagging along the wispy line.

Ignoring his dry mouth and growing fatigue, he picked his way through the trees and shrubs, his feet occasionally causing wisps of the insubstantial trail to break free. They dissipated in a flash of colour, each time strengthening the aroma. The substance became thicker and easier to see.

The shadows lengthened and grew darker, reminding him that even if he turned back, it would be nightfall before he was home, but the passing of time meant little compared to the pull of the mist.

The slope rose more steeply, stretching the back of his legs, forcing him to slow. The trail oozed like a fragrant soup from somewhere above, moving through and over the bracken and grasses cloaking the ground. As it moved, colours arose, soft pastel pinks and yellows suffused with green and blue, like a predawn sky. He pushed on.

Without warning, he arrived at the edge of a clearing in the trees filled with a

1

swirling, pulsating fog. Tendrils of vapour and odour emerged from the mass like writhing snakes. He stepped back with a gasp.

The fog seemed to gather force as if aware of his presence, the pastel colours filled with a flickering, ethereal light. He reached out to push it away as it neared, but his fingers met a solid, spongy substance his hand couldn't penetrate. He pushed harder.

Again, it resisted.

The aroma filled his nostrils. "Wine-rotted stuff."

The fog muffled his voice, as if absorbing his words. A shape moved towards him through the mist.

"You've come." The voice was slow and indistinct.

The figure gained form as it stepped forward; sharp, dark eyes in a lined, age-weary face. A hand extended in a gesture of familiarity, touching but not penetrating the boundary where fog met air.

"Who are you?"

"I am Quon. I called you. Give me your hand."

The pull of the aroma was so strong he obeyed without thought, but the rubbery presence of the barrier prevented him from grasping the proffered hand.

"Try, for Ean's sake. Try!" Urgency punctuated Quon's words.

The need to reach through the barrier became overwhelming. His whole body ached with effort as he pushed harder. His hand moulded to the other's until only a skin-thin layer held them apart. Colours swirled around him, red streaked with yellow and a deep purple, vibrancy reinforcing urgency.

"Now!" the man called, veins cording his neck.

The barrier snapped. He came through, banging his head into the gravel at Quon's feet. He struggled to sit, groaning and all he could sense was a flood of natural background scents—the aroma was gone.

"What happened?" He looked up, brushing sand from his forehead. "Who are you?"

The older man, thin body dressed in a well-worn grey robe, made no effort to help. He rubbed his chin as he looked down. "You are not what was expected. You are young and show limited control. But you must be the one." He shook his head.

"I've no idea what you're talking about."

Quon's eyes tightened before his head swung away.

A buzzing, barely discernible against the quiet of the clearing, grew louder.

"Quiet. Get away! Hide!" A dark haze of odour rose from Quon's head.

Confused at the order, the young man stumbled away until the trunk of a large tree stopped him.

"No! No!" Quon moaned. The old man dropped to his knees, covering his face with his arms.

A grinding, clattering sound filled the air. A mass of black and yellow burst through the trees. A swarm of creatures, insect-like but twice the size of a man's head, all legs, eyes and jaws, flew straight at Quon, hitting his upraised arms with a heavy thwack. A spray of blood exploded into the air, tendrils of red spreading out like the parody of a whirlwind.

The creatures clung on, ripping at the old man's body in an obscene feeding frenzy.

The watcher retched, his stomach rebelling at the gruesome scene.

The crunching and squelching ceased abruptly. The whirr of wings stilled. Multifaceted eyes and jagged mouthparts swivelled towards him.

Frozen in place, he gripped his stomach, biting his tongue.

With a buzzing of large wings, the creatures heaved themselves into the air, scattering the old man's blood and flesh around the clearing.

The watcher opened his mouth to scream.

Chapter One

A grumble of thunder chased Kyel down the cobbled street. He resisted the temptation to look back as he slowed to adjust his tunic top and resettle his pack. A muffled squawk of protest reminded him of his companion.

"Shush," he whispered, "we'll be stopping soon."

The funnel-like street emerged into the rubbish-strewn marketplace at the less desirable end of Korla. Kyel hoped the smell of decay would overwhelm the senses of those tracking him and the coming rain would wash away his scent.

The timeworn buildings showed little evidence of the stone and brick used in the more respectable areas of town. Built more for functionality than style and permanence, only luck gave them a semblance of being vertical, while some had leant so far they met and created narrow, dark tunnels.

Almost like back home in Lesslas, he thought, scanning the buildings around him. Only in these parts of town could people be anonymous. No one would see or remember him. Most stalls had been cleared and secured against the approaching storm. A few people scurried into shelter, heads down against the flurries of dust already whipping into the gloomy atmosphere.

Kyel targeted a small gap between two buildings which looked like a waste hole for the buildings' refuse. Although dark and uninviting, it offered a place to wait out the storm. He dashed across the square and squeezed into the sphincter-like opening, trying to ignore the smell.

He squatted against the rough wooden wall and squinted across the dusty square. No one seemed to have noticed him, so he wriggled off the pack and eased it to the ground. As he opened the flap, a lizard poked its scaly head out, mouth open, nostrils flaring.

Kyel reached out to scratch it. *Sadir's going to fret. She'll know the seekers are after me but won't know I'm here.*

His mouth tightened. He pushed on the lizard to shove it back into the pack, but a sharp spine stabbed his hand.

He yelped, choking off a cry as the frill around the lizard's neck rose.

The sinuous grey body quivered in alarm, dark eyes staring into the gloom of the passage.

Kyel inhaled deep breaths through his open mouth, his nostrils wide. The acrid odour of sewage hid other, lighter scents, but nothing unusual. Then the first drops of rain added the crisp smell of water.

He shook his head. "False alarm, Tel. Nothing to worry about. Settle down." He grabbed the lizard and pulled him onto his lap.

Tel strained, looking into the darkness. He hissed and stiffened his frill.

Kyel leant forward, alert again. He had great respect for Tel's abilities. Conduvian lizards were more than pets. They had eyes that could see things others couldn't and a well-developed sense of smell. The people of Ean had learned to train the reptiles into highly effective warning systems.

"Better check what's bothering you or we'll get no rest." He peered into the darkness as he stood. Tel scrambled onto his shoulders, clinging tightly, his rough frill scraping Kyel's cheek.

Still Kyel could detect no "wrong" scent. Despite there being no indication of anything unusual, he crept forward in silence.

A rhythmic noise echoed faintly.

Kyel paused, pressed against the rough wood of the wall, as rigid as his companion. The dark ahead threatened. His stomach gurgled as if to relieve the tension, much too loud in the confined space.

"Lizards' teeth!" he squeaked, clutching at his middle. Belatedly he covered his mouth, angry at his breaking voice.

The sound continued; its rhythm more noticeable.

Kyel pressed harder against the wall.

Tel chirped and folded his frill. He scrabbled down Kyel's arm, plopped onto the dirt and waddled forward.

Kyel snatched at the lizard's tail but missed in the gloom. "Tel! Tel!" he hissed, straining to see his companion.

The rain was now drumming against the rooves. Dripping water masked the sound he was trying to locate.

The lizard's distinctive scent, easily picked out among the dust and odours of spiders and other small creatures, led to a gap just discernible between the wooden wall and the ground. The dark space seemed impenetrable. Only his confidence in his companion and the fact it would be a dry refuge made him squeeze under the building.

Kyel shivered. No light penetrated the space. No unexpected smells lingered in the air. Only the noise of the rain and occasional rumble of thunder broke the silence. He hunched over, one hand grasping a wooden support, all senses alert. In the dimness, he could smell Tel.

Now a hint of something else. He peered uselessly into the dark and shivered again.

"Just got to do something."

He felt for a firestarter in his pack, eased it out, and struck it against the side of the support. The sudden light threw back the shadows. In front of him, a large black mass moved.

Kyel jerked back, crashing his head into a beam, almost dropping the light. Pain coursed through his skull. He held out the flickering flame.

A figure, large in the light, backed away, his arms gripped tightly across his body, head half turned and pulled down to hide between broad shoulders. The man in the cramped space should have been pumping out odours, making a palpable stench, but there was nothing beyond background smells of dirt and sweat.

The light flickered. The man's breathing quickened.

"Be calm." Kyel extended his open palm. "I'm not going to hurt you."

The whites of the stranger's eyes flashed.

"Who are you? Where're you from?" Kyel asked.

The firestarter snapped out, plunging them into darkness.

Kyel held his breath. He heard Tel move, his claws scratching on cloth. He could sense the lizard's contentment, heard him settle and give a satisfied purr.

A rasping noise, slow and measured, rose above the background rumble of the rain.

Then, as if a stopper was removed from a jar, the stranger emitted a flood of scent. One moment hidden, the next overwhelming.

Kyel detected the expected emotions—anxiety, stress, alarm—but there was also an acrid tang of old blood, excrement, a residue of unfamiliar smoke, and faintly, very faintly, a must of foreign smells.

Kyel felt for dry pieces of tinder, anything that would burn. When he had a small heap, he struck another firestarter and thrust it into the pile. The flames flared to weakly light the surroundings.

The stranger, slowly stroking Tel's scaly back, stared at Kyel. Worn and dirty, he had a shadow of stubbly beard, and dark hair fell across his forehead. He wore a coarse-weaved coat, dark trousers and solid boots.

Kyel had not sensed his like before.

Chapter Two

The comforting dark cocooned the man against a confusion of intense colours. An unobtrusive sound rumbled in the background until he forced the colours aside. Now the rumble became recognisable, infiltrating his mind as he focused.

He breathed shallowly, but it still came, manoeuvring through the tangle of colours. When it reached him, he grasped it and wallowed in the familiarity of the sound and smell, a bastion, a buffer. *He had experienced it many times before, but when and where?*

His fingers felt textures—soil, small stones, things that crunched, snapped. A tentacle of silk snagged his hand. *Spiders?* "Yes, spiders," he murmured, his voice hoarse.

He moved his other hand and rubbed his chin. The bristles prickled. He pulled his hand away to touch the encrusted tangle of his hair.

He refocused and detected the scent of water on a slight shift of air, an almost pleasurable light tang mixed with fresh mud. Just above his head, wood roofed a vague outline of beams. A fine web covered everything. He leant against a wooden pillar.

A sound diverted him. He peered at a lighter patch in the darkness. Colours leapt, cascading into his brain, odours pouring over him.

With his eyes screwed tight, he smashed his head into the pillar, repeatedly. *When had he lost his memory? What trauma had he experienced?* The pain numbed his confusion, but a trickle of blood told him to stop.

Then he tried to regain his focus. *Rain?*

The sound and smell became a factor. He was back, living the memory, big, heavy drops crashing into his face, streaming over his skin, down his neck, under his collar, gathering at his belt.

He smiled for an instant, in control.

But he anticipated colours waiting for the moment when his attention waivered. A possibility occurred to him. A crack, a chink in his focus, might work,

9

might slow them. It was as if that thought created the action. *Simple.*

A strand of mustard yellow snaked through the gloom, questing like a vine seeking light. It came to him, moved softly up his body to be absorbed. A memory identified the colour: *fungus*. He tasted the individual notes, initial sweetness with a bitter principle as it rolled past his tongue. Ripe flavours with a substrate of rotting wood. The success encouraged him. Many colours pushed to pass his barrier.

But a small tendril, stone grey, was different. It moved purposefully, vibrating as it neared. He tasted it: dry, vaguely pungent with a musty note. It triggered an old memory, one locked deep down: *lizard.* The scent pushed at him; its source closer.

Sounds came, colours flickered. His assurance vanished.

He blocked out the colours, closed them off, and hid behind his barrier, returning to darkness, to self.

A crash of light grabbed and held his awareness. He recoiled, pushing back against the pillar into the narrow space, trapping himself among decaying wood. The light flickered, allowing tendrils of scent to pour out, but he did not dare let them in.

Something nudged his leg.

The grey tendril. The lizard?

Empathy flowed from it, the scents comforting. He focused on the flame and the figure holding it, keeping his arms tightly around his body. He backed harder into the pillar and watched the stranger.

Then the light snapped out.

His attention returned to his leg. Before he could react, the lizard climbed, sharp claws penetrating the thick cloth of his trousers. As it settled it purred, a contented, non-threatening sensation, releasing a comforting scent. He stretched out a tentative hand and touched rough skin. The animal arched its back into his palm as if it belonged there.

A light flared. A sandy-haired youth peered at him from beside a small fire, thin face lit by the flickering flames.

The lizard, black eyes glistening from a visage of grey scales, wriggled higher, stretching, inviting attention.

The youth glanced at the lizard, then at him. He spoke while clicking his fingers towards the animal. The words had a familiarity, but he could not make out their meaning.

The lizard did not respond, lying quietly on his chest.

The youth appeared settled, non-threatening, as he occasionally fed the weak flames with scraps of wood. Background noises added a hypnotic feel to the air.

The man's eyelids drooped.

He woke some time later, his mouth dry, stomach empty and cramping.

Darkness still surrounded him, though a dim light came from further away. The colours had not returned. His control had held. The weight on his chest was gone.

The boy eased away, the lizard a dark shape at his feet.

The man struggled up, brushing against the rough wood as he crawled forward. "Wait!"

The youth turned, hesitated, and beckoned. "Come on, then."

His gesture made sense even if his words were hard to understand. The man scrambled out into the muddy gap. He stood, stretching his back, neck and legs, groaning.

"Shhhh," the youth hissed while moving on.

They crept through the slush in the gloomy, narrow space and paused at the end. An empty, open area spread before them. A light wind blew under an overcast sky, the rain gone.

Half closing his eyes, the man could almost see the thick, noxious vapours from the marketplace mixing into a slurry, outdoing competing odours. A small stream had gathered offerings from the boggy ground and deposited them in a low-lying corner.

He frowned and shook his head.

The youth tugged his sleeve and gestured urgently. "Come!"

Huddled close to the wooden walls of the buildings, they slipped along slightly firmer ground until they reached a laneway where water-filled gutters had left the centre relatively dry.

He was thirsty and hungry, legs feeling the strain as they pushed up the narrow street and past buildings in better repair. It was quiet and deserted.

He put a hand on his companion, stopping him. "Where're we going? What's the hurry?"

The youth frowned at him from a dirt-streaked face. Then he touched his chest. "I'm Kyel. Who're you?"

"Kyel?" The taste of the word rolled around his tongue. He searched through his memories to see if he had a name and grabbed at something familiar. "Targ. I'm called Targ, I think."

"Well, Targ,"—Kyel grabbed at his coat with one hand while pointing up the lane—"If you're coming with me, we've got to go now. No time to talk." He hurried off, leaving Targ to follow.

Odours continually intruded, solid and visible, providing a grey background in the dull light. He shook his head and hurried after Kyel. The odd trickle of familiar, tip-of-the-tongue scents almost caused him to stop to explore their source. Only when they paused at the corner of a wider street did the scents become familiar. Targ drew one in to smother his face like a fresh, warm towel. He concentrated until he could see the pale tendrils—the smell of baking, rich oils and salts. Saliva filled his mouth.

"Kyel, I need food." He rubbed his stomach and pointed to his mouth. The youth shrugged, and then nodded.

With an ease that betrayed familiarity, Targ kept hold of the tendril with his mind and began to track it to its source. He hastened up the street and into a small, cobbled alley where he pointed at a shuttered window. "There."

Kyel touched Targ on the shoulder and held his finger to his lips before tapping on the shutters.

A moment later, a weathered face peered out. The woman's black eyes glanced to each side and then behind them. "Come, come," a large floury hand beckoned them.

"Quick!" Kyel grabbed Targ's sleeve.

They reached a small door set in the old brickwork as it swung inwards. The smell of new loaves gushed out, enticing Targ into a comfortable room dominated by a wooden table and a hot, blackened stove. Lines of flat bread rested on the table.

The face he had seen belonged to a short, plump woman in a light, beige-coloured smock that reached her feet. A dusting of flour covered a faded white apron and the sleeves of her smock. Her eyes widened at the sight of Targ. She twisted the folds of her apron between her hands as she spoke with Kyel.

"It's your time, isn't it boy?" she rumbled.

Kyel nodded.

"And they're after you, I suppose?"

"Yes, not far behind, I reckon. We need some food to get away. Can you help us?"

"What about him?" She glared at Targ.

"He's not able to look after himself. He's not a seeker, though he knows about scent. Sorry."

The old woman harumphed and reached into a cupboard. "Guess you know what you're doing, but you can't stay. You'll have to go. Even now they might smell you've been here."

Targ had edged over to stand near the warmth of the stove and watched the woman handing Kyel small packets of what looked like preserved meats and cheese, which he put into his pack along with several bottles of pale liquid.

He gave up trying to listen in and concentrated on the lizard, who was snacking on the small insects crawling along the windowsill. Then he saw a loaf of bread on the table and reached for it.

"Targ."

He jumped and guiltily stepped back.

"No, Cer, no. Please eat," the woman gushed as she came over. "Take it with you." She thrust the bread back at him.

Targ snatched the food, half-ashamed at his reaction but too hungry to care.

Kyel signalled for him to follow. "You'll have to come with me, I guess. Can't stay here."

Targ groaned and pushed stiffly to his feet. "Speak…slower."

"No time. There're seekers nearby, chasin' me. We've got to go."

The woman thrust several loaves of bread at Kyel and embraced him before helping him on with the bulging pack.

"You better take Tel," Kyel said, as he saw Targ going to the door.

Targ bent down and clicked his fingers at the lizard. Tel leapt to the floor, across the tiles and up the front of Targ's coat.

"Must like my odour more than me," he muttered, mindful that his clothes were stiff with grime. The lizard, which had draped itself around his neck, was like a heavy set of shoulder pads.

The woman quietly opened the door and peered out before motioning them through. She handed Targ a brown cloth bundle, patted his arm, sniffed, and gently shook her head. "Good fortune Cer, and to you, boy," she muttered, touching the side of her nose.

Targ nodded, understanding that she wished them well.

The door snapped shut behind them, closing off the comforting smells.

"What now?" Targ addressed the top of Kyel's hooded head.

People dressed in sombre greys and browns, were picking their way through the odorous slush left by the rain, self-absorbed, rarely looking around. A man passed, leading a couple of large, rank animals, furry and dirty grey, with long necks and calm expressions on their faces. Targ thought he recognised what they were, but a blanket covered his memories beyond the day, filtering bits of the past, giving only frustrating impressions.

A tug from Kyel moved him out of the alley and into the procession of people, Targ making a conscious effort to avoid the strong smell of the animals they passed.

A rough queue of people, animals and carts packed together blocked the way ahead. Kyel pressed closer, leaning into Targ.

Tel hissed. His frill cut into Targ's neck and claws dug into his shoulder. "Damn thing," he shouted, as he attempted to pull the lizard off. Wiry arms pinned his own and slowed his frantic movements.

"Stop!" Kyel whispered, shaking his head. Curious eyes looked their way as Kyel dragged him to one side.

Kyel's distress appeared as odours, hints of yellow and red eddyied around him.

Targ ignored the traffic moving past them as he strove to come to terms with what he saw. The claws hurt, but became an irrelevance as he stared into the river of aromas around him, opening his mind to the intricate confusion of this tantalising experience. The scents, their colours and feel, all had meaning. He could determine their source and their emotions if he focused.

The pull on his arm jogged him from his thoughts.

"What?" He looked into the wide, brown eyes of Kyel.

"They're up there, ahead, just there," he hissed. "We can't be found!"

"What do you mean?"

Kyel huffed and pushed hard back against a wall, his eyes staring at the queue of people. "The seekers," he whispered.

Targ followed his gaze to a disturbance in the movement of the scents around them. Like eels going against the water's flow, solid odour tendrils moved low against the cobblestones, black with poisonous yellow bandings pulsing as they approached.

His barrier of the previous night returned instinctively, forming around both of them. He knew it as it grew. His protective shield was like looking through glass and knowing nothing could break through.

He held his breath as the tendrils reached them. They butted against the barrier, touching, feeling, tasting and then, as if losing interest, moved on. Animals started when touched but no one else reacted. Tel's frill grated against Targ's neck as the lizard watched, following the tendrils until their questing heads moved out of sight. When the lizard's frill dropped, Targ relaxed and his barrier dissipated.

Kyel stared at him. "What are you?" he demanded. "You can't be a seeker. You don't act or smell like them."

Targ shrugged. *How could he explain what he had done, done without thought, if he could not understand it himself? He had no memory of what it meant.*

"I don't know if I should be with you. But"—Kyel took a deep breath as he looked up the road—"we still need to get past there. If we do that, you're on your own. Right?"

Targ nodded as he got the gist of Kyel's words, knowing that danger lay ahead. "What are seekers?"

"We can't stay here," said Kyel, evasively.

"We've got to get through before they notice we've stopped. You're big. If we want to get out of Korla, you have to look like everyone else. Use what the old woman gave you." Kyel tugged at the forgotten bundle still held under Targ's arm.

Targ sighed and opened the bundle to reveal a well-worn, brown travel coat. "Put it on. Quick."

It almost fitted, but his wrists showed past the sleeves and the coat only went halfway down his thighs. A hood at the back covered his head.

"It'll have to do." Kyel nodded briefly. "C'mon, we've got to move. We've stopped here too long."

They slipped back into the traffic.

Targ stood on tiptoe, peering over the crowd, looking for the cause of the hold-up.

"Down!" Kyel motioned, pulling on Targ's shoulder. "You're too big. They'll see you."

Targ slouched down to fit in with the crowd. But he'd seen what was slowing things—men ahead of them were clearly checking for something.

The tendrils of black-and-yellow odour and the men were linked; they had to be, and that was what Kyel and the lizard were reacting to. He risked another quick look. The men inspected everyone closely.

"They musn't catch us, but we've got to get past." Kyel's fears were palpable.

Targ realised he might be able to use this physical form of scent. He gestured at a nearby animal. "Can we get one of these?"

Kyel looked puzzled. "A perac?" He paused, then nodded slowly.

Targ watched the boy edge his way towards a herder who had three of the dirty grey animals. The man looked across at Targ while Kyel spoke to him, then shook his head and started to move on. Kyel grabbed at the man's shoulder and spoke more emphatically, thrusting his finger in the direction they were going. As the herder pulled away, Kyel snatched the tether of one of the animals and hauled the perac towards Targ.

He handed him the lead. "That what you want?"

The herder started towards them, looked to the front of the queue, then hesitated. His anger showed as dark odours, but he did nothing more.

The line inched forward.

Targ pushed the lizard down under his coat, then gritted his teeth before placing an arm on Kyel. He could see Kyel's fear, tendrils of odour twisting and curling, standing out against the background scents around them, even against the brown, ropey stench of the perac. *The men might see it too.*

His mind grabbed the tendrils and forced them down into the spongy mass of the perac's reek. Fashioning a thin, wire-like tendril from an extraneous scent, he stitched the fear into the brown mass, tangling them together like a ball of wool.

The queue moved. The seekers, as Kyel called them, were closer: five solid men dressed in grey with black cloaks, all with daggers on their belts and clubs in their hands. Two held spears. One pushed his club at people whose fear exploded out before disappearing, like breath on a cold day, when they passed.

Scent snakes writhed forth from two other men, their mouths and noses spewing thick black coils that gained the distinct yellow bands as they fell and flowed down the line of people.

Targ's stomach tightened, and he licked his lips, glancing at Kyel pressed into the animal's side, frightened eyes wide, his body made smaller by the bulk of the perac.

Head down under his hood, Targ saw dispassionate eyes glaring at him. A club flexed as it pushed into his midriff.

The head of the club drew out vapours of scent, identifying his smell. He grabbed a ball of background odours and mentally thrust them at the device. When it came to Kyel's turn, Targ did the same for him.

The seeker grunted, gesturing them to move on. Targ almost pulled the perac from its feet to get it into motion. Keeping a lid on their emotional signature strained him. When the greens and browns of the town outskirts beckoned, it was hard not to break into a run.

They breathed a little easier near the town gate.

Then the noise started.

Targ's heart sank as he turned and recognised the man detained by a seeker. The herder yelled and pointed at them.

A swirl of emotions arose from the men, vivid pulsating coils of scarlet and purple—*anger*. Other people shouted and moved towards them.

"No!" Kyel cried.

The strain overpowered Targ. He sank to his knees, the battering of emotions obscene.

"Targ! Help!"

Hands grabbed Targ, pushed him down, grinding his face into the dirt. He cried out as his arms were wrenched behind him. Cords bit into his wrists.

He lost consciousness.

Chapter Three

The culmination of painstaking years of effort, aided by his drive and vision, had seen the land of Ean firmly under Jakus's control, something no previous ruler from Sutan had achieved.

The cities and towns of Ean were now linked by the network of collection towers and efficient scent messaging. Any rebellion had been removed by the capture of scent-talented native youth and their indoctrination into Sutanite ways, those who failed to assimilate discretely disappearing. However, there were still rumours of rebel scent masters.

Jakus gripped the balustrade of the balcony, watching a shimmer of heat rising from the baked brown clay that formed most of the houses in Nebleth. The buildings surrounding the great tower with their cappings of white marble were stately compared to the dwellings in the lower areas. At this hour, only a few traders and their animals were moving, seeking shelter from the sun in the sparse shade of the alleyways.

The stench of humanity was visible in the odorous air, drowning out the duller tones of the rock, sand, and unsavoury wastes, twisting tendrils vying for control. The challenge, the thrill of delving in and selecting the ripest of those essences to mould and use, almost drew him in.

Jakus turned at the movement behind him, knowing it was Septus even before he detected the Head Seeker's distasteful essence oozing through his myriad of masking agents.

"They're ready, Shada," said Septus.

"Lead on, then," Jakus commanded, looking down at the shorter man.

Septus's bent form stumbled as he led the way through imposing wooden doors and down the dim corridor. The dark gave an unsavoury aspect to the man, as if the heavy stone was giving up some of its joyless past.

Others were surprised that Septus was one of the most powerful people in the country, but his relationship with the ruling families, and his talent, were undeniable. He was the obvious choice to be head of the seekers and second-in-command of the city.

The age-darkened beams ended at a square, stone wall, covered by a faded tapestry. Septus pushed open a door recessed in the corner with a muted creak of the hinges. Jakus followed Septus down the stone steps, using the support of the solid, finger-stained wall.

Odours wafted up towards them, evidence that the lower door was open.

"Who's been here before me?" snapped Jakus.

"I had to check all was ready. I didn't let anything happen, my Shada."

The stronger notes of fear within the rising odours distracted Jakus.

They passed into a large hall lit by candles in blackened holders on soot-covered walls, the roof lost in the gloom. By contrast, the floor was clean enough to allow the natural scents of the stone to come through.

A dozen pairs of eyes stared at them, their unkempt young owners huddled together with hands bound. Jakus picked out the sombre tendrils of fear and apprehension whirling about them.

A number of seekers, large and mostly solid men with hoods raised, and uniformly garbed in black cloaks, loose-fitting grey trousers and tunic tops, were assembled around the walls. Each had a long dagger, truncheon and pouch suspended from his belt.

Jakus automatically sent out a tendril of enquiry to them, seeking their state of mind, reinforcing their loyalty. He frowned at the lack of reaction from his head seeker, Jelm. "Is this all, Jelm?"

"All the potentials that could be found in and around the town of Korla, my Shada. Unfortunately, several evaded capture, but Genur's on their trail." Jelm, a tall, spare man, continued to exhibit an irritating confidence.

Jakus's eyes bored into Jelm's. "Then why aren't you helping? Surely, it didn't need four seekers to bring in this pitiful group? Move the potentials into the processing room. Now!"

The floor of the processing room crunched under their feet, dust rising from the brittle black surface. The stone walls were clean, while slate tiles covered the ceiling. A number of wooden chairs with metal restraints on the armrests and legs encircled a leather-covered stool.

The seekers worked quickly, cutting the captives' bonds, then clamping each into a chair. Jakus motioned the guards from the room when the task was completed. Septus quietly opened several large stone jars, releasing a vapour that rose in spirals towards the ceiling.

Jakus stepped into the centre of the captive group, stretching out his tall, thin body so his black robes seemed to fill the space, emphasising his power with an aura dominated by swirls of purple and black.

Emanations of resignation and fright oozed from the captives.

He slipped his hood back to expose his shaved head and looked down his aquiline nose.

"My young friends," he said, baring his teeth, "you have been chosen to help your country, help your friends and families live a better, richer, fuller life. You are the future."

Jakus kept the youthful minds focused. A dozen dirt-stained faces, mouths half open, stared at him. The almost translucent vapour descending from the ceiling fell over their bodies. They began to relax.

Jakus felt an unfamiliar feeling, paternal warmth, as he looked at his audience. "My young friends," he repeated dreamily.

His body jerked as alarm rushed through him.

"Septus!" he hissed. "You fool! It is enough. Close the lids."

Jakus reached into a pouch suspended from his waist belt, took a pinch of dark red crystals, and slipped them into his mouth.

The substance's astringency hit his brain, expanding his senses in a euphoric whirl. With startling swiftness, the emanations grew more visible. The walls exuded a wave of natural scents, lighter notes drifted from the ceiling and mingled. The floor efficiently absorbed the outflow. He could see Septus giving in to his emotions.

Jakus refocused on the young bodies, relaxed and open around him. Scents slowly descended from them to the floor. The released vapour had done its work—they were calm, tractable, and yielding.

He concentrated, sending a tendril from his mouth and nose towards his target. She was on the verge of womanhood, curves under shabby clothing, a scatter of fair hair circling an oval face, brown eyes vacant and open.

The tendril moved towards her face, slipping easily into a nostril. She jerked, wincing with unease. He pushed into the smell centres of her brain.

He could find little evidence of deceit in her scent memories. The sexual pheromones were hers, no others. Recent fright and terror showed; little had disturbed her life. He sucked back scent memories to keep and savour later.

He paused at the intoxicating innocence and budding femininity. The emotions grew as he pressed. He could feel her whole body quivering. He had to find his control, and quickly, or he'd be lost in the euphoria.

Ah, the tractable key is there, he thought. *I'll be able to use this one.*

He pulsed a scent of duty, obedience and dependency into the virgin area, marked her, and reluctantly withdrew. He paused to watch the girl obediently swallow red crystals from Septus's hand, then moved on.

The next youth was even younger than the girl. *Perhaps too young? No,* thought Jakus, *my seekers wouldn't make that mistake.* Clothing was indeterminate: torn trousers, loose top covering a skinny, underdeveloped body. Hair, dark and lank, fell over his pale face.

Jakus extended his probe into the youth's nose. The violent jerk of the young man's head made Jakus curb his impatience. He tightened his grip, insinuating himself into the smell memories, lingering, finding differences to the girl. The youth had come from a cereal-growing area. The heady aromas of crushing, cooking and malting were a light relief to the familiar, yet intoxicating, odours of fear and flight. Taking a sample for himself, he continued to seek the same tractability as before. It was there, to be manipulated and used.

He moved on and allowed Septus to administer a few crystals.

The next youngster was more solid than the previous two, with a squarer face. His clothes were slightly better, though soiled by the journey.

Jakus moved in, slowly. The probe found the memories without difficulty. The stone scents made this one different. The distinctive, acrid notes of granite and basalt contrasted with the earthiness of slate and mudstone, showing the boy had lived in different circumstances. He searched for the tractability site containing the area of control, of loyalty, without success.

Jakus withdrew and looked up to see Septus. Heaving a mental sigh, he nodded.

Septus smiled.

Chapter Four

The colours and ache behind Targ's eyes woke him. A continuous cramp across his shoulder blades and down his arms strengthened the pain pulsing through his head. He could not move.

A chunk of gravel migrated to the front of his mouth. He spat it out, tasting the earthy notes. The surrounding clumps of scent seemed natural, expected. But there were alien flavours, too: a faint tang of metal and oil, a dribble of body stench, animal dung and the poignant, intangible drift of musk. He could see the last overlaying all the others, dominating: oily grey speckled with pink.

With an effort, he rolled onto his side. His hands stayed pinioned behind his back, but he could see his feet bound tightly with a thin cord.

"Hisst."

Targ strained his head towards the sound. Recollections of the youth came flooding back. He could recall memories of streets, of people—Kyel particularly—and of the strange appearance of odours. The memories were not right, not usual.

"Targ?" whispered the boy.

Kyel was lying near him, eyes large in a tear-stained face, arms fastened behind his back and legs tied.

"Hey!" yelled a voice. A sharp stab of pain in Targ's side emphasised the yell.

"Damn! What're you doing?" Targ exclaimed

Another flare of pain hit his ribs, harder than before. Targ's breath hissed through clenched teeth.

His attacker grunted and moved away.

A memory flashed into his mind. It prompted anger and gave him a focus. He had met such people when younger—*schooling, perhaps?* Scarlet coils of anger escaped before he could suppress them. If he could see them, then his guard probably could, too.

He caught sight of the man who had kicked him. The solid-looking man gave a laugh as he joined others at the roadblock. They glanced at Targ before resuming their inspection of the slow trickle of people moving past towards the gate. The queue had thinned as the shadows lengthened and the air chilled.

He was lying on damp grass surrounded by various bundles, including Kyel's pack. A strong smell of perac came from a roughly-built wooden building nearby. A grey tail sticking from beneath the flap of the pack drew his eye.

"Tel's safe," he mouthed to Kyel.

Kyel lifted his head, frowning, eyes dark in his pale face. He looked long and hard at Targ, then nodded. "We're not the only ones caught," he whispered, and jerked his head to the bundles behind him.

Targ could see someone lying further away, initially concealed by the loose scattering of gear. The shape, smaller than Kyel, moved as if aware of his scrutiny and a white face, surrounded by light hair, looked over. He could see little in the thickening shadows but recognised some of the scents. The aura was different to Kyel's, softer. She was a youth, and obviously upset.

What had she done? He wondered what any of them had done and what their captors had planned for them. He had no intention of going along with it.

The crunch of footsteps preceded an emanation of metal, oil and stale sweat. He saw five men silhouetted against the fading light.

"On your feet!"

Targ staggered up, wincing with the effort. The man half-hopped him along the wooden wall until they reached a dark opening; the stink of animal dung and rotting straw greeted him. A rough shove sent him tumbling into an empty, straw-covered animal stall.

The impact of two other bodies knocked the wind out of him. Targ grunted, Kyel swore, and a light sob came from the other captive.

Targ lay still as the men moved their gear past them into the building, dumping it in the next stall. When they had gone further in, he hissed.

"What's this about, Kyel? Tell me!"

"Can't yet," Kyel whispered. "Just wait… Look out, they're coming'.

Two of their captors approached carrying a burning torch.

"Stay there," one growled. "We've got bread and water. Can't have you say we didn't treat you proper. Now stand up, then turn round so's we can untie your hands!"

They ate quickly when released, while the guards waited.

"Right, now, turn around."

Targ pointed out the door as a guard held out the cord to retie the bonds.

"I need to go; have to go," he said, miming the action.

The guards looked at each other, and then laughed. "You can go in here. It stinks anyway."

"Please?"

One guard shrugged and gestured towards the open door.

"What about my feet?" Targ indicated the bindings.

The guard jerked his thumb at the door.

Targ relieved himself on the grass, noticing the door fastened simply with a long wooden bar fitted between metal supports. He was returned to the stall, his hands retied behind him before the others had their turn. The doors were then barred.

It was dark, the only illumination coming fitfully from a small fire inside the building, the men around it blocking most of the light.

They waited trying to get what little comfort there was on the straw. Targ started when a small body scrabbled over him and onto the youth.

"Tel," breathed Kyel.

"So, who's the girl?" whispered Targ.

"She told me her name's Luna," said Kyel. "From here, in Korla."

"Kyel, slower, you're hard to understand." He looked back at the girl. "Hi, Luna," said Targ gently.

"Targ?" she said, her voice small and sad. "You're caught too?"

The tiny, frightened voice struck a chord in Targ. He felt protective towards this defenceless girl. It seemed that he, as the oldest of the three, should help them escape, but he was having enough trouble helping himself.

Gentle animal noises rose as the nearby perac settled for the night. A low murmur of voices came from their captors. Kyel and Luna were whispering. Apart from the kicks in his side, they had not been mistreated. It was puzzling there was no one watching them, but he put that to the back of his mind while he thought of what to do.

It was dark and he could not see the scents, which limited his potential to use his abilities. He knew scents were there, but how to grab them, manipulate them?

The light from the fire revealed indistinct odours, like specks floating across his eyes. It was hard to make them out, and concentrating made his head swim.

Eventually he isolated the guard's body smell; it almost gagged him. He easily grabbed it with his mind and reeled it in. He compressed it into a fine wire of scent, all the while afraid he could not hold it, and that it might slip away. He manoeuvred it by feel into the cord on his bound hands. The strength of the tendril pulled at the knot. It was like using a springy wire: it had give, but would not break while he controlled it. His determination overrode any feeling of awe at this skill.

One of the men got up and trudged over. Light from his burning brand washed over them before he grunted and turned away. Soon the only sounds were the creaking of settling timbers and the gentle movements of the animals.

Targ could see the glow of the fire by peering out past the edge of the stall, occasional sparks flaring when prodded by the lone guard on watch. It was a problem they were not all asleep, but he could not have expected it to be too easy.

He pulled the loosened cord from his hands and then untied his feet before moving over to Kyel.

"Give…me…your…hands," he whispered, reaching forward. He heard Kyel's gasp of astonishment before the youth turned his back and lifted his bound wrists.

"Keep quiet, Kyel," whispered Targ as he undid the tight knots using his fingernails. "Help her."

Leaving his companions to work on the remaining bonds, Targ slowly got to his feet. As he leant around the edge of the stall, there was a stab of small claws in his thigh.

'Damn,' he hissed. *What's that wine-rotted lizard up to?*

He could see Tel's pale shape standing upright, holding onto his leg; the lizard's frill extended alarm.

Targ squinted hard at his surroundings, but he could see nothing in the dark. He'd seen the lizard detect things before he could, so he knew it must be reacting to something. He concentrated, squeezing his eyes tight as he did so, creating flashes of light through his mind. A musky odour moved out of the background scents.

He opened his eyes, now aware of faint flashes of pink lined up in a grid-like pattern along the length of the corridor alongside the stalls; the spaces between the lines were not much more than a boot length. "Ah!" he gasped in understanding, and reached down to pat his friend. *A warning system. Smart lizard.*

Targ saw the guard leaning against a post. His four companions were asleep around the fire. Every so often the man looked at the floor and then down the length of the building.

The scents were clearer now. Foggy emanations were rising from the sleeping men, smells of sleep. He found it relatively easy to grab and mould them into an almost solid mass. It took little effort to gradually lift the scents and then allow them to drift down, like a haze of smoke, to settle over the man's head. The guard soon slumped against the post, asleep.

Targ remained focused as he wove more of the sleep smells over the remaining men. The background grid of faint pink lines slowly faded, leaving the floor dark. He stepped cautiously out from the stall but all remained quiet, just the crackle of the fire and the sounds of the sleeping men.

"Come," he hissed, before moving to the next stall and searching through the dark pile of baggage until he found Kyel's pack, untouched. He took it and another pack containing more foodstuffs and several blankets. "Here's your pack. Let's get out of here!"

Targ heard the others behind him and the gentle enquiry of curious animals before he lifted the bar to unlock the doors. The cloudless night sky shed enough light to see that no one was around.

He beckoned to the others to come through and then pushed the doors closed. "Where...to?" he asked.

Kyel adjusted the pack on his shoulders. "Follow me," he said, grabbing Luna's hand as he led them away from the barn and into the darkness.

As Targ turned to go he felt a familiar shape climb his leg and onto his shoulders before settling on the pack he was carrying. He smiled and followed.

They walked through a land lit only by starlight, their footing uncertain on the rutted road.

Luna pulled her hand out of Kyel's and stopped walking. "I'm not going with you. I belong here. This's where I live." She stamped a foot, knuckled fists just discernible on her hips. "I'm not going!"

Kyel huffed. "Look..." He reached out a tentative hand to touch her shoulder; she pushed it away. "Luna," he warned, "we don't have time for this. The seekers will be right behind. We have to get as far as possible. We just can't..." His voice trailed off as he heard Luna sniff, and he detected a gleam of tears in her eyes. "Aw," he said, pulling her resisting body to him and leaning his head on hers, "we just got to go."

"But my family's here," she gulped. "All I've got, and I don't know what they've done to my aunt. She won't know what's happening." They stood together until a crunch of gravel alerted him to Targ just behind them.

"And you," Kyel said to Targ, "where do you think we should be going?"

"What's the problem?" Targ asked.

"Ah, lizards' teeth, Luna," Kyel continued, pulling the girl into a stumbling run.

"I guess that means we don't go back," Targ shrugged and followed.

Kyel led them at a fast pace along the rough track, still holding Luna's hand despite the uneven ground. The rocky outcrops and clumps of trees looked alien in the dark, their strangeness reinforced by unfamiliar scents. Targ was tired, his ribs were sore, he was hungry and nothing was familiar.

They finally paused on the summit of a small hill. Tel scrambled off Targ's shoulders. They took off their packs and sank to the ground. Targ was content to catch his breath, even though he was curious about Luna.

They sat in silence as they ate bread and cheese and shared a bottle of fruity drink. A faint light outlining the hills in the distance revealed dawn was not far away.

"Hello, Luna," said Targ, turning to the girl, "we haven't had time to talk."

She was slight, only as tall as Targ's shoulder, with a dirt-smeared, cute face. Her eyes were dark and uncertain under a fringe of curly blonde hair and the brown hood of a travel cloak.

"I'm…Luna," she said.

"Yes, I know. And you're from around here, aren't you?" asked Targ slowly. "Is that why you didn't want to go with us?"

"Yes, that's right," she replied after a slight hesitation, her accent thick but becoming easier to understand. "My aunt lives in the village, but she doesn't know where I am. She'll be worried." Luna sniffed, spreading more dirt across her face as she rubbed at her nose. "Where're you from, then?"

"Ah… I don't really know. My memory's not working." Targ tried to think back. It had to do with something from before, something bad. He remembered things at odd times but nothing was complete.

"Yeah, Targ," added Kyel helpfully. "I found you near the markets. You were acting weird and your smell weren't right. You can't be a seeker, though you can do things like them." He looked at Targ's stubble-darkened face. "And you don't look like anyone from here. You're too big for a start, and your nose isn't large enough for a Sutanite; your eyes are too light, also."

"Fine. Thanks a lot," said Targ. He took a deep breath. "What are seekers and Sutanites? And please try to speak slower, I'm having some trouble understanding what you say."

Kyel looked around. The sun was making an appearance, the strong rays lighting the tops of the hills in the distance. It was a rugged landscape where innumerable hills formed by millennia of erosion made travel very difficult. Sparse bushes and trees were fighting to hold on in a dry and unforgiving country. There was little green, the predominant colours being rusty reds and oranges of the soil and rocks.

"I'll have to tell you later. The seekers will be after us now it's light. Just know that they want us, those of us with scent talent, to take to the city. Then things happen, bad things," Kyel gulped. "We've got to go now."

Kyel pointed along a rough, winding gully that was almost identical to others surrounding it. "I think Luna'll be able to help us, being a local." Luna gave Kyel a brief shrug before looking where he indicated.

Tel, perched on a high boulder to catch the first rays of the rising sun, quivered. "Just like a lizard," said Targ, as a stray memory surfaced.

"We'll have to get moving," prompted Kyel. "The seekers won't give up."

Tel hissed, startlingly loud in the quiet, and bounced rapidly from foot to foot as if the rock was suddenly hot. With his frill extended, he looked down the track.

"Too late!" yelped Kyel.

They packed hurriedly while scanning the slopes for danger.

It remained unnaturally quiet; nothing showed. Targ noticed both Kyel and Luna had their mouths open as if to draw in any vestige of scent. But he didn't need to, he knew the seekers were nearby because he could see the black odour tendrils, highlighted by flashes of yellow, moving in the shadows of the rough track, their blind heads flicking back and forth as they sought their prey.

His companions anxiously sniffed and looked without seeing, Tel's alarm adding an air of panic.

Targ divorced himself from the others as a trickle of belief came from somewhere and worked instinctively, processing a combination of scents from his recent memories. He extracted the powerful body stench of the guards, the reek of the marketplace and the outflow of cesspits, and combined it all into a rock-rotting stench.

His teeth itched as he manoeuvred the odour ball through his mouth and nose. He separated it into four thin spikes and targeted the seekers' scent snakes. Without hesitation, he thrust the spikes into the snakes' heads, like hooks into worms.

He overcame any resistance and ruthlessly drove the spikes through the lengths of the snakes and into the smell centres of their owners' brains. These were not evil men, and he felt a brief twinge of sympathy before he crashed into their unprepared senses. They gasped, overwhelmed, as something reached into them and stole their life energy. When their awareness closed down Targ felt relief, not regret.

Tel, his frill folded back, skittered over the rocks in an almost comical dance before looking towards his companions, as if seeking praise for his efforts. He resumed basking, the sun picking out brown highlights in his grey skin.

The danger was obviously over.

Chapter Five

Jakus shuddered at the warm, sticky atmosphere, the endless hum and smell of decay in the cavernous home of the large creatures. Natural light filtering through numerous shafts high in the walls revealed the constantly moving hymetta as they tended their brood and groomed their jointed, stick-thin legs and shiny yellow bodies. The gaze of so many huge, black eyes was unnerving. Jakus automatically reinforced his control scent before moving further into the nest with Septus.

"Shada...Head," called a voice. A large, fat man came puffing up to them. "Good you could come."

"Your report, Keeper," ordered Jakus.

"It's the hymetta, Cers. Some've returned with the rebel scent," he gasped. "You wanted to know if that happened."

Jakus smiled and rubbed his hands together. It meant that the hymetta, bred to track and destroy, had been successful, finding and eliminating a potential enemy of the country.

"Which hymetta?"

"Them." His jowls shook as he pointed over his shoulder. "Uh...follow me."

The keeper led them past several of the hexagonal brood chambers to a trio of hymetta. The creatures, each near the length of his torso with bulbous abdomen, powerful winged thorax and melon-sized head dominated by black compound eyes, were tethered by the neck and drinking at a half-filled trough. They raised their heads at the disturbance, globs of viscous liquid dripping from their large jaws. Their bodies lifted as if ready to spring. One buzzed its wings, raising a flurry of dust and releasing a waft of rancid scent. Jakus was reminded of a fly being watched by a spider. He pulsed out a scent of dominance and stood his ground; Septus, he noted, stayed behind the keeper.

"Here, Cers. There's the blood." He pointed to a dark stain on one's head and thorax. "I've stopped them grooming it off."

"Get me a sample!" ordered Jakus, his eyes bright with anticipation.

29

The keeper pulled out a knife and bent forward to scrape at the material. The hymetta regarded, with some interest, the man's unprotected neck while he worked. Jakus took a step back to avoid any blood spray should the keeper's control on the creature fail.

"This enough?" He proffered the knife to Jakus.

"I'll take that," interrupted Septus.

"Yes, you can…after me." Jakus shifted to block Septus and lifted the knife to his large, beaked nose.

It was like sucking a sweetmeat. A multitude of flavours hit the palate, stronger elements standing out before the lesser ones.

The overpowering, coppery tang of blood gave way to an underlying odour of need and attraction. It bespoke power, more power than he had come across before. It pulled at him, tantalised him with a promise so ethereal he could not grasp it; it was there, just out of reach.

The two men watching him were aware that something significant was happening. Septus almost snatched the knife when his turn came. Jakus gritted his teeth before focusing on what he had learnt. Despite the promise of power, it was not good.

A rebel had been tracked and killed by his hymetta, that much was certain. However, the scents confirmed another rebel with unusual power.

Production of a scent of this intricacy meant there was an organised group at work. Why and how had they had been producing such a powerful, unfamiliar attractant? It spelt danger. The one consolation was that it had caught the attention of his hymetta. *The sooner this was investigated the better.*

Septus groaned, eyes rolling back in his head.

"Snap out of it, Septus," Jakus spat. "Your thoughts?"

"You've got problems."

"*We've* got problems! This could have big implications for you, and the games you play."

"Games, my Shada?" Septus, eyes wide, glanced up at Jakus. "What do you mean?"

"Septus…" Jakus glared.

"Shada, we've been too soft, too reasonable. There's no appreciation for our administration. It's time to be tougher on the natives, yes, much tougher." He paused. "We need to find out where the Resistance is and crush it. Use the hymetta. Let them get a taste for the natives, that's all, and soon there'll be nothing to worry about." Septus nodded, his eyes glittering.

"Mmmm," said Jakus. He knew his offsider's leanings and usually quashed them, but he was uncertain, distracted by what might be hiding in the vast, lightly-inhabited areas of the country.

"We'll give 'em a taste," continued Septus, fixing his gaze on the hymetta and taking Jakus's silence for assent. "Keeper, get the rejects ready. The hymetta need to know their enemy." His black figure hobbled off into the gloom of the cavern, bald head gleaming in the dark.

"How many, Shada?" asked the keeper.

"What?" snapped Jakus.

"How many of them do you want to be put in the pit?"

The question refocused him. He belatedly realised he'd agreed to Septus's proposal and felt a brief annoyance at the waste of the potentials who'd failed; still, it was better to snuff out any possibility of rebellion before it developed.

"All!" he commanded and stepped back as the hymetta were led past.

The creatures were fixated on the attractant scent sticks held by the keeper and his assistants. They were single-minded, a trait that made them effective predators. Once they had a scent they would follow it until exhausted. The trick was making sure they were controlled. They were most effective when their reward was linked to an appropriate scent. While he could not claim credit for the hymetta's existence, he used them effectively.

The creatures and their handlers were moving through the cavern to a tunnel at the lower end. Jakus took a separate, higher route, partly to avoid breathing the musty stench of the hymetta but also to get a good view of what was to occur. He stopped at a small balcony off the main cavern.

The space below the balcony reminded him of a hole he had once seen where a large section of ground had dropped into an underground cave system. The fall had left a circular pit, many paces across, containing the bones of trapped animals.

This hole was similar. However, the sheer walls were smooth, the floor black and composed of the same smell-absorbing compound as the processing room. Nevertheless, extraneous odours were still wafting about. He could see their insubstantial forms and taste the faded emotions of previous events.

The hymetta had been shepherded into a holding pen, the buzzing sound of their wings revealing their anticipation.

"They're ready," Septus said into his ear.

Jakus started. "No mistakes? *And* you've got only the rejects?"

"Of course, Shada. I'll signal the keepers now?"

"Do it!" Jakus felt a surge of anticipation that overwhelmed a strange feeling of regret. He could not fathom whether it was the wasting of potential, or just that Septus seemed to be drooling at the prospect.

Septus hung over the balcony, gesturing at the men beneath. Jakus half raised his hands at the temptation to push before dropping them to his sides. *No*, he thought, *the man still has his uses.*

The failed potentials from the processing, four boys and a girl, were led out into the centre of the circular black pit and left huddled together. They slowly looked around, eyes glazed from the effects of the soporific drug released during processing, only vaguely interested in their surroundings.

Jakus knew better than anyone they were not appropriate for further training once he had detected a potential in their scent talent that could negate control. It was far better to remove such threats before they developed; and their sacrifice would help train the hymetta. He felt a pang of loss for the girl of the group as he'd like to have had more time with her.

"Now?" asked Septus.

Jakus inclined his head and Septus signalled to the waiting men. They pulled the pen gates open before retreating into the tunnel.

It was like opening the gate to a herd of water-crazed perac. The hymetta crashed through the space to quickly overwhelm the five unresisting youngsters and snuff out their screams. The floor became a seething mass of yellow bodies and translucent wings as the hymetta fought to get the choicest bits, fluids scattering as they eagerly tore off pieces of flesh.

Jakus, regretful at the lack of resistance, suddenly saw the gush of scents. The tang of blood and freshly ripped flesh, the bile-like outpourings of the gut were massive attractants. He took a pinch of the red crystal magnesa before he extended himself.

It was euphoria at its best. His mind lost itself in the complex of flavours, weaving into ecstasy. It heightened all his smell memories and made them real, physical. He could take any of them and move to where they once were, see any part he wanted along a myriad of paths and go there, become lost in the scents, stimulate the most pleasurable of memories and build an untouchable motivation.

Chapter Six

The sun was high, burning down on unprotected necks. Targ had knotted a square of material he had found in his pocket so it sat over his head; this had caused a fit of laughter from the others. He had stripped down to his shirt, coat slung over his shoulders, when he stumbled as his foot caught on the uneven path.

"Damn! Wine-rotted road!"

The others turned. Kyel raised an eyebrow while Luna spat out a lock of blonde hair she had been chewing.

"What?" Targ shouted at them. They glanced at each other and then kept on walking.

"Ah, damn," he muttered. He did not know who he was or where he was going. He was struggling to understand the language with its thick accent and many unfamiliar words. He wanted to be in control, but he was fed up and swearing helped.

The others had almost moved out of sight. Their resilience amazed him. Kyel carried a full pack and still made a brisk pace, even overloaded by a relaxed lizard. Luna, with the other pack slung over her shoulder, led the way.

He sighed and strove to catch up.

The day had done little to change his early impressions of the rugged nature of the land. Seen close up, the rocks were pitted by erosion and shattered by temperature extremes. This created a hazardous surface for walking and meant there was little opportunity to look around. Other than a light scattering of grass, there were few trees. The bark was rough and hard on his hands when he used a handy tree to clamber over a difficult area of the track. He kept looking for evidence of local wildlife, anything flying or walking in the dull green scrub that clumped together into occasional thickets. Sometimes he caught a flicker of movement in the corner of his vision, but nothing else.

The rough path led to where some trees offered shade. He was hungry and thought it safe to stop for a while.

His ability to shut out personal stink intrigued him. But, just thinking about it made the smells come; days of not washing mixed with extraneous scents, ranging from the coppery tang of blood to perac pong. Targ could see a vague fog overloading the others. How Tel could stand being with any of them was beyond him.

Kyel and Luna slumped to the ground in the shade. Water from a small stream had gathered into a pool deep enough to sit in, ideal for a soak and clean-up.

Targ took off his boots and stiffly grimed socks, and rolled up his trouser legs. He squatted at the water's edge.

"No!" screamed two voices.

Kyel scrambled to his feet and grabbed Targ by the arm.

"No," he repeated, shaking his head at him. "You mustn't. There're dangerous things in there."

"What now?" he snapped as he shook off Kyel's hand. "Something that'll get me, eh?"

"Could be. Just can't take a chance, is all," replied Kyel, stepping backwards, clearly a little bewildered by Targ's protest.

"First," said Luna, "Something to eat and drink." Her attempt at light-heartedness lit up her face. She saw Targ looking at her and glanced down, a slight blush colouring her cheeks.

Targ took a chunk of spicy meat, cheese and a hard biscuit. A swig of drink, provided by the old woman in Korla, helped it go down.

He noticed Tel was lying alongside the pool, staring intently into the water. *Obviously, "don't go near the water!" doesn't apply to him*, he thought.

The lizard lay perfectly still, its colouring making it look like any other rock.

A movement near the water's edge caught his eye, something clambering up one of the weed-like sticks in the pool. It was just close enough for Targ to see a mud-brown body and thin legs.

The lizard was almost too fast to see. One moment there was a creature of some kind, the next it was gone; only the working of Tel's jaw and a puff of scent gave a clue as to what had happened.

Targ nodded, impressed.

Kyel rummaged in his pack and produced a small wood-handled knife. He stood and moved to a tree topped by large leaves spreading out in a fan-like pattern, each leaf about a forearm in length, coming from the end of a long stem. There were twenty or so of these stems high on the rough-barked trunk.

Kyel stretched up and hacked at the stems above his head, taking little time and effort to cut off two leaves. He pulled some of the leaves together with a strand of cord to form a cup shape on the long stem.

"Targ, try and get some water using this; save getting too close."

Targ grunted and took it from Kyel. He walked back to the pool and forced the cup under the surface. With both hands supporting the weight, he carried it back to the others.

"This all right?"

Both nodded and helped balance the ladle between several rocks. They shared sips of the water.

Targ could taste a mix of flavours, mostly salts the water had leached from the rocks over which it had flowed. He could pick the muddy flavour of the pond bottom, the scents of some life, small and natural. There was also a lingering flavour of something unfamiliar; it had a concentrated feel to it, a focus that made Targ think of a predator.

Luna reached over and picked up his coat. She inspected the weave, the buttons and the stitching.

"Targ, where's this from?" she asked, her voice soft. Targ just shrugged and leant back to rest on his arms. Luna looked to Kyel. "This's like nothing I've seen. It's not perac wool, and finely made. Look at his boots. Trousers, too. You're right, he's not from anywhere round here." Her nose wrinkled as she held the coat closer. "Perhaps we should wash while we can. Kyel, you've got soap?"

The soap Kyel pulled out of the pack looked like a block of cheese. It was a solid yellow square with a distinct perac odour.

"Unused?" Luna raised an eyebrow at Kyel as she took the soap and offered it to Targ.

"Here, you should be first since you need it more than us."

Targ grunted as he accepted the soap, then opened his shirt and rolled up his sleeves. He took the square of material he had used as a hat to wet and rub the soap before using it to wash off some of the grime. It did little to remove the dirt but it helped to cool down his face and neck.

Kyel pulled off his tunic top and rubbed soap over his chest and arms, developing muscles showing on his thin body. Luna just pulled her top down to the swell of her small breasts and washed her white shoulders and neck, wetting her fair hair so the curls plastered against her skull. She washed more meticulously than Kyel, before using his spare shirt to dry off. He did not appear to mind.

"We're heading to me town of Lesslas," Kyel said as he watched Luna repack the bags. "It's another day away but I think we should be safe from the seekers, since they've been through this area already. I was runnin' from there in the first place. Thought Korla would be safer, but it wasn't." He played briefly with an index finger, inspecting a chewed nail, and then glanced at Targ. "You haven't heard of Lesslas, have you?"

Targ shook his head, causing some hair to flop across his forehead.

"Yeah," interrupted Luna, her small voice straining with emotion, "Both Kyel 'nd I were escaping. However, once they've got you, that's it! We've friends who've been caught."

"Yeah," continued Kyel, "I'd got to Korla and thought I'd escaped, but they follow. They catch your scent and never let go."

"Why do they want you? What have you done?" Targ asked.

"They're evil, that's what. They take you and drain you, don't they?" Luna, face white, pulled at a curl of hair before looking at Kyel.

"Yeah, they do," he agreed. "A friend of mine, Riyar, was caught—never seen since. No," Kyel shook his head, "once they've got you it's all over."

"So that's the difference, is it? You've got this scent talent and others haven't?" Targ had noticed other youths in Korla who had not seemed concerned about the seekers.

"We've got scent sense. You have too, though yours is older and, uh, much more full than ours. Therefore, they want us. But we won't get another chance if they catch us again." Kyel puffed out a long slow breath.

"They won't!" Targ said emphatically. "Something happened when they came after us. They came and I sent them back; don't ask me how."

"Something's queer about you and what you do, right enough. We'll see if my sister, Sadir, can sort it when we get home." Kyel looked sideways at him, his face a grimace of concern.

"I've heard the word…Sutanites," said Targ. "Are they seekers?"

"Well you're right about that. The Sutanites are not from here—Ean I mean, though some are born here. No one's happy about them being the bosses of Ean."

"Come on. Let's get moving." Luna stretched, hands rubbing the small of her back. "We've got a way to go and we don't know if something's after us or not."

The breeze became a light wind rustling the branches and grasses as they crunched over the gravel and rocks of the indistinct track. The murmur of the youngsters came to his ears, but there were no other sounds. It seemed a desolate land.

The heat was still intense, with waves of hot air rising from the ground. He half expected to see Tel-like lizards basking on the hot rocks, but there were just three bareheaded people in the sun. He reknotted the damp material at each corner so it gave some protection to his head, but the heat and the rough trail were so energy-sapping he was soon walking in an unthinking rhythm.

The country changed as the day wore on. Hills became mountains and the valley they were following narrowed. The vegetation grew thicker and a darker green, the odd tall tree often surrounded by dense bushes. A river, too deep to cross, blocked their path at a junction between two valleys so they walked along the valley sides, moving further into the mountains, appreciating the temperature drop as the high peaks cut off the sun.

"What do you reckon?" Kyel pointed to the narrow entrance of a small cave overhung by the bony brow of a cliff face and half hidden from the track by a number of spindly bushes with small, olive-green leaves. "Do you think it'll be all right?"

They both looked at Targ.

A variation in the background odours around them caught his eye. While he could see a stream of normal scents from the undisturbed, dank rocks in the cave, there was nothing else of note. He made a show of looking inside and saw a gravel floor littered with leaves and twigs but with no sign of inhabitants.

"Yes, it's good," Targ said with all the authority he could muster. "Now let's have a fire. Something hot." A chill had descended and the thought of a fire with hot food brought a comfortable memory. He scouted around for dry wood with Kyel while Luna cleaned out the cave.

It quickly grew dark and the cold settled. They had a good fire burning at the entrance and sat against a side wall. Exhaustion seeped through Targ's bones as he watched Luna spike chunks of the spiced Korla meat on thin twigs. She seemed a competent young woman, not given to talking too much, even though she must have been through a lot. Targ smiled as he noticed the tip of her tongue protruding as she worked.

Luna grinned back when she saw him smile. "Won't be long," she said.

Kyel looked up. "Next day we'll get to my village, and my sister Sadir. We'll work something out then, we will."

They watched the glowing coals as they ate, sharing the last of the fruit drink. Targ could see the odours of the burning wood mingling amongst the spurt of sparks and rising into the air to whirl past the overhang. Away from the glow of the fire, a blanket of stars stood out, like a myriad of eyes in the blackness. There was nothing there to jog his memory.

They had put on all the clothing they had and wrapped themselves in the blankets Targ had taken from the stable. The ground was hard, and Targ could feel his hips complaining as he tried to get comfortable.

The fire died down to a glimmer of coals but no one was awake to refuel it.

A fog appeared, coalescing about the rock face, and slowly descending. As it reached the ground, it broke into many fine tendrils that progressed in questing, leech-like movements, quite unlike fog. The tendrils gave the fire a wide berth. They hesitated, as if tasting the scents, and then crept over the blanketed occupants.

This time Tel did not warn them.

Chapter Seven

Jakus felt the burgeoning headache a small price to pay for the sensory euphoria he had experienced. He lay back, appreciative of the darkened room and the soft bed.

"You may go, Nefaria."

He was exhausted. Even the sight of the naked back and buttocks of his sleeping companion did not rouse him as she slipped on her dark brown robe and crept out of his chamber.

The stimulation of the emotions released at the hymetta feeding had been overwhelming, increasing his store of scent memories. With little effort he could recall the strongest emanations released. These were in their most unadulterated form, produced without reservation, without stricture, so strong that they caused an intense mental and physical reaction. Sex as a follow-up was something of a letdown, but he had no quarrel with his acolyte Nefaria, for she had tried her best.

Jakus soon rose, performed his ablutions and ate a light meal. On finishing, he strolled to the main hall and sat down at the meeting table.

Septus was the first to arrive, thin face haggard from the previous day's excitement. Jakus pointed to a seat at the large wooden table and they sat in silence, waiting while the others arrived. Jakus reviewed his memory of odours, categorising them to reminisce on later, resenting the fact that this mental high would soon end. He eventually focused on the people sitting at the table, satisfied that all were attentive.

A scribe sat by his left hand, while Septus sat on his right. A short distance from Septus was Strona, a senior scent master. She was a tall woman with a humourless face dominated by her Sutanite nose and greying, close-cropped hair. On the opposite side of the table were Jelm, one of the head seekers, and Rancer, the heavily-built master-at-arms. There was a distinct contrast between them. Jelm was a tall, fair man of thin rather than solid build, unlike a typical seeker, while the bearded guardsman was heavier, broad with leathery, sun-hardened skin. Further down the table were the head keeper, the perac master, whose distinct animal odour identified his occupation, and a third-year acolyte.

"There is a problem that must be resolved." Jakus's dark eyes glittered as he scanned the attentive faces before him. "Unusual rebel activity has been found in the hinterland. This activity, which we detected by chance,"—he paused, as if daring someone to look away—"shows that there is a more significant resistance operating than any intelligence you've provided. The evidence, brought by our keepers' pets, indicates a previously unknown level of talent. It is a threat that cannot be tolerated. The source must be found and destroyed." As he scanned the table he pulsed out an ambient odour to reinforce his command and sense of urgency.

He saw Septus smirk.

"The map!" ordered Jakus, stretching his hand towards the acolyte at the bottom of the table next to Strona. The youngster hurriedly passed a roll of fine leather to her. She flipped it open so that it unrolled towards Jakus.

"Is this updated?" she asked the acolyte in a commanding tone.

"Yes, senior seeker." The young acolyte glanced briefly at her, then up to Septus and Jakus. "It…it has the latest scent collector information."

Jakus noted that the acolyte had added fine lines to the map showing the direction of the recent prevailing winds. The scents tracked by the hymetta had originated from the area north-west of Nebleth.

"Hmmm." He scratched at stubble on his pointed chin. "We'll need patrols to investigate most of the inhabited region, from the Sensory Mountains, through the Hills of Lesslas to the North Wash. This will include all of our towns,"— Jakus tapped the map—"a significant distance to cover."

"I'll be leading one patrol, Septus another, and Jelm the third. This is a decision I have not taken lightly, and neither should you," Jakus barked. "You"— he caught Strona's eye—"will remain here. You are well able to keep things running while Septus and I are away."

Strona briefly inclined her head. "I will do as you say, Shada."

Jakus relaxed in his chair, massaging his temple while Septus organised the patrols. Each patrol consisted of a scent master supported by troops, a keeper for hymetta and a perac handler-cum-cook.

He shivered slightly. The possibility of coming up against something that could be a challenge was stimulating and began to supplant the euphoria of the previous day. He'd had few challenges recently. The rebels, such as they were, had never been able to provide more than the most basic opposition. They had managed to hide the odd potential from his collecting teams, even caused some difficulties for the town authorities on occasion, but had provided no significant opposition.

"Septus," he interrupted, leaning forward, "I think the seekers stationed in the towns will suffice if we need additional talent. We're only investigating an unusual occurrence, one that may have been dealt with already, so teams that have at least one effective scent master, with the usual support, will be sufficient."

Jakus leant back in his chair and thought for a moment before interrupting again.

"Septus, you and the scribe come to me as soon as you're finished." He got up from the table, hearing the conversation recommence as he left the room.

The barber scraped his curved blade in decisive sweeps across Jakus's skull and face, removing any vestiges of hair. Jakus bore the attention with minimal irritation as his mind was occupied, the repetitive action soothing. He knew that hair trapped smell, and any impediment to control was unacceptable.

Following a rubdown with bland oil, Jakus dismissed the barber and walked over to the open window to enjoy the cool breeze. He moved onto the balcony, opening his senses to the air.

It was near noon with the usual noises and smells of the traders taking advantage of the moderate temperatures. He liked his city. He believed his rule, though strict, was accepted by the people who enjoyed the benefits of prosperous living through trade and the wealth of the country. His forebears had had considerable foresight in establishing Nebleth as a centre of commerce north of the coast and at the crossroads of trade from the hinterland. The proximity of the port of Saltus, half a day's ride to the south, meant that any of the more noisome aspects of the salt trade were hidden from the Capital.

"Shada."

Jakus felt a flash of annoyance at being caught daydreaming by his deputy.

"Well?" he snapped as he swung around to see Septus walking in with the nervous scribe behind him. Septus kept his scents suppressed, obviously keen to conceal his feelings.

"Shada, we'll be ready to move out of Nebleth by dawn, and then complete the teams when we arrive at Regulus."

Jakus nodded.

"That is all then. Scribe. Leave the notes on the table. Septus, you can attend me later. Oh, and Septus," Jakus added, causing Septus to turn, "send Nefaria to me."

Jakus returned to his contemplations as he leant against the balcony rail and tried to regain some of the serenity he had felt before Septus's arrival.

He could see one of the circular openings above him, positioned strategically on the tower. He thought about checking the latest odours collected to glean further information on activities in the north-west. One of the problems with the scent-collecting operation was its non-specific nature. Scents needed to be analysed in conjunction with known variables before useful intelligence could be interpreted; the impact of wind patterns was significant.

The rebels, for instance, could have been developing scent weaponry for a long period with no vestige of odour reaching any of the collectors. The problem highlighted the need for superior analytical ability at each of the collection points, particularly those away from Nebleth and the garrison city of Regulus. While all Ean towns had their own collectors, the talents of their chief administrators might be insufficient to accurately analyse the daily collections, even with the judicious use of the magnesa crystals. The pulsing of the odour collections to Nebleth, when wind conditions were favourable, had become a necessary practice. A hard-riding messenger from one of the outlying towns was often used as a back-up.

"My Shada," came a pleasant voice.

He turned and saw his favourite acolyte waiting for him. He enjoyed Nefaria's soft aroma of welcome and anticipation, choosing to ignore the faint thread of unease in her scent aura.

He briefly analysed his feelings for Nefaria. Certainly, she was beautiful, with a nest of dark curls outlining the shapely skull and the intriguing large hazel eyes above a small nose and full lips. Her smooth brown robe woven from only the finest wools outlined a figure that was decidedly feminine. Jakus was drawn to her and desired to keep her on hand.

One day, he thought, *I might even elevate her to the position of Favoured Acolyte. But I'll keep her training to a low level. The hair suits her even if it limits her scent talent.*

"Nefaria, you will attend me," Jakus ordered.

A bustle of activity greeted Jakus as he entered the main courtyard of the tower. Septus and Jelm were in conversation with Rancer, while the keeper was helping the perac master with three cages, each containing one hymetta. The perac, ears laid back, groaned with distress at the proximity of the creatures.

Jakus briefly considered the emanations from the group before going over to Septus.

"All well?"

"Ah, yes, Shada, except for these useless animals." He flung a hand towards the commotion.

Jakus turned to his master guardsman. "Rancer, your troops are expecting us at Regulus?"

"Word went out last day, Shada. They'll be ready."

"Jelm, what of the towns? Have you informed the administrators?"

"Yes, Shada. Favourable winds have been located and the message scent pulsed. Can't tell if they've been received yet, but will when we're at the garrison."

They turned as the noise escalated. The keeper and the perac master were struggling to quieten the perac.

"We'll be ready as soon as they can control those things," snapped Septus, half stumbling as his boot caught in the uneven cobbles.

"Ah, Strona, it's appropriate that you're here," Jakus said, looking at the tall woman entering the courtyard. "I'll expect regular reports; contact me using Heritis's scent tower in Regulus, but," he added, "only items of worth."

"My Shada," said Strona quietly, mouth pursed in an almost disapproving line, "I would not expect to bother you unnecessarily. I'm here to wish you well in your endeavours."

The troop followed a quick, sure path through the cobbled streets of the sleeping city, the perac fresh and eager at the start of the journey. It was cool and still dark, and the few people about quickly moved aside for the party.

They made the river in good time using the largest and best-maintained road in the capital, having to provide, as it did, for trade and access to the river's transport barges. It also connected the road to Nebleth and the garrison city of Regulus.

As they reached the river Jakus couldn't help an involuntary shiver. He, like most of his countrymen, disliked the sullen, grey water. His forebears had encouraged this attitude and he half suspected they had helped to develop the scent fish, the haggar. The haggar's habit of finding prey through any type of water, tracking it over large distances and then silently sucking it dry, was revolting. Often the victims had circles of puncture marks in skin stretched taught over nothing but bones.

He grudgingly admired the intrepid bargemen who travelled the river.

Chapter Eight

"Argh…" Targ coughed as he hawked up a glob of phlegm and spat. "Damn. My head's on fire and I'm freezing!"

He felt like he had been drinking all night; his head ached, his hips hurt and he had no energy. He levered himself up to look around. A faint light broke into the gloom of the cave, but everything seemed to be in a fog. He blinked to clear his vision, but it did not work. He sank down and shut his eyes; his aches soon forced them open again.

The ceiling of the cave became clearer as the daylight intensified, but the floor remained covered in fog. His eyes idly traced the line of the fog from where it entered the cave. It bypassed Tel's form resting on the cold ashes and covered his companions in a fine, web-like blanket.

He yawned, then flicked a piece of rock at the lizard. It landed close, raising a puff of ash. One scaly eyelid opened, and a black pupil traced the source of the disturbance.

The lizard sprang up as if stung, catapulting off the pile of ash and onto the wall of the overhang. He ran in an extraordinary zigzag along the wall and out of the cave. Targ could hear him scrabbling around outside. Suddenly, he was back, landing with a thump on Targ's chest, frill fully extended.

"Blast! Blooded lizard. I was getting up anyway! Come on, you two," he called, "let's get the fire going."

Kyel and Luna did not move.

Targ realised something was wrong.

He pushed the lizard to the ground and kicked his feet through the fog. It broke into many tendrils, snapping away from the youngsters' bodies before retreating along the cave floor and to the outside. Targ knelt and shook his companions. A faint gush of air came from Kyel's cold form.

He raked through the ashes seeking live coals, then grabbed some dry grass near the entrance to drop into the fireplace. He blew gently until fire appeared, before adding a few sticks to build it up.

Targ pulled Kyel and Luna's cold bodies towards the fire, feeling as if something had drained the heat out of them. He sat with an arm around each, holding them into his chest, feeling for signs of life. He willed the fire to warm them.

"I don't like this land," he muttered. "The fog's evil, smells hold secrets and every time I turn around something strange happens. I'm sure it'd make some sense if I could remember...anything; but why can't I remember?"

The fire crackled and the light smoke drifted to catch at the rocky overhang before reluctantly flowing up into the early day's chill. Tel was a grey shape, frill down, motionless in a patch of sun at the cave's entrance. The light intensified as he waited.

His body started to cramp at the awkward position he was in, but he did not dare move, staring into the flames with the unresponsive bodies held against him.

"Targ?" said Luna's faint voice.

"What! You're alive?"

"Yeah, Targ. You're hurting me," Kyel said quietly.

"Sorry." He released his grip on Kyel's arm. "How do you feel? Are you all right?"

"Awful," came Luna's small voice. "Can't seem to wake up. So cold."

"I'll build up the fire and get some food," said Targ. "I'm so happy you're alive." He winced as he extracted himself from between the two huddled and shaking figures.

K yel leant towards the fire nibbling at some cheese, suspecting they had been attacked by a kind of parasitic fungus, a mycene, but he couldn't be sure.

He looked up to see Targ frowning at him, eyes light in a pale, dark-stubbled face.

"Forgot about the fire, we all did," Kyel sighed. "Didn't think we'd be in danger; should have checked it out better. Looks like we were attacked by mycene—at least I think so —sneaky things they are. How'd you stop them, Targ? Did Tel wake you?"

"Uh... No, Kyel, he didn't, though he got me up in a hurry. What's a mycene, anyway?"

"When we're ready I'll take you out and show you. Just got to get my energy back first. Can you get more food? Hey Luna, what are you doing?"

Luna sat next to him hugging her knees, her head resting on them. Her shoulders were shaking.

"Luna? Hey." Kyel reached out and patted her curly blonde hair. "What's the matter?"

She raised her head, face streaked with tears. "What's the matter?" she asked. "What's the matter? What d'you think's the matter?" She sniffed loudly. "You've..."

she gulped, "you've at least got your sister…and *him*"—she jerked her head towards a bemused Targ— "but me… I don't even know if my aunt's all right. And she doesn't know about me. What if them seekers force her to tell? What'll happen, eh?" Her eyes glistened. "Then I'll be all alone again, but no, you'll be all right. Just eat some food and it'll be all right!" Luna snapped, and then banged her head back to her knees, her shoulders shaking.

"I…I'm sorry. I didn't think." Kyel looked up at Targ before shuffling closer and putting his arm around her. "We'll help you, won't we, Targ? We'll help you. Just got to get to Sadir." He chewed at a dirty fingernail.

Luna kept sobbing but leant into him.

It was some time before they left the cave to climb further up the hillside.

"Check the boulders, especially the bigger, rounder types,' said Kyel, pointing towards the rock-strewn ground. "It looks like one of them and it's got to be nearby."

"Hey," called Luna after a short time. "Here's the hideous thing."

They gathered around the mycene. It was shaped like a huge boulder, as high as Kyel's shoulder, with a russet-brown, scaly appearance. The odour was like mushroom, and it gave slightly when prodded, but was anchored solidly in the stony soil.

"What does it do?" asked Targ.

"Do? It sucks the life juices out of you, that's what it does," answered Luna, her tear-stained face looking up at him. "A man from the village was got by a mycene. Found him all dried up near it."

"It doesn't really suck your life juices away, Luna," said Kyel. "These mycene only use you. They take your energy, but the really big ones can kill you. This mycene's big enough, but it had three of us to use, so we were lucky."

"Can we stop it, kill it somehow?" Targ asked.

"If we had an axe, Targ, but we haven't time. We've got a ways to go."

"You reckon," Luna whispered to Kyel as they started up the hillside, "Targ's not from here? He didn't even know about the mycene. You sure you don't know where he's from?"

"No idea, Luna. Maybe Sadir'll work him out?"

"I suppose," she said. "Still, would rather be at my aunt's place. I really want to understand what's happened, and Korla was much closer than Lesslas."

"We already discussed that. The seekers know where you lived. Just wasn't possible to go there. Sadir'll like you, anyway."

"Me? Probably, but what about him?" she said, looking back at the tall figure behind them.

"Targ? Na. Sadir works at the tavern; she's used to strange men."

A yapping echoed through the high-walled canyon they had just entered; how near was impossible to tell.

Targ felt a vague connection with the sound. This was an animal noise, one he thought he knew.

"What was that?" he asked.

"Just a k'dorian. Don't you know it?" queried Kyel. "If you try you can just get the smell, though I reckon it's downwind."

"No, I don't know it, but I'd like to see it."

"Probably can, but we don't want to get too close. It'd eat Tel in one gulp and has a nasty bite, too; might even take us on."

Targ concentrated on finding the smell of the creature as they continued, the background scents forming a kind of soup around him. Their own ripe odours rode a light breeze into the canyon, advertising their presence, but there was an underlying stink, like something had marked its territory. The musty smell had a rancid quality that caught in the back of his throat.

"We better climb out of here," said Kyel. "I don't like the way Tel's trying to hide under my tunic."

A section of the canyon wall had collapsed to form a scree-filled slope, making it hazardous to climb. Kyel led the way, helping Luna over the looser sections. Targ followed with a groan, now regretting he had offered to carry a pack.

"Let's sit for a bit," he suggested when they reached the top. They were in an area of huge boulders that had remained after the softer rock eroded away. Targ absorbed the stark, harsh country highlighted with the red, brown and oranges of the rock. It had a certain beauty to it.

The bark of a k'dorian sounded closer this time.

"Quick. No time now. Let's go," said Kyel.

They hurried across the stony ground until Targ saw a smoky grey rope, crossing the spaces between the large boulders like a spider's web. Their path led towards that ropey barrier. He hesitated, waiting for the others to stop.

"Hey, slow down!"

"What?"

"Stop!"

They stopped just short of the rope.

"Can't you see it? There. That!"

Both Kyel and Luna leant forward, peering where Targ pointed.

"Yeah, there's somethin' there, sort of misty string," said Kyel.

"No, it's quite solid; greasy looking. Can't you get the odour?"

"Yes, it's stronger here. It's k'dorian pong, heavier than down in the canyon. It smells like it's all around."

"Yes, Kyel. It's coming from that web."

"I've heard about those," said Luna, spitting out a lock of her hair. "They're traps. If we go through, the k'dorians will know we're here. But they don't bother people, do they Kyel?"

"Depends on how hungry they are, I s'pose."

"Lizards' teeth!" cried Kyel, as a fierce yapping broke out behind them. "How'd it get there? No choice; we'll have to go on."

Targ saw the ropes snap, then wither away like hair in a fire, gone in an instant.

"I think their owner knows we're here."

"Better move quick then," responded Kyel.

"It's there! It's there!" shouted Luna.

"Where?"

They were in a small clearing flanked by large rocks. A forked tongue flicking out caught their attention. A large black eye stared at them.

"Wine's rot!" exclaimed Targ. He was looking at a huge lizard. It was as high as his waist, covered in grey pebbly skin, with odour tendrils drifting smokily from its nostrils. The head, turned side on to them, showed tooth-filled jaws atop a solid chest and wide shoulders. Large talons made this an efficient-looking hunter.

"We'd better go back," whispered Kyel.

"Yap, yap yap!" A fetid smell drifted nauseatingly from behind them.

They froze.

"You didn't say they hunted in packs," whispered Targ.

They moved quickly, slipping sideways to a large wall of boulders. Two heads followed their progress.

A second k'dorian matched its mate in size. The sandpaper skin looked as tough as leather plating. A black, forked tongue flicked in and out as if tasting them; penetrating eyes held their own.

They became part of this frozen tableau, no one moving as they sized each other up.

"Do one of your tricks," whispered Kyel.

"Sure! What do you suggest?" hissed Targ. But he knew he had to do something quickly. The giant lizards were not using odour offensively, so he could not throw it back at them. In addition, the animals were too big to physically attack.

The memory of animals marking their territory struck him: that stench left by the dominant males. The coils of k'dorian smell drifting around them formed a loose fog over the clearing. Both animals were pumping it out in quantity.

I could use that, he thought.

He flung his senses out, grabbing and intensifying the smell as he moulded it into a solid mass. Then he separated it into two balls.

"Tel! No!" screamed Kyel.

"What?" Targ looked down in time to see Tel scrabbling his way across the clearing. Two big heads followed the lizard's flight, before jumping in pursuit. A flurry of rocks scattered in their wake.

"No, Tel; no!" yelled Kyel. Ignoring the danger, they followed the k'dorians.

They quickly caught up. The creatures had stopped, intent on a scrap of bloodied meat at their feet. Kyel and Luna screamed. Targ was furious. He tapped a hidden power, reaching and combining chunks of k'dorian odour into dark grey balls. He flung them at the heads of the giant lizards, sending puffs of overpowering k'dorian stink into the air. The concentration of smell made the k'dorians paw furiously at their heads as if in pain. They bared their teeth before slinking away amongst the boulders.

Targ ran with the others to the patch of blood on the ground.

Chapter Nine

Lesslas lay below, its narrow winding streets shadowed by the sinking sun. The wood-tile rooves of the buildings contrasted against the light stone walls. A large square, two-storeyed building surmounted by a squat tower dominated the highest point, its open sides appearing as black holes against the stone walls. From the trio's vantage point, the town was a patchwork of blocks and lines outlined by the dark wooden palisade in a brown grassland sea.

"There," Kyel pointed, "you can see our house, just over two streets past the big hall. Sadir should be home. They won't have been to her, I hope." He sighed. "She'll be pleased to see us." He reached for Luna's hand, smiling as she returned his grip. "Might as well get down before it gets too dark, just break our necks otherwise."

The loss of Tel hung over them as they picked their way down the rough hillside towards the town.

Targ followed the two youngsters as they made their way to the town along a barely discernible track. It took little effort to scale the wooden wall before they were inside and able to slip along the narrow, deserted streets. The descending twilight made it hard to see but he could not detect any sign of recent seeker activity. There was, though, a disquieting feel, as if a bad essence still lingered in the air. Kyel appeared unconcerned, as he kept up a swift pace until they reached a junction between two streets.

A figure, dark and almost invisible, waited in the shadows.

Targ's heart skipped a beat. He prepared for an attack.

Curiously, an errant beam of sunlight angled through and lit the eastern side of the row of cojoined cottages. As it did, it caught the top of the figure, turning its head into a golden ball of flame and highlighting a soft pink-and-blue aura with orange-yellow flecking. While Targ puzzled at this, Kyel suddenly yelled.

"Sadir!"

He ran down the cobbled street, arms outstretched, and threw himself at the woman standing there.

Targ felt Luna lean against him, and her hand slipped up to take his as they watched the reunion.

"Come on," called Kyel, his voice husky. "Sadir says to get inside. Now!"

The words broke the moment, and Targ led Luna to the cottage Kyel had gone into with his sister. He quickly glanced along the quiet street before ushering Luna inside and closing the door. Kyel beckoned from the end of a short hallway.

"Sadir's got some hot food on the stove. She's had it ready." He rubbed his head. "Don't know how she knew, though."

They stepped into a welcoming warmth. Several candles lit the room, light reflecting off their holders' polished metal sides. A blackened stove stood against an inner wall, a pot on it releasing an appetising aroma. Wooden chairs, a table and several cloth-covered armchairs almost filled the remainder of the room. The dark beams overhead were supported by lime-washed walls whose starkness was relieved by a number of woollen wall hangings with earthy tones. Similarly-made curtains covered the only window. A door next to the stove drew his attention. At that door stood a woman, her hand possessively on Kyel's shoulder, eyes firmly fixed on him.

She was a similar height and build to her brother, but there the resemblance ended. Her figure was decidedly feminine, revealed by the soft folds of the sky-blue, full-length dress, the horizontal cut above her compact breasts showing a lightly tanned neck and oval face framed by wavy brown hair. She looked trim and competent, and Targ could see little sign of ageing in her face. She continued to stare at him, one eyebrow raised as if asking him to explain himself.

Targ smiled, aware of how he looked—dark, dirty and foreign—and noticed Luna move away out of the corner of his eye as if trying to distance herself from Sadir's inspection.

"Sorry, Sadir," Kyel said, pushing away from her and walking over to Targ. "This here's Targ," he said, touching him on the shoulder, "and Luna." He smiled over at her. "We've all been on the run from the seekers, all the way from Korla, and lots happened, too."

"Kyel," said Sadir, her soft voice mellow and calm, "before we talk about your friends, are you sure you haven't been followed?"

"No. He—I mean Targ—stopped them. Just as if he was one of them, a seeker,' he hurried on, "but he's not though… He's not the same as us, neither… or…"

"Just a moment, Kyel," Targ said as he looked at her. "Kyel's right, I'm not one of them…er…a seeker."

Kyel and Luna laughed, interrupting him. He looked puzzled.

"Definitely not from round here," smiled Sadir. "Your accent gives you away as not being a local; I don't believe I've ever heard such before." She noticed Targ's eyes straying towards the stove. "Before we go further, you must wash your hands, eat, then bathe. Your smell is obvious, even from here. The soap and water over there are for your hands."

Targ nodded, and then moved further into the room towards a small sink set unobtrusively in one corner.

He was sitting in a sun-soaked nook of a small courtyard at the back of the cottage, dressed in a large coarse-wool robe and sipping a cup of hot, spicy tea. The sky was a brilliant blue with the sun's warmth welcome in the early part of the day. It was the first time he had felt truly relaxed since his memories began.

He was taken with the way Sadir had handled their arrival. Her joy at seeing her younger brother again was reflected by how she made them all welcome. Washing off the dirt from his journey, then food and a long sleep on a soft bed pushed the madness of his time in this land of Ean to the back of his mind.

"Targ?" called a soft voice. He looked up at Sadir, a cloud of mellow scents surrounding her with a feminine aura. "Can I join you?"

"Please," he said as he moved to give her space on the seat.

They sat in companionable silence, sipping tea, the only sounds some far-off chirping and the buzz of insects in a patch of flowers growing out of the paving stones.

"Kyel and Luna are still sleeping," began Sadir, turning to face Targ. "Tell me more about yourself, and where you're from."

Her words were clear, her unconscious scent projections emphasising her meaning.

"Sadir," he said, savouring the word on his tongue, "I don't know." He paused, looking away, "I have no real memory of the past. I do strange things at times, but I don't know why or how…"

"Kyel told me how he found you and what you did to get here, but you're different, too. Your clothes… When I washed them, I saw…the material's different, the stitching more precise than anyone here can do… It's strange… Let me see your hands."

She held his broad, smooth hands with her slim, work-roughened ones.

"Hmmm," she murmured as she turned them over. Targ took the opportunity to investigate her scents. He was appreciating this strange, yet tantalisingly familiar power and its ability to see into the character of a person. Sadir's aura revealed her temperament and personality; he wondered just how much of his character he was revealing to her.

"Your hands don't show signs of hard work, so you're not a tradesman," Sadir continued. "I think you must be around my age… I'm twenty-one." She smiled up at him. "You don't look much like any race I've come across. Our parents, before we…lost them…travelled over much of Ean, even to the capital Nebleth and the port beyond. Even those related to the Sutanites, with their hook noses and looks of starving k'dorians, are not as tall and wide as you; then there's others… Yes, you could be from a country even further away than Sutan." She sat back, her deep brown eyes assessing him. "While there's something about you in your scent aura…"

Sadir paused, thinking about the strange powers Kyel had said this man had and wondering why he was here at this time, when the fight against the Sutanites was faltering. Could he have abilities that would turn the tide in their favour? *Maybe he's the one. Yes.* They *must see.*

Sadir nodded to herself. "I think you're well beyond any help I can give…for your memory. Best we get you to those who can."

"What do you mean?" Targ asked, more sharply than he'd intended. He sighed and looked into his cup before rubbing a hand through his hair. "Sorry. Sorry. I'm just fed up with not knowing. Kyel told me something of these Sutanites and the seekers but I don't know much of what's going on."

"No, I should be the one apologising." Sadir put a hand on his knee. "I can see that you're distressed, and I owe you a better explanation. The Sutanites and their seekers have ruled Ean for generations—each town has them. You came across a *collection* team of seekers who were looking for our talented children. And we're the Resistance, the Eanites, the people who belong. Our leaders, our Resistance, have to hide from the Sutanites. Any time we break their laws, people disappear. Any upset and people vanish."

Sadir took hold of Targ's hand again while looking into his face. "You already know how these Sutanites work, don't you?"

Targ nodded.

"Well, they're always watching, smelling us out. If children have talent, they take them. We don't usually see them again…" Sadir's voice trailed off as she looked away towards the sun. "Some are found…later…turned into seekers… but they're tainted, forever."

She looked vulnerable, eyes reflecting the light as soft tears threatened to overflow.

"I thought I'd lost Kyel…"

Targ felt for this young woman. He leant closer, unexpected emotions rising, and he longed to reassure her, to hold her and hug the sadness away.

"You mentioned…" he prompted, "the people we're going to see, the people who might be able to help?"

"Sorry Targ." She let go his hand. "It may be best to try to meet up with the Resistance. The leader's a man called Lan. They're in the hills a ways from here. *They'll* know what to do. First, though, I'll contact a friend where I work. He'll get you on the right road, plus see what he can do for my brother and Luna."

"Chirp."

Targ started at the sound.

"Chirp." Closer now, just beyond the stone wall.

"Sadir, how do I get out? Is there a door?"

"There," Sadir said, pointing to a wooden door set discreetly in a corner of the wall. "A latch, near the top."

He slammed his mug down, rushed to the door, and heaved at the resisting fastener. It gave and he yanked the door open.

"Chirp."

A familiar figure leapt onto his woollen robe and scrabbled up his body.

"Tel!" exclaimed Targ. "Blood's grace, Tel, you're alive! Where've you been? And your tail? What's happened to you?" Tel's skin was marked with healing scabs, a ragged end showed where his long tail had been. The lizard pushed into Targ's shoulder.

"It's so good to see you," he gushed, running his hands over the scaly body before calling over his shoulder. "Sadir, it's Tel. He's back!"

As Kyel and Luna took turns to hug Tel, Targ could see the animal revelling in the attention. There was a show of new scents surrounding the trio, the soft oranges and yellows tinged with light blue reflecting the warmth of their feelings.

"Pity about his tail," he smiled.

"No, Targ. Look." Kyel pointed to a scabbed point in the torn flesh. "There's a new tail growing. Conduvian lizards can regrow tails, you know."

He laughed. "No, I didn't. Can all lizards grow new tails?"

"Suppose so," shrugged Kyel.

"Can we take him inside and feed him, Sadir?" asked Luna.

"Of course, we can," she laughed.

They sat around the table in the warm, cosy room while Tel drank water from a saucer and devoured some scraps of red meat. Targ reflected on the lizard's tenacity and obvious intelligence; its contribution and impact were out of proportion to its size.

Sadir placed a platter of freshly buttered toast with a liberal spreading of thick honey before them. "All of this excitement must've given you a hunger."

Targ murmured his thanks before he eagerly took a bite. The flavours were familiar. He'd had this before in another lifetime, it seemed. The butter was stronger, more pungent but the honey's sweetness triggered memories.

"Mmmm." He closed his eyes, trying to let loose his trapped thoughts.

"Targ? Targ!"

He jumped at the sound of Sadir's voice. "Sorry, it's just…a memory was almost there. I've had this before, the honey." He waved a half-eaten piece of toast. "Don't know about the butter, though. It's different, stronger."

"Perac butter takes some getting used to, especially for foreigners. Which reminds me…" Sadir leant forward, elbows on the table and chin resting on her hands. She looked directly at Targ, her gaze slightly disconcerting him. "You're a strange one. Could be that you'd be a good prize for the Sutanites… Yes," she nodded, "and I don't think we have a lot of time before they track you, and my brother…down. I must go out now, make arrangements. You, all of you,"—she swept her gaze across the three of them—"will stay here while I'm gone. That means you don't open the door or look out of the window till I'm back."

"Fine, we'll do that," Targ said, "just stay here and do nothing." He noticed her smile.

"Well, you could tidy up a bit," she said, her eyes twinkling. "Kyel knows where I keep a razor." She stood up, took a thick peracwool overcoat from a peg in the small hall and opened the front door. "I'll try not to be too long," she whispered as she stepped through and shut the door.

"Phew," Targ breathed out, "she's quite a woman, your sister."

"So?" sighed Kyel, "I suppose I'd better get the razor, though I don't know why Sadir wants you to clean up."

"I'm not really sure either, but the beard's tickling and your sister seems to know what she's doing."

"**H**ey!" called Kyel. "Damn, I almost cut myself!" exclaimed Targ.

"Y'know, you're not as old as I thought," continued Kyel. "Without your beard, I mean. What do you reckon, Luna?"

"Yeah, he's not really so old after all," she smiled impishly up at the freshly shaven Targ.

"Come on, you two," he pleaded, "let me finish. Sadir will be back soon."

"Must look good for my sister," chuckled Kyel as he and Luna moved away.

Sadir clicked the door shut behind her as she took in the three curious faces. "Uh, Targ?" She hesitated. Targ dropped his eyes. "You know you look quite handsome now that you've cleaned up."

"Yeah, took a while to get the whiskers off though," piped in Kyel.

"Kyel, don't be so rude," she admonished, "and you ought to talk; look at your nails, bitten to the quick."

"Well at least I don't chew my hair, like Luna," he shot back. Luna spat out a curl and blushed.

"Don't worry about them, Sadir," said Targ. "They're both fine, though a bit cheeky."

"Enough now," responded Sadir, "we'll have to get moving. Kyel's been lucky so far, but don't forget: the seekers will find he's from Lesslas and soon be here. No, we're not safe."

"You're coming, Sadir, aren't you?"

"Yes, Kyel…yes." She reached out and covered his hands with hers, gripping firmly. "Besides, they might link you with me, so I don't have much choice. When all your clothing's fully dry, we'll go to the tavern. Till then, eat."

She moved to the stove and ladled food from a large hotpot onto four plates; spicy meat on chunks of fresh bread made a satisfying meal. They all enjoyed the convivial atmosphere at the dining table and tried not to think of the future.

Sadir's house was one of a number along both sides of a small street, tucked away from the main business district of Lesslas. The houses ran in a line, joined by common stone walls, any appearance of affluence being countered by the aged, wooden-tiled roofing. Narrow, shuttered windows opened out onto a cobbled street. Gutters flanked both sides and served as the common waste disposal.

The small group quietly closed the door behind them and left quickly, merging into the flow of traffic, travelling hoods up and eyes down. Sadir nodded to several people as they passed but kept up a brisk pace down the gently sloping street. The rows of houses petered out at an intersection. The city hall gradually became apparent as they walked. On top of the building stood a squat brick tower, black openings on each side revealing its scent-gathering purpose.

They turned up a wider street running at right angles where there was a large, squat stone building, distinguished by a row of perac tied to a wooden railing.

"Wait here," whispered Sadir, pulling the hood of her travel coat back from her head, "I won't be long." She hesitated at the entrance, glanced along the street before pushing through the wooden doors.

The perac, in colours ranging from grey through to an orange-brown, attracted Targ's interest. They were different to those he had seen before—the animals were slimmer, more streamlined and carried saddles. He saw a wagon coming towards him pulled by yet another sort of perac, broader and heavier. The driver, a solid figure in loose, faded clothing avoided eye contact as he passed.

"Come in," called Sadir from the tavern door.

They entered through a battered, solid-wood door into a large, dimly lit room. The wooden beams overhead faded into the gloom and the light from a number of irregularly spaced candles left many dark corners. Talk stilled, cautious eyes turned their way. Sadir hustled the group over to a table near the bar.

"Sit here and I'll go and see Jeth—get us somethin' to drink as well."

The room began to fill with conversation once more.

She spoke quietly with the large man behind the bar, who was industriously wiping a large earthenware mug with a colourless cloth. He was middle-aged, with a worn, comfortable face, and the look of ownership. Targ noticed caution behind the bartender's businesslike attitude. The barman filled some mugs before following Sadir back to the table. He plumped the drinks in front of each of them.

A powerful, rich aroma evoked strong memories. Targ reached for his mug and buried his mouth in its foamy contents. The malt-flavoured drink was cool and refreshing as he gulped the contents down.

"You must've needed that," said Sadir, eyebrow raised.

"Um, yes," replied Targ as he wiped the foam from his mouth.

"Like another?" offered Jeth, face impassive.

Targ felt the others watching him, as if daring him to break a local custom, but he nodded anyway.

While the bartender was gone, Sadir leant forward.

"Jeth is going to help us. He has a number of contacts. But we haven't got long. The Administrator's been very active lately…'cause of the seekers here and over at Korla; they seem to have a way of knowin' what's happening."

"Your drink." Jeth banged a mug in front of Targ. "Finish that, then you'd better go."

Targ drank deeply. He could feel his body relaxing, the drink again evoking some distant memories and the effect of the liquor was calming. He looked up to see Jeth twisting his cleaning cloth. Targ looked at Sadir.

"Now?"

Sadir nodded.

Jeth hurried them to the back of the room and into a kitchen cluttered with a wood-heated stove, various pots, plates and mugs. A large washstand and table and assorted storage barrels stood along a wall. He unbolted a door in a small alcove—Targ immediately recognised the peculiar perac pong before he saw three powerful-looking animals in the alley. Each wore an intricate saddle that allowed a pack bag to hang from both sides. Halters went around their muzzles and over their heads, with two tied off on each other's saddle. The lead animal's halter was held by a small, hooded man in loose, well-faded clothing.

"This here's Cernba. He's volunteered to take you on your way," Jeth said in a low voice, looking up the alley towards the road.

Colourless eyes, almost covered by their lids, peered up from beneath the travel cloak's hood. The weather-beaten face gave a tight nod. Targ noticed Cernba's aura was hidden, but it gave a purposeful feel.

"Sadir," resumed Jeth, hand on her shoulder, "you shouldn't ride unless you really need to. Your friend's too big for these perac. They're loaded with enough feed and water for two, three days at most, since you'll be going the back way. You should be near Galan by then, barring mishap." He touched the bridge of his nose with the middle finger of his right hand. "Tie your gear on the saddles, and take these now, to eat as you go." He handed each of them a stuffed bread roll. "May the waft of the road be the waft of your home."

Sadir gave him a hug. "Thank you Jeth, you're a true friend."

As they headed down the alley, Targ raised an arm in farewell. Jeth's back showed a cloud of scents rolling in waves about him. It left a leaden feeling in his stomach.

They slipped into the light traffic, taking a direction that led them away from the town centre. Targ held on to the oily fleece of his perac, letting the animal lead while he took the opportunity to look around.

Suddenly he noticed a disturbance in the background emanations ahead. Waves of dark scents were moving towards them, scarlets and purples so deep they were almost black. Counter-odours, light reds with flecks of yellow, reflected alarm and anxiety around the disturbance. It was like a rock pushing through water.

Targ looked at his companions. They too had noticed the disturbance and were starting to react. Without conscious thought, he reached out with his mind and grabbed their betraying scents, firmly squashing them into the background emanations.

From next to his perac, Targ could see the black figure of an officious-looking, bald-headed man with a prominent hooked nose, standing on an elevated plinth in the centre of the roadway. Two more sombre men next to him were measuring the passing crowd with their eyes. He recognised them as seekers, since they were dressed in the same black and grey as the guards in Korla.

Thankfully, the trio seemed to remain unaware of the group's anxiety as they passed by. Targ glanced back and saw one hesitate, a frown creasing his brow as he looked their way. Targ immediately averted his eyes, tightening his hold on the concealed scents, striving to be innocuous. He saw the seeker shake his head slightly, then turn the other way. Targ let out his breath.

His companions exchanged glances and relaxed. Kyel looked at Targ, eyebrow raised. Targ nodded, "We're through."

"We're lucky," came Cernba's unexpectedly gravelly voice. "Keep moving and we'll be outside by midday."

Chapter Ten

The town hall seemed like a broad barge riding a brown sea of grass as they left Lesslas to travel northwards, pushing against the flow of people and animals heading into town with items of trade. Some acknowledged them with a nod or a wave, but few said anything.

There were herders, grain growers, wool merchants and labourers generally wearing loose-sleeved tops and baggy trousers in greys and browns.

Groups of grazing perac, attended by one or more youngsters, became increasingly frequent the further they travelled. The animals were stockier and more muscled, with a soft-looking fleece, colours ranging from off-white to dark brown and black. A few stopped grazing the thick, tall grass to watch as they went past.

"Cernba, are those perac for wool?"

Cernba looked back at Targ. "Them? The perac? They're for wool, but also meat. Lesslas is a main centre for perac. There'll be plenty more before we turn off."

Targ reflected on the calmness of the grazing animals before moving up to Sadir.

"Can you tell me more about where we're going? I assume we're heading further north, into more mountains?"

"Yes. Sorry, I didn't think you wouldn't know," she smiled at him.

"Not too loud," hissed Cernba. "Best not to draw attention since the river's near."

"Should leave explanations till we stop after sun down," Sadir whispered. "He may be overly cautious, but…"

The road led to a stone bridge wide enough to allow a wagon and foot traffic to pass, rising in an arc to clear a fast-flowing stream. Their path was momentarily clear of oncoming traffic.

"Quick. Get across, fast." Cernba pulled the reluctant peracs into a trot.

"Targ. Hurry!" Luna called back to him.

"Why the rush?"

"Don't you remember?" Kyel called over his shoulder as he came off the bridge. "We told you ages back, when we were at the pool."

"No," Targ said, shaking his head as he caught up, "you warned me about something to do with the water. Is it here too?"

"It's the haggars; slimy pink worms that live in the water," interrupted Luna. She was looking back, her face tight with concern. "You're dead if they touch you. We've got to keep going; we're still too near the water."

"You've got to listen to the girl," said Cernba. "We've got a ways to go into the Short Ranges by sun down. I don't want us travelling in the dark."

"I still don't see why you're all so nervous," persisted Targ as they climbed up a slight rise away from the river. "There's obviously nothing there, yet we're almost running."

"Your friend is a strange one, foreign too," Cernba said loudly to Sadir. He stopped and blocked Targ's progress, his body tense. He let go the perac's lead and pulled up his rough tunic top, revealing his flat, hairless stomach. "See. You see!" He stabbed down with his finger.

Despite himself, Targ gazed at Cernba's belly, or more accurately at a puckered, scarred hole the size of a small fist in his left side. "What the... What did that? You're lucky you survived whatever it was."

"Lucky? You could say that." Cernba let his top drop back. "All because I camped too near the water and it was a foggy night, moist enough so it could move aways. The thing was fastened onto me before I were awake. Lucky I were near a fire and could burn it." He shuddered, eyes glazing over. "I were lucky." He touched the bridge of his nose with his finger. "I'll never be near water again without the feel of that thing sucking me innards out. Never again."

He swung around, picked up the perac's lead and walked briskly. "We'll be turning off the road, just ahead, if you can hurry," he called back.

Their path became a small track leading to their left into some low hills, covered with scrubby bush, the odd spindly tree and scattered grasses.

"There'll be better shelter soon and feed for the perac," commented Cernba.

Being in the company of the animals was rather pleasant once you got used to the smell. Perac were amiable, content to chew their cud while keeping an interested, ear-pricking gaze on their surroundings. They made little noise, if you ignored the odd stomach rumble, their feet falling softly on the stone and grass of the track.

"Luna," asked Kyel as they walked, "are you happier now?"

"I suppose," she nodded, looking at the country around them. The boulders were larger and more frequent, similar in colour to the land between Korla and Lesslas. "Gettin' a bit sick of running, though. Hope something good comes at the end of all this."

She sniffed and reached to Kyel's shoulder to give Tel a pat. "Of all the things that's happened I reckon he's the best. If only I could be as brave as him. There's just so much to worry about."

"Well, the people we're going to see are supposed to be able to help us. Perhaps train us up, even. I'm not really sure, but at least it shouldn't be any worse than it's already been."

"No, I don't suppose so," Luna replied. She gave a little shiver and leant into Kyel as he put a comforting hand over her shoulder.

"You'll be right, just you wait and see," Kyel replied.

The journey passed without incident. Targ saw that Kyel and Luna were keeping together, hoods down, heads close and talking occasionally. He smiled back at Tel, noticing how the truncated lizard was having a rough ride keeping balance on Kyel's shoulder.

At one stage, when they were passing through a copse of trees, a group of long, thin lizards leapt out and glided into low trees further away on translucent skin membranes. He saw the odd flying insect and an occasional large black beetle buzzing purposefully by.

Luna came up to Targ and touched his arm, interrupting his thoughts. "See," she pointed, "over there. Look at those rocks on the hillside."

Targ saw nothing but an assortment of rocks, reddish in colour with a sprinkling of orange and brown. He looked at Luna, noting her moisture-filled eyes and pale face.

"There!" she said tightly, pointing again.

He used his smell sense and immediately recognised a recent adversary. Looking inconspicuous amongst the rocks was a boulder-shaped object, quietly exuding its scent into the light breeze.

"Ah, I see. Won't forget them in a hurry, eh Luna?" He put his arm around her and gave a slight squeeze. She surprised him by pressing in and burying her face under his arm, her whole body briefly shaking. "Hey, don't worry. Don't worry. We're here to protect you. Nothing will happen with all of us together."

"No, Luna," said Sadir as she moved next to her and put a hand on her curly, blonde hair. "Targ's right. You'll be safe with us. 'Sides, Cernba's a local and he knows the country."

"Well seen, Luna," said Cernba, "there's not many of them about. First thing you do when you camp is check for them. Anyway, we have a ways to go before dark, so better keep going."

"Shouldn't you chop them out?" asked Targ.

"Nah. It'd just spread the seed, is all. Best leave them to themselves."

The sun was already hidden by the line of mountains in the west when Cernba selected a campsite amongst a thicket of bushes in the lee of a hill. He cleared the level area of any branches and small rocks before spreading a thin line of salt around the perimeter.

"It's to keep off any creatures who might think we look tasty," he said in response to Targ's unspoken query. "See those ants round that bush there? They can smell you out, and they can bite."

Targ could see a number of ants, as large as an index finger with bulbous heads and pincer-like jaws, determinedly foraging.

"They'll bring their friends if they taste you," continued Cernba, "though could be they're out because there's bad weather coming. Give us some help with the fire, Targ? We can have a sizable one since we're well hidden."

Targ sat with Sadir close to him, shoulders occasionally touching while they watched the leaping red and yellow flames seeking to outdo each other before disappearing into the blackness of the night. Through the flickering light Targ could see unfamiliar constellations of stars sprinkling the sky as he relaxed in the feel of the moment.

An aromatic smell hit his nostrils, a complexity almost defying analysis.

"Here you go then." Cernba passed him a plate holding strips of meat and a mash of tubers. "This's good, what Lesslas is known for. Tea's in the pot."

The taste was as good as the aroma and Targ concentrated on his food, satisfying his hunger while enjoying the unusual flavours.

"Phew, Cernba, you're a great cook. Really nice spices. I suppose the meat was...perac?"

The man nodded, jaws working rhythmically while he determinedly chewed his food.

"Cernba? How long before we get to where we're going?"

Cernba continued to chew slowly, giving Targ a long, measured stare from a shadowed face, eyes reflecting the firelight. He audibly swallowed the mouthful before putting his plate on the ground. "If Jeth thought not to tell you then it's not really me place to say much. Not really me place," he repeated, then paused as he put another branch on the fire. "Though you're here now," he continued, nodding, "and you should know."

Targ waited for Cernba to explain, feeling impatient at his ponderous style and thick accent. He was pleased to feel Sadir's hand close over his.

"I'm to take you to meet a very special group of people in a very special place about a day's trek from here. It's a place where the talented can go without fear of being sniffed out—without being taken by the Sutanites. So it's hidden and safe, and we keep it so."

Targ could see Cernba's grim expression in the firelight.

"Few gets to see them, and even fewer knows how to find them," Cernba continued. "I were surprised to get Jeth's call that I should take you there. He and Sadir here must be sure you're worth it." Targ felt Sadir squeeze his hand.

"Last thing I will say though is that they seem to be going out of their way to help you. Either you're something special or it's time to get something happening." He then stood, stretched and, refusing any offers of help, took the plates to clean and pack.

Targ noticed that Kyel and Luna had already settled for the night, two huddled figures close together. He spread his blankets near Sadir's, and put down a pack for a pillow. He stretched out and then smiled across at her vague profile in the dark. She was a comfortable presence in the turmoil of his life, and he felt he should express himself, say something, but nothing came. So, he just laid back and continued searching for the familiar in the stars, always feeling that something was missing.

He finally slept, leaving that puzzle for another day.

Chapter Eleven

The wide road allowed the frequent convoys of wagons to move unimpeded to and from the capital; the traffic was disciplined enough to keep to one side when fast-riding groups needed to pass. The perac gave a comfortable ride once one was familiar with the rhythm and had the stamina to make the long distance to Regulus without a stopover.

The route Jakus proposed took in the country north of the garrison city where the patrols would split up and seek out the unusual, anything to indicate rebel influence. The mountains hid much, including creatures that could make movement through the terrain hazardous. It was those same hills and mountains that allowed the rebels to stay hidden, developing their plans against the legitimate rulers.

The patrols were formidable with the addition of seekers and guardsmen from Regulus. He and Septus were without equal in their skills of detection and attack. And they came with the advantage of an effective shock weapon to decimate any resistance—the hymetta.

The creatures were not normally used by patrols for capture since the hymetta were difficult to work with. Once released they relentlessly sought the target, focusing on a strong scent or a line-of-sight attack. The biggest drawback to using them was that they did not return; once fed on the kill they flew back to their home nest in Nebleth. However, they remained a terrifying weapon.

The walls of Regulus rose above the road, the dark eyes of the scent tower on the castle casting a threatening demeanour in the twilight. The road led under the tower and down the city's throat.

Regulus was located on the site of a trading post strategically situated between the mountains to the north and the southern coast. It sat astride the Great Southern River, on the small plain between the Sensory and Belt ranges controlling all trade to and from the hinterland and filtering the movement of the populous. It was the centre of regulation, run by teams of administrators and

67

seekers. Taxes were collected to finance the government, with all goods tariffed when entering the city.

Jakus's cousin, Heritis, with his consort Regna, effectively ruled the city in the way of the elite of the Sutanites. Jakus knew that he would not want for anything that night.

Wafts of steam carried sweet scents; their colours white in the vapour. They beaded on his skin and took away the stink of the journey. The strong, supple fingers of a youthful Eanite massaged his aches; her scents indicated a strong desire to please. She was a beautiful second-year acolyte with nut-brown skin and short, black, wet hair. He wondered where Heritis had been keeping her, but appreciated the gesture, nonetheless. An exploratory tendril gently inserted into the girl's nostril brought the information he sought: she was from an intake three seasons back.

Jakus relaxed to her expertise, content to keep his mind on the present.

The dinner had featured a large tarquin, a local fish from Nebleth Bay, filled with a highly spiced grain. It, and the small yellow tubers complementing the white flesh, were lightly covered with a fine honey glaze.

Jakus leant back with a sigh of contentment.

"You enjoyed the meal, Shada Jakus?" Heritis's consort was tall, almost matching his cousin in height, dark hair piled high on her head exposing her regal neck. Her brown eyes flicked up at him as her fingers tapped on the tabletop.

"Pleasant, Regna," he conceded. "Your cooks do Heritis proud. You may leave us now." He gave a brief nod as she rose.

"Jakus," asked Heritis as the door closed behind her, "would you care to move into more comfortable quarters? I have a fine wine which I think you will enjoy—western vintage."

"Ah, yes, cousin, I well remember the earlier vintage you sent me, some time ago now. Maybe this'll be of equal merit?"

The men stood and walked to the door. Their bloodline showed—both were tall, with shaved heads accentuating aquiline noses and sharp featured faces. Where Jakus's face revealed his power, Heritis's face had a softer cast, as if he had a lower inner energy.

"Should I send for Septus, Shada Jakus?"

"Yes," he said, "our discussions will concern him, and he will have had enough time with your lead seeker…"

"Genur," said Heritis.

The fire was restful, the chair comfortable and the wine relaxing. A firm knock preceded the door opening. Septus entered with Jelm, Genur and a seeker cloaked in a nervous scent aura.

"You'd better hear what this man has to say, Shada Jakus, Shad Heritis," said Septus. "Go on," he said, pushing the man forward

"Shada and…err…Cers," the seeker stammered, "reports have just come in of further problems c…caused by those who escaped recruitment in the Korla region. Those trying to recapture them were stopped, prevented somehow."

Jakus sat forward. "Why has it taken so long to hear of this?"

"Ah…th…the winds weren't favourable," he stammered, head bowed, odours pumping.

"There are other ways, you fool!" Septus interrupted. "Why weren't these considered? Well, answer the Shada." He glanced back at Jakus.

Jakus's eyes tightened as the seeker's legs started to buckle. He flicked his hand. "We'll get no more out of this fool now. Take him out and get him to pull himself together!"

His sumptuous meal sat heavily on his stomach while he considered this train of unusual happenings over several days in the same region.

"What an appalling state of affairs; a hint of this and that, but nothing concrete, no detail. You run a poor operation, Heritis."

"I think events have conspired against us, Shada Jakus," responded Heritis. "Genur, your thoughts," he said to his lead seeker.

"Shada," the thin, plain-faced man addressed Jakus, looking from under a bony brow ridge, odours tightly controlled. "The situation is appalling. While our seekers are expected to operate independently and report directly, when initiates are brought in, or via scent pulse, this unexpected attack will have thrown them— it's not normal. However, they're there now, searching for those traitors. It's no excuse for the lack of contact though, and for that I apologise."

"But," broke in Septus, "you knew there was trouble in the Korla region, and that we were coming. You should have been prepared for us."

"Head, the confusion is not acceptable, for that I am sorry," countered Genur, bowing, firelight reflecting from the top of his shaven head.

He's like Septus's double, clever of tongue, thought Jakus.

"Well, it needs to be fixed. Take Jelm with you. And prepare for a very early departure." Septus glanced at Jakus. "With the Shada's permission."

"Agreed." Jakus eyed the two seekers. "Jelm, you'll report to me; ensure Genur does likewise."

"I will make sure of it, Shada," Jelm replied.

"Heritis," Jakus continued, "I think you should accompany us next day. Your knowledge of this region will be useful."

"My thoughts too, Shada," replied Heritis. "It will be appropriate."

During the night, Jakus and Septus updated Heritis on what they'd learnt at Nebleth. Two good bottles of Western vintage aided their discussions.

They left Regulus in pre-dawn; it was chilly and dark, a forerunner to the colder season. Breath plumed in the air as they formed into a single column of men and beasts. The group comprised twenty-five men, scent masters all in black, seekers distinctive with black cloaks over grey uniforms, guardsmen and keepers in greys and browns. The men rode light, with most of the baggage and the hymetta carried by five spare perac.

The party's authority, enhanced by a visible scent aura, ensured no one would hinder their progress. They rode hard on good road to a permanent encampment, Main Camp, established at the junction of the Great Southern and Western Wash rivers. The day ahead promised to be clear and warm, with little chance of bad weather. This suited their campaign, since the gravel roads deteriorated further north, and rain would add an unnecessary impediment.

They made good time travelling over the thinly-grassed floodplains alongside the Great Southern, arriving at the bridge crossing the Western Wash by midday. Main Camp was a well-provisioned stop, allowing the group to feed and rest their animals while organising the next stage of their journey. The group broke into three patrols, Jelm and Genur taking the Korla route to the west, Jakus and Heritis going north-west via Lesslas and then on to Galan, while Septus was heading directly north to the distant town of Telas.

Each patrol comprised an additional seeker, three guardsmen, a perac handler-cum-cook, one hymetta and its keeper, plus two spare mounts. Septus's patrol included the third-year seeker/mapmaker, since it was heading to the less travelled regions.

The sun was slanting to the west when Jakus swung himself up on his perac. "I expect," he said firmly, "that anything out of the ordinary will be reported to me immediately and to the leaders of the other patrols. If a scent pulse is not possible, then a rider must be sent to make contact. Have I made myself clear?" Jakus looked pointedly at Jelm and Genur. "Then we must move. Time is of the essence."

Jelm and Genur's patrol diverted from the group almost immediately to follow a clear road along the Western Wash, keeping the river with its imposing backdrop of the Sensory Mountains on their left. Once they reached Korla they would interrogate Genur's men from the seeker patrol for any useful intelligence.

The remaining patrols headed north for a time until the road divided. Then Septus continued on to make the long trek to Telas, the most northerly town in Ean, while Jakus and Heritis took the road heading north-west towards the town of Lesslas.

They travelled through the grey-brown sea of grass of the region which contained few trees, with nomadic herds of perac appearing as isolated mounds.

Jakus knew that anyone fleeing Korla would most likely have come through

Lesslas before moving elsewhere. If there were traces, he would find them.

They reached the town as the shadows of the hills behind Lesslas were creeping over the buildings. The patrol pushed through the gate past a few straggling wagons and foot traffic. A bearded guardsman fumbled his lance as he recognised the party.

"Sorry Cers, sorry." The man almost bent in half. "I…I didn't know you were coming this night, sorry. Can I get you an escort to the Hall?"

Jakus dismounted without comment, left his mount for one of the guardsmen to retrieve and strode with Heritis up the sparsely populated cobbled street. He anticipated surprising the Administrator, an officious man named Helmus. But Helmus was waiting for them at the doors to the Administration building, hands gripped together and his short, plump body taut.

"Shada Jakus, Shad Heritis, what a pleasure to have you with us. Please, come this way." Helmus's aura gave lie to his words.

Jakus swept past. "We'll have refreshments. What news?" They entered the common room, sat down. Mulled wine and a variety of savouries were on the table.

"Uh, Shada," said the Administrator, "I have worked diligently with the seekers since I learnt of the escapes at Korla. There were very few clues here, as might be expected, few if any scent trails; nothing really out of the ordinary. But…we have found something…" Helmus smiled briefly.

"And?" asked Heritis.

"Err, we found a slight disturbance in the background scents leading out of the town, one unusual mote, just detectable. I also learned that a group with three perac went out the north gate around noon last day. That was an unusual time to be travelling away from town. No one seemed to know who they were or where they were going. We tried all methods of persuasion—no one concealed anything."

"Which way, man?" demanded Jakus, leaning forward.

The man smiled fleetingly, shifting his feet. "Uh, northwards—we just tracked them to the river."

"Hmmm." Jakus pondered as he sat back, his eyes fixing on a spot just above the Administrator's head.

"This could be just the lead we're looking for, Jakus," broke in Heritis.

"Yes, I agree," said Jakus, noting the fleeting expression of surprise on Helmus's face. "Anything further, Administrator? Details of the animals? Thoughts on the people involved? No, of course you haven't." He looked over at Helmus. "Then we'll leave early. Attend us before dawn." Heritis rose as Jakus stood. "Now take me to my quarters."

He reached his arm across the sheets, searching for the warmth of a companion; and clasped empty air. He pulled his arm back as he realised he was in a strange and empty bed.

Jakus grumbled as he swung his feet out from under the bedclothes and into his wool-lined boots. He shivered as he splashed cold water from the vanity basin over his face, before pulling on thick linen underclothes and a woollen vest. The black robe completed his dressing.

He pushed open the door to the startled face of an attendant.

"Y…your pardon, Shada," the servant said quickly. "How can I attend you? Do you wish to have your dawn meal now?"

Jakus ignored the man as they walked down a short corridor to the common room.

Heritis stood at the polished wood dining table, upon which was set a bowl of mixed fruit, a large tureen of cereal porridge, steam still rising, and a long, fresh loaf covered with scents of its making. Butter and honey sat in separate dishes. He gave a brief nod to Jakus as he served himself. "Our host has provided well."

"Mmmm." Jakus scanned the table. "We'll need to be on our way. Our quarry will not wait."

They left before the sun rose over the far-off Long Ranges that ran north–south on the eastern boundary to Ean. Moving fast, they passed a few shadowy early risers heading into town and crossed the Lesslas bridge. The growing light showed an undulating country, reflecting the influence of the hills that backed up behind the town. Trees and bushes dotting the landscape became thicker in the eroded gullies of the Short Ranges that loomed to the north-west.

They sampled the background odours while they travelled, but even with the skills he and Heritis possessed, there was little that could be regarded as unusual or worth investigation. The scent evidence of groups moving along the track had merged over the night to blur any real distinction, so they followed the obvious thoroughfare.

"Hold!" barked Jakus. He ignored the movement of the animals as he studied the ground. Newly made scent tracks showed that a small group with at least three perac had recently joined the road.

"Heritis, this may be them."

"I agree. There is something unusual in the trace scent. This is of interest."

"Move faster," yelled Jakus.

They eagerly scanned the land ahead at every high point in the ground as the scent trail grew stronger. They could now taste feminine scents, adult and young—two women. A youth with a trace showing some scent talent. Another of a man with a strong regional taste, smelling of earth and animal. There were other scents, mixed in with the perac. One was unusual, fleetingly present and then gone.

"There, Shada Jakus!" called Heritis, pointing at a number of distant figures in the process of crossing a stream.

"Keeper!" Jakus turned to the hymetta minder, "Time for your little pet, I think. Now, before we get closer, and they see us. Use this. It'll be quicker than waiting for you." Jakus pushed a coalesced odour ball made of the newly discovered scents to the keeper.

The patrol backed away as the keeper readied the creature by drifting the odour over the hymetta's head, before unlatching the cage. It pulled itself onto the top of the structure, where it proceeded to groom, all the while buzzing its wings.

"It should go for the strongest scent, probably the man," predicted the keeper.

The hymetta stiffened at his words. Its head swivelled as it focused on the scent. The wings buzzed at a frenetic pace, as if struggling to lift the large body. It rose slowly into the air, circled once, and then sped away in the direction of the distant group.

"Follow! Quickly," ordered Jakus, "before it destroys our man."

Chapter Twelve

They had broken camp at dawn and left the relative protection of the Short Ranges foothills to travel through the sparse vegetation that became undulating grasslands spreading away to the east.

Cernba looked over his shoulder, then squinted at the sun. "We'll keep that on our right and should reach Distant Stream by midday. By sundown we'll be nearing Galan, and where we're going. This should be an easy run," he said, touching his middle finger to the bridge of his nose, "though I've heard that said before."

The stream seemed to chuckle as they approached, its waters burbling and gushing around a line of large, flat-topped boulders that made an insecure-looking crossing.

"Just follow me. Hold onto the perac, they're sure-footed," Cernba said with a shiver, fixing a gimlet eye on the innocent-seeming water, "and keep your wits about you."

Cernba led his animal onto the first of the spray-covered rocks, pulling the other two as their halters grew taut. Kyel and Luna held firmly to the animals' fleece as they stepped with them onto the slippery surface. Targ and Sadir came last.

"You're almost there. Just another step," called Cernba.

Targ, his head buzzing, concentrated on taking the last step. One more and he would be on dry land. When he reached the bank he looked up, blinked and squeezed his eyes tight, then stared, mouth falling open.

The buzzing was not in his head!

Something about Cernba, only a few steps away, had changed, wasn't right. His head had blown grotesquely out of shape, his face just a cage of angular lines, elongated with lumps of black and yellow, oozing red. Then Cernba screamed, a weird keening sound that pierced the air. It cut off abruptly as he slumped on the side of the stream.

Targ pumped air into his lungs, his mind whirling with recognition. His heart thumped as if forcing itself from his chest while his eyes denied the scene in front of him.

His scent sense abruptly overloaded and he closed down, pulling his world around himself. It was dark and safe.

The crowd in front of him was tense and expectant. Then one, a greying old man with small eyes in a pallid face, spoke.

"Well, Targas, what do you think?"

"Ah, yes," he heard himself say, "it's a Roundhill malting, around eighteen years old—most of that time maturing in a well-toasted cask." He held the glass to the light, moving the splash of liquid to highlight its golden colour. "Its nose is vinous, floral and smoky. The flavours integrate well but, with dilution, a vanilla, grassy edge comes through before a savoury dryness settles in the mouth. Overall, I'd suggest it be bottled now, as any further maturation would not improve its quality. I think, my friends, that this malas is one to recommend."

He acknowledged a smattering of applause with a slight bow of his head.

"Targas, could you give your opinion on this?"

The old man passed over a tasting glass, containing an inch of amber fluid, and then irritatingly gripped his arm.

Before tasting he detected a curious fishy note, far too much for the good of the spirit.

The applause recommenced; another irritation.

"Could you stop holding my arm?"

He turned towards the man as the pulling became painful. "Let go!"

He started, for that face had changed. The eyes had curiously vanished in the folds of skin that wrinkled across the pale face. The head extended into a long, grotesque body, like a thigh-thick pipe, lying alongside and past his arm. It rippled in waves of contraction as it tugged at him.

The applause also changed its note and became a chuckling, splashing sound that he remembered. The fishy smell was so overpowering it was weakening him.

The pulling on his arm hurt; cold enveloping and moving up his shoulder. His body bending further, becoming wetter and colder. The bitter damp reached his neck.

He yanked back, panicking. He instinctively gripped his own scents, raising them from under the blanket layer of enveloping smell. He pushed it higher until he could mould it with his mind into a small, solid dart. Then he pulsed it down, smashing into the eyeless head of the flesh-coloured creature. It reared away, releasing its pressure in an instant.

The relief hit him, and he lay there, in cold moving water, the sound rumbling in his ears until pain overrode the numbness.

He pulled himself onto his hands and knees, crawled out of the stream and onto the bank. He was freezing, wet, hurt and alone.

The sun was drying, warming away the cold, leaving only pain. Targ pulled off his travelling cloak and jacket, and rolled up his sleeve. The damage was limited to a fresh bruise extending from his wrist to his elbow. He hissed with effort as he stretched to pull off his wet boots.

Then the memories flooded in. *Targ?* His name was not Targ, after all. No, he was *Targas*, an analyser and taster of spirits for the House of Versent, and he was here? Where was his city and, more to the point, where was Tenstria, his homeland, and his family? His brow crinkled as he brought to mind a smiling woman, grey-haired and surrounded by the fragrant aromas of cooking. A man was there, big, slightly stooped with age, his large hands working wood. He did not smile much but gave the aura of solidarity and permanence. A feeling of loss was associated with him. Then even his mother faded. He desperately searched his memories for someone, anyone else, but no one came to mind, just several leather-aproned men redolent with the spiced and mellow odours of the local spirit, malas; recollections of dark-stained wooden barrels stacked in dimly lit rooms, the taste of many spirits with solid peaty and fruity overtones left after the firey first bite of a fresh malting.

He shook his head, feeling the flop of wet hair, and looked around him at the unfamiliar desolate countryside. Recent memories took over, firmly thrusting his painful recollections to the back of his mind. He remembered what had happened to him in this strange new land, the unbelievable skills, the pursuit of the seekers and how he used his sensory abilities in a strange—and frightening—way.

Where are they? My friends...

Targas mentally shook himself, closing off the questions, the emotions, the old memories. He was here. He was now. No time to wonder and recollect. There were important things to do. He was sitting on a boulder, near a stream, in the middle of a foreign country; and he was alone.

"Chirp!" A scrabbling up his leg brought a familiar weight to his body. "Tel!" Targas grabbed the lizard to his chest until it hissed in protest. "What's happened? Where're the others?" he shouted into the creature's face.

The lizard looked at him unwinkingly.

The ground nearby was scuffed, with tufts of grass and broken soil. A lot had happened here. He looked at the ground, reminding himself he could track well. As a youngster, he had followed a wounded furred beast, a softpaw he recalled, over a kilometre by seeing the odd mark, splash of blood; his eyes were still as sharp.

A parallel set of marks showed something had been dragged into the stream. Not far away, rocking slightly in the water was a dark, man-sized shape caught against a rock. He moved closer.

He pulled back, startled as a large pale tentacle humped itself up to thump down on the back of the body in the water. Another rose, hovering inquiringly, turning its blind, flesh-coloured face towards him. A third joined it.

"Enough!" he yelled. He instinctively pulled a mass of dark scents from within himself, a torrent of anger fuelling his revulsion. Shaping them into darts, he speared them at the grotesque pink worms, hitting them with visible impact.

The result was instantaneous. Like ants scurrying from a fire, the worms reared up and flipped into the water. The ripples swiftly dissipated.

Without thinking, merely accepting what he had done, Targas trudged towards the shape, dimly aware of Tel's tense form by his ear. Light movements caused by the current rocked the mass that had been left by the worms. The clothing was familiar. He recognised it.

"Wine's rot! I wasn't dreaming."

He forced himself to approach, stretching a hand to push gently. It was headless and rocked far too easily. He steeled himself to pull it to the bank. The body revealed a bare torso punctured by numerous hand-sized holes. He could see the gleam of ribs through several and then recognised an old, circular scar on the left side of the abdomen.

He sat back, sucked in his breath and pulled his arms tight into his chest, ignoring the sudden spasm of pain from his bruised arm. Only the previous day they had spoken about the dangers of the haggar and Cernba had warned him, a warning he had taken too lightly. Now the husk, sucked out by those very worms, was no longer that man. Cernba was gone.

He had not known the man for long, just enough time to be impressed with his knowledge and commitment. However, his death, with no warning, was devastating.

He gently pushed Cernba's body out into the stream and allowed it to be taken by the current.

What's happened? Where is everyone? Tel would never have left Kyel. What about Sadir? Where is she? And that thing that attacked? Why hadn't Cernba known, been prepared? It was his country.

And why am I still here, alone?

He contemplated the patch of disturbed land, seeing the wisps of scent rising, his mind in turmoil.

The questions and his indecision did nothing, it merely delayed things. He needed to be decisive, not wallow in self-pity. The memories of his previous life came and went like a cork bobbing in the waves, delaying the future, but he needed to be decisive. With a strength of will he pushed those memories back, the very memories he had been searching for, and focused on the present, the here and the now.

The broken earth showed a confused track leading away southeast across the stream, recently disturbed odours highlighting the trail against the background. Whatever had happened came from that direction and was now returning.

His hand absently stroked the lizard, the rough skin reminding him of what they had been through together. He analysed the scene and came to terms with what to do; the past faded with this new purpose.

Avoiding the bloody patch near the water, he examined the melee of perac tracks. He found a clear group of foreign perac tracks coming from the crossing Some force had crossed the stream to catch up with his group. Then it appeared they had all returned across the water. Some of the group were walking and the scents indicated that Sadir and the youngsters were part of it. His reading could not tell what had happened and the scent traces were confused. He just hoped that they had not been harmed.

So far the country had thrown some horrors at him, and he had survived, his abilities being stretched with surprising results, but what lay ahead was unknown, and powerful. What they had used to kill Cernba really scared him, digging out suppressed memories. However, he knew he had to follow, he had to get his friends back; there was no choice.

Physically he felt good. He had had a substantial breakfast that day—a lump formed in his throat as he thought of Cernba—and there was plenty of water available. However, there was little time.

He moved upstream and drank from cupped hands, keeping an eye on the water as he did so. Tel watched with interest but made no move to get off his perch on Targas's shoulders.

"Nothing to carry water in but we'll manage, Tel. Let's get going." He felt his resolve weakening as the thoughts of all that had happened, and his current situation started leaking into his head. He took a huge breath and fixed on what he had to do, locking out any recriminations. He studied the stream, the crossing and the land beyond.

After tying his coat and travelling cloak into a manageable bundle, he carefully crossed the stream and then climbed the slope of a low hillock. The track headed southeast, as indicated by the scent trail, until it disappeared against the sky with its developing heat haze. Targas noticed that the group was following a level, less direct path, as if they were not worried about pursuit. Cutting over and between some of the hills would be shorter if he could keep up the pace. He was fit from regular walking, and any excess weight had been burnt off by the last few days.

"Okay Tel. Hold on."

Targas ran down the grassy side of the hill and fell into a loping jog over the undulating ground. His mind kept pushing memories of a different land at him.

He expected to see people appear, to nod or call "good day", even to discuss the weather. However, none of this happened because wherever he was, wasn't there or then, wasn't his home. He pushed those memories out of his mind and focused.

He jogged to the top of a small hill and stood catching his breath while scanning the horizon. A dark line of mounted people moving at walking pace was not far ahead, a small cloud of dust trailing them. He could see three shapes on foot towards the back of the group.

He quickly calculated in what direction he would need to go to be ahead of them, then ran on down the hill.

An ambush. That's what I need. One of me against all of them. Little chance.

Targas knew that he was at a disadvantage, but he had to try. He had overcome difficulties before, and he seemed to react instinctively when stressed.

He tracked their progress by keeping an eye out for their dust and odours, setting a pace that eventually took him at a distance parallel, then past, the line of people. He allowed no sign of his presence since he was sure the enemy had good scent detection capabilities. He eventually collapsed down onto an earthy bank along their path.

The wait seemed forever as he sprawled on the crumbly, clay soil. The soft, earthy smells merged with his own scent, binding him even more firmly to the surroundings. He lay with more patience than he had ever known, focused, not allowing his thoughts to stray.

A feeling gave the first sign. It was almost like a vibration in the bedrock—a gentle insinuation of presence. The absence of sound added weight to the feeling. They had arrived.

The crisp crunch of perac feet broke the silence, vibrating through the shale. Targas risked a look.

Their outlines appeared over the ridge. The leader, a tall bald-headed man, black-robed, had an arrogant profile and a seemingly easy confidence. He imagined the flared nostrils and the hawk-like gaze. There was minimal aura about this man.

His black-and-grey-clad offsiders showed less composure, constantly moving their heads from side to side, exuding a nervousness he could see. The captives' stress showed clearly, following behind in the dust, bound hands tied to a solid animal controlled by a perac-riding guard.

As they came closer he could see that the journey had not been kind to Sadir, or Luna and Kyel, but they appeared unhurt.

The vibration increased—they were almost on top of him. Targas lay motionless, heart beating loudly as he strengthened his concealing odour shield.

Their gazes swept over him, mouths half open, nostrils quivering, but there was no reaction as they moved past.

He was stiff from being in one position for a time, any noise covered by the trudge of the party, and scent concealed by the clouds of dust rising into the still air.

He moved out of hiding.

Leaving Tel behind, Targas hurried after the group, keeping directly in line behind the walkers. He used his developing skills to hold a large swirl of clay scents around him, forming it like a shield so that anyone looking back would just see a thicker dust cloud. As he caught up he could see his friends, dirt-covered, heads down and stumbling along at the rear. They looked so exhausted that it would be hard to help them get free.

He maintained a tight hold on his covering odour while he investigated the solid leather leash binding the animal to the guard's saddle. He had nothing to cut it with so waited for the animal to walk past so he could see if his companions' ropes were any easier to untie. Sadir was closest.

Targas put a cautious hand on her arm. Her head jerked up and he looked into her dark brown eyes, the whites startling in her dirt-covered face.

"Sadir…"

"Targ," she croaked, confused she couldn't see him. "I thought you were dead. Are you all right? Where are you?"

"Shhh," he whispered urgently. "You must be quiet."

She lifted her bound hands as she was jerked forward by the perac's progress. "Help us," she pleaded.

Targas looked at the ground for inspiration and found a shard of flint-like rock with an edge. "This'll have to do," he muttered.

It was hard to keep cutting at the one place on the leather with the constant movement, while tightly controlling his concealing shield. Then Kyel and Luna became aware that something was happening and automatically pulled, putting more pressure on the animal leading them. Targas paused as the perac grunted its discomfort.

"Shush. They'll see. Quick, Sadir."

He sawed feverishly at Sadir's bonds while she pulled back against the tether. He pushed out with his mind, gathered abrasive grit from the surroundings and forced it across the rope in time with the sawing. With a sudden jerk the tether snapped, releasing her. They both fell to the ground, dust rising all around. But the animal's distress had caused the guard to stop, and he could hear shouting through the opaque cloud of dust.

"Hurry!" yelled Targas as he grabbed Sadir's hand. He pulled her to one side, up a small slope and away from the noise.

"Here!" He pushed her into a small gravelly depression and then lay next to her desperately pulling in his surrounding odours, tightening them, forming a blanket above them. He distantly marveled at his control of his developing powers.

"Shhh," he puffed as Sadir's gasping seemed so loud in the confined space.

The noise near them ebbed and flowed. There was a lot of shouting, one voice particularly strident. He cringed when he heard the youngsters cry out in pain, and then it grew quiet. He held Sadir tightly, locking away his failure at rescuing all of them, while breathing her familiar scent.

The silence was even more worrying. He knew the enemy was nearby; the animals made scuffling sounds; their vibrations obvious through the earth. Other vibrations were even more disconcerting, like small tremors moving across the ground. He could feel them getting closer, so he tightened his cover, pulling every odour molecule from the surrounding rocks into a tightly woven barrier. A large thump on the blanket pressed down, hard, and then passed. Their cover held, though the pressure sent sweat pouring out of him.

After an interminable time, the vibrations receded; he could hear the animals moving away. Then complete silence.

Sadir's repeated coughs into his arm became dry, shuddering sobs. Targ loosened his arms to give her more room.

"Shhh," he hissed urgently into her ear. "Please."

"The others! Can't we…get my brother?"

"No, sorry. So sorry," he whispered.

They lay entwined, their hearts beating so loudly that he was afraid that the enemy would hear.

"Targ," murmured Sadir, "what're we going to do?"

Chapter Thirteen

The guardsman was a bloody mess, so flat his body moulded to the shapes of rocks beneath.

Whammm! The body shivered under the impact of another odour bolt.

Heritis's face was a choleric red as he targeted an odour bolt towards the youngsters cowering next to a nervous perac. The piercing scream as the animal took the brunt of his burst of power snapped him out of his rage.

"Ahhh, blood's stink!" he shouted as he powered a bolt at a boulder, shattering off several chunks. He pushed clenched hands firmly down his sides and ground his teeth.

"Jakus…" he muttered, looking in the direction their leader had taken earlier, following the capture of the youngsters and the woman. There was nothing he could do to recover the missing woman, and Jakus was sure to make him pay. Heritis recalled watching his cousin pacing the ground back at the stream, sniffing and studying the air, puzzling through the scents for that elusive mote of odour that he had tasted from his hymetta in the caverns of Nebleth. He had told Heritis he would return to Regulus, via Lesslas, taking a guardsman as escort, since what he was seeking in the scents was missing.

"And Heritis," he'd ordered, "bring the captives and follow. Guard them well."

Heritis stood glaring at the rest of the patrol as they searched the ground, a trickle of sweat running down the side of his face adding to the sticky humidity of his black robe.

"Shad Heritis," called his seeker, nervously easing his perac forward. "I believe we'll need to move soon. It's a long way to the main road and a suitable campsite."

Heritis took a last look over the stony, desolate ground. *How did she escape? Did she have help? Jakus will want to know.*

"Shad?"

"What!" retorted Heritis, swinging around and glaring at the seeker. "Right, let's move. No! Leave him," Heritis yelled at the remaining guardsman and seeker as they moved to retrieve their companion's body.

The perac stopped abruptly grunting its protest at an increased load. Luna and Kyel lay senseless in the dirt, scratches and dishevelled clothes showing they had been dragged some distance by their bound hands.

"Blood's stink! Pick them up. Get them onto the animals." snapped Heritis. "Throw off what's not needed."

The men moved, efficiently pulling off the empty hymetta cage. Then they strapped the male captive in its place; the female they bound across a spare perac.

Heritis watched irritably, knowing that he could not delay informing Jakus of the situation by scent pulse any longer. *The Shada has to be told or it will be the worse for me,* he reflected.

The scent pulse was not complicated and had been developed into an effective means of communication, even though it was dependent on the weather pattern. The message was composed of linked scents bound in a form that would hold together until trapped and interpreted by a scent catcher or trained scent user.

Heritis used essences from the area of capture (as defined on the constantly updated Ean odour maps), and a combination denoting time of day, a twist of capture/danger odour, extracted captive smells of the prisoners, all stamped with his imprint. An underlying link clearly noted the escape of one. The scent message was pulsed into the air currents on a broad, thin band.

He was confident that minute odour motes would be received by Regulus, and most likely by Septus in the north if the winds swirled back against the Long Ranges that formed Ean's eastern border—but it was unlikely that they would reach the south-west where Jelm and Genur led their patrols.

Wispy clouds coming from the west would soon cover the sun—a quick taste of the air confirmed the potential changes in the weather. Rain was coming.

"Let's move," ordered Heritis. "We need to get as close to Main Camp as we can before dark."

Targas's mind was calm. He was in the comfortable arms of the woman, cocooned by the scents around him. Both remained motionless.

The vibrations had ceased some time ago.

A trickle of gravel pattered onto his cheek; a scaly nose pushed through his dissipating odour blanket and brushed his ear. He became aware of Tel, the heat of the day and a raging thirst all at once.

"Sadir?" He reluctantly extracted himself from her grasp.

"Mmmm."

"We must get moving."

"Targ?" croaked Sadir, staggering as Targas helped her to her feet.

"First we need water, then…" He stood, holding Sadir while scanning the surroundings for any sign of their attackers. A confused melee of fading scents was the only sign of their presence.

"Uh, stay here. I'll have a look; see if they've gone." He kept low as he crunched over the uneven surface to where he could see the trail leading south. As he did so he heard a loud buzzing, then saw a dark reek of odour nearby.

"No!" he gasped. There was a grey-clad body, pulped beyond recognition, blood spread widely over the clothing and on the ground, large flies already feeding.

"That's the guard!" gasped Sadir, coming up behind him. "The one who had us. It's him. Only him that's there, isn't it?" Sadir reached for Targas and buried her mouth in his shoulder. "Tell me there's no one else!"

"No!" said Targas, firmly pulling her away. "Just the guard; you can see his boots. Let's go."

He focused on the southwards-leading trail, trying to concentrate and break the mass of scents into their individual components, compromised as they were by the surroundings and the overpowering animal and people smells.

"Yes, they're still with them, not hurt as far as I can tell."

"Can we get them, rescue them?" Sadir pulled at his arm.

"Arr!" Targas jerked away.

"You're hurt. Where?"

"Got into a fight," he shrugged, rubbing his arm, "nothing to worry about. I don't know what we can do about the youngsters, Sadir. Those…Sutanites are too much for us to attack."

Sadir looked along the trail. "We can't just leave them…" She staggered slightly, leaning against Targas. He put an arm around her.

"I don't want to leave them either," he said, "but we need help. Food. Water."

He paused and shook his head as if to clear it. As much as he felt for Kyel and Luna and knew they must attempt to rescue them, the strangers had shown just how powerful they were. And what was he, anyway? Would it do any good if they attempted a rescue against such odds?

Yes, he rationalised, *if we can just rest, then maybe find help.*

"Where's the nearest stream?"

"Back where we've come from, I think, but it's away from Kyel and Luna."

"We've no choice, Sadir, we'll be in a bad way if we don't get water, and we'll have to get shelter too." She slumped back into his shoulder, and they turned away towards the north.

The sound of running water was a magnet. They dropped to their knees at the stream's edge and thrust their faces into a deep depression, drinking their fill, the need overcoming caution. In his relief, Targas didn't think to scent the water.

"No!" said Sadir. "The water's too dangerous. Oh!" She rocked back on her heels, her face ashen, hand on her mouth and tears brimming in her eyes.

Targas got quickly to his feet and reached down for her. "What's the matter?" he asked.

"It's Cernba. I've just remembered Cernba," she sobbed. "He's dead, isn't he?"

"Oh damn," said Targas, "I'm sorry." He shook his head, then gently squeezed her shoulder. "Yes, he is… Did you know him well?"

"No," she murmured. "No, I didn't, but he was nice. That dreadful hymetta got him. Didn't you see it?"

"See it? That thing?" He remembered Cernbar's head covered by the legs and body of a creature, the same thing that had killed the man he had met when he first came to the country. "They're…*hymetta?*"

"Yes. The enemy use them. They're cruel and vicious."

Targas shuddered as the memory also brought back the haggar. "Hold on for a moment." He scooped up a handful of water, tasted it, and recognised immediately the rapacious hunger of the creatures below. "Yes, the haggar are here too. I've an idea."

He went deep into his scent memories for the only other dangerous animal he knew intimately in the country. He knew the strength and power of the k'dorian odour, and determined to infiltrate it into the stream.

With his mouth under the surface, he felt the predators' interest as he moved the k'dorian scent through the water. The viscosity and currents were different, but similar to the process in the air. He pushed the odour out in a broad wave with all his force.

The hungry haggar came closer, wary of the presence of k'dorian stink.

Targas increased the scent, concentrating it, pushing harder. The haggar were now moving side to side as if unable to go forward. He insinuated his most powerful k'dorian scent memory, the moment when the giant lizards had seen the easy meal of Tel. The water rippled as the haggar rose, twisting away and fleeing down the small rapids. The predators had gone.

He paused to wonder how easily he had done it, using his skills in this untried way.

"Targ?" Sadir's voice drew him to the present.

He sat in the deep depression in the streambed naked to the waist, enjoying the splash of the chilly water on his skin, keeping the memories of similar times out of his mind. He plunged his head under to wash the dust and grit from his hair, and sat up refreshed, now taking time to look at the woman sitting next to him.

She had stripped down to a fine linen top tied at the waist and a pair of light-coloured briefs. He watched her long, slim neck and contoured back as the water darkened her brown hair and pressed the shirt against her skin. As she came upright, the wet material outlined her small breasts and firm stomach. She was desirable, and his body reacted.

"Sadir?" he said quietly.

She turned to him, glanced down at his chest before looking up. Her dark eyes were dancing, as if the water had washed away their concerns.

They moved together, noses touching, inhaling each other's scent, sensing each other's need. He pulled her closer and lost himself in the urgency of her kiss.

His mind focused on her, absorbing her, breathing her in. They used each other, clinging, feeling, comforting, supporting as he pulled her onto the bank, but a small part of his mind warned him against full body contact. His feelings for her could not allow the moment to change into something he would later regret. He stretched out with her on the soft grass.

Targas noticed the sky slowly filling in a disconcertingly familiar way, with light wispy clouds edging towards the westering sun. Sadir lay in the crook of his arm gently moving her hand over his skin, curling fingers in his chest hair.

"Targ, I don't want to think, don't want to worry. I feel safe just now and for the moment. And I know we'll be able to save Kyel, and Luna…won't we?" Sadir looked up at his face and then rested her cheek on his chest, afraid to see the answer in his eyes.

He squeezed her shoulder as they lay resting, refusing to look beyond the moment.

"Sadir," Targas murmured, "I think I've got most of my memory back." He felt Sadir stiffen. He hurried on. "It was when we were attacked, and when I… you know…closed off somehow, like…like I did before in Korla, when Kyel and I"—he swallowed—"when we were captured. However, this time the seekers didn't see or scent me, and I was just left partly in the water. Somehow it was that, and the haggars, forcing back my memories. One was pulling at me, and I thought I was back home at a gathering, telling people about the properties of our spirit drinks. Then the haggar started to hurt."

Sadir lifted her head to look directly at him.

"My name is Targas, not Targ, though it's close enough, and I come from a country called Tenstria. I'd never heard of Ean but…I have heard of Sutan, where the Sutanites come from; I think Tenstria must be somewhere beyond Sutan."

"Go on," she prompted.

"Well, I can remember my parents, though it seems vague, as if they've died— at least I don't have real feelings for them. I sensed there could be someone else, but I couldn't find them." He looked sideways at Sadir.

A light breeze chilled the air. The fine clouds had now caught the sun, dimming its brilliance, its warmth.

"We need to get away from here, I think." he said squinting at the sun. "Better get dressed."

Sadir gasped as she noticed his arm. "That round mark on your arm—where the bruises are, did that come from the haggars?"

"Yes," said Targas. "It wasn't pleasant, but I managed to stop them. At least they helped me get some of my memory back. However, enough of that." He thought back to his gruesome find. "We need to find somewhere to stay for the night."

"Yes," Sadir agreed. "Can you taste the air? There's a change—bad weather coming. We'll be needing shelter soon."

A vague sunset fought the descending gloom by the time they found a small cave where a large flat boulder had fallen against others.

"We're going to get cold, maybe wet," shivered Sadir.

"What about a fire?"

"We haven't got any fire starters, Targ...Targas."

"Have you got some flint? You know, rocks that give a spark when struck together?"

"I suppose there could be some around here. But I've got a small knife if that'll help. It's got a steel blade. Sorry, I just remembered I had it." She smiled fleetingly, then pushed her hand into an almost unnoticeable slit in her trousers and produced a small, wooden-handled knife.

"Yes, that'll help," said Targas. "Better late than never."

He prepared a small fireplace, and piled dried grass and small sticks together while Sadir searched for wood. Striking the metal with a small, flint-like rock brought back memories of living off the land as a boy, catching softpaws in home-made snares, cooking them over fires, and sleeping under the stars. He looked up at the sky with that thought, seeing the dark clouds bringing an early end to the day and smelling the vague traces of ozone and freshness giving a hint of what was to come. Then he concentrated on trying to make a spark.

"Damn thing!" It did not work, and he was loath to fail his fire-starting before Sadir returned.

He recalled how he had added solidity to an odour when he was freeing Sadir. He focused on the rock, seeking the hard crystals that caused the spark. He grabbed the odours, building up then compressing them into a solid ball. He rasped it down the metal.

Sparks flew. These he trapped, coalesced into a glowing ember that slowly floated onto the tinder when he released his hold. The fire almost exploded out through the grass and twigs.

"Oh!" Sadir approached out of the gloom, arms laden with sticks. "How'd you do that?"

"Err, not sure," replied Targas with a grin, "but it's effective."

They lay squashed together, Sadir cuddling into the crook of Targas's shoulder, while Tel took up his usual position next to the fire.

"Be nice to have something to eat. How about roast lizard?" Targas joked. "That lizard can live off the land, but we've got nothing."

"Targas, we've got a ways to go before we find anyone, and any food. But we must by next day; the youngsters are depending on us."

"Sorry Sadir, I shouldn't be thinking of myself."

"No. I didn't mean…" She fell silent, pressed against his length. Both of them were lost in thought.

Targas pursued his memories. He still couldn't remember having a partner or having a relationship before; only that he'd been alone for a while, wrapped up in his work, self-absorbed, only occasionally aware that something may be missing from his life. It felt good having Sadir lying alongside him, relying on him. He sighed contentedly.

Plock! A large drop of water hit his head, splashing across his eyes.

"What?" Targas exclaimed groggily.

Sadir, murmuring in her sleep, flung an arm across his chest.

A small glow marked the fire at the entrance, a breeze was making its presence felt and a light drift of rain touched the edge of his boots. It was cold and a line of water drops hanging off the edge of the boulder began to fall. He got up to stack the fire.

"Targas, it's cold and it's wet," complained a sleepy voice.

Targas lay back down and listened as the fire, hissing and spluttering, fought the rain. He tried to recapture some warmth until Tel moved closer, pressing his cold body between them.

"Tel. You're missing Kyel too. Oh, I hope they're all right."

"Sure to be," said Targas reassuringly. "They wouldn't go to all that trouble, then harm the youngsters."

They lay huddled together while the rain grew heavier, and the fire lost its battle.

Leaving the site's security to his seeker, Heritis went straight to his perac-hide tent. It had been erected on high ground where it was partially protected by trees. Inside was enough room for a small, covered fire, a camp bed, a table and low seat.

Once refreshed with a passable meal, he had the two captives brought in. They were untied and pushed down against the central supporting pole. He could see their terror rising in waves above the general background of pain, hunger and thirst. The youngsters focused on him, just their eyes relieving the monotony of their dusty covering.

He lifted an earthenware jug from the table and poured a stream of water into his cup. He drank, deliberately spilling drops down his chin.

Heritis pulled his hood off, allowing the light to reflect from his shaven head, leaving his face in shadow. He kept his voice low.

"I need answers; just a few. Then you may clean up, have some water, something to eat perhaps." He reinforced his suggestion with a gentle pulse of entreaty and trustworthiness.

He noted a level of defiance that spoke of hidden knowledge. He would have liked to investigate it, but he did not have the time. Jakus would want to break these two, and of course Septus would be there.

"Names first."

He pondered the names he was given. Kyel and Luna were village-derived, no lead there.

"Parents and village? Kyel."

"Just my sister, Cer. We live in Lesslas now. Our father was a trader; died when I was small."

Heritis caught Luna's eye.

"None, Cer. Something happened when I were young. Brought up by an aunt in Korla." She glanced at Kyel with wide, frightened eyes. "Just visiting with Kyel and his sister."

"Where were you going?"

"Excuse me Cer, can we have water?"

"Certainly, after a few more answers." Heritis pulsed out an essence of amiability. "You must have an understanding of where you were going."

"The town of Galan, Cer; leastways I think that's where we're headed. We weren't told much."

Heritis could see Kyel was telling the truth, but his aura revealed that he also concealed something.

"That's fairly obvious," he said, "but why were you going to Galan?"

"To see friends, relatives." Kyel's aura boiled with unease.

"Hmmm," Heritis murmured. "Luna, who was with you?"

"What do you mean, Cer?" Luna was like a small lizard trying to face down a hungry k'dorian.

He threw off his amiability and spoke through clenched teeth. "There were others with you. We know you had a local with you—smelt like a perac herder. Who was he?"

Luna's eyes squeezed shut and her head dropped. But Kyel stared hard at Heritis, eyes bright with tears. "That was Cernba, our friend," he said in a hollow voice. "You killed him!"

"Nothing to do with me. The hymetta can't be easily controlled. Who else was with you?"

Kyel sniffed and wiped his nose with a sleeve. "My sister, she…she was with us," he sobbed. "She's the one you lost. Where is she?"

"We'll leave it for now, shall we?" Heritis said.

He saw waves of relief coming from the youngsters.

"Just one other thing," he began quietly, rising from his seat. "You *will* tell me who else was with you…soon." He projected a large, looming presence, pulsing fear and aggression at them in a powerful wave.

They pushed back against the post, eyes wide, shrinking into each other. Their auras revealed anxiety and that they were concealing something.

It was clear these two were part of a secret linked with the rebels around Korla. *Jakus will be pleased to know of this,* Heritis thought.

"Guard!" he called.

The guardsman pushed his head through the flap of the tent.

"Take these two, bind them and keep them where you can see them. Feed and water them, too. You'll see to it that they don't escape, of course."

The man pulled Kyel and Luna to their feet and hustled them out.

As Heritis prepared for sleep, mind whirling with the possibilities of what knowledge these captives held, rain began to hit the tent.

Chapter Fourteen

"Shad?" The voice broke into his dreams.

"What is it?"

"Your dawn meal."

The seeker came into the tent with water running through his cropped black hair, down his youthful face and onto the overcoat of perac wool. He held a platter of food covered with a waterproof cloth.

"All well during the night? The captives give any trouble?"

"No concerns during the night, Shad Heritis. The prisoners were brought into shelter when the rain became too heavy."

"Good. We'll have a wet trip this day. I need someone to ride ahead to Main Camp to prepare our quarters. We leave when I've finished eating." Heritis paused. "The keeper's little to do now. He can go."

No matter how well designed, the rain found a way through the clothing. Perac wool was an effective, if somewhat odorous rain repellent but it became heavy, and leaked more the wetter it became. The black dye in the cloaks also had a tendency to run and stain the skin.

Heritis was soon soaked, and found it hard to appreciate the sure-footedness of his perac on the muddy road. Water filled the ruts and potholes, leaving an unpredictable surface and making for a day of slow travel. Each rider allowed their animal to pick its way along the road.

Looking back through the misty rain, he could just see the captives sitting hunched over on their perac. The guardsman followed closely behind.

A grey light showed an extensive, misty rain giving the wet couple little hope of relief. Even Tel, sheltering inside Targas's coat, was starting to complain. Growling stomachs and the chill finally prompted them to move from their inadequate shelter.

Sadir looked up at Targas, the damp hood of her tunic top framing her moisture-beaded face. "Wish I still had my wool overcoat," she said as a shiver ran through her. "Don't s'pose there's much hope for the youngsters out in this?"

"They'll be all right," he said, assisting her to her feet. "But what we need is help and a large dose of luck as well." He peered out at the wall of rain. "Not looking good."

"It's not going to stop," said Sadir. "We'll have to go. Just freeze and starve if we stay. We should head towards the mountains. We'll meet the track to Galan that way. We'll have to go there—they'll help us."

It had been raining all night and the ground was voiding runnels of water into slight hollows. Trying to avoid them was impossible. Boots filled with water, every part of their bodies was wet and eventually mud-covered from a number of falls. Tel had moved to Targas's shoulder to better prepare for the next tumble.

Sadir and Targas clung together as they climbed the rough terrain alongside the stream. They were saturated and cold, the chill causing them to shiver uncontrollably.

"At last," groaned Sadir when they reached a muddy track, the only piece of level ground. "I've just got to rest for a moment," she said, starting to sink down onto a convenient rock.

"No," Targas said, shaking his head tiredly, "we can't. I'll never get up if we do. Which way now? Anywhere we can get dry and warm."

"This way, I think." Sadir clung to Targas's arm.

Targas, too tired and cold to object, linked arms with her and together they staggered along the sodden track.

The day had lightened, although the rain continued at an energy-sapping rate. It was all they could do to put one foot in front of the other, and Tel's weight across his shoulders was becoming oppressive. Their shivering had stopped, and he was having trouble concentrating. He knew something about hypothermia and was worried. They had to get out of the rain and get warm soon.

A dark shape loomed up next to the path. Two large boulders standing at right angles with beams of wood fastened on top would give a modicum of shelter. They moved into it and slumped against the stone. There was no heat generated between them as they huddled together, their ability to create warmth having vanished during their trek. Tel semi-hibernated on them.

We have to rest a bit, before going further, thought Targas as he held Sadir to him. He knew that to stop could mean their deaths, but he was so cold and so tired, the effort of moving just too hard. *Perhaps we'll be all right if we rest a little.*

The cold invaded his mind and his thoughts ceased.

"Come," whispered a voice in his dreams, "we'll take you to shelter, get you warm."

His body was pulled up and draped across something with a familiar smell. He recognised the rhythmic movement and felt the glorious warmth of an animal underneath him. All the while the shivering continued. A time later he was pulled off and carried into a dark, warm space, redolent with smells. Hands busied themselves with his buttons, clothing, boots, removing everything. Then he was moved into a space where an all-encompassing warmth enveloped him, pressing his skin, thawing his bones.

"Drink this," whispered a voice. A cup was put to his lips, and he drank reflexively, the liquid leaving a trail of fire down his throat. He heaved and coughed, finally becoming aware of his surroundings.

He smelt a resinous tang in warm water vapour all around him and felt a gentle massaging of his flesh by supple hands. His body responded by cramping, but each time a muscle contraction threatened the hands knew and kneaded his flesh.

"Shush," croaked a voice as he attempted to speak. His eyelids felt heavy, but he forced them open to see a wizened old face with kind, black eyes. He started when he realised she was female, but then relaxed and closed his eyes again.

The wise old face grinned lopsidedly down at him.

Coughing not far away drew his attention. Rolling his head to the side he saw Sadir responding to similar treatment. She lay on a wooden bench on the far side of the room, being massaged by a young female in a short white shift.

Later they sat in a warm room, wrapped in soft, grey wool robes. They sipped a thin soup and sleepily watched the flames of an open fire in a stone hearth. He had enjoyed the massage and felt that he and Sadir were now safe.

He was puzzled when Sadir looked behind him and tried to stand.

"No, sit, Sadir," a soft voice said, "you've been through enough already."

The short, grey-robed old man who stepped around in front of Targas was bald and thin with a heavily-lined oval face. He bowed and spoke in a slow, precise way.

"I am very pleased to finally meet you. Welcome to our haven in the hills. I am Lan of Sanctus." A smile lit his face.

The knocking on the hut door was loud enough to trip his security grid. Heritis recognised the intruder's scent.

"Septus. What is he doing here?" muttered Heritis. "Wait!"

Heritis got off the bunk and went to unlock the door. Septus barged in, his wet, thin face excited.

"Where're the captives? What have they told you?"

"Sit, Septus. Something hot? Acolyte!" he called through the open door.

Septus looked like a drowned perac, his black robe a second skin plastered to his gaunt frame.

"Are you mad, man? Have you travelled in these cursed conditions, and through the night, just to find out what I've discovered? I sent you a message to say we'd wait for you at Regulus."

Septus took a spare perac wool blanket off the bed and draped it around himself, then snatched a steaming mug brought in by the acolyte.

"I...got the scent message. I was coming back a-any...w-way." His teeth started to chatter. "My men are still up around Telas, searching."

"You left your patrol and came all this way without escort?" asked Heritis.

Septus frowned, taking half a step towards Heritis. "W-what're you s-suggesting?"

"Forget it, Septus. We have other concerns. You didn't by any chance happen to detect any signs of a woman when you came back, specifically in the region just north of Lesslas river?"

"N-no. Why?"

"One of the captives has escaped, albeit in strange circumstances."

A tendril of alarm shot from Septus through the background of chill and exhaustion. "How?"

"That, Septus, is a matter between Shada Jakus and myself," said Heritis stonily. "I have advised him that the woman captive escaped and the guardsman responsible has been dealt with. A point this raised, however," he continued, "relates to the circumstances of the escape. The woman disappeared without trace. Her scent vanished despite an extensive search. The other captives are two youngsters at their change of life, same age as other potentials. They have given little yet, but I know that they have more information. We will extract that at Regulus." Heritis gave a tight smile.

Septus drew back his lips in the semblance of a smile, his teeth making his face more harsh than usual.

Just your looks will be enough to frighten it out of them, thought Heritis.

Chapter Fifteen

The weight on his chest woke him. Ungumming his eyes, he looked into the impassive face of Tel sitting calmly on the bed cover. Memories rushed in.

"You're good at disturbing people, and haven't gotten any lighter," Targas groaned.

Tel looked away, distracted. Another weight was slowly making its way along Targas's body. Another "Tel" peered down at him.

"Don't tell me you've multiplied during the night? No, this one's too pretty to be you."

The new arrival had a slimmer head and was a slightly darker shade of grey. The odour was distinctly lizard but there were subtle undertones.

"Get off, both of you. I have to find Sadir."

He pushed them aside, wincing as his body threatened to cramp, then slid out of bed. The comparative warmth of the stone floor was welcome to his feet. He stretched, then realised he was naked.

"And I've no rotted clothes. Surely they've left me something?" he said, looking around the small chamber.

The light coming in from the doorway revealed the bed taking up most of the space—there was nothing else.

He glanced at the two lizards sitting on his bed, unperturbed by the activity.

"You could at least help me look." He peered into the dark space under the bed.

"Targas?" The voice came from somewhere behind him.

"Sadir! Ouch!" His head hit the edge of the bed as he reacted. "Hold on!" He looked around and then grabbed Tel, holding him protectively in front.

"Oh!" exclaimed Sadir as she paused at the doorway.

Targas's face reddened. "Can you find some clothes? Mine have gone."

"There's your robe. It's fallen off the back of the bed. Shall I get it for you?"

"No! I'm quite capable, thanks. Just give me a moment."

Sadir gave him a quick glance as she stepped out. He heard her stifled laughter outside.

After placing Tel on the bed, he pulled on the soft, grey peracwool robe, which extended down to mid shin and sandals from under the bed.

She smiled as she came back in. "You looked so funny. At least we know what else lizards are good for."

"Huh," he replied. "But it's great to hear you laugh."

The smile leached from her face. "Come," she said, almost formally, "I've spoken to Lan. He wants to speak with you over the dawn meal."

Sadir turned to go, paused and then reached back with her hand. Targas took her small, cold fingers in his.

She led him down a short corridor of grey, granite walls and ceiling that had a feeling of permanence and security. They passed other, similar bedrooms before turning through a wood-lined stone arch into a larger, brighter room. Many timber tables, some with grey-robed people sitting at them, lined the sides; it looked like a communal meeting room.

He recognised Lan sitting at a table that was well lit from several window slits in the rock wall.

"Welcome, Targas. Targas…that is the way to say your name, no?" He gestured to the seats opposite him. "Please. Come and sit.

"Targas… That name is unusual here in Ean. Sadir has told me something of your journey. You are truly a remarkable man. From Tenstria—a country unknown to us… Most unexpected, though you were called…"

The man's speaking in riddles, thought Targas. "Uh, I should thank you for what you've done for us. The last few days have been hard."

"Please. Enough that you are well…and we have met. Sit down. Eat. Then we will talk." He smiled at them while gesturing to an array of breads, cheeses and fruits.

Targas found he was hungry; the journey had taken a lot out of him. He ate a chunk of bread and cheese, then washed it down with a gulp of hot tea. The tea was so familiar that it instantly brought back memories: sitting in a sun-drenched kitchen, drinking tea, eating toasted bread, but so long ago. He felt confused, as if there were two minds operating inside his head: one, a professional working in a field he loved where he could assimilate flavours and tastes, combining them for a promising maturation and then savouring the results over a period of time, the other an incompetent bumbler in an unfamiliar land.

"Targas?"

"Sorry, I was just thinking about what has happened." He looked across into Lan's warm, brown eyes.

"All in good time, my friend. For the present we should discuss Sadir's Kyel, and Luna."

"Damn, I mean sorry. Please, we need to help them." He held his upturned hand out to Lan. "We couldn't free them before…too many…and we need to, urgently. Can you find out where they are? Tell us what we can do?" Targas paused for breath, aware that he was sounding confused.

"Everyone here at Sanctus is scent-talented; refugees from all over Ean. As I have explained to Sadir, we are not yet ready to allow the enemy to know more of us." Lan gave a slight smile while gently shaking his head. "But one or both of your youngsters have a role in our journey... It may not be fully understood until their part is over. With *Knowings,* or the foretellings we occasionally have, sometimes there is just a shadow to guide us.

"For Kyel and Luna we have already commenced a process, a process which may save them, although there is risk."

Targas looked at Sadir, seeing the moisture forming in her large, dark-brown eyes, "We aren't afraid—we'll do what it takes,' he said. "So, when are we going?"

"No, our plan for the youngsters does not include you, or Sadir... Not for this day, at least." Lan looked from one to the other. "We truly sympathise, but we are doing everything possible. We have another priority here and we believe that is you, Targas. We have much to do with you," he continued. "Sadir, thank you for bringing Targas to us—the cost has been high. But"—Lan held up his hand— "the timing is most opportune." His eyes searched Targas's and he nodded. "Our task is to bring you into our ways... For you to understand our ways, our talent and to help you develop those powers that are in you. Meanwhile, please eat."

Targas smiled curtly and turned his attention to the food.

"Come," said Lan when they had finished. They followed Lan through another wood-lined doorway into a long, narrow room. Light from thin window slits along one wall cleverly lit several rock sinks filled with steaming water. Two grey-clad women, sleeves rolled above their elbows, looked up as they entered.

"Lethnal and Hynal, two of our most talented companions," said Lan as he acknowledged them. "Sadir you know. Let me introduce Targas."

The women's auras, suffused with a rosy pink and soft green, were obvious in the bright light as they came to greet them.

"Welcome," said Lethnal.

Hynal nodded and added, "We're pleased that you've both recovered so well."

They embraced Sadir then Targas, almost touching noses. Targas noticed a flare-like scent coming first from one, then the other. He saw an answering scent from Lan out of the corner of his eye and raised his eyebrows in question.

"You'll see," laughed Lan. "Thank you, my friends, we will take our leave." He turned to Sadir and Targas. "Follow me."

The first impression was of a watery sun struggling to provide light and warmth through a haze-filled sky. Its efforts turned a panoramic scene into colourless country painted with a grey wash. The view would have been uplifting, were it clear and sunny, but the day just reflected their mood.

Sanctus faced east on a hillside formed of jumbled grey granite boulders. The buildings merged into the background; even the doors and windows appeared to be mere cracks in the rock. Targas could see no sign of people anywhere, even though the size of the buildings suited a considerable number.

They followed the grey of Lan's robe through a grey field of stone on a grey day—even their own robes blended in. It surprised Targas that the odours also merged together into a general background of natural earth and rock, life being revealed only in small patches that quickly dissipated. Any buildings were soon lost from view behind towering monoliths as they followed a barely discernible track. Their progress was halted by a narrow ravine where a small stream coursed, splashing over the edge to hit lower down with some force. Targas gave an involuntary shudder as he remembered the sound.

Lan turned abruptly along a trail skirting the lip of the ravine, then walked towards a wall of granite, huge and forbidding in the pale light. He ducked into a small, dark opening in the rock face and disappeared. First Sadir and then Targas followed, stepping onto a wooden ramp crossing over a small rivulet issuing from the same opening.

Their feet crunched on coarse sand as they walked into the dimness of a large, open area; it was surprisingly warm. There were torches all around the walls, burning with a steady light and near invisible flame. Lan stopped, letting them adjust to the conditions.

Targas could hear sound above the trickle of the small stream, the murmur of people—a considerable crowd, if he was any judge. He was sensitised to it; it was more than odour, it was *feel*. He waited, pleased when he felt Sadir's hand seeking his.

They were in a large, roofed-in rock cavern, with a high ceiling and smooth, concave walls. The space was oval-shaped with a number of large pockets along its length, eroded over the ages by a persistent stream scouring through the rock. Flowing water had ground out the cavern and smaller caves where the stone had been softer; the spoils littered the floor as sand and gravel.

Lan coughed gently to get his attention, and said: "Targas, our people wish to meet you." He faced inwards towards a crowd of men and women. "Fellow Eanites, may I make known to you the man who accompanied Sadir from Lesslas. This is Targas of the country of Tenstria. His coming signals the change."

Targas snapped out of his thoughts and looked at the people coming towards him in the dim light. There was an ethereal quality to them, all in grey robes and many of them with little hair or completely bald, both men and women. He felt unkempt in front of them with his tangle of dark hair and unshaven face.

Their scents created an overwhelming background to their welcome. The next few minutes were spent in embracing each of them nose to nose. These were genuine, loving people, all of whom he felt could be friends.

Lan seemed to sense when Targas needed rescuing, and soon led him to one side.

"I am sorry, all this is new to you. So many of our people at once is hard, but they are most pleased to meet you. It is foretold you are their hope for the future." Lan smiled at him, "You have done well in understanding us to this point; our accent, our scent. It is time now to help you increase your understanding. Come somewhere quieter and I will tell you what we should do."

Targas gripped Sadir's hand and followed Lan through an opening in a side wall. It led into an almost spherical room that was a dramatic contrast to the rest of the cavern. The floor under the curved granite ceiling was composed of white sand. A trickle of water widened into a small pool before disappearing into a minute fissure at the opposite end. The sand was soft, with a clean, crisp smell, reminiscent of the first breath taken after rain has washed away the dust of the day. Lan sat comfortably cross-legged on the sand and patted the ground. With some awkwardness, Targas and Sadir settled on the ground near him.

His voice resonated in the enclosed space.

"Targas, we recognise you hold a great potential. You have shown some of that already. We must act to help you use your power against the Sutanities before it is too late. But time is short, so we need to act with haste."

"But Lan, you talk about skills and potential. I'm not the one you're looking for, the foretold one. I don't even know how I got here. Since then, I've been doing things I couldn't do before in Tenstria, as far as I remember, but I don't know how I'm doing it. I've just been reacting when something happens. Sometimes I seem to be able to control what I do, but…

"I can't help you if I don't know what's happening to me, what all this scent power means. I'm a blender of malas, nothing more.

"There must be someone else."

Lan saw the confusion in Targas's face, hands outstretched as he pleaded for understanding. The silence widened.

"You know not what your skills are? What they mean, how to use them?" The creases on Lan's brow deepened as he spoke quietly, as if to himself. "We were expecting more awareness from the one called to our aid.

"That is disturbing, Targas…but you *are* the one, so we will have to use what you have, train you and help develop what you are. Maybe with time you will be aware of what is within you.

"Perhaps because of you some of our best will be able to learn to work in ways unknown before you came."

Targas opened his mouth to speak but the look on Lan's face brooked no challenge. Shoulders slumped; he waited in resignation.

"Targas, you will learn and understand. I will answer the questions I see in your face, but we will need to prepare first. Will you trust me in this?"

Targas hesitated and sighed. "What do I have to do?"

Lan lowered his voice and Targas leant nearer. "Here you are exposed to natural odours where we can direct scent groups into your head to help open doors, develop knowledge. It will take some time, but your abilities will build as we proceed."

Lan turned to Sadir. "Sadir, if you would leave us? And please ask Zahnal to come."

"Yes, Lan." Sadir smiled fleetingly at Targas, then rose and left the room.

"In a moment you'll be re-acquainted with Zahnal," said Lan.

Targas turned at a slight sound and immediately recognised the small woman who had tended him the night before. Her wrinkled face smiled in welcome from under a head of short grey hair.

"Zahnal will be shaving you. She is very experienced."

Targas's eyes widened as the old woman theatrically raised a large knife and winked.

She made Targas sit on a convenient boulder near the pool, then proceeded to produce a scentless lather from a mash of plant material in a large earthenware bowl. Her brush was stiff perac hair bound to a wooden handle. She occasionally added water as she lathered, humming a tuneless song under her breath; every so often she would look up and wink at Targas out of an eye almost lost in wrinkles.

"Ready, young man?"

She poured a handful of lather on his head and down his face, massaging it in with strong, practised fingers. Targas found it hard to relax.

The long swipes of the blade easily removed his growing beard, then his hair, leaving his head and face hairless. He could see Lan nodding out of the corner of his eye.

"Up, young man. Please remove your robe."

"What?" Targas shifted back.

"All hair is a scent trap. It is usually removed, all or in part,' Lan answered quietly.

Targas bit his lip on an automatic response. "All right," he growled, "do your worst." He looked warningly at the old woman brandishing the knife in front of him and pulled off his robe.

"Step into the pool and sit," Zahnal ordered. "The water's warm enough."

As he did so she dropped her own robe, unashamedly revealing her brown, wrinkled body, and came into the pool carrying the knife and bowl of lather.

Targas closed his eyes.

S adir walked into the large cavern with the feel of many people. The relative darkness encouraged her to move back against a wall, so she leant against the stone and closed her eyes, willing her mind to quieten. She jumped as a hand touched her shoulder.

"Sadir, sorry if I startled you. You remember me, Hynal?"

"Yes," Sadir replied, "we met in the washing area." The scents of the tall, solidly built woman were familiar.

"I just wondered whether you wanted some company," Hynal continued, "I mean with your partner in there…"

"No, he's not," Sadir objected, then hesitated. "I s'pose he is, really." She smiled into the darkness, "I mean, someone's gotta take care of him."

"Well, Sadir," said Hynal, "I just wanted to let you know I'll help where I can. It must be hard on you in this strange place with all that's happened."

"Thanks, Hynal," replied Sadir, and meant it. "What should I do now?"

"Why don't you come with me?" Hynal linked her arm with Sadir's. "We'll go back to the main building and have a look at your scent powers. Might get tea or something else while we're there?" She pulled Sadir away from the wall and together they trudged through the sand of the cavern and into the daylight.

"N ow Targas, make yourself comfortable…" said Lan. "Lean against the wall. Feel into it; be part of it. Just relax your mind. Trust me."

Targas concentrated on the soft sand, the sloping wall of rock and the feel of the room. His body relaxed after Zahnal's onslaught, and he tried not to think of his new bald look.

"Open your mouth slightly and close your eyes. Relax. Don't worry when you sense me moving in your head."

With some difficulty Targas let himself go, allowing his thoughts to drift.

He felt a solid block of substance pushing against the roof of his mouth, then further, into his sinuses, and higher. He was lost; tugging movements briefly registered, then there was silence. He fell into a sleep, a sleep of nightmares.

Chapter Sixteen

Heritis led the patrol through the tall wooden palisade of Regulus and into the city. A nervous guard met them inside the heavily timbered gates, confirming that Jakus had already returned.

"The Shada wants me to attend him?" Heritis snapped.

"Yes, Shad," the man responded with an enthusiastic nod as he stepped to one side.

Heritis looked back to Septus. "Take the prisoners to the dungeons. They need to be prepared for interrogation, but their wellbeing, Septus, is vital, so take care. The Shada will be seeing them soon."

Heritis kept up his outward calm as Septus led the small group away without responding. The two youngsters remained slumped forward in their saddles.

Heritis knew that Jakus would be angry at the loss of the captive woman. His cousin was a dangerous man, and being a relative had little benefit.

However, he still had misgivings over Jakus's early return to Regulus. The ways of the man were strange, almost furtive. Heritis sighed, shook his head and then dismounted. *I hope Regna hasn't had to put up with Jakus's advances. But there's no future in worrying if he's been with Regna. This is not the time to do something about it.*

He saw Jakus's long, black figure at the window as he hurried into the castle. A dark aura showed above his shaven head, but Heritis thought he could see a measure of control in the scent, which boded well.

Jakus turned and glowered at him. "So, you have come back without the woman? I would not have expected the Shad of Regulus to have had difficulty controlling a woman and children," he spat, scent clouds billowing darkly. "And you have no knowledge of how she escaped or where she went? Or even know who she was? You fool!"

"I offer no excuses for the disappearance of the boy's sister, for that's who she was," said Heritis calmly. "I carried out exhaustive searches of the area immediately she disappeared, and found nothing. I've never encountered such a complete absence of scent trace." He paused, composing his face. "I can offer no explanation except to be certain that it was rebel-caused. I questioned the two captives on my way to you and found some useful information, if you wish to hear it." Heritis waited until Jakus gave a curt nod before giving details of what he had learnt.

The Shada stared at Heritis. "Useful? Maybe. I'll interrogate the captives without you; you've been too soft. We will continue this discussion later. Leave me!"

Heritis backed out of the door, concentrating hard to avoid revealing his feelings.

He was pummelled from all sides, assaulted by thick fingers pushing through his hair, probing every part of his body, dragging a soapy black scum with them. The two men had overpowered him, stripped off his clothing and then proceeded to clean him with little thought to his comfort or dignity.

A yelp at a particularly thoughtless probe brought a splash of tainted water in his mouth. He endured the rest in silence.

The buffeting stopped and he stood there dripping into a puddle of black scum, arms gripped protectively around his middle, waiting. A whimper made him look to his side.

Luna was next to him swaying with exhaustion, naked and small.

"Here!" A bundle of clothes was thrust at him.

Kyel pulled the tunic top and loose trousers over his wet body with difficulty, and then turned to Luna. She had not moved. She just held her own bunched clothing against her stomach, trembling, eyes blank.

"Let me help you, Luna." He gently disentangled her fingers and opened the bundle. As he forced the clothing over her wet, pale body, she seemed to recognise him and gripped him hard. Kyel knew that as bad as the experience had been for him, it would have been worse for Luna.

Soon their watching guards pulled them apart and walked them out of the washing area, through an age-eroded doorway and into a small side room. The black floor crunched as they crossed to a rough wooden bench and sat on it. After a time, a guard brought them two bowls of thin, lukewarm soup and left them alone in the dim light.

They leant against the wall huddled together, feet tucked up to avoid the cold and harshness of the scentless charcoal floor. They did not talk, each wrapped up in their own thoughts, exhausted and still hungry.

"Luna… Listen, we've got to get ready for them. We've got to try and fool them somehow."

Luna shivered in response and pushed into him.

Kyel looked at the top of her wet, blonde hair and nodded; he understood. There was not much they could do against scent masters, and they would be stripped of all their knowledge. He tightened his hold on her.

There were important questions in his mind. *What had happened to Targ?* When the hymetta had killed poor Cernba, Targ had disappeared. He was behind them, last across the stream, but was lost in the confusion. *And why had Targ been missed by old lizard-nose?* He shook his head as he absently focused on the rough stone wall in front of him.

And how did Sadir, his sister, get free? He reckoned Targ had something to do with that. All he knew was that his captors had been very upset. He had never seen such power—the way that guard had been destroyed was terrifying.

Kyel knew they were soon to face their captors and that there was little he could do to prepare.

"Luna?" She did not respond, just sat small and waif-like, staring at her knees, her blonde, wet-darkened hair outlining her face. He squeezed her, trying to get a response. She looked up at him, a flicker of recognition in her eyes.

"Luna," he repeated, grasping her head between his hands, "we have to do something to get ready for when they come."

Luna sighed.

"Come on, girl. Try!" He rubbed her cheeks, trying to get some warmth and colour to return. In desperation, he kissed her cold lips. She pulled back slightly, then hugged him.

They stayed huddled together for a while.

"Kyel?"

"Mmmm."

"I'm sorry."

"What? No, Luna, no. It's their fault, not yours. We just have to try and get ready. What I reckon is that since they'll be able to find out what we know, we should try and change it a bit."

Luna looked at him questioningly.

"It's about Targ isn't it?" she asked, her eyes widening as she spoke. "You don't suppose he's still around?"

"Could be. Don't know, though," he sighed and touched her cheek. "But Targ's strange, wouldn't you say?"

Luna nodded.

"We haven't seen anyone like him before. He's strange," Kyel reiterated.

"Oh, I don't know," said Luna, shaking her head.

"Yes you do," insisted Kyel, seeking eye contact.

"Do you?" countered Luna.

"Yes." Kyel raised his voice. "I do, really, and so do you. He's definitely strange. He's done some stupid things. But he's probably dead by now, right? Right!"

Luna saw the animation in Kyel's thin face and nodded slowly.

"Yesss…he's probably dead," she agreed. "I liked him, though."

"We both did. Poor, sad Targ."

Then they fell quiet, as silent as the walls around them, shivering together.

The door hit the wall with a crash. Light poured in. Rough hands pulled them to their feet and hustled them out of the room, along dark corridors and down stone stairs to an aged wooden door. They pushed it open and thrust them into a square room lit by several lamps.

The complete absence of smell, of any odour, was Kyel's first impression as they crunched barefoot across another black floor. Against a stone wall were several cross-shaped, wooden frames leaning at an angle. Kyel was pushed backwards, his hands and feet spread out and secured to the arms of a frame, leaving him spreadeagled, unable to move. He could see the men adjusting the straps on another frame to allow for Luna's small size, before fastening her to it.

The straps were tightened, the men left the room and the door closed behind them.

An odour began to insinuate itself into his brain: a pleasant, calming aroma that spoke of warm, sun-drenched days, a comforting tiredness, supporting friends—not seen, but there.

Clouds formed, grey and fleecy in a blue sky, gently moving across the sun. The light dimmed with a gentle drift of rain, just enough to bring a subtle end to the peacefulness. One cloud grew darker, larger than the rest, firming in shape, filling his vision.

"Hello, Kyel," said a soft voice.

"Mmmm," he murmured.

"How are you? Are you and your friends all right? Hope you haven't been put to too much trouble?"

"No, not much." It was difficult to answer any other way.

"Where are your friends?"

"Ah, Luna's here."

"What about your other friends? Who are they?"

"Best friend is my sister," he began slowly, "then there's Tel."

"Who's Tel?" the voice continued in a soft monotone.

"My friend. He's been hurt though, but he'll get better."

"Where is he?"

"Don't know. Hope he's all right. He's tough…"

"Is he special?" probed the voice. "Is he powerful?"

"Yeah. He knows when things're wrong. He helps us." Kyel paused, getting tired of the questions and wanting to go to sleep.

"Who is he?" The voice had become harder, more insistent.

"He's my friend," mumbled Kyel. "And he's been hurt; growing a new tail, though."

"What!" The voice changed pitch, becoming strident.

"Uh!" Kyel's eyes flew open and in front of him, blocking the light, was a huge figure, black and forbidding. Kyel frantically glanced around, at once aware of his surroundings.

He was still strapped to the cross-shaped frame. Luna was similarly bound alongside him, but she was not looking his way. Instead, she was transfixed by a hunched black form crouched, spider-like, only an arm's length away, white face highlighted by the red gash of a smile, with humourless eyes.

"Septus, leave her for now. You can help me with this one. We'll try the easy way first."

Jakus turned his attention back to Kyel. "Now you'll tell me what you were doing out there. When you were captured you were heading north, with others. And you both had been caught before by one of my patrols in Korla, eh? But then you got away. You must be special."

Kyel tried to look away, avoid breathing in the man's sour breath, but firm fingers gripped and turned his jaw. He held his face rigid.

"Who was that man with you?" Jakus's eyes bored in at Kyel.

Kyel tried to resist, pulling against the restraints, away from that face. However, this powerful scent master puzzled him for he wasn't using odour with his questioning. Kyel swallowed and tried to appear calmer and helpful.

"H…he's just a man, Cer—a man I found in the town. He followed me when I was leaving. He was there still, with me, when the seekers took us. Then he went weird. Didn't seem to know anything; he was…" Kyel stopped, not sure what was going on behind that impassive stare.

"It was him, wasn't it?" a voice hissed into his ear.

"Ah!" gasped Kyel at Septus's sneak attack. His vague control collapsed, and his bladder relaxed.

"Blood's stink! Guard!" called Jakus. A man in grey guardsman's garb rushed in. "Decontaminate this with new charcoal." He pointed at the black floor. "You were supposed to make sure they were clean. Is this clean?" He pointed at the floor below Kyel.

Kyel shut his eyes. He was not embarrassed, just vaguely pleased at causing them a small problem. However, he knew there was worse to come.

"Septus," snapped Jakus, "don't scare him again."

"Better, Kyel?" said Jakus, after new charcoal had been spread. "Septus asked you a question, you remember? Was that man the cause of you staying free for so long?"

Kyel tried to pull away from Jakus, who had moved even closer, now sitting on a stool between the lower legs of the frame. Blood started to seep from his wrists as the skin tore. He knew that these men were going to get what they wanted from him—if not him, then Luna.

"Don't know," he said evasively. "He did some strange things…but he really didn't help us; were just lucky, I guess."

"Fine," said Jakus. "We can play it that way if you want. Septus, would you like to ask another question?"

Septus grinned, reaching out to place a pallid hand on Luna's knee. "We aren't asking for much, so, if you feel you can't help we'll just ask this young woman. I'm sure I can persuade her to tell us what she knows." He gave a slow smile, tongue darting lizard-like over pale lips. "Where is he, this stranger?"

"I don't know." He shook his head, then hurried on as he saw a frown ripple over Septus's face. "I mean he was with us. We left Lesslas with him, and he was with us. When your thing killed Cernba…"—Kyel gulped—"When Cernba died, everything happened at once. I think Targ fell into the water." Kyel's mouth snapped shut as he realised he'd revealed Targ's name.

"This…*Targ*," smiled Jakus, "was he really powerful? What did he do?"

Kyel hesitated before answering. "He…he seemed to want to help us, but didn't know much about here. I reckon he's not normal, a bit gone in the head."

Jakus turned to Septus. "Strange or not he has power, and if he's not dead then we've got to find him." He looked back at the prisoners. "It's time to get into their minds. No relaxant to make them more tractable. Straight in."

"Shada, I want the female."

Jakus looked at Septus, and then at Luna. "This time, Septus…but be controlled. I don't want her ruined. We may have need of them later."

Kyel strained his neck to see Luna. She was panting through a tight mouth in a white face dominated by her dark, wide eyes. Septus came to her, pulling at the legs of the frame.

Then a long-nosed face blocked his view as Jakus descended onto him, thick odours emerging from an open mouth. An invasive pain bored up into his sinuses, emerging into his brain. Colours exploded; he was pulled in all directions and knew he was lost.

Chapter Seventeen

Colours cascaded into his brain as his eyes flashed open. The surrounding scents were more intense than he had ever experienced. He snapped his eyes shut, but then a suffusing perfume pushed at his memories, calming him.

"Targas?" The speaker was Lan. Targas recognised the scent from when they'd first met, but now it was as if the other was standing right behind his eyelids.

He squinted out of one eye. A general background of pink, containing a run of blues and greens, was suffused with sparkles of yellow gradating through to orange. He closed the eye.

"Targas. Do not worry; let it go. Let the memories go. Relax… Allow it," soothed Lan. "This tea will assist."

He was propped up on a soft pillow in his room of the previous night. He gratefully accepted the warmth, and absorbed flavours from the tea. He recognised a potpourri of spices from his previous life: soothing and zestful, the sharpness overlain with the tang of mint and the acidity of lemon. He savoured each sip.

A familiar aura delightfully pushed through the wall of scents into his mind, demanding to be recognised.

"Sadir, I'm glad you're here." Targas tried to open an eye in her direction. The canvas of colour had changed, bringing more yellow than pink; light blues and greens were present but there was a line of violet closely associated with her femininity. He recognised it and was pleased. A stronger purple flickering in her background showed an underlying stress.

He was making a rapid adjustment to this change and was able to keep his eyes open this time as the colours gradually faded away, like water evaporating on a hot rock.

"Come, my…love," said Targas, holding out his hand, pleased by his warmth for Sadir and the way her aura had shown her feelings for him. She sat next to him and caressed his freshly shaven head.

"It feels nice," she whispered in his ear.

Targas spent the remainder of the day assimilating his new scent awareness. He felt strangely alive as the energy flowed through him. Being given a greater range and depth to his scent senses meant he needed time to develop and experiment, but the urgency of their situation hung like a pall over him; the need for haste overrode everything else.

The large communal room had its share of people, but all seemed too polite to approach him: a brief nod and flare of scent was all the recognition they gave if he caught their eye. However, there was one response he found disquieting. An older man had hurried past with just a quick, blank glance. He puzzled over the feeling that he knew this man.

Sadir slid in next to him with two bowls of savoury stew, the smell reminding him that the day was almost over. He smiled, enjoying the intertwined odours of the meal together with that delightful aroma of the woman he found he cared for. A quick sorting of her aura revealed that while she was pleased to be in his company, she was pre-occupied.

"Nothing further about Kyel and Luna?" he prompted.

"No, Targas. I've found out the Council heard from their agent, and he's now headed for Regulus—that's a city on the river about three days from here. The youngsters have made it there, but it's got a reputation. There's nasty things that happen there, nasty." She shook her head, eyes brimming with tears. "Surely we can do something for them. Oh, I know what Lan says, but he's looking at bigger things, not just two youngsters."

Targas put a comforting arm over her shoulder.

"I asked, Targas, I truly did," she sniffed. "But Lan has plans for you. You've just got to work on your abilities, and I, I've got to be patient. And we've both got to get strong again. You know, he says we almost died last day?"

"Yes, we were lucky to be found," reflected Targas.

"I'll get you some more food, shall I?" said Sadir, "and drinks."

Targas nodded, yawning. "Please."

"Then we'll get to bed. I can hardly keep awake as well."

As Sadir left the room, his eyes followed her trim figure. He felt a closeness that was more than just companionship.

The sun was high enough to have heated the massive rocks. It promised to be a clear, cloudless day.

Targas closed both hands around the mug of hot herbal tea, warming them while he walked. Lan was waiting in a small alcove formed by the towering granite boulders, a suntrap for cold days.

Targas pushed through the last patches of covering bush to see the elder seated on a half-buried boulder. His calm, weathered face smiled up at him.

"My friend, sit with me...please."

Targas sat, feeling the warmth of the sun, and the permanence and peace emanating from the man and the surroundings. The view southwards across the wide valley where the foothills of the Short Ranges pushed in from the west was breathtaking.

He took a sip of his tea and exhaled noisily.

"You have taken a liking to our drink? A good place to sit, eh? A good place to think." Lan nodded towards the view.

"I was just thinking how I've always enjoyed a hot drink first thing in the day. It's been quite a while."

"Well, you have earned it. I expect it has not been easy for you. But just being here is significant. You are a resourceful person, Targas." Lan looked quizzically at him. "I surmise it is time to give you an explanation, eh?"

"Yes," Targas agreed, "at moments I think I know how I got here. I remember bits, but it seems too fantastic, like I'm making it up. I remember what's happened since I arrived though, but I don't know why it's me. I need to know."

"Just relax, my friend," interrupted Lan. "We will talk on this." Then he turned to look out into the distance as if seeking inspiration.

While Targas waited he saw vague movements in the small trees down the slope where the local wildlife was foraging. Squinting against the light, he could easily pick out the land's odours rising from infinite sources in questing tendrils, a light breeze directing them.

"Ean…is a troubled land, and has been over generations. There is a group, which is strong," Lan nodded to himself, "very strong. They have substantial powers, and they use them to get what they want. I suppose," he continued in his slow and measured way, "it is the problem of light versus dark. To locate with, and to use smell is often a well-developed skill here, more so than in other lands such as your own. It is what the people of Ean have always been able to do. Those whose ability is greater usually hold positions of responsibility within the community. Wise people, healers and protectors, guide us, help us survive and develop. Our scent mastery is a vital part of who we are."

Lan smiled at Targas. "When the Sutanites invaded several generations ago they crushed any resistance by native Eanites. Our land, our resources were taken and used. Their scent mastery was strong, and it was used to a new and frightening level. The Sutanites have been led by ruthless individuals. The current Shada, Jakus, continues the tradition. He, and the head of his scent users, Septus, are powerful scent masters. They have developed the practice of seeking out, snaring talented natives, young men and women, indoctrinating them." Lan sighed and gazed into the distance before continuing.

"Kyel and Luna were in the latest capture and, but for your interference, would have disappeared, like others before. I believe your presence is beginning to cause them concern."

"Yes, I understand what you're saying, Lan," Targas agreed, "but the real question is, how did I come to be part of it? I'm not from this country and my memories of getting here are pretty horrific."

"Patience,' Lan said, raising a hand, "I will come to that. It is important to understand more about the Sutanites. Their rule has been based on secrecy…on fear. They expand their powers in unnatural ways. They use these powers to control the people." Lan paused and looked down at his sandaled feet. "Ean's animal life has suffered as well…I know also that you have had experience of the hymetta."

Targas shuddered.

"The most insidious aspect of this," Lan continued, "is their program of control. Again, you experienced this. They will not be hindered and react to any threat, real or imagined. Unfortunately"—he shook his head—"their seekers taking our youngsters at their change of life is one of their methods. It is most damaging to our people… Anyone who tries to stop them is killed. Those found to have value are kept, the others just disappear." Lan looked into Targas's eyes. "That is unacceptable, and we must do whatever we can to stop it. Whatever!"

"Lan, I agree, particularly now," said Targas. "But where do I fit in? And again, how did I get here? It shouldn't be possible."

Lan reached over and took his hand. "You have talents, powerful talents, some unknown to us, Targas. They add layers to reinforce and control… You seem to have the ability to alter the makeup and structure of bonds as if changing the very essence of scent. Those talents may just make a difference. Like the Sutanites, who have spent years, many years, establishing and developing their control in Ean, we have been seeking ways to counter that control.

"A generation ago the Sutanites began taking our children. One of their soothsayers predicted a scent master with exceptional skills would arise in Ean and destroy their power. By taking our talented ones they would control all scent power and prevent that happening.

"We tried to hide our children of talent, but they knew how to find them and in the finding many others were killed. Their reprisals were savage, their destruction of our scent talent ruthless.

"Our most adept scent masters sought to find a way of locating the one foretold, before the Sutanites did—it offered us hope.

"As you know, like the Sutanite scent masters, we control smell as a physical form. We can manipulate it. We can use it. Our plan was to send, uh…tendrils of an attraction scent. Not the kind you have already experienced from the seekers," said Lan, "but physical scents…attractants. There was an inherent danger—there has to be one, does there not?" Lan smiled sadly.

"We combined our knowledge and skills and sent out a search web of attractant tendrils. To our shame, we were ill-prepared and acted before we understood the power of the force we created."

Lan paused, his face strangely still as he remembered.

"We drew another like you to us…but she was with child. The journey drained her life force as she arrived. The baby was taken from her…alive.

"We hoped that the abilities we called for would show in the little one, but it was not to be. The *Knowing* in the first week of life showed it was absent.

"Perhaps it was foolish at that time to try such a path without fully understanding its power, but our land was suffering…"

"What happened to the child?"

"She lived and was raised by a family that loved her as they would have loved the baby they had just lost…"

Targas waited, unwilling to break the silence and draw Lan back to the present. A question pushed in his mind. He needed an answer.

"Lan, you refer to Knowings. I assume they're a kind of foretelling of the future? Do you take much stock of such things?"

Lan paused and looked hard at him.

"Yes, we do. One does not know how such prophecies occur, other than some of our people are able to interpret the future through a scent-based skill. Wise women in Ean and further afield are vessels for such, and in every generation Knowings come and are recorded. Your arrival was noted in such an event."

Targas shook his head and let the issue go for another time. He had more important things to consider.

Lan continued with the issue at hand. "We have used the years to perfect the passage rites that would not take the life force of its target, so that we would be ready when the time was right."

Lan pointed back over his shoulder.

"Behind us is Sanctus, a closely hidden place, where gifted Eanites can develop their powers in relative safety. While potential for scent power is recognised at birth, it fades to allow development, then re-appears as maturity approaches to be fully revealed in adulthood. Time has allowed us to gather the most powerful scent masters in Ean…in one place and in secret. Preparing and waiting." Lan half nodded to himself.

"Recently we detected a *tang*, very faint, no more than a mote or two, not of Ean. It had power and expression, unlike anything we knew. We were equally certain that our enemy did not have it…and because it offered a possible link to the predicted scent master, we worked at locating it." Lan paused, looking at Targas.

"Unfortunately, while we were developing the attraction tendrils into a more effective web, the Sutanites had been constructing more effective smell detectors, such as those now located in the scent towers in each town. Therefore, the risks we were taking had increased significantly. Then we chose one of our people best suited to carry out the search…Quon. Ah, Quon was a highly trained scent master and a very brave man." Lan shook his head sadly. "My friend, Quon, went to a place near Korla, where there was the greatest likelihood that we could reach that minute *tang*. There he sent out the attractants focused on the motes we had located."

Targas leant forward.

"Yes, and while we knew this could likely attract the notice of the enemy, we had to act. We were advised by the mystic that the timing was most auspicious. And Quon gave his life." Lan paused and gazed over the valley for a long moment.

Targas's thoughts unwillingly returned to his nightmare memories with vivid recollections of the old man, Quon, being torn to pieces by the attack of the hymetta. He clasped his arms tightly around a rebelling stomach.

Lan continued. "How we managed to get you from a far country, I do not know. We were anticipating someone closer. An attractant scent has an ability to pull other, target scents to it"—Lan scratched his head—"like two sticks will come together in water. Only this time Quon managed to bring you from so far away." Lan patted his hand. "But I am of a mind to think it relates to the unusual abilities…those you have already shown us."

Targas sat, staring into his now empty mug, shaking his head. *How can that be? How can* breaking *through an insubstantial cloud of fog cause me to travel from Tenstria to Ean in a moment of time?* he thought. *And how can they expect me to be able to solve their problems when it's so hard to even accept what I'm being told?*

Chapter Eighteen

"**D**amn that blood-drenched haggar!" Jakus slammed his fist against the wall. "Septus!" he bellowed.

But he was alone in the interrogation room with the two captives.

Jakus shook and clenched his teeth as he looked at the body Septus had left. *No wonder; no blood-stinking wonder he's not here.*

Luna lay there, her white, naked body already showing bruising. He noticed a puddle of blood congealing beneath her and the slight movement of her flat chest.

He rinsed a cloth in the already reddened water and pushed at the blood. *How did the man wound her there? He should have been concentrating on her mind, there was no purpose in destroying her body.*

He lifted her eyelid to confirm what he could already tell. She was unconscious and badly hurt. He hoped that the girl was more resilient than she looked.

He absently licked his fingers, startled at the rush of flavours hitting his palate. He stopped his involuntary movement towards the pool of blood.

"Guard!"

A guardsman appeared through the door in moments, snapping to attention.

"We have finished here. Take the boy to the cell. You'll not speak of what you've seen."

Jakus waited for the guard to leave before covering Luna with a blanket and carrying her out of the room to the infirmary.

Once he left Luna there he found Septus's scent trace easily enough. It led towards the meeting and dining rooms where they'd spent days organising their expedition north. He pushed the doors open and saw Heritis and Septus standing by a warm fire drinking wine out of silver cups, food spread on a small table nearby. An attendant acolyte hovered.

"Ah, so you're both here," said Jakus, keeping his voice even as he moved into the room. He glared at Septus but spoke to Heritis. "I've been clearing up after Septus and his self-indulgence. He seems to have forgotten what we have the captives for, at least those you didn't lose, Heritis."

"Wine!" he snapped at the acolyte.

Jakus took a gulp from the hastily proffered cup. "We'll need to discuss what we've found out, Heritis. I'm sure Septus has gathered valuable intelligence to share with us?" He looked pointedly at his deputy.

"As you no doubt have, Shada," responded Septus.

Jakus reacted, snapping a strong, thin odour tendril around Septus's skinny neck, beating his automatic shield. The man's eyes bulged, hands tugging ineffectually at the tendril. He spluttered, attempting to speak.

Jakus shut off the attack just as quickly, as Septus fell to one knee.

"Let's sit, shall we?" smiled Jakus as he waved his hand to dismiss the startled acolyte.

They moved to comfortable seats around the table, Septus still rubbing his neck, eyes glistening.

"Will you share your findings, Shada?" enquired Heritis conversationally.

Jakus looked into his cup, swirling the liquor with its blood-red colour and heady aromas. "The two prisoners have proven useful, despite being mishandled," he snapped. "It appears we were right to be concerned. Unusual events in the north, in the Korla and Lesslas regions, indicate that the entire area is worth closer scrutiny. That the prisoners were captured further north, near Galan, confirms this."

"Might I interrupt?" asked Heritis. "I've received notice that the patrol at Korla has information. One of the leaders is returning with it."

"Good," nodded Jakus, then he stared at Septus. "Now Septus, I trust that your heavy-handed interrogation of the girl has been worth the damage. Perhaps you could share the result?"

Jakus watched the man compose himself.

"Shada, Heritis," Septus's voice hissed, as if overcoming pain in his throat, "I have confirmed that the young woman was part of the escape from Korla." He smiled confidently. "She had been taken in a collection of those showing possible scent talent, along with a youth, the one in the dungeons, and his older male companion. Her description of this man is confused—big, strangely dressed and hard to understand, not local. He helped them escape. Also helped them avoid some of our more…uh, *dangerous* wildlife along the way. I can get more detail if you wish." His tongue slithered briefly along his pale lips.

"So, the boy and the man are important to her," Heritis stated.

"*But!*" snapped Septus, "she seems to think that the stranger is dead. He was with them when they were captured, then he was not." He shook his head. "Must have lost another one, Shada?"

"Just keep to the point," Jakus stated. "Do you have anything further to add?"

"There are intimate details if you want"—Septus's sallow face darkened—"but I think we should hear from you, Shada. After all, it was your patrol who found them."

"Mmmm," Jakus nodded. "My questioning of the youth, Kyel, has confirmed some of what the girl revealed. The feeling that this Targ was unusual and probably dead, was part of his memories too, but underneath Kyel revealed a great deal of faith in Targ and a belief he will still help them."

He rubbed his chin before standing. "Heritis, thank Regna for her hospitality. I did appreciate it." Jakus saw Heritis frown. "Also arrange for the young female acolyte to bring my dawn meal to me early. She is most pleasing."

Jakus caught Septus's eye. "Luna is with the healer. He is attempting to undo the damage you've done. You will not go near her. Understand?"

He reinforced the instruction with a flare of anger.

A delicious triggering of his alarm grid woke Jakus. He stretched, automatically dampening the strong breath odours that sleep had caused, substituting a pleasant mouth-freshening aroma.

"Your meal, Shada." Her voice sounded husky and confident, but a trickle of unease added spice to her presence. "I have your massage oils if you desire."

Jakus smiled as he pulsed an attractant towards her. No words were needed.

His first stop was with the healer. Luna had fallen into a deep sleep during the night, but her condition was stable. Jakus emphasised that no one was to disturb her by placing a strong barrier scent outside the room.

The boy, in contrast, was defiant. He sat in the corner of his cell scowling at Jakus, his aura reflecting his mood.

He has a fair potential, if properly trained.

"Where is she? What've you done to her?"

"Boy…ah…Kyel, if you mean your young companion, then she is comfortable and resting in another room." Jakus pulsed a subtle message of friendship and dependability over the youth.

"You w…won't let that black k'dorian get near her again, will you?"

"No," smiled Jakus, "but I require some help from you in return. I have some questions. Come, Kyel," his voice rumbled, "let's take you out of this place and find you something to eat."

He led Kyel to the inner courtyard, which was a striking contrast to the grim interior. There were several raised beds with flowers in a variety of blue shades, leaves almost absent, a wall of aroma discernibly rising in the chill of the early dawn air. It was bright and cheery; the only depressing feature was the dominating shadow of the square scent tower thrown on the brickwork of the opposite side of the building by the rising sun.

119

"Sit, Kyel," Jakus said, continuing the flow of attractant scent. "I know the bricks are cold, but the guardsman is bringing something for your feet."

Kyel chose a position where the sun could stream over his back, but the look on his face showed he was puzzled.

Jakus smiled and leant back.

"Cer, where's Luna? Why can't she be here?"

"You may call me *Shada*, which means *leader* or *ruler*, Kyel," responded Jakus. "Luna is still sleeping. Septus...the black k'dorian...was not gentle with her, but she will mend."

"What do you mean?" Kyel started to rise. Jakus touched his arm, pushing him back onto his seat.

"He was a little overzealous, but she will be fine. Trust me on this." His assurance was interrupted by the arrival of a uniformed man. "Ah, the food and footwear." He gestured the guardsman to put the food on the small table, then took the sandals. "Leave us," he commanded.

Jakus waited until the man had left and moved next to Kyel.

"Here, put these sandals on and help yourself, I'm sure you're hungry."

He saw Kyel hesitate but the food—fried rhodan eggs, slivers of cooked, marinated meats, slices of cheese and a flatbread—gave out such inviting aromas that resistance was brief.

They shared a jug of honey-sweetened juice made from a tart fruit grown on the foothills of the Sensory Mountains. Jakus slipped a few crystals of the special substance, magnesa, into Kyel's drink.

Bees buzzed to the flowers, accepting the sun's warmth as a signal to forage. He wondered whether the pria, large creatures similar to the bee, still existed in the wilds of the mountains. A number of over-large animal types had been reported over the years, some of particular ferocity, and only a few had been domesticated—although he would hardly call *hymetta* domesticated. He made a mental note to check if the hymetta used in the capture had returned to its nest.

Kyel sat back. His eyes had the slightly glazed look that showed the magnesa was beginning to take hold.

"Kyel," Jakus began, leaning forward, his face open, "we must work together, make things right. You'll help me to understand how to do that, won't you?"

"What about Luna?" interrupted Kyel.

"This is not about her," countered Jakus, "she is happy, resting at this moment—it's about you. You have potential to become a scent master, maybe even one of the best in Ean. You just need to let that potential out, and to trust me to help you do that."

Jakus could see the magnesa causing conflict in Kyel's mind. He gently pulsed an amiable scent into the air.

"You'll come with me to the capital, to Nebleth. There you can achieve that greatness. Then you might come back to your friends and help them. You would like that, wouldn't you?" His voice was steady and soft.

Kyel nodded hesitantly.

"You'd be able to help Targ and Sadir, and Cernba and…"

"No! Cernba's dead. That thing killed him." Kyel started to look confused.

Jakus exerted his power, trapping Kyel's fear, replacing it with warm odours of invitation. "Relax, Kyel. You will help your friends. But first you must tell me more about them. Tell me more about Targ. I know he's not dead."

"No, don't think so," Kyel panted. "He's really great. Always finds a way to help us. Probably helped my sister, too."

"So, you think he took your sister, do you?" This was the first confirmation that this Targ had been involved in her rescue. If so, he'd done it right under Heritis's nose, undetected.

"Yeah," Kyel nodded.

"Where will he have taken her?"

"Don't know, but it's somewhere near Galan. They were going to meet *Them*," he said quietly.

"Them?"

"Don't know about Them, just that's where they were going."

"Is Targ a strong scent master? He has helped you a lot. He must be powerful?"

"He stopped the k'dorians, easy. He stopped those men from following us— don't know how, but… Don't understand why he didn't know about some other things, though." Kyel's eyelids began to droop.

So which part of Ean did he come from? Or is he from southern lands, Sutan even? thought Jakus. *And the Them. If this Targ and Them get together then the rebels could be a major problem.* "Bah!" he huffed in frustration. "How can I find out more? What am I missing?"

"Huh?" asked Kyel.

"Never mind, you can go for a rest. We'll talk later."

A shiver of premonition ran down Jakus's spine.

Chapter Nineteen

It was noon and the day was still and clear when Targas and Sadir slipped away for some time to themselves.

The Sanctus robes he wore were surprisingly comfortable and now he wanted to relax after Lan's revelations; having Sadir with him helped.

They walked on stony ground, sparsely covered with short grass that grew amongst the boulders dotting the hillside; every now and then they found a well-camouflaged building or outhouse. Puffs of odours with distinct Conduvian lizard tinges were frequent along their path.

Targas sat on a large flat rock with Sadir. Huge boulders marching off in a variety of directions gave them comparative privacy.

"It's good to have a better understanding of my scent sense. I'm not sure how Lan did it but it's like a new world has been opened up." He hugged Sadir to him. "I can see the patterns in odours. Before I just sensed them and combined them by a sort of…*instinct*. Now I can see how one part might lock into another. But I just don't know how far I can push myself yet."

Sadir nodded and reached up to rub her hand over his shaven face and head. "You'll have to cover that up. You're going pink in the sun. Your face is getting prickly too," she smiled. "Targas, you're nice to be with. I hope things work out for us, all of us. When you're with me I really believe we'll find Kyel again."

They sat in silence, feeling a light breeze brush their skin and just a touch of coolness coming into the air.

"Sadir," Targas said, finally breaking the quiet, "can you help me understand where everything is? I know that Korla, Lesslas and now Galan are, I suppose, at the foothills of all these mountains, where every sort of strange thing is supposed to come from. Then there's rivers and streams crossing the plains to go into the Great Southern River. And Regulus is down south, on the river. Further down is the capital. So, what else is there?"

"You're right so far, Targas. Regulus is where they'd have Kyel…and Luna—oh, I hope they'll soon get them out of there." Sadir nestled into his side. Targas automatically put an arm around her shoulder. "And Nebleth, the capital, is even further down the river, on the plains through the mountains…the Sensory Mountains. The people who go through Regulus are usually traders heading for the coast. My father used to travel there all the time, even going to Port Saltus."

"Your father, Sadir, you haven't spoken much about him, or your mother."

"I don't remember my mother. My father raised us but then he went missing, died I suppose, a long time ago now," she sighed. "He traded perac wool, though somehow he became involved with the Sutanite's salt trade. I think he may have found or seen something he shouldn't. He…he just disappeared; never found." Sadir paused.

The sound of scurrying Conduvian lizards, interspersed with the familiar chirping, suddenly appeared to be all around them.

"Since then," she continued, "I've had to work in that tavern, usually with Jeth, to give Kyel a home without parents. However, what about you, Targas? Are you joined?"

"No, Sadir. I'm only just into my twenties and my apprenticeship was a long one."

"What's your trade? It must be important."

"I suppose it is to a lot of people. I am—or was—an analyser and tester of spirits in the House of Versent, one of the most famous Houses in Tenstria. That's my country…though where it is"—he gazed around as if searching for a familiar landmark—"I don't know. I am skilled in the various distillations of malas, a very popular drink, and can determine the quality of that drink, how to improve it and when it should be bottled. It's a very competitive field and I was lucky enough to be very good at it. They said I had a natural talent to be able to discern and combine a range of flavours."

He paused, a frown creasing his forehead.

"I suppose it's a bit like being able to combine scents here to form something totally different. The cloaking shields and scent bolts I used when we escaped…" he slowly added, "seemed to happen without thinking, as if I'd absorbed elements that were needed to make something special…maybe what Lan said…" A slight shiver reminded him that Sadir was waiting.

"But enough of what I was. What about here, and now?"

Before Sadir could reply there was a "chirp" at their feet.

"Tel, you've found us," Targas exclaimed. He reached down and picked up the lizard, which immediately settled down on his knee.

"Look Targas, his tail is really starting to grow again."

"I've noticed that the place seems to be riddled with these lizards," he said.

"I know you're a lot better than me with the scent talent, Targas, but I can smell them all over these rocks. Can you guess why there's so many here?"

"I bet they're a warning system. Tel here,"—he gave a long stroke on the lizard's rough skin—"showed us that early on. Clever," he said. "Anyway, back to the layout of Ean."

"Well, there's a huge sea beyond Port Saltus. All the shipping comes across it and into Nebleth Bay," Sadir continued. "That's where the Great Southern River finishes. It's also the place where the Sutanites came to our country a long time ago, and where the great battle—or rightly the massacre—happened; it's called the Plain of the Guardians. Once the Sutanites were here they started a huge trade in salt, since we have lots of salt in the desert that's on the other side of the Long Ranges. They're mountains east of the Great Southern," she added.

"Couldn't they just have gotten salt from the sea?" asked Targas.

"How, Targas? There's little enough salt in the sea. Anyway, mining salt is hard work, so the Eanites became their slaves. We're made up of many peoples; other than us in towns and farmers and herders, there's the mountain people of the Long Ranges, and the river and marsh people—also the wanderers that live in the desert. We used to keep to ourselves, sometimes meeting for trade and markets, but the Sutanites changed all that." Sadir reached over and stroked Tel. "They have used us and affected how we live; and a lot of it's to do with the salt. We have to mine and move the salt for them. Even the port, Port Saltus, is named after it."

"So, you have a lot to hate the Sutanites for."

"Yes, but that's not all." She jerked forward to turn and look into his face, her eyes flashing. "They use us even more, not just as workers. What's happened to my Kyel shows that. It's our scent talent, Targas; they're taking our very selves."

The remainder of the day passed quickly and only the change in the light, as the sun moved behind the mountains, reminded them.

It was almost dark when movement in the lizard odour signals indicated someone approaching. He did not need to look to know it was Lan.

"Targas and Sadir, it is time. We need to prepare for the night. Come with me."

As Lan walked them back to the main building he explained what they needed to do, but didn't elaborate on what was to happen.

Targas found the bathhouse without difficulty, recognising it from the first night when the healer, Zahnal, had brought him back from near death. This time he was determined to clean up without her help.

A number of men of all ages relaxed in the steam, rubbed themselves down with cloth and soap, or washed in the warm pool. He noticed they had very little hair. Several had short stubble on their scalp, but the rest were bald, no hair anywhere on their bodies. They had little surplus fat and their skin colour ranged from pale white to light brown. They smiled politely but went about their business without attempting conversation, even though their scents showed they were curious about him. One man rapidly left the room, odours tightly controlled. Targas recognised him from the day before and again felt a shiver of unease at his reaction. He shook his head and focused on his cleaning.

At one stage a woman walked in with a bundle of clean light grey robes and placed them on a table. No one reacted to her presence.

He put on a clean robe and sandals before moving towards the buzz of conversation in the common room. He noticed almost equal numbers of robed women and men. While some of the women were bald he was relieved to see that most had short-cropped hair. He started when he saw what had been done to Sadir; her attractive brown hair had been cropped to within an inch of her skull.

"Targas," she called, her face reddening at his surprised look, "I did manage to stop them cutting it all off." Sadir came up to him, her natural odours heightened by a fresh and clean smell.

"It looks good on you," he blurted out, "but I still don't know what this is all about."

"It's a very special ceremony of renewal that the scent-talented have here at this period, but we'll find out more together," said Sadir as she put an arm through his.

Lan led Targas and Sadir out of the building and down a now familiar path. They were quietly followed by the throng of people. Targas could sense their anticipation.

They walked the path along the small stream until they came to the great wall of granite marking the entrance to the cavern. Targas followed Sadir through the narrow opening after Lan.

The temperature was pleasant after the chill night air. As they crunched across the coarse sand, he noticed a glow lighting the cavern. There was also a pervasive smell, sweet, almost vanilla-like that had not been there before.

A noise sounded above the crunch of everyone's feet, reminiscent of a bee's hum. He could feel it above him and looked towards the high rocky roof.

"I will explain," said Lan as he saw Targas. "You would be hearing a tina…it is a night-flying insect. The scent we have released will attract a few of them this night. Do not be alarmed, they are harmless, even if a little large."

"You don't mean hymetta-big?"

"Not quite, but close," responded Lan.

Ah, more giant insects, Targas thought.

"Your places, my Ean friends," called Lan. Targas, still holding Sadir's hand, stood with Lan as everyone shuffled around them. In a short time, they had formed a large circle towards the back of the cavern and stood waiting silently.

"Come with me," whispered Lan. "You will trust me, please…follow my direction." The three of them moved to the centre of the large circle.

Targas's eyes had adjusted to the dim light and the many tones of grey colouring the surroundings. The people stood like pale statues, ghostlike in the gloom, faces darkly hidden under their hoods. The scent had become more cloying, stifling, and the background flutter of tina flying above them added to the strangeness.

The light intensified. Targas looked for its source and noticed a man-sized hole in the roof, directly above their heads. Thickened wafts of scent were rising from around them, up through the pale glow that was entering the cavern. He gasped silently when he saw a huge moth enter through the hole on the odour's trail.

No one moved as the glow grew brighter.

"It begins!" came the slap of Lan's voice. "We replenish. We renew."

A flurry of activity happened. The people surrounding them pulled off their robes and sat down, cross-legged on the sand, before linking hands. A double circle of pale bodies ringed the three of them at the centre. The noise ceased.

"Disrobe and then sit," said Lan quietly to them both. "Link hands with me."

They followed Lan's lead after a little hesitation and were soon sitting cross-legged, in an expanding pool of light, naked under the gaze of over one hundred people.

Sadir's hand gave his a quick squeeze. He risked a glance but had little time to appreciate her before the growing light distracted him.

The moon, the source of the light, edged over the hole in the roof. It was like being in a spotlight. Targas felt drawn to it, so far away and yet familiar.

A background vibration added to the atmosphere. The scent grew stronger, visible in the light. The vibration coming from those around him helped to force the scent deeper into his head, making the air around him seem thick, like a glowing soup. And he found himself drinking that "soup", opening himself up until it was a second skin around and running through him. He became lost in it, floating with the light, completely exposed to its influence. His throat responded as he joined in.

His head opened with every fibre, every cell lying exposed. Information strands flowed like bees into a hive, each knowing its own destination. Gentle influences worked, pushing and prodding. He moved on as the light grew, seeking to go with it, but an experienced hand anchored him and kept him from following that siren call. So, he filled up on the scent, following the new pathways and channels, pulling countless scent memories to join and be it. He was complete, part of everything, one with the people around him, divorced from the minutia of the day. Fulfilled.

Slowly the light diminished as the moon moved on, the power faded, and his senses closed down. He seemed suspended in an unknown place, not hearing or feeling—at total peace—not wanting to leave. Gradually he was drawn back, floating gossamer-like to the ground.

The presence of everyone, individual but together, was overwhelming. Their strengths, weaknesses and overall focus, and belief in what they were, made a wall of contentment around him. Lan was a rock that drew him, a solidarity to cling to, while Sadir was something more. He had never felt as close to someone as he did to Sadir at that moment.

After some time, he felt a hand rest gently on his shoulder. "Come Targas," said Lan. "It is time to leave…but do not speak, just be."

The glow had faded, and an eerie stillness pervaded the cavern, broken only by the rustle of people dressing. Targas pulled on his robe and, holding Sadir's hand, followed Lan out of the cavern.

As the path widened, Sadir leant against Targas; he put an arm around her shoulders, and they walked in a dream through the moonlit night.

Chapter Twenty

Jelm reported to Jakus soon after sun down. He was one of two leaders of the patrol heading west to Korla and the highest ranking of the Nebleth seekers. They found the trail of the fugitives, now known to be their current two captives together with the mysterious Targ, who had initially been lost in the foothills above Korla. The simultaneous collapse of two of the seekers in the original collection team was disturbing. They had been using the locate-and-control technique with solid scent tendrils and only now were lucid enough to describe what had happened. They reported that their senses had been suddenly overwhelmed, like hitting a wall before rebounding into their brains.

The investigation by Jelm and Genur had led them to the site of the original hymetta attack, a clearing on top of a small hill. The soil showed signs of a struggle and the remains of a body. Scavengers had rendered it unidentifiable, but odour traces revealed an Eanite of some scent ability. Another presence had been detected, one with strange undertones that disappeared abruptly. A trail of broken vegetation led towards Korla, but no scent trail was found. The report confirmed Jakus's belief that Targ was part of something significant.

He ordered Jelm to stay and assist Heritis and Septus analyse information that came in through the Regulus scent towers and from interrogation of the city's road and river traffic, while he returned to the capital Nebleth with Kyel, leaving Luna behind to recover. The effective communication channels between Nebleth and Regulus would limit any disadvantage caused by his absence.

Jakus, Kyel and a guardsman left Regulus at pre-dawn on three sturdy perac. They travelled light, since several way stations provided for official travellers along the highway.

He was anticipating the first rays of sun over the Main Belt Mountains east of Regulus when he noticed wisps of fog spreading tenuously from the river across their path. The Great Southern, still grey and swollen from the rains in the north, had an annoying tendency to develop fogs as the country entered the cold season. He quelled his instinct to move faster as the mist thickened, for such a natural event could cover another, more insidious foe.

While scent masters could use fog to carry manipulative alarm and control odours, the flesh-eating haggars found it benefited them as well. The water vapours allowed haggars to move out of their river habitat and seek their prey over substantial distances on land. It was fortunate for the city dwellers that they had a natural tendency to avoid built-up areas.

Jakus and Kyel rode abreast as the fog thickened. Soon the guardsman was merely a shadow behind them, and their steeds' pads were muffled on the main road. Moisture accumulated and dripped off their perac wool cloaks, down exposed flesh and gradually dampening their clothing.

Jakus kept up the rapid pace he had set when leaving Regulus. The first way station was not far, and the thought of a warm fire and hot food were inviting. Jakus's odour memories of his journeys were like an in-built version of the scent maps of the country. Way stations had the distinct odour of perac, fire, men, river and stale food.

The station was constructed on high ground like others on the river road. Logs driven into the ground formed a curve facing away from the water. The front was a wall of rough-hewn planks broken by a doorway and a small, shuttered window. A solid set of stables was set alongside, while hard clay tiles roofed the structure. The station was of a basic, strong construction, capable of being easily defended and also stopping any stray haggar looking for an easy meal.

"Good day to you, Cers, though hard to tell," called a voice. A thickset individual, difficult to see in hood and an accumulation of non-descript clothing, came out of the building and through the fog towards them. "You're early on the road, Cers," he continued, reaching a hand towards the perac's bridle.

"We'll need warmth and food," commanded Jakus as he automatically sent a control tendril into the way station attendant.

"Yescer, yescer," the man grovelled. "I'll stable your perac if you go on in. The fire's going."

Jakus ushered Kyel inside and directed him to one of the stools by the fire, the guardsman following. The interior was a functional shelter, the main room large enough to act as an eating and sleeping area. A small room off one side proved to be quarters for the attendant and his woman. The building was heated by a fire set in a riverstone hearth; a large pot hung over it.

The attendant's partner waited with steaming mugs of tea. She was similarly thickset and showed her river people origins, broad face stretched in a smile outlined by a web of wrinkles.

"Tea, Cers. May I also get yer some cooked oatmeal?" she asked as she passed over the mugs.

Their clothes steamed with the fire's heat as they ate the stodgy food. The fog seemed as thick as ever and Jakus became impatient. He had much to do, and the delay irritated. He stared into the flames. *The boy has not spoken since leaving Regulus,* he thought, *and it might be a useful opportunity to extract more information.*

However, the flames were calming and the atmosphere warm. No noise from the attendant, nothing from the animals and even the fire was quiet.

He was suddenly fully alert. The atmosphere had changed. There was a faint smell intruding, a fish smell, salty, just above the general pervasiveness of the river's odour. And there was no sound.

Jakus quickly rose to his feet and moved to the door. He was reaching for the latch when the door crashed inwards, hitting him.

Grey figures, spectre-like in the inrushing mist, charged straight at Jakus, now sprawled on the floor, their lances driving at his body.

He instinctively forced all his most violent odour memories into a single outpouring and thrust a wide and strong scent wall at the intruders. While the lances started to penetrate the barrier, their bodies were stopped. The wall continued its rapid expansion, rippling out in an arc of power, carrying all before it. Bodies were thrust back by the force; meaty impacts were followed by the splintering of the wooden walls and the shattering of the window shutters. Structural timbers snapped and hit the ground. A groan, almost too quiet to hear in the welter of noise, preceded the collapse of the roof. A roil of odour brought the smell of wood and dirt mixed with an overpowering reek of gut contents.

The broken building settled until only the grunting of frightened perac continued.

Jakus rose shakily from a clear space where the debris had been held off by his power, and began to investigate. The fog was rapidly disappearing, allowing the daylight to penetrate and reveal the extensive damage he had caused. The entire front of the building had blown out, leaving broken planking and shattered tiles stretched over a wide area. Somewhere within that rubble were the bodies of his attackers, and presumably those of the attendant and his woman.

Jakus checked on Kyel. Apart from a bloodied head, the youth was relatively unscathed. His guardsman was less fortunate; it appeared that he had caught the full blast of Jakus's defence.

Useless; little loss, he thought.

The last remnants of the fog vanished.

Jakus was grimly satisfied at the result of his powerful response to his attackers as he began to pick through the debris looking for bodies. He extended his senses for any unusual smell, but found little. He did a wider search of the area and located drag marks leading to the river. These had been partially disguised, but a shallow depression in the mud suggested there'd been a small boat on the riverbank. There was little else.

Jakus hurriedly composed a message of the attack and pulsed it into the air, hoping for favourable breezes for Regulus or Nebleth. He pulled Kyel to his feet and then lashed him into his saddle on the perac. Tempted though he was to continue investigating, he felt vulnerable enough to want to put as much distance as he could from the site of the attack. He left the remaining perac and the guardsman's body.

The sun had now dissipated the mist, clearly outlining the flat countryside with its reed-like grasses along the river and thickets of low bushes flanking the paved road. Jakus rode hard, pushing both perac to the limit.

If I'd been less skilful the attempt could have been successful. How has it happened this close to Regulus; and on the safe, main way? Who organised and carried it out? Obviously powerful enough to manipulate the fog, and remove their dead and injured so quickly and quietly.

But was it a rescue attempt on the boy? Is he more important than I first realised?

A final thought gave him pause. *Who knew I was travelling to Nebleth? The names are limited, and none of them would dare to be disloyal. Would Septus have the nerve to try, or has Heritis found out about Regna and leaked my travel details to the rebels?*

Jakus shook his head. *No. It's far more likely that someone in the city has been opportunistic. So at least I now know to focus more on the rebels. And…to be more concerned with my own safety.*

Jakus's face set in a grim mask and a visible dark aura plumed above him as he spurred the perac down the road. Those travelling in the opposite direction quickly pulled over to let him pass.

The gates of Nebleth were welcome. They had ridden at an energy-sapping pace for most of the day. He had stopped once to re-strap Kyel into his saddle and then continued to drive the animals by fear odours. But there was only so much an animal could do when performing at such a high level, and they were exhausted by the time they neared the city.

"Ah!" exclaimed Jakus as he saw a welcoming group coming to meet them. They would have been in no doubt as to the state of his mind revealed by his dark aura.

He pulled up and transferred to fresh mounts, directing that the semi-conscious Kyel be taken straight to a healer.

"Strona," he said to the tall, black figure of the senior seeker, "everything in order?"

"Yes, Shada," she replied. "We were horrified by your message of the attack on your person. It is inexplicable." She gulped as Jakus's face hardened. "What is your wish?"

"Organise a council," he ordered. "For dawn, in the main hall. I will not accept any excuses. We have much to discuss. And," he continued as she was about to hurry off, "send a messenger to Heritis to ensure that he received my scent message of the attack. Let him know that I want it investigated immediately, and that there will be repercussions. Use one of the scent masters to ensure that my message is reproduced in full."

Jakus goaded his new mount through the gates of the city. As he cantered towards the tower he permitted himself a slight smile. *The enemy has shown their hand. In addition, I have the knowledge to retaliate more exactly to crush any rebellion.*

Time was short. An imperative request to rescue the youngsters had come, too late to circumvent interrogation but an urgent directive to act, to take even the smallest opportunity.

Too late for the boy; Jakus had already left with him. So, he had no choice but to leave Kyel's rescue to others. All he could do was to try and get Luna away from Regulus. That was dangerous enough in itself, for if his identity was revealed many years of planning would be ruined, putting the strategy of the Eanites at risk. But the request was explicit, the need great; it had to be done.

He took one shuddering breath before he pulled the hood of his cloak over his head and slipped down the dark corridors of the castle he knew so well.

Chapter Twenty-One

Luna was carried at a brisk pace, light and dark flashes patterning through her closed eyelids. Her body flexed with the speed and roughness of the movement. Pain came in white-hot bursts, stabbing through her head and down her body. She cramped continuously.

Her groans grew louder.

"Shush," said a deep male voice next to her ear. "Relax, just try to relax." The voice, accompanied by a soft, smoky scent, caused her to drift away. She offered no resistance, just let herself be carried.

After a time, the vibrations affecting her body changed; sounds of footfalls on wood echoed dully and she winced as the man carrying her staggered.

Scents drifted into her consciousness: the pong of stagnant water, an undercurrent of rotting wood and urine. She lay on a soft surface that crackled. It had a clean smell with a vague phosphoric odour.

A murmur of whispered voices roused her, urgent but unthreatening. One was the stranger who carried her, his odour of perac and sweat distinctive. The other had a slightly salty, sharp scent with light, soft undertones.

Footsteps receded. A rocking sensation, then silence. The softer tread returned, bringing the feminine smell of an older woman, vague floral notes.

Her clothing was gently removed, and she heard a sharp intake of breath.

"Me poor darlin'. What's been done t' yer?" The woman's voice was soft and caring.

Warm water was dabbed over her, fragrant plants applied—scents she remembered from her aunt, a long time ago, healing aromas.

A warm, damp cloth moved over her body. She winced at the sting.

'Sorry, luv. Didn't mean t' hurt yer."

The footsteps retreated. Silence returned.

She dozed.

Another presence, male, startled her.

"Quiet, luv. Yer'll be fine," said the woman gently. "Just have t' do this. Woll, we've got t' do it," she continued in an urgent whisper.

"Yer right, Cynth. Yer usually are. Let's get on with it," the man sighed.

The smell was acrid, salty and masculine. It swirled thickly around her body, covering her like a second skin, filling every orifice. Her lungs drew in the mixture. She coughed harshly.

"Don't worry luv, it's for th' best. Gotta remove his influence. Yer don't want him t' have that hold over yer," Cynth cooed sympathetically.

The procedure ended and she slumped, exhausted. A soft blanket eased over her, and she fell into a dreamless sleep.

A gentle rocking woke her. Her head felt better, but a driving thirst drove Luna to stand. She felt giddy, unsteady and wherever it was, was moving.

The room was dark, dimly lit from light seeping under the door. The curved wooden walls met at a point opposite the door. There was a table below that point and a small metal oven with a flue exiting the low, wood-beamed roof. Another bed, with two smaller benches against the only flat wall, made up the remainder of the furniture.

She shuffled to the mug on the table, wincing with the effort; every part of her seemed to be stiff and sore. The water tasted slightly salty, but good.

The feeble light revealed a small mound of clothing on her bed. She slowly pulled on the baggy pants and loose top with a vaguely familiar feminine scent; there was nothing for her feet.

Luna pulled on the handle. The door swung inwards and hung there, gently moving. She blinked at the light pouring in from a square hatch in the roof. A short set of wooden steps led upwards in the small alcove; another door was set behind the steps. The breeze coming through the hatch smelt of water, mixed with mud and rotted grass, a salty odour dominant.

A fire burnt in her groin and her chest. Her neck hurt and she had no energy. She clung to the steps until she heard footsteps on the roof. Luna dragged herself up the steps and poked her head out into the open air.

The light coming from a low sun lit up the long, flat cargo boat. They were on a broad grey river lined with untidy drab green trees and bushes; paths along both banks separated the vegetation from the water. A figure moved towards her across the deck, easily coping with its slight rocking. The shadows made it hard to see the face under a shapeless wool hat, but the form in bulky clothing was unmistakably female. As the figure neared, a scent waft confirmed that it was the person from her formless memories.

Luna smiled tentatively.

"Up and about me luv?" came the figure's genial voice. "Good t' see. Do yer want t' climb up alongside?" Cynth smiled at Luna and extended a broad, roughened hand.

"Take it easy; no hurry. Oh, it's pleasin' t' see yer better."

Cynth pulled Luna up and then hugged her with strong arms. Her motherly scent and the dominant smells of the river, the salt and the mustiness of the craft, were starting to make sense. She was on a river barge, a salt-carrying river barge.

"Me poor little fish, yer've been through a lot." Cynth gave another strong hug. "How do yer feel?"

"I...I'm aching...all over. Something happened. It wasn't a man, it was a...skull and he...he was sucking at me," Luna shuddered, and tears began to run down her face. She buried her head in the woman's ample bosom. "What happened... Why am I here...please...tell me?'

"Suppose I must," said Cynth. "Yer've been rescued from th' dungeons of th' river garrison. Yer must have powerful friends t' get away, because it was someone special who brought yer t' us, at great risk t' himself too. We've been on th' go all day t' get away, 'n upriver," she added.

"No! No...sorry. Can't you just tell me?" yelped Luna, voice straining between her sobs, "I've got to know."

"Yer a persistent one," sighed Cynth. "Well, yer was hurt 'nd worse," she said gently. "That man, Septus... But don't worry," she hurried as she saw the horrified look on Luna's face, "we've stopped that, made yer body forget him."

"What?" cried Luna, "What do you mean?"

"Hey!" called a deep voice from behind them. Luna swung around to see a man, dark and bulky at the stern of the barge. "Get back down! They'll smell th' girl."

"Oh, hag's dung, I forgot!" exclaimed Cynth. "Just gettin' inside, Woll," she added.

She looked down at Luna. "Now, me gel, down them stairs quick."

As Luna started to descend she could see the bank, now in shadow. There was a large perac walking slowly alongside, attended by two skinny youngsters; a thick rope ran from its harness to the bow of the barge. As she reached the floor, she could hear Woll shouting at the children.

The boards creaked as Cynth followed her, so she moved out of the way behind the stairs.

"Come luv, yer can see into th' hold next day," she said, misinterpreting Luna's movement. "We'll go 'n get food now. Th' others'll be hungry when they've got Maw on board 'n tied off."

"Maw?" asked Luna as she followed Cynth back into the same room she'd recently left.

"Our sorry excuse for a perac, that's Maw. Just sit on th' bed, out of th' way while I get cookin'."

The noise began with an erratic thumping on the roof over their heads, then a thunderous banging on the stairs as if a hailstorm had hit. The door swung open and two wide-eyed, dirty-faced youngsters ran in, and stopped dead to stare at her. Luna pushed herself further back onto the bed.

"Wash in th' basin. Yer covered in perac 'nd mud." Cynth waved a vague hand towards the corner of the room. The youngsters followed her direction, backing away from Luna.

Another thumping broke the brief silence and a large, blocky man pushed in through the door. His face broke into a broad smile when he saw Luna staring at him.

"Don't worry about me family, luv," he explained, "they're easy t' control. Tallest is Lynthe, 'nd th' brightness in her mother's eye is Tishal. You've met Cynth, 'nd I'm Woll." The man smiled again and looked at his wife. "How's th' meal goin'? This young woman here looks like she needs a feed."

Woll winked back at Luna, before going to the basin. "Out of th' way now; man's gotta wash."

Luna sat in a virtual cocoon of space, chewing a lock of hair while watching the never-ending action that focused on the basin. Each member of the family matter-of-factly stripped to the waist to wash. She could see their father in both youngsters; the same dark curls haloing their heads, skin with a permanent suntanned hue and brown eyes with a slight squint. Their bone structure promised the strength that both adults showed. The boy, Lynthe, was not much younger than her, while Tishal was only just starting her change of life. Every so often one of them would glance sideways at her.

"Come 'nd get it," called Cynth as she plunked five bowls of fish stew onto the small table. Woll moved out two benches from under the beds.

"Sit next t' me, gel," ordered Cynth. "Tishal, th' other side; we'll stare at th' men."

Luna got up stiffly and moved to sit close to Cynth, the aroma of the food pulling at her. Brother and sister giggled at each other.

"Ah," nodded Cynth. "Can't keep this one up too long, she's been through a lot. She'll get yer bed, Tishal; yer'll sleep with me. Don't yer make those fish eyes at me, that's final. Now eat up."

"I'm sorry I can't eat any more,' said Luna. "The food's good though... Sorry."

"That's river fish," said Woll, quickly. "Ugly as a haggar, but smart enough not t' get eaten by it."

"The haggar!" exclaimed Luna, face whitening. "They'll get us."

"Don't yer worry about th' hags. Us 'nd the haggars have 'n understandin'. We don't bother them 'n they don't bother us." He saw Luna's puzzled look. "Really, we just make sure we keep up th' salt 'nd they can't get on board. There's a line of salt that runs right around th' boat 'nd I check it each night. No, we don't have a problem with th' hags." Woll leant over the table, looming over Luna. "But don't tell our secret, will yer?"

"Nooo, no I won't."

"Don't scare th' poor gel, Woll. Now I'll just get her t' bed. She's got a lot of catchin' up t' do."

The noise continued around her as she warmed up in Tishal's cramped little bunk bed, but it didn't stop her falling into a restless sleep full of skull-faced men and wormlike haggars. The occasional bump of a log and other debris in the passing water added substance to her dreams.

"Shush." A rough hand with the familiar scent of Cynth clamped firmly over her mouth. "Keep still," she warned, head cocked, listening. "I think it's them. Get up quick gel, we've got t' hide yer."

Luna winced as she climbed out of the bed and went with Cynth to the door; Woll followed them.

"You on the barge, show yourselves. We're coming on board." The voice was authoritative and commanding.

Luna shivered and quickly followed Cynth through the door and behind the steps.

"Get that gel out of sight," hissed Woll as he started to climb the stairs. "I'll see t' them."

The door on the other side of the alcove opened into a long, wide space lit by a faint luminescence. The walls were the planks and ribs of the sides of the barge, while evenly spaced pillars supported the low roof. They moved into the room, crunching through an acrid-smelling salt crust on the floor, until they reached a central pillar.

"Wait." Cynth pulled a flat bar of metal from a deep pocket, plunged it into the salty floor and heaved. A section rose through the salt to reveal a square opening where water glistened darkly in its depths. Luna recoiled from a vile reek of salt and old fish.

"What's happening? Tell me. They can't get me!" Luna tasted bile in her throat.

"Trust me, Luna. Yer safe. Yer've got to go in, just for a while, till those seekers go. Won't be for long. Just keep yer head near th' pillar where it goes through th' floor—the air's freshest there."

Luna looked wildly about her as if seeking an escape. Cynth gently put her arm around her and held her. "Trust me, please."

Luna put a bare foot down the hole until she touched a slimy beam of wood with her toes.

"C'mon now, Woll can't hold them forever."

Luna gulped and slipped down into the noisome hole until her feet entered chilly bilge water.

"Won't be long. Be brave," whispered Cynth as she slid the hatch cover into place.

The blackness was almost solid as Luna pushed her head onto the hard wooden pillar where the stench seemed to be less. The dark water rippling around her shins and the cold eating into her bones made her head swim as she fought for fresher air. She drove her fingernails into the slippery pillar and held on.

Muffled voices echoed in the room above; footsteps sounded over her head, then moved away. She was cold and alone.

The barge's movement gently massaged Luna. The clean, lightly scented air wafted over her. She drew in a deep breath, sneezed loudly and stretched in Tishal's bed.

Soft wool blankets covered her. Faint sounds of water rippling alongside the sides of the barge brought comfort.

She became aware something was different, something had moved, changed. Luna carefully swung her bare feet to the floor of the dimly lit room and stood gingerly; she was wearing another set of Cynth's clothes.

Luna pulled open the door and stiffly climbed the stairs. She peeked out of the hatchway and saw a wan sun, now behind the barge. The river was no more than a narrow stream of clear water, rather than the muddy flow of the previous day. The trees had thinned out and were drooping as if lacking water. Despite the conditions, the colours seemed bright, and she could see vapour-like scent rising slowly.

"Hey gel," called Woll's voice from the stern. "Good t' see yer up 'nd about. D'yer want t' come back here or join th' others on th' bank?"

Luna glanced over to where Cynth and the youngsters were walking the barge-pulling perac. They waved at Luna, and she tentatively raised a hand.

Luna focused on Woll and moved onto the gently-sloping deck, carefully walking along a central plank that ran down the length of the craft. He pointed to the flat hatch covers that she was passing.

"That's how we get th' salt blocks. It's loaded in sections, block by block till we're full. Now come 'nd sit down 'ere," Woll said, patting the bench next to him on the other side of a long wooden tiller. "Yer can steer if yer like," he offered.

Luna shook her head and sat on the bench, huddling into herself and twisting her hair around a finger.

"Not too close t' th' edge, mind. Never know when haggars are around, though they know barges 'nd we don't see 'em much," Woll smiled at Luna as she edged away from the rail.

They sat in silence.

"Woll?" she asked after a while. "How did you stop them…the seekers?"

"Ah, we have our ways," Woll said. "Our own smells are very strong 'nd them little scent sticks of theirs got overwhelmed, didn't they? Besides, they couldn't get yer above th' stench."

He pointed over the bow. "Hey, yer see them mountains? That's where we're goin'. That's where we load th' salt."

A series of stark mountains, ahead to the left, stood out like giant stepping stones in the vague light of the late day. Sparse vegetation covered their dry slopes.

"We follow th' Salt Way a ways yet," Woll continued, "though it's a lot narrower, as yer can see." As he spoke, his male scent wafted over Luna.

"Woll…?" she began slowly. "Did you…do something to me?"

"What?" asked Woll with a puzzled frown.

"I remember something happened…something you and Cynth did."

"Ah!" Woll glanced at Cynth patiently leading Maw along the towpath and a blush began to extend from his face to the back of his neck.

"Ah," he repeated, and then rubbed his arm across his forehead. "Cynth is a good woman 'nd a good healer. She's helped many people 'nd with what happened t' yer—well—she asked me t' help."

He looked at Luna but she remained silent. He shrugged. "We had t' use me, t' use me man smell, t' get rid of what he did to yer; had t' make yer body react. I'm really, really sorry, luv," he said, looking down at his feet.

Luna bent forward and covered her face with her hands. Her groan unsettled Woll.

"Don't worry, gel. Please don't worry," he said, reaching a tentative hand towards her bowed shoulder, before stopping.

Woll looked over at Cynth. Cynth would know what to do.

Chapter Twenty-Two

The grey robe, near invisible in the dim light, shivered from pale shoulders and pooled on the floor. Her dark eyes glistened as a smile broke shyly over her face. She approached, her arms moving hesitantly away from her small breasts and sliding down across the soft belly to her naked flanks. The tip of a pink tongue appeared fleetingly as her lips tightened.

Without thinking he shrugged off his robe, allowing light, soft scents of contentment and promise to drift across the narrowing gap. He shuddered as she slid between his outstretched arms. Their hands flowed over each other's body and lips became familiar, adding to the rapidly thickening odour of desire, its colours of pinks and yellows combining with a soft green.

Her small hands gripped his shoulders as she moved to straddle him. His mouth traced the firm line of her throat to her lips, their bodies beginning to move rhythmically together.

Their tongues touched and their bodies melded. His hands held her while they moved. They briefly broke apart, breathing heavily, her dancing eyes partially obscured by the darker, orange-red scents of their lovemaking.

Their sweat-lubricated movements added sensations, building on others. He clasped her tighter to slow her slippery, trembling body, but the race of emotions continued as they moved on an unstoppable course.

They fell softly back to the mattress, still holding each other. His hand gently cupped her face, tilting her head to graze his lips over hers, smiling into those wide, dark eyes. Their breathing slowed and their pounding hearts quietened.

Hands and legs still linked, they rolled apart before falling into a deep and comforting sleep.

He awoke with a weight on his chest.

Tel?

A hand moved over his face, rubbing the bristles on his chin.

"Targas?"

"Mmmm…Sadir. I thought you were Tel for a minute,' said Targas, smiling as he moved his shoulder to better accommodate her head.

"What? I'm a little better than a lizard, aren't I?" Sadir stretched against him, moving a hand over his chest, nibbling on his ear.

"Mmm…I don't know. We'll have to see." Targas lifted the blanket and ran exploring hands down her body.

"What are you doing?" she laughed.

"Just looking."

"Uh, no you don't." Sadir wriggled further down the bed, pulling the blanket over her head.

"Ahem… When you two have finished…"

Targas reacted, almost kneeing Sadir as he tried to sit up.

"No need to worry, Targas," said Lan, a smile creasing his face. "And I am sorry to interrupt. We should speak when you come for your meal. You too, Sadir."

Sadir's head peeped up from under the blankets, red-faced.

Lan turned and walked away, a broader smile on his face.

"**D**amn! I was having fun."

"Me too," said Sadir as she wriggled up alongside him.

"I'm very tempted to stay but I suppose we can't keep Lan waiting," he sighed, and slid out of the bed.

"Targas," she murmured pointedly, "you can't go looking like that, can you?"

"Don't tempt me," he said as he quickly grabbed both discarded robes to the front of him. "Now which one is mine?'

"Targas, pass mine, please," said Sadir, jumping up.

"No," said Targas, "you don't need one. I like you just the way you are." He held off Sadir's attempts to get to the robe, grabbing around her waist and throwing her back on the bed.

"I just might go like this," she pouted, with her arms crossed under her breasts.

"This robe doesn't really suit you, you know," Targas said as he handed it over.

Sadir smiled and pulled his face down to hers.

Waking up with Sadir was the culmination of a very satisfying night. He felt so full, bursting with thoughts, feeling and knowledge. If he had never felt part of this new land before, he did now. It was as if he had thousands of strings of knowledge; he just had to focus on one and an opening would form to bring that subject to mind.

Sadir looked at him as they walked to the common room, and her brief smile triggered an instant scent pulse between them. The room was full, and he blushed at how obvious their lovemaking was.

"Sit with us…eat; you will both be needing to build up your energy." The side of Lan's mouth twitched.

He was near the window at his usual table, on which lay platters of food and steaming mugs. Lethnal, the old healer Zahnal and two men were with him.

Targas's face froze, for seated at the table with a tight look on his face was the same man he had come across several times before.

If Lan had noticed, he showed no sign but just gestured to the seat opposite. Targas let Sadir slip up the bench alongside Zahnal before he sat next to her.

"You'll be needin' a shave again soon, young man," Zahnal chuckled.

Targas smiled fleetingly and felt for Sadir's hand under the table.

Lan nodded towards the food on the table and paused while they helped themselves to bread and several sliced fruits.

"You'll know of the inner council here. Lethnal, of the mountain people, Brin, who has links with the river people, through his mother's side. Zahnal is, well… Zahnal and Quonir from Korla, the twin of the heroic Quon; we have a lot to thank Quon for."

Targas started as he looked across the table into Quonir's dark, assessing eyes, at the man who closely resembled Quon; Quon, who had been tragically destroyed in that frenzied attack from the large wasp-like creatures, and the man who was responsible for where he was now.

Targas gripped Sadir's hand tighter and focused on his food.

Lan kept talking.

"There is not much to discuss from last night. We achieved what we wanted…and more. Lunight, our renewal, was the most powerful we have had for generations—your doing Targas, I believe. Our chances of countering the enemy's control over our people have improved."

Lan smiled at Sadir, eyes creasing, "And thank you, Sadir, for being so patient. Your needs are more immediate, more important in the fullness of this cycle…I am speaking of Kyel, and of Luna. There have been rescue attempts, but we do not yet know if they have been successful. But we know the youngsters have been questioned," he continued. Sadir stifled a sob and pushed into Targas's shoulder.

"We do not know the extent of the questioning or what may have been revealed," Lan hastened. "Still, events are moving, and we are being directed by them. We would not have precipitated them at this time, but now we must follow the course."

"They're not hurt?" Sadir leant forward. "You know that much, don't you?"

Lan hesitated.

"Don't you!" she spat.

Targas put his arm around her shoulders and gently pulled her back.

"I am sorry, Sadir," Lan responded quietly. "We do not believe they were injured; I suspect we should know that at least. Please relax if you can. We are doing all that is possible."

Lan took a sip of tea, his weathered face wrinkled in thought. The others sat quietly listening, Quonir still staring at Targas.

"The self-styled Shada, Jakus, will be aware of your existence and will be reacting," Lan said. "This may affect the long-term chances of our success against the Sutanites. Their immediate response may be reprisals against our people, without us being in the best position to counter such actions." He ran a weathered hand over the edge of the table before continuing. "Our plans included cutting off the Sutanites' wealth by stopping the flow of salt for the trade. This has begun, but unfortunately without all pieces being in place. We were close...are close." Lan slowly shook his head. "But you, Targas, you are developing your powers and are still relatively untried. However, that is as may be. Our forces have yet to be brought together and we will have to work quickly. So," Lan said, slowly looking around the table, "we will be leaving Sanctus at dawn, for where we need to go."

Targas frowned.

"You look puzzled, my friend," Lan observed.

"It's the distance. If Regulus is around three days from Sanctus, how do you get messages so quickly?"

"Ah," Lan nodded, "I think this is one I will leave to Lethnal."

"It's pleasing to get a word in, since I speak at a quicker pace than our leader." Lethnal's smile lit up her thin face, making her look younger. Targas thought that she would be 10 to 15 years older than he and Sadir, since her short hair was liberally peppered with grey. "It really shouldn't be me who is telling you this but my colleague, Rasnal. She's really in charge of them. Oh, well," she sighed.

"We've always linked with nature. We haven't really exploited it, just lived in harmony as much as possible. Unlike the Sutanites," Lethnal's eyes flashed. "They want something, they take it. Their greatest wrong against our country has been the way they have changed the natural way of things. The worst result... you already know, for you, and Quonir's brother Quon," she added quickly, "have had experience of it."

Targas broke in. "You mean the...hymetta? They're too big, aren't they? They're wrong somehow. Back in Tenstria, such creatures don't get much bigger than a little finger."

"I only wish that were so here," said Lethnal, shaking her head. "They're a real danger to us. It may be that the Sutanites interfered with nature in a despicable way, but we didn't know of the creatures until after they came. Luckily these hymetta breed far from here and are very nest-bound, though that makes them harder to manipulate, I understand. But, we've our own link, our own 'big' creature, the *tina*. You saw them last night. We've known of tina throughout th' history of our people but only in recent times…"—she paused, looking across the room—"have we learnt how to use them. They give us a distinct advantage over the Sutanites, and that's the ability to send a fast message over a long distance, without the scent messages being trapped by those foul scent towers the Sutanites have in every town."

"So, you use the scent attractant, to *tell* the…tina to go to a place, right?" Targas saw the answering nod, "And have it carry a scent message? That's clever, really clever. I suppose you'd have to be a scent master to decipher the message, though?"

"Yer have t' be trained, yes," said Brin, speaking for the first time. He was as short as Lan, but broader, with large shoulders and thick wrists. His face was also rounder and darker. "Me people have some different ways of usin' their smell sense but just a little trainin' allows anyone of skill t' read th' message."

He leant forward, past Zahnal and Sadir, to look at Targas. "Yer already know I'm from th' river from me scent pattern, 'nd me accent, but what yer may not know is that I am of th' barge people. We're th' race th' Sutanites kindly use t' transport *our* salt down th' Great Southern t' Port Saltus, 'nd it's a hard life for me people."

"Quonir," broke in Lan, "you have been quiet. Do you have anything to add?"

Quonir's gaze fastened on Targas, his body rigid. He looked like a near-identical version of his brother, who Targas had met in his nightmare entry into Ean. The shaved head made it hard to guess age, but his creased face, high cheekbones and narrow eyes, dark in leathery skin, gave him an inscrutable appearance.

"Seems like we've put a lot of faith in him, a lot of faith at great cost," he said gruffly, glancing sideways at Lan. "I hope it hasn't been misplaced."

"Uh huh." Lan cleared his throat and smiled apologetically at Targas. He then took a deep breath, placed both hands on the table and pushed himself to his feet. "Time will tell as it must. Before we finish I must put into words what we already know, from last night, for Targas. We all shared special experiences with you and you with us. Your presence in Ean has given us impetus to put our plans into action, to bring them forward to counter our enemy.

"Normally our system of teaching scent control takes years, with many levels of learning before you reach scent master. But we cannot teach you much, in such a short time." Lan smiled. "We can hope the ability we have detected in you and helped expose, to utilise the motes of scent in diverse and extensive patterns, will serve us in the forthcoming conflict."

The silence at the table continued as everyone appeared to wait for Targas to respond. He stood and forced himself to look around the table. "From where I am," he said, "there's little alternative, so I hope I can play a part in what lies ahead. I don't know what else I could do, anyway, as I seem to be involved." He smiled nervously down at Sadir. "And there are some things that have become very important to me."

"That is good," responded Lan. "Come, we have spent enough time at the table. There is much to do before we depart."

"Another fine, sunny day," said Lan, leading the way across the hillside. "And I must apologise for my friend Quonir, he has been through much. I am pleased anyway, you two"— he nodded towards Sadir—"have…ah… bonded so well; it is comforting. Something I find I miss."

They came to the small alcove amongst the boulders.

"Oh, this's lovely!" exclaimed Sadir as she sat on a sun-drenched boulder with Targas next to her. "You know, I feel guilty to be happy while my brother is in the hands of those people, but I'm so glad I've found Targas, even if he has some unusual ways, and is not of Ean—everything seems to work the same, though." She looked sideways at her partner.

Targas put his arm around her.

Lan nodded at Sadir. "You've needed the time here…and we have made good use of it. Your man has the skills we believe will increase our chances." He remained standing, leaning against a towering grey monolith.

"Events are moving, without enough control or co-ordination. Our hand has been forced. The river people have commenced the salt blockade, perhaps before time. They are a well-trained and resourceful people. However, their opponents, the guardsmen and seekers at Regulus, are more numerous, so we have to act and support them. But what is especially concerning," Lan continued, "is the involvement of the salt miners. The mountain and river peoples have trained for this time…but the miners are different. They have a difficult life in the mines. The Sutanite garrison exerts a strong control over them. And our ability to contact and help them has been limited. The enemy is ruthless, and we fear for the miners' safety as events unfold,' he sighed, looking around at the peaceful scene.

"Targas, I will not say more, but know too that we have learnt from you. I would suspect that you were a scent master in your own way, in Tenstria… although we have seen that it is not a focus for your people. So, I'll leave you both." He paused for a moment, looking between them. "Take care of Sadir, Targas, she is important to us." As he turned to go, Tel appeared in the entrance to the alcove. "We have found Conduvian lizards an important part of Sanctus, and our defences… Also, good companions."

Lan walked past Tel. "Return when you wish."

Tel pushed his way to sit on the rock between them, wriggling to Targas's absent-minded pat on the rough skin. Sadir's short hair tickled his chin as she leant over the lizard to cuddle him. Targas sighed contentedly and moved his arm to hold her.

He could see the movements of animals in the trees down the slope like the day before. The same tendrils of scent rising, forming patterns as they twisted and became entwined. As they rose the light breeze added a force stronger than the bonds that held it, making the tendrils thin and become almost mushroom-shaped where the breeze increased. The wind pushed the scents, breaking and mixing them until a virtual porridge of odours was moving in the one direction.

Targas found he could keep track of a scent and recognise its nature in that mix, but the further away, the more difficult it became. He could go with it, recognising its origin and whether it was natural or the result of strong emotion. He grinned as he followed along, enjoying the play on his senses.

A stronger scent infiltrated, the darkness of worry infused with light reds, pinks and soft yellows. He recognised Sadir and immediately pulsed reassurance and love. He let the strengths of her aura take him, allowed himself to savour her scents where he could be lost and hide safely away from the dangers ahead.

Even as this thought occurred, he saw the potential of the physical scents around him, like pieces of a game board. All could be identified, categorised according to compatibility, and used. One could be dragged, overlain with another, strengthened, and become part of a bigger thing. Just like the joining of many essences in a liquor; by themselves meaning little, but together giving a quality finish.

So, he worked, instinctively knowing which scents would fit, taking one, binding it with another, entwining it with others until he had an interlocking of odours. His heightened skills allowed him to grasp it, fashion it into a net that had enough physical presence to catch and hold other scents. He manoeuvred it through the air until it collided with the treetops and broke into a puff of vapour. The challenge continued; the new net was made with more powerful bonds, held together with greater purpose, stronger will. This time the trees bent aside as it pushed through, and it retained its shape.

He brought it to him with a small, thin lizard trapped in its folds. The net dissolved above his lap, dropping the creature. As it fell, the lizard pushed out a pair of transparent flaps of skin and glided away. Tel snapped at it, too late.

Sadir's lips opened in awe. Her aura was a mixture of scents, and he could see her abilities at work. It took just a moment to rub up against them, take some with her consent and bring her with him as he revealed his control. The exhilaration he felt was magnified by the linking of her femininity with his masculine essence and her participation in his ride of the scents. He could feel her curiosity as he took her with him on this exploration, her amazement as the boundaries of her knowledge widened. He knew when he was pushing her too fast, was leaving her behind, and understood her limits.

They were mentally gasping for breath when he released his control on the scents and returned to normality. They looked at each other with understanding. He let out a sigh, knowing that things were starting to crystallise for him, that he could bind so many scents into whole functioning units, over a large area and with control. And with the knowledge that working with the intricate capabilities of scent was a natural extension of his abilities.

It was late in the night when they returned to the main building of Sanctus. Time had passed so quickly, only the hardness of the rock seat and a chill settling over the valley had made them move.

Targas found his original clothing repaired and cleaned on the bed. While the robes were comfortable he was pleased to have his coat, shirt, trousers and boots back for travelling.

Again, it was the common room where everyone congregated in small groups after the nighttime meal.

Lethnal came over. "Would you like to see how we receive messages from the tina?"

"Yes," replied Targas. "Sadir can come too?"

"I'd be pleased to show you both," said Lethnal as they walked. "You may not know that the tina are controlled with a very special scent; a scent you've already discovered. They're attracted to it over a very large distance if the winds are right, and when released will find, and remember, the next source of the scent. By careful use we can quickly send messages between places."

They took the familiar path to the cavern, but this time moved on through the large underground space to one of the smaller caves further in. Lethnal spoke briefly to a short, thick-set woman, who they recognised as Rasnal. She stood aside to allow them to enter.

It was warm and dark, but easy to navigate. His smell sense had been so enhanced that it was possible for him to judge where he was by the slight changes in odour, as the scents increased in strength the nearer to their source. He held on to Sadir's hand, and drew in the smells. The musty vanilla odour he had detected the previous night became stronger. Slight movements on the walls of the cave revealed the large creatures crammed together, wings folded flat across their backs, legs gripping the rough wall.

"Fantastic," he breathed. "Can I touch?"

"Gently," said Rasnal. "Just don't rub off their fluff. Suppress your own odour too if you wouldn't mind."

They were big and dark, with large compound eyes below fan-shaped antennae. Their bodies buzzed almost silently, which seemed to be creating small gusts of air. Both he and Sadir touched the softness of the wings.

"What's causing this draft, Rasnal?"

"Just the tina breathing," she replied. "They don't breathe like we do. They have to vibrate their bodies, and when you're with a crowd of them the air's never still."

A breeze suddenly sprang up. The buzzing grew louder as a dark shape flew around them and landed to drink from a cup-shaped hollow in the wall, the source of the sweet vanilla-like smell.

"There," Lethnal pointed to the tina. "That's what we've been waiting for. Rasnal will check for a message."

Targas and Sadir watched in the dim light as Rasnal gently stroked the sides of the large creature, relaxing it so she could reach its thorax. She pulled off a small strip of what looked like leather and unrolled it before handing it to Lethnal.

Scents wafted up from the strip, a complex tangle, each strand with its own meaning.

"Can you smell these? They all mean something. You can detect the male and female odour?" Lethnal paused. "And there's a link to Regulus—you wouldn't know that scent yet; then the girl Luna is linked to our agent and the river barges. By Ean, he's succeeded! I hope it's not placed him in danger. But the young woman is not well, though the river people are very capable healers," she added hastily. "The male—I mean your brother—is linked to the leader, Jakus, and Nebleth. However, there's a scent of failure. I'm sorry Sadir, it seems that Kyel is still with the leader. No indication of injury, so there's hope."

Targas could feel Sadir's concern and held her to him. "We'll get him back, my love," he murmured.

"Thanks, Rasnal," said Lethnal. "I'll take this message above. We'll no doubt be leaving at dawn."

Tomorrow, thought Targas, *we'll be on the road again and the brief peace we've shared will be over.*

Chapter Twenty-Three

Kyel sat on the side of his small bed and pulled on a dark brown robe. As he slipped on sandals, his stomach rumbled at the thought of food.

I wonder if there's some of that pie from last night, he thought. *First that, then I'll see what my friend's doing.*

A guard outside his door escorted him through a maze of corridors to Jakus's rooms. He knocked at the large wooden doors and then ushered the youth in before leaving.

Jakus frowned as Kyel entered, but his words were welcoming. "Ah, my young trainee, how does it feel to wear the robes of a new acolyte, mmmm?"

Kyel stopped at the sight of his friend, Jakus, sitting in a large chair in the last stages of being shaved, the barber rubbing oil into his freshly shaven scalp.

"Leave me." Jakus waved the man towards the door, then turned, a smile pasted on his face. "You'll need a shave sometime soon, won't you?"

"Ah, I suppose so," said Kyel, feeling his chin. "I've got hair already."

"Yes, yes," Jakus responded absently. "You're hungry? Nefaria," he called, "you will serve for us."

Kyel looked to the adjoining room, his jaw dropping when a beautiful woman walked in. She was wearing the brown robes of an acolyte, but they looked different. The material was a finer weave, clinging to her body in a way that made him blush. Kyel's eyes followed the slight movements of her breasts under the fabric. The dark hair, cut short, left the white column of her neck exposed. Something on her eyes and lips highlighted them in a way that made her face striking.

Kyel fell instantly in love.

"Looks like you have another convert, Nefaria?" Jakus mocked.

She laughed, a musical, tinkling sound that sent shivers up Kyel's spine. "And shall I feed him for you?" Her voice was soft and low.

"No. Eat while we talk. Kyel, pay attention." Jakus pulsed a scent dart at him.

"Ouch!" Kyel pulled his gaze away from Nefaria, rubbing his arm where the dart had hit.

"You will be starting with the other trainees today, and judging by your scent display, discipline should be on the agenda. I'll be leaving for Port Saltus on business, so report to me on my return after sun down.

"Take our young friend to meet his teacher; I don't think his mind is on food."

"Certainly, my Shada. I will see you on your return?"

"Of course. Kyel, go with Nefaria."

Kyel followed Nefaria from the room, not noticing where she was taking him. He followed her along the dark corridors, concentrating on the roll of her hips and appreciating the view whenever the slanting light from window slits lit her body. He wanted to follow her forever.

"Come Kyel, your scents would be obvious even to the untalented," said Nefaria, not looking back at him. "I think you need Akerus to teach you some control. Ah, we're here."

She pushed open a well-used door on to a room full of young people, all in brown robes. Noise ceased as they entered.

"Ah, Nefaria, one of my favourite ex-pupils. I wish you could return to class and give me a hand." The speaker was a bald-headed, plain-looking man of around fifty, dressed in a black robe. A smile lit his face.

"Akerus, I have other duties," she laughed, "after delivering you your new trainee. This is Kyel. I'll leave him in your care."

She gently pushed Kyel toward Akerus and then swiftly left the room. As the door closed, Kyel looked at a sea of curious faces.

"Kyel, take a spare desk, and please try some control. We all have a special spot for her, but don't make your desires so obvious."

Kyel quickly found a seat and dropped his head to hide his blushes.

The day passed slowly, with Akerus teaching at a level mostly above Kyel's understanding. Some areas were basic, but the analysis of scent signals, control of one aroma above another, and the levels that led to being a scent master, were difficult. He found it hard to concentrate.

His elbow was suddenly knocked from under him, causing his head to almost hit the desk.

"Kyel, pay attention," yelled a voice in his ear. "Now what are these for?"

A black cylindrical object was thrust under his nose. It was achingly familiar and caused him to recoil in horror. The last time he had seen a scent truncheon so close up was when he'd been escaping from Korla with Targ and Luna.

Lizards' teeth! What's happened to them? Why am I here?

He yelled in disbelief and started to get up, looking wildly around the room at a group of bemused faces. One stood out in his panic, a face he had known from long ago. He focused.

"Ryiar? Thought you were dead; you were taken ages ago. Why are you here?"

A heavy hand clamped down on his shoulder. A strong, calming scent flowed over him. A pinch of the bitter crystals was pushed into his mouth. As he started to sink into a drowsy state he heard Akerus mutter behind him. "Too soon. Jakus, you gave him to me too soon. The magnesa level's out of balance."

Jakus banged the door open to hit the wooden wall. The guardsmen scrambled to their feet, knocking over a chair.

"The guardsman in charge?" he snapped.

The three men in the guardhouse looked at each other, before one turned back to Jakus.

"Shada, I'll fetch him," he said, straightening to attention before edging out the door.

"Refreshment!" ordered Jakus. He sat on the more comfortable of the chairs and pushed back his hood, his prominent bald head adding weight to his authority. He ignored the actions of the remaining guardsmen as he thought through what he needed to do while in Port Saltus.

"Shada?" came an anxious voice.

Jakus looked up to see the commander of the Port Saltus garrison before him.

"Ah, Master Guardsman Daltir."

"I apologise for not being here, Shada. If you'd given me more warning…"

"Why?" asked Jakus, eyebrows raised. "Did I interrupt something?"

"No, no," Daltir rushed his words, "I would have preferred to welcome you personally, that's all."

"Hmmm." Jakus locked eyes with Daltir as the big man straightened under his scrutiny, pulling his grey jerkin tighter. "No matter; you may join me."

Jakus inspected the food and drink placed on the table as Daltir took a seat opposite him.

"Leave us!" The two guardsmen left as Jakus focused on Daltir. "You know of the rebel activity in Ean? The troops here are in readiness?" The solid features of Daltir tightened.

"Assuredly. Shada. Our men are ready, and we can move upwards of three hundred at a moment's notice. We have few scent masters here, as you…would know, but our fighting men are at their peak."

"We may need to move soon," replied Jakus. He then gave details of the situation while Daltir sat rigidly nodding at the appropriate moments.

"You will inform only those you can trust not to talk to the ranks. This must be an orderly operation, if it comes to that. Now, what is the state of my ship?" Jakus questioned.

"Your ship…Shada?" asked Daltir.

"Speak, man!"

"Your ship…is in readiness as always, Shada."

"Good." Jakus pulsed a command and loyalty scent, satisfied as Daltir's eyes glazed over.

Jakus left the room, refusing the offer of an escort. Leaving his mount at the guardhouse, he walked out of the gates and turned down one of the smaller streets leading towards the docks. As he moved he seemed to shrink, become less obvious, the black robe blending in with the pre-midday traffic.

He slowed, adopted a shorter stride and a less purposeful gait until he entered a narrow street that ran parallel with the waterfront. Two-storey buildings blocked the view of a number of the sea-going trading vessels that moved cargo in and out of Port Saltus. A gloom pervaded the street, allowing little light to enter the small, shuttered windows that typified the wooden buildings.

Jakus stopped at a solid, age-scarred door, looked up and down the street before entering. He quietly climbed a set of steep stairs in virtual darkness, using his senses to find his way rather than relying on the flickering light of the two burning candles in their holders. He nodded to himself before throwing open the door at the top of the landing.

"Blood's stink!" yelled a beak-nosed, narrow-faced man with thinning lank hair as he jumped from his seat.

Jakus, face set, saw the other occupant of the room back into a shelf-lined wall, a dagger gleaming in his hand. A map falling to the floor did not distract him.

"Saemid, relax. It is only our partner and…protector. Welcome, Jakus." The man skirted the small table to greet him.

Jakus smiled tightly, before stopping him with a burst of control scent.

"I don't believe I've seen the other side of my operation, Tibitus," said Jakus, nodding his head towards Saemid, who was replacing his dagger under a large, worn coat. "You might care to introduce us."

"It's Saemid…Captain Saemid," said Tibitus with a nervous smile. "You wouldn't have met him since he is usually trading away from Ean."

Jakus peered at the features of the man hidden under a flop of long, dark hair. He was a Sutanite half-caste with weathered face and eyes overhung by bony eyebrows, and a large nose. While he had some scent control, Jakus easily read the man's secrets.

"Uh…could I offer you some wine?" asked Tibitus, holding up a dark bottle. "It's well matured and just in from the eastern lands."

"Hmmm." Jakus nodded and sat where he could see both men. His eyes tightened at Saemid's belated scent control as he moved to resume his seat at the table. Tibitus poured the aromatic liquid.

"You have had success then?" Jakus sipped the wine, enjoying the flavour hitting his senses.

"Uh...yes and...no,' said Tibitus as he resumed his seat, one uneasy eye on Saemid. "The Captain has just arrived, having successfully offloaded our salt. In return he has brought much fabric, spices, beverages"—he raised his glass to the light—"and gold...uh... magnesite was in short supply. I was this moment preparing a message to inform you..." Tibitus glanced at the tense figure of Saemid.

Jakus smiled fleetingly before reaching into his pouch. He held his hand out to show the red crystals nestling on his palm.

"Magnesite is made into this and is more valuable than anything else you've brought back. It is the prime reason I put up with you, Tibitus, as a business partner.

"And Saemid, do you know what I need it for...mmmm?" Jakus noted his puzzled look. "Let me show you."

Jakus extruded his red tongue and licked up the crystals. His eyes momentarily glazed over as he pushed the hood off his head, his gleaming scalp clashing with the room's gloom.

"In the hands of a novice, the crystals are a useful sense enhancer. In the hands of a master, it can be used in many ways." He slowly rose to his feet. "Captain Saemid," he said, looking over at the man. Saemid pushed back his chair, eyes wide. "Did Tibitus fail to mention that all magnesite belongs to me? Did you think I would tolerate a thief working for me?"

Saemid lunged out of his chair, dagger outstretched. A physical thickening of the air in front of Jakus's stomach met and blocked the knife.

A tendril, black and thick, grew instantly in front of Jakus's face, before spearing at Saemid and diving down the man's open mouth. Veins corded on Jakus's forehead as he manoeuvred the odour tendril inside Saemid.

The dagger clanged to the floor, gurgled cries cut off and Saemid's eyes bulged. He pulled at his throat as he staggered back into the shelves. His stomach was distending and moving as if something was fighting to get out; his hands dropped to grab at his belly. The scent tendril broke through, forcing his gut contents to spill. A vile smell followed.

Saemid's body crashed, still thrashing, to the floor. Tibitus, crouched in a corner, did not move.

"I believe I am owed a quantity of magnesite?" muttered Jakus, breathing evenly.

Tibitus managed a stiff nod, ignoring Saemid's final spasms.

Jakus, in the one unsullied part of the room, smiled before quaffing his glass of wine.

He paused at the door and looked back at Tibitus. "Choose more wisely for our next venture."

"Kyel," whispered a familiar voice. The scent brought an automatic feeling of desire. "The Shada's back."

He sleepily opened his eyes.

He could just see a slim white hand reaching down to him in the darkness of his room. He took it and struggled to his feet.

"He's just back and wants you." The urgency in Nefaria's voice shook the grogginess from his head and made him hurry. He kept hold of her hand as they moved along the dark corridors.

Jakus's dark aura was obvious when they entered.

"Boy! I need more information from you. Akerus tells me that you disrupted his class this day. That he had to calm you down?"

"Yes, Cer," Kyel answered, hanging his head, "but I'm better now, though I can't remember much about it."

"Enough!" snapped Jakus. "It appears I made an error of judgement. You must be stronger than you look."

"I don't understand..."

"No, I don't expect you do. Sit there. We'll talk," he said. "Nefaria, bring wine."

He sat opposite Kyel and scrutinised him. "I had a hard day at Port Saltus. I even had to remind people my wishes should be respected. On my return I hear that your girl has escaped from Regulus."

"What?" asked Kyel.

"Blood's stink!" Jakus slammed his hand on his knee. "Think, boy!"

Kyel's heart leapt as he saw the frown on Jakus's face. "Oh, you mean Luna? Don't know. Wasn't there."

"No, you weren't, were you? What's she like, this Luna?" pushed Jakus. "She didn't seem very decisive, very capable."

Kyel remembered Luna. She had been a good companion when they had been together. She was helpful and seemed to know what she was doing. In addition, there were moments when they had held hands and really enjoyed each other's company. Then when they had been caught... *Yeah, caught...* His mind started to follow that line of thought. *We'd been together, with each other. We'd been scared too. She was good to be with. However, Nefaria... She's much different. I reckon I could...*

A blast of repulsive scent hit him in the face. "Snap out of it, boy! Tell me what you know. Now!"

He thought hard and told Jakus all he could. Even in a foggy haze he wanted more and more to please him—*after all he's me friend.*

"Hmmm," murmured Jakus, "then why is she important enough to be worth the risk of rescue? You, I can understand…but she, she showed limited scent talent.

"Ah, the wine. Leave it there."

Nefaria nodded to Jakus and smiled briefly at Kyel before going into the adjacent room.

The wine was a new experience, bringing warm tingling feelings to Kyel's toes as he tried to answer the man. However, while his words seemed muddled and often ran together, eventually Jakus seemed satisfied.

"Next day I'll be busy," he instructed, "so you'll continue your learning. Be here for the morning meal."

Kyel left, puzzling about Jakus's preoccupation with Luna as he wandered through the maze of corridors back to his room.

The next few days passed in a blur of training activity. He was always busy and, except for a shared morning meal with its daily dose of those bitter-tasting crystals, he had little to do with Jakus.

He found it strange he could concentrate on the lessons and remember the techniques he was being taught, but when he tried to think beyond the everyday he could remember little. It did not usually worry him, unless it was at night when his dark dreams began.

Nefaria was another distraction. He hadn't been put off her by Jakus, or by the age difference, and had quickly learnt to hide his reaction to her presence. He found many excuses to be with her, even limited as they were by her duties and his training.

It was through her that he finally understood the hierarchy of the rulers. At the bottom were the potentials, the brown-robed trainees. They had to work their way up to be third year acolytes. From there, if they wanted advancement, they joined the ranks of the grey-and-black-garbed seekers that acted as the police force throughout Ean. Exemplary performance as a seeker led on to further training as a scent master and the kudos that went with it. Kyel quailed at the thought of becoming one of those black-robed, cold people. They always scared him, and encounters with scent masters were never pleasant.

No, he thought, *I'd much rather stay in th' brown robes, be amongst people like Nefaria and Tamas.*

Tamas was a serious young man, with slightly squinting eyes but an open, round face. He had finished his third year of training and was now the acolyte in charge of the reference map in Nebleth. The map was usually kept in the tower and continually updated according to information received from the scent towers, seekers and scent masters around Ean. Tamas explained features of the map to Kyel. He had never seen a map before other than the odd shapes scratched in the sand, let alone a large linen canvas outlining details of the entire country. Tamas pointed to various parts of the landscape marked on the map and allowed Kyel to smell the range of scents on specific locations. But one thing Tamas wouldn't reveal was how odours were set into a fabric and the process for accurately identifying a specific region.

"Just a matter of training," was all he would say. "You have to know your scents, know how they go together to make the message and find the location."

Kyel learnt to trace the great river bisecting the country. He saw how the mountains virtually cupped all the towns and Regulus in their arms, and understood that Korla and Lesslas were a long distance from Nebleth. The odours did vary across the map, but it was too hard for him to single out a precise location by detecting the difference in them. If he concentrated, blocked out his other senses and just used smell to do the work, he could appreciate scent variations on the map. Kyel began to *see* that the clumps of scent, constantly being updated, had more similarities the closer they were together, but also distinct differences. It was like a river starting off with one source, *one scent* of water and gradually picking up other waters as it travelled and grew. The river, at the finish of its journey, would still have the original water but would be so augmented and mixed with waters of different amounts and origins that the final character contained all elements. The trick was to follow each of those elements back to their source. He could see it would take much training and knowledge of regional odours.

And his interest in these extraneous things, even being tardy for his lessons with Akerus, was tolerated by Jakus.

All this changed after several days. News had come that left the castle in an uproar. His lessons were cancelled. The strength of a very negative blocking odour kept him in his room while urgency and menace pervaded the corridor. It was late in the day when a harried-looking Nefaria came into his room.

"You're to come," she said, and grabbed his hand to hurry him along. He stepped in close and looked into her eyes.

She seemed startled, then reached out and ruffled his hair.

"Ah, Kyel," she breathed, giving out a companionable scent. "You're so like someone I knew."

"Who...who are you talking about? What's happening?" he asked, swallowing a sudden pang of disappointment.

"Oh." Nefaria's eyes tightened. "Another time and place; no matter," she shook her head. "As for what's happening?" she repeated Kyel's question. "It should be for the Shada to say, but there's been bad news. The rebels have blocked off the salt." Nefaria went silent as they walked. She stopped and gripped his hands as they came to the door. "Just come in here and wait, but mind you keep out of his way unless he wants you."

Kyel walked into a room full of people and then stood inconspicuously against one of the walls, the solid stone giving a measure of comfort.

The aura circling Jakus as he spoke was dark. Surrounding him were many of the black robes, cropped and bald heads contrasting against the dark colour. A tall, thin woman with short-cropped grey hair seemed close to the Shada. She had an air of command, even the other scent masters, including his teacher, Akerus, appearing to defer to her.

"Who's that?" he whispered, pointing.

"*That*," hissed Nefaria as she slapped down Kyel's arm, "is Strona, a powerful scent master. You don't want to get her attention; not as bad as that slimy Septus but best to avoid if you can."

Nefaria put her arm on his shoulder as they watched.

Only three were obvious soldiers in the grey tunics but several seekers were also present in their grey-and-black garb.

One seeker spotted Kyel and Nefaria. He smiled and came over.

"Nefaria," he whispered, "a pleasure to see you as always." The man moved his head close and exchanged an intimate scent greeting. Kyel was a little surprised at the man's familiarity, especially with Jakus in the room, but a quick glance showed they were unobserved.

"And this must be Kyel?"

"Yes, Jelm, it is," smiled Nefaria, looking at the tall man while trying to keep an eye on the centre of the room. "Good to see you're back from the mountains."

"It's been a long, hard patrol, Nefaria. And from what the Shada is saying it looks like we have a harder time ahead of us. The rebels blocking off the salt supplies will force Jakus's hand.

"Now boy, let's look at you. Hmmm, you look well cared for, though glazed in the eyes. Magnesa, Nefaria?"

She nodded.

"Out! Everyone!" yelled Jakus, instantly silencing the buzz of conversation. "Meet here at dawn. Not you, Jelm or Nefaria."

Jakus locked eyes with Jelm as he and Nefaria approached; Kyel followed unobtrusively. "We may have to leave for Regulus soon to follow up on the pitiful salt blockade. Jelm, what's this about Septus? Has he gone to break the blockade? What support has he taken?"

"Can I speak freely, Shada?" asked Jelm.

"Speak!"

"Shad Heritis and Septus have acted to investigate the situation. Septus left with a force of seekers and guardsmen to restore the supply of salt."

Jakus frowned. "Your opinion?"

161

"Uh, Shada," began Jelm, "it may be as the Shad surmises. The salt supply might be easily restored, although there has been no recent communication with the salt mines. The force with Septus should be strong enough to counter any problems, though it may have been more…*sensible* to have gathered further intelligence."

"Enough," snapped Jakus. "Heritis should be able to make such decisions. But it's a pity I was not informed sooner; my own recent experiences may have influenced his actions." He suddenly seemed to notice Kyel. "No further news concerning the boy's companion?"

"No, my Shada."

Jakus glared into Jelm's face, his aura visibly thickening. Kyel could see beads of sweat break out across the seeker's brow as his face whitened.

"I can't be everywhere. Can't do everything. Surely some of you are capable of thinking in Regulus?" Jakus's gaze switched to look at Nefaria and Kyel.

"Well then, I don't need the boy or you, Jelm… Leave. Nefaria… Stay."

Kyel was happy to escape the oppressive room with the tall seeker, but as he saw Nefaria moving towards Jakus, he felt an unfamiliar pang in his heart.

Chapter Twenty-Four

The grasslands were bisected by a swollen, silt-laden river flowing southwards. Like a vast swathe of molten lava, it barred the easterly path of the entire Sanctus resistance party. Ahead loomed a tall mountain range, harsh and forbidding. A purple bank of cloud was rapidly coming behind them out of rugged western hills they'd left the day before.

"I hope we don't have to cross that, Sadir," Targas shivered. "And there's the smell of rain, too."

"Don't know if we have to cross the Great Southern, but those clouds are bringing rain, Targas. You can see all the odours almost flying before it. Yes, I think it's going to be windy and wet before long." As if to emphasise her words, a flurry of wind whipped dust and grit into their eyes, tugging at their clothing. The fringes of Sadir's cropped brown hair ruffled as she pulled her hood tighter and double knotted the cord around her midriff to prevent the robe from flying up and leaving a gap above her woollen trousers.

The pace had been punishing and there were sore spots on Targas's thighs and buttocks; perac gave a smooth ride once you were used to it, but getting used to it was the problem. At least their night in the open had been far more comfortable than the last time they had camped out—they had taken pleasure in each other in their small tent.

Targas pulled the grey hood down over his head and tightened the cloak around his body, grateful for the extra protection it gave over his coat and trousers, before heading over towards Lan.

The leader squinted at them from where he stood with Brin and smiled. "You will be wondering how we are to cross the Great Southern? Concerned about the weather also?"

"I was hoping that we wouldn't have to cross, but I know you've something planned." Targas looked back at the huddle of people and animals around them. "There's so many of us to move, too."

"What is bad for us…is good for us,' replied Lan. "While this weather change will make conditions bad for traversing the river, it is at least blowing any odour traces away from our enemy…and that is important with all our scent masters in one place…"

Targas was about to ask a question when he noticed that Lan and Brin were distracted by several large, dark shapes edging along the river's edge towards them.

"Friends," Lan shouted into the gusting wind, "help is at hand." He pointed at the river barges. Soon over a hundred people with their animals and supplies began to move down the slope towards the river.

Targas could see the shapes were imposing, flat craft riding low in the water and slowed by the current. Several large perac were being led along a rough track on the bank to provide the barges' forward power as they strained against thick, connecting ropes. Each craft was guided by a man at the rear on the tiller.

The crowd soon reached the craft and enthusiastically greeted the bargemen. Brin pushed through to talk with his countrymen.

Targas walked alongside the barges with Sadir, pacing it out. *Going to be a tight squeeze for everyone, plus animals, and how in blood's grace can we get these craft across the river?*

A fresh squall of wind with a smattering of rain hit the group.

"Quick, everyone," Brin called, his voice booming against the rising sound of the storm, "start leadin' th' perac up th' plank. Yer'll have t' all go int' th' cargo area. Won't be for too long. I hope," he added, looking anxiously skyward.

The people began an orderly embarkation, maintaining a calming scent on their animals as they boarded.

"Wait a moment," Brin called to Targas. "You'll be needed."

"What can I do? I've never been on one of these before."

"Could yer stay in th' stern of th' first barge with me 'nd Lan? We'll need t' keep 'n eye on th' joinin' rope, 'nd th' water, because it's goin' t' be a dangerous crossin'." As if to emphasise his words the wind picked up and rain slanted down, rattling off the wooden decks and wetting those not under cover.

"Sadir, love, I suppose you better go inside as well," said Targas. "Take Tel too, he'll just be in the way out here."

"If I must. Don't risk yourself." She touched his arm, her eyes large with concern, before joining the queue for the first barge.

"No time for introductions t' me countrymen, just get on board. Th' bargemen will use their poles t' push off," said Brin.

Targas grimaced. The Sanctus resistance, in barges on a rough, fast-flowing river, was ripe for the enemy to pick off in one go. *Though the elements might just do the job for them*, he thought wryly as he settled on a worn, wet seat, pulling his travelling cloak tighter and nervously waited while the stragglers moved aboard.

The hatches were slammed and fastened. The bargemen pushed in unison at the riverbank with their long poles.

The barges seemed reluctant to join the flow of the Great Southern as they held to the bank. The energetic efforts of the men eventually caused the current to catch the bow of the first barge and pull it into the strong flow. The rest followed, joining ropes thrumming with tension.

Rain masked the other barges, making them black shadows behind them. Ahead there was nothing but a grey wall through which they bounced and shuddered. Waves began to wash across the low deck and into the cockpit. Targas and his companions were soon saturated.

"Don't like th' look of this," yelled Brin into his ear. "We're too heavy in th' water. They're built well, but not that well."

"Targas," said Lan into his other ear, "we need to calm it somehow. If we focus we may be able to flatten the water."

Targas suddenly, and unexpectedly, felt a rush of fear; an unwanted memory surfaced. As a child he'd almost drowned when he'd fallen into a bog hole. Every time he'd tried to get out, the sides of the hole had collapsed, trapping him further. He'd been in the cold bog water for a long time before he was found.

He gritted his teeth as blackness edged into his vision.

"Targas!" shouted Lan, shaking his shoulder. "Brin! There's something wrong with Targas."

Targas was dimly aware of Lan and Brin as they tried to push an odour wall out and around the craft, to flatten the cresting waves. However, the surface was too rough; it was clearly too hard a task.

A particularly forceful spray of water hit him in the face, snapping him into awareness. His stomach recoiled as the large vessel tossed violently. A noise of animals screaming in panic broke through the crashing of the waves.

Sadir, he thought suddenly. *Enough!*

He reached out into the odour form that Lan and Brin were using and joined them. He assessed the mass of scents, then pushed. Targas found he could pick out the most minuscule of components and knew instinctively which ones to link with the others. The stronger elements had long chains which would be almost unbreakable with the right connections. He pulled the significant bits together and expanded the process, multiplying the effect dramatically to reinforce the whole. The rough walls of water eased off. The water flattened around the barges, leaving a smooth, rocking platform dragged along by the fast-flowing current.

Targas concentrated on keeping the odour blanket from fraying. He held his companions in with him, the rain a dull, cold pain across his forehead.

One danger was over, but they had no control of their destination.

The journey was a nightmare for Targas. The strain of holding the odour mass tight and on the water was beginning to tell. Sweat mingled with the rain running down his face. His stomach still protested violently. The headlong rush into the driving mists of rain and the ceaseless motion of the barges continued.

A new force suddenly intervened. The barges shuddered into a different direction as a powerful current hit them. Still no visibility and no obvious destination, but at least a change. Time passed. The currents holding them slackened and their speed slowed. Targas sensed rather than saw Lan and Brin pulling themselves out of the union of scents. A firm hand hit his shoulder.

"Yer can let it go," said Brin. "We need t' use th' poles now."

It was easy. Just like turning off a tap. The scents broke apart and dissipated. The waves and the rocking returned, but not with the same impact.

Targas panted, head down to his knees, aware of the bargemen using their poles to manoeuvre the massive vessels into quieter waters.

The barge crunched on a gravely bottom. He allowed himself to be led down the ramp and onto a sodden riverbank, before flopping to the ground, hardly noticing the animals and people moving past him. A welcome pair of arms circled his neck from behind.

"Targas, you're soaked through. You can't stay here," Sadir coaxed gently. "We have to move under cover." Sadir pulled him to his feet and guided him into a nearby thicket of tall trees that provided some protection from the driving rain.

The people worked efficiently. Waterproofed shelters had been set up, small fires somehow lit to provide hot drinks, and temporary seating arranged. Everyone, despite the weather, was animated after their ordeal.

"Hot tea for you two, though I fancy you'd like something stronger, Targas," said Lethnal, passing over two mugs. "You helped save us back then, you know."

Targas looked up tiredly.

"Yes, he's good isn't he?" Sadir jumped in before Targas could say anything.

Lan's quiet voice came from behind. "Yes, Targas, you have power. We needed your skills out there. You gave everything. For that we thank you."

Targas sipped on the hot drink Lethnal had given him. "I couldn't have held much longer, Lan. It was starting to loosen. Without that big push we had all of a sudden..."

"We can thank the bargemen's knowledge of the way these rivers work for that. It was merely the influence of the floodwaters from the Lesslas River. When we met them we were pushed to the other side of the Great Southern, close enough for our friends to get us ashore. Fortune is on our side. Come, let us see if we can get you dry."

With hot cereal filling his now settled stomach, Targas felt guilty sitting in front of a small fire while others worked around him. Every time he attempted to help he was pushed back on his seat and told he needed to regain his strength. He dozed, sitting with his back against the rough bark of a small tree.

Sadir leant against him. Tel lay at their feet, virtually in the fire.

"Tel likes the heat, and at least you're starting to dry," said Sadir, putting an arm around his waist. "I don't like it when you're wet." She looked up at him, streaks of water on her face making her quite desirable. He no longer felt so tired.

"Well, you're not too sleepy, I see," she smiled impishly.

"You made my thoughts go elsewhere for a moment. Wish we had some time alone."

"Me too," Sadir replied, "but we've a long way to go before we get to the Salt Way, and Luna too, I hope. Leastways that's where the bargemen say she was being taken."

"It's good to find they've got Luna out safely," said Targas. "Let's see Lan and the others. They must be deciding what to do next."

Targas started to rise before he stopped and frowned. He was struck by another of those moments. He had lurched from crisis to crisis, solved them to someone else's satisfaction and then waited for the next event. These were good, well-meaning people, their cause just, but he felt he was not really part of it. His home was far away, in time and memory, and now this country and these people were quietly replacing what he had left. His past was fading just as he found it.

A warm hand squeezed his, breaking his thoughts. "Come love, you're with me now."

"Mmmm?" he murmured, returning to the present. *At least Sadir's with me*, he thought, hugging her to him.

"Dry enough? Our weather saves havin' a wash, doesn't it?" Zahnal came up behind Targas and kneaded his tense shoulder muscles with wiry fingers. "I should give you thanks, young man, since you made my job much easier, just a few bruises and nausea. Do you need a rub down by any chance?" she chuckled.

He laughed weakly.

"Targas," interrupted Lan. "You should be part of our current planning."

Still holding Sadir's hand, he moved away from the old healer's ministrations.

"We are a day from the salt mines, the other side of the Long Ranges to the east…and more than a day from the loading docks on the Salt Way River down south. We believe Luna and her rescuers should be at those docks by now and expect to receive word from one of our scouts," Lan told them.

"But that is of no matter, for we must make for the mines. That is where we are needed. Later we will move to the docks and re-unite you," he smiled apologetically. "Matters have come to a head, rightly or wrongly, and we must take this opportunity to strike a telling blow."

"How?" questioned Targas. "The enemy is extremely capable from what I've seen."

"That is one of our problems. We are not a warlike race and have limited experience in battle." He ran a hand over his shaven head. "Our hope is in our mastery of scent, in a number of ways different to our enemy's, and our thinking. Many of our people are trained in the use of basic weapons. With this and our scent talent, we have hope."

"They're not going to let you just take over. There must be guards at the mines if the salt trade is so important to them."

"The mines, Targas," said Lan, "are protected by around twenty guardsmen and several seekers, a formidable but not insurmountable force with our numbers. We now have river people with us, those from the mountains to join us and… there are the miners themselves. But you have the right of it. The enemy will be alert since they must know that the docks are taken, an unfortunate development and too soon." He slowly shook his head.

"And…?" Targas asked, impatiently.

"Uh? Oh, forgive my distraction." Lan looked towards the grey bulk of the mountains now becoming more visible as the weather cleared. He pointed at a valley between two formidable peaks. "We must go through the Long Ranges. If we are successful at the mines, and have the miners join us, we will move to support the Salt Way docks before there is a major reaction from the enemy. The river people, the bargemen, are a strong and well-trained group, but inclined to act rather than consider. This stopping of the salt trade will be like pulling on a k'dorian's tail, foolhardy at best."

"And I've come at the right time?" asked Targas pointedly.

"On that, we agree," said Lan, not reacting, "although your impact is yet to be really tested. The rain is light now," he continued. "I suggest we move on until sun down. It is best to keep going as we do not know when the enemy may get scent of us."

The terrain became increasingly rugged as they moved east through the mountain range. Despite the rain, the country was harsh and dry, with much exposed rock and little vegetation, giving a forbidding aspect to the surroundings.

Darkness came swiftly, aided by the misty rain and the bulk of the mountains. They set up camp on the hard ground in the gloom and ate cold food. Sleep was almost impossible as he and Sadir sought comfort in each other's warmth.

It was still overcast and dry at dawn, a fog blocking the light of the rising sun. They snatched a cold meal before hurriedly organising the animals and packing their camping equipment. The pace was slow, dictated by the terrain and their numbers. Tel huddled under Targas's coat, trading comfort for warmth.

Targas was still damp on this grey day, and everyone was preoccupied. He hummed a tune as he rode.

"What's that, Targas?"

"Eh? Sorry, I was far away. What did you say, Sadir?"

"You were humming."

"Yes I was, wasn't I? Music from home; one of our old drinking songs. Come to think of it, I've never heard any music here, unless you count what happened in the caverns."

"We do have music, but you usually need to be happy to sing, and I don't think many of us are. Besides, our rulers would probably think it suspicious."

Targas's inclination to hum deserted him.

Sadir noticed a familiar, close-cut fair head just ahead, so urged her perac on. "Hynal," she said as she came alongside the taller woman, "we haven't had a chance to catch up."

"No," Hynal smiled, "I think you've been rather occupied with your man." She looked over at Targas. "He is rather...um, engaging, isn't he?"

Sadir heard Hynal chuckle. "I don't know what you mean," she laughed, and then hesitated. "I don't suppose...ah, I don't suppose you've heard anything?"

"No, Sadir, I'd tell you if I knew. With good fortune we'll hear from Salt Way docks soon. That's the best hope we have. Just"—she turned and looked into Sadir's sad eyes— "enjoy the moment while you can." Hynal reached over and patted her knee.

Sadir smiled back and sighed.

The mountains had receded to scrubby hills, the land flattening out into a stark landscape. A shimmer far ahead caught Targas's eye. When the group stopped on a low rise, he moved his perac next to Brin.

"This is dry-looking country, Brin," he said. "Where are the salt mines, and what's that in the distance? Looks like water."

"That ain't water, that's salt pans. Usually dry 'n hot out there; little water. Don't like this side of th' mountains, never rains here, though I'm not complainin' this day," said Brin, gazing across the vast, empty spaces. "Yer asked about th' mines? They're not far. Reckon we'll be stoppin' here, since we'll need t' be careful before we go any closer."

"Haven't had a chance to speak much with you two," said Lethnal as she came alongside Targas and Sadir. She pushed her hood back, eyes squinting against the growing glare from the desert ahead, her short grey hair contrasting with her suntanned skin, lined face crinkled in a smile. "I know this region better than Brin; his people can't stray far from the water." She looked at Brin, still smiling. "But he's right. We're not too distant from the garrison, which guards the mines. You can't see the mines since they're underground. The garrison itself," Lethnal continued, "and the buildings around it weren't built for looks. They're grey stone, coloured like the surrounding desert; not a place you'd want to visit. Anyway, you'll see. Uh"—she looked over towards Lan—"I think we'd better see what our leader's planning."

"Feel up to a short walk, Targas?" asked Lan, as the four of them approached. "We will be staying here, overnight. It is not far from the garrison but protected by the last of the hills... The breeze heads north." Lan stopped at Targas's puzzled look. "The movement of air will carry our scent away and not reveal our presence to the enemy. They are to the east and also south of us."

Lan continued, "Our walk will take us near the garrison. We must find out who controls it and confirm how many there are. Then this night we plan, tomorrow we fight. I am sorry Sadir, but could you stay behind?" He smiled apologetically, "A small group to seek the enemy is best—Brin, Lethnal, and Targas. You, Sadir will be involved in establishing the camp. You do understand?"

"I will be fine with that, Lan. Please be careful." Sadir looked at Targas.

Targas smiled and gave Sadir's hand a quick squeeze, before turning away.

A watercourse, dry and stony, offered a convenient route between the small hills. It was now well after noon, shadows already lengthening as the mountains behind them intercepted the sun's light.

They emerged onto a barren, rock-strewn hillside gently sloping towards the flat plains of the desert. A harsh jumble of what appeared to be large boulders broke the landscape in the distance. Targas noticed that they were mainly in straight lines, showing they had to be fabricated.

"Hissst," whispered Lan. "Down."

They crouched on the uncomfortable surface facing the garrison. Targas, grateful he was wearing his thick trousers, wondered how well the loose pants of perac wool under their robes protected his companions.

"What now?" whispered Targas, looking across at Brin and Lethnal from his position next to Lan.

"Now," said Lan, "we watch. We wait. We learn."

Chapter Twenty-Five

His eyesight had always been exceptional, so the slight blurring of vision was frustrating as he tried to pick out individual scents in the fog of odours from the garrison.

"Can't we get closer?" Targas whispered. "It's hard to see much from this far."

"No, it is too dangerous," said Lan. "They have skilled scent users inside the garrison. And we do not need to, for we have other senses that will suffice."

"Oh, of course. I find it hard to think that way."

Targas extended himself, pushing at and infiltrating the odours. He felt the presence of his companions: Lan was blue-green, suffused by pink, strong but mellow, Brin more subdued, with blues and greens dominant; Lethnal was paler with a mix of greys and olive-green. Their company was both calming and strengthening, aiding his exploration.

He recognised common factors in the mix of scents. While everyone was unique, the soldiers had a familiar aura of weaponry, perac, leather and garlic. Several others stood out by their controlled aura, as if the very release of odour allowed a vital essence to escape, again recognisable.

Targas's senses manoeuvered through the more insubstantial odours of the rock and wood of the garrison to the human scents. A large block of perac, damp wool and dung revealed the stables, while the soldiers appeared in a range of locations. The seekers' auras showed them congregated in the same area.

"Keep back!" A warning flashed yellow across his awareness. Targas pulled away, absently aware of the garrison receding from his senses. He shook his head as his companions stirred.

"Well?" asked Brin, raising his eyebrows at Targas, "What do yer think of that?"

"I…I don't know how to explain it," he said, "I could feel all of you with me and I was there; you could even tell what their owners were feeling. There were guardsmen, and seekers too…"

"Targas," interrupted Lan, "how many were there? Could you place their location, mmmm?"

Targas shrugged.

"Don't make it harder for him, Lan," said Lethnal. "He's done well. Listen, Targas, you saw each person's aura?"

He nodded.

"And you could see where each individual was, roughly? Then all you had to do was follow the scent source to the owner; that would reveal them and their location. And we counted"—Lethnal looked at Brin and Lan—"seventeen guardsmen and three seekers at the garrison."

"Yer fergettin' th' miners," said Brin. "There weren't any in those buildings around th' garrison. Something's strange about that, because there were no families either."

"They must be in the mines," said Lethnal excitedly. "They have to be."

"I believe," cut in Lan, "you are right. I noticed activity in that direction, and it would be logical. It is too hard to confirm that now." He glanced up. "It is darker; the mountains have brought an early end to the day."

"Why are the miners and their families in the mines, I wonder." Lan puzzled as they picked their way across the rocky ground towards their camp. "I believe this may make our task even more difficult."

They ate their food huddled in blankets with no warming fires. They were confident they would not be detected but were taking no chances, with scent masters guarding the perimeters of the camp and masking the site. Lan, Lethnal, Quonir and Brin sat in the middle of around two hundred people whose mass and scents provided a feeling of companionship. Targas shared a blanket with Sadir and Tel.

The moon broke through a final wisp of cloud, chasing away the darker shadows and casting a pallid light over everyone. Lan attracted their attention as he stood, features stark but softened by his aura.

A shiver ran down Targas's spine.

"We have assessed the situation," said Lan, projecting his voice. "We know the garrison is manned; this was expected. Further, we believe the miners and their families are being kept in the mines...probably guarded by a few guardsmen and at least one seeker. That tells us our enemy is aware of the unrest, and likely the blockade at the Salt Way docks. But it also tells us that there has not been any reinforcement, which will work in our favour.

"We will split into two groups, as arranged. Scent masters, including you, Targas"—Lan nodded in his direction—"will be taking the garrison, since most opposition will be there. Brin and Lethnal will lead the rest to the mines. I would suggest that Zahnal and her healers go with them, since we do not know the condition of our friends."

Targas could see scents moving from Lan as he concluded: "We will be leaving before dawn, so I recommend you get some rest. First, we renew. Let yourselves relax." After a long pause, he spoke in a penetrating whisper, "It begins!"

An aroma arose, tantalisingly familiar. A vibration surrounded them as everyone commenced humming, and Targas's throat responded in empathy. He was enclosed in a vanilla-like scent with everyone, sharing their thoughts, joining, bonding and becoming one. The moon cast a softening light over them, pulling his gaze and filling him with a sense of belonging. He melded comfortably into Sadir's side as his stubbly cheek and her soft skin met. He felt complete.

They moved noiselessly, a grey tide rolling over a rocky shore in the dim light. The Sanctus-led assault on the garrison and the mines had begun.

They split into two pre-arranged groups, at the final ridge before the desert. Targas adjusted his cloak over his coat and snatched a quick hug from Sadir. She breathed a scent of longing and encouragement at him, before leaving for the mines. The dark rapidly swallowed her.

He was part of a large group, almost forty strong, their mission to take the garrison and prevent any warning being sent back to the Sutanites in Regulus.

"Blast," muttered Targas as he stubbed his toe on a hidden rock and almost fell into the back of Lan. Lan had stopped, hand held up in warning.

"My friends," Lan hissed, "we are near... We must take care not to warn the enemy. All is not as it should be."

Targas strained his senses and understood Lan's feeling of unease. A familiar odour nudged his memory, sounding warnings in his head: an odour of his time in Korla.

"Don't move, anyone," Targas said in a strained whisper. "There! In front of you, on the ground." Targas recognised a much larger version of the alarm grid he had experienced before, minute flashes of pink outlining a black lattice that extended into the darkness.

"Touch that"—he pointed at the ground—"and they'll know we're here."

"Mmmm," responded Lan. "Although this was expected, it will complicate matters."

Fedik yawned, stretched back in his chair to ease aching muscles and pushed his boots across the scuffed floor. The light through the open window strengthened, signalling an end to a cold night's vigil. Since notice of the unrest, he'd taken responsibility for the night watch and maintenance of the warning system.

He thought about relaxing the alarm grid now that the day had arrived, but the idea of salt meat and hard bread gave him no reason to hurry.

He yawned again, shaking his head to push away reluctant cobwebs. It had been a long night and his replacement was due.

Fedik was a seeker in his thirties on his third placement. After training in Nebleth he had been sent to guard the salt stores and shipping areas in Regulus. Next, after a stint as Administrator support in Ean's most isolated and coldest northern town, Telas, he had been offered a promotion to the garrison. He had taken it despite rumours of its bleakness.

"Those rumours were true," he muttered, "all too true. At least Telas had some night life."

Fedik's eyes started to close, and his head dropped towards his chest. A noise broke through just before he relaxed his hold on the warning grid.

"What?" Immediately concerned at his loss of control, he stood and pushed with all his skill at the suffocating feeling and the pressure to fall asleep. Fedik staggered to the window and took a gulp of the chill morning air. Grey shapes moving inside the battlements caught his attention.

He briefly puzzled how intruders could have gotten through the scent snares and why his men had not sounded an alarm, before moving to the door. He dropped the wooden locking beam and focused on composing an urgent scent message to alert the command at Regulus. A loud thump at the door almost broke his concentration before he finished the message. He rapidly pulsed it out of the window for the southern breezes to take the scent message through the mountain passes to the city.

The door burst open. Fedik swung around with a raised scent shield, but a rush of bodies quickly overwhelmed his hasty defence.

Fedik's last sight was of two grey-clad men running to the window and looking into the sky.

Targas and Lan searched the sky for signs of any enemy scent message.

They had successfully overrun the garrison, binding their captives and rendering the scent users helpless by inserting plugs of a powerful aromatic up their nostrils. But their efforts to prevent the seeker in charge from sending a warning of the attack had failed.

They soon could see the long line of the scent message spreading out, following the breeze, extending far into the sky. Odour pulses fired to break it up had had some effect, but they feared it was not enough.

"What is done cannot be undone," said Lan wearily. He turned from the window and put his hand on Targas's shoulder. "But we have achieved much and without cost. We can only hope that Lethnal and Brin's assault on the mines will be as successful."

Earlier, Targas had contributed his skill to manoeuvre a large cloud of sleep emanations over the garrison, gradually infiltrating the rooms within the complex and subduing the guards and seekers. They had succeeded, but with one exception. The seeker maintaining the warning grid had resisted. His protections had been sufficient to thwart their best efforts and keep the alarm grid intact, so another method to counter the alarm system had been needed.

Experience from the recent river crossing helped develop an odour blanket, which was then moved out across the ground towards the garrison. Odours were combined until they solidified to a block several handspans across that hovered above the Sutanite grid. Targas had then woven the strongest strands together, pulling them so tight that they became a solid sheet just above the ground. The strength of this structure enabled Lan's army to walk in single file over the warning grid, without triggering it.

Targas had been the last to cross with Lan guiding him, such was the strength of concentration needed to keep the structure in place.

A well-defined track led to several low hills some distance behind the garrison in the otherwise featureless desert. Two figures, black against the rising sun, moved down from one of them.

"Thank Ean," queried a familiar voice, "you're here and you're safe."

"That we are, without loss…Lethnal," called Lan, squinting up at the woman and a solid-looking bargeman next to her. "The remainder stayed at the garrison." He gestured back at the group of twenty people lined behind him. "Have you had much difficulty?"

"Sorry," puffed Lethnal as she stumbled down the slope and came to them, "I couldn't hear." She leant forward, panting, her hands on her hips.

"You were successful?" she gasped. "Good. We weren't as lucky. Once we were in position we attacked the mines, but…they were waitin' for us."

"How?" blurted Targas, "Where's Sadir? Is she hurt?"

"A moment, Targas," puffed Lethnal, "please. Stakol, could you…", indicating with her head.

The burly bargeman by Lethnal's side moved forward. A welt marked his weathered face and grey dust covered his hair; his bloodied hand gripped a long spear.

"It's been hard," he began, looking at Targas, "worst I've been through. There's several dead," he gulped, "'n some that's injured." Stakol paused, but seeing Targas opening his mouth, hurried on. "Sorry, Cer but I should have said, your Sadir's with th' healers, lookin' after those that need it. She ain't hurt."

"Stakol," interrupted Lan, "can you lead us to them?" He looked at Lethnal. "Are you ready?"

"Was winded for a moment," she replied as she straightened. "I'm not as young as I was."

Lethnal and Stakol turned and led the group along the track between the hills.

"We've found the miners, and their families," she said over her shoulder. "They're well, but frightened. Don't think it'll be easy to get them to move."

They reached what looked like a construction site. White-grey, knee-high grainy blocks were piled in loose stacks over a large area, as if waiting to be used in building; lengths of dark, squared wood lay in several piles. They passed through the bleached stacks, some that reached head height, before Targas saw a dark opening in a wall of rock.

"There is the Sutanites' reason for the subjugation of our people," Lan said, waving his hand around him. "These blocks represent the start of the salt trade…"

The path began to descend, leading under large wooden beams that outlined the mine's entrance.

"Come, Cers." Stakol moved into the dark, his grey-clad form disappearing almost immediately.

"Not far," called Lethnal grimly. "There's a large holding room just inside. I suggest only several come in as there isn't much room."

Lan looked at the group behind him, singling out the silent Quonir.

"Could you keep the rest here for the present?"

Quonir grunted and abruptly turned to head back to the stack of salt blocks with the remainder of the group.

Lan turned to Targas. "You will be coming with me, I suspect?"

As he ducked through the opening Targas briefly wondered why Quonir was still unfriendly towards him, then the dark closed around him. It was hard to see but the iron tang of blood overlying the salty smell of iodine told the story of what had happened. He searched through the conglomeration of scents until he recognised Sadir's.

Following scent trails and avoiding the many people lying and sitting on the floor was difficult. He could hear cries, detect flares of pain and even a dark cloud of death emanating from one corner.

Sadir and Zahnal were crouched over a groaning patient as he approached.

"Welcome my boy," grunted Zahnal, "I trust you've not brought us more work?"

"Targas," breathed Sadir, reaching up to grab his hand. "So glad you're safe."

"Ours was easy compared to what you've gone through," he said as he crouched beside her. "Are there many hurt?"

"Some," she replied. "Our people were brave, but the guardsmen were very strong. If it hadn't been for some help from the miners we might've had many more injured." Targas felt, rather than heard her turn away. "Sorry," she said, her voice muffled, "I've got to help here."

The atmosphere was oppressive with the pressure of many conflicting scents, so Targas was grateful to leave Zahnal and Sadir to their task. He traced his way back to the opening and out into the light. After taking a deep, cleansing breath he moved over to where Quonir and the others were sitting in the shade of a large stack of salt blocks.

He gratefully accepted a mug of water before sitting against the cool blocks. The smell was more invigorating out in the open, reminiscent of the ocean— memories of sun on his face, a breeze whipping through his hair, rope rough in his hands and salt spray on his lips. He pushed his head back, hearing the slight crunch of crystals before telling those around him what he'd experienced.

Quonir sat a short distance away looking into his mug, not showing interest.

The sun was nearly overhead before a mass of people began to disgorge from the mine. Those they'd come to rescue seemed built for mining, being shorter and leaner than what he'd expected, as if their occupation extracted flesh instead of building muscle. They had dark hair and pale skin mainly covered in swathes of loose clothing that made it hard to see where their shirts finished, and trousers began. The miners milled around, blinking in the harsh light. There were children too, smaller versions of the adults, several of whom ran off squealing in shrill voices.

He was relieved to see Sadir emerge, walking alongside a wounded bargeman being stretchered by two of the miners. Her face broke into a smile when she noticed him. "Stay there," she signalled.

The stacks of salt offered some shade for the large group that soon gathered. Sadir slumped beside Targas and gratefully accepted a mug of water. Her aura reflected her exhaustion and sombre mood.

The noise level grew as people continued to exit the mine. Targas distractedly listened to the accents, picking out the similarities with the broad speech of the river people. He didn't immediately notice Lan, Brin and Lethnal coming towards him with several miners.

"Quonir, Targas, Sadir," called Lan, as he neared them, "this is Davd and his companion, Wilm. They are able to speak for the stone people, the miners."

Davd and Wilm reminded Targas of the wandering peoples back home. They had the thin-lined features and dark eyes that he remembered, and an in-built restlessness.

"Davd and Wilm," asked Lan gently, "can you tell us what happened in the mines, why our people met with such trouble?"

Davd looked at Lan for a brief moment before breaking eye contact. He glanced at Wilm next to him and then spoke to his feet.

"We watched, we did," his words came out as a rusty hiss. "We knew we did, knew somethin' was happenin'. The salties forgot us; they was lookin' out, knew yer was there." Davd paused, flicking his eyes at Lan before continuing. "Saw th' smell user push on, up at th' light. Saw th' salties with him, spears out, ready.

"Couldn't warn, just couldn't." Davd held clawed hands to his face. Wilm held onto his sleeve. "If did, our childen would suffer. Please forgive."

He looked out between his fingers. "Yer smell people 're strong, but late; sorry yer got stuck. Salties are hard fighters."

"Thank you, Davd, for telling us this," said Lan quietly. "We put no blame on your people. We are all Eanites together in this struggle. Those who gave their lives gave them willingly." He paused, squinting at the sun. "This night we will fare them well."

They squatted in the lengthening shade, and shared out food and drink. Small knots of people were settling, the healers working on a number of wounded.

"Davd," continued Lan, "your people know the rebellion has begun, yes?" His eyes held the smaller man's. "And you know the Sutanites' attention is on us? Our action here, this day, has committed us all."

Davd looked at Wilm and then at a group of fellow miners listening nearby with blank faces before turning back to Lan, his shoulders slumped.

Lan in turn scanned the group, sending out minute pulses of enquiry to members of his council. Targas's heart gave a jump when he focused on him, eyebrows raised. His shrug seemed to satisfy Lan, who turned back to the nervous miner.

"We have no choice but to continue. You, Davd, and the stone people are involved and will be a necessary part of our future success." As Lan watched the miner, his eyebrows came together, and he frowned. "Mmmm," he said, "we will return to the garrison with our wounded and dead. Davd, we will expect your answer."

Davd pulled Wilm to her feet and shuffled over to the group of miners.

Targas shook his head at their apathy.

Chapter Twenty-Six

"Ho th' shore!" called Woll, his voice echoing over the deserted docks. Numerous barges were secured in pairs along the rows of wooden piles lining the riverbank, but there was no sign of life.

Luna, beside the solid figure of Woll at the tiller, became aware of the change in her surroundings. The slow, hypnotic movement of the craft pulled by Maw, the perac, had helped her to keep her mind steady, free of thoughts of what had happened, thoughts threatening to bubble up in her mind like globs of marsh gas.

Wooden planks laid side by side on the bank made a firm surface for the loading of the barges. Further back, a number of large sheds provided storage for the salt from the mines and accommodation for the dock workers. Low, rolling hills that met the distant mountains kept the structures from extending too far from the river. It was a dry, colourless place with a desolate air, as if it had been preserved in its own salt.

"Ho th' docks," called Woll again, his voice breaking. Cynth and the children huddled against the perac on the edge of the wharf and snatched looks at the buildings.

"Should we come back on board?" she hissed.

"Na. They're here. No sign of anythin' else. Just wait."

Luna's senses took over, sifting through the background odours for recognisable scents. People had been here recently, animals too; a darker mass of scents behind the large buildings revealed their location. A common scent thread showed a link to the barges, to Woll and Cynth. The hidden people were barge- or river-based, and should be friendly.

The smells coming from one of the smaller warehouses had a familiarity that sent a shudder through her, one that quivered down her spine and ended up in her stomach, threatening to force her down to the barge's privy. She recognised guardsmen's odour from that building, a dark taint she could never forget.

Luna started to shake from side to side, holding her head between her hands. Woll looked up helplessly at Cynth on the docks.

A shout distracted him.

"Ho the barge!"

A sudden trickle of people from behind the buildings quickly became a flood. Woll's face creased into a grin; Cynth laughed in relief; Tishal and Lynthe screamed excitedly and ran to meet others of similar age. Luna sat and wondered why she did not feel involved.

"Come, gel," said Woll, turning back to Luna and extending his hand. "Come 'n meet me friends."

She reached out her hand to hesitantly grasp his fingers and let her be pulled to her feet. She forced herself to move.

The camaraderie and genuine happiness almost overwhelmed Luna as she withstood the inundation of river people. Everyone, except the multitude of children, seemed taller and bulkier than her. The occasional splash of colour, mainly yellows and blues, highlighted their sombre costumes. Most were dressed in the common loose trousers and tops, and some of the women wore bulky skirts. They all had perac leather boots. Standing in the middle of a whirlwind of people reminded Luna of her first meeting with Cynth's family.

"Luna. Luna," called Cynth, "Come 'n meet me cousins." Her rough hand grabbed and pulled Luna into another group of warm, suffocating people.

"This here's me cousin Zylth, her man Janhl 'n…" Cynth looked around. "Where have those youngsters gone? I suspect…never mind, luv. Musn't forget Ginrel—he's in charge here. Then there's…"

Luna kept a tight, fixed smile on her face and looked with unseeing eyes at the movement and shadows around her.

Her nose itched, like a worm was crawling on it. She could feel it humping its way along the bridge of her nose. It paused near her eye, so she flicked an eyelid to distract it. A slight tremble from its weight concerned her. It seemed to be growing, as if the idea of her blood gave it substance.

Luna thought to swipe it away, but her arm wouldn't move. She panicked, pulling at her other arm but it was tied down, the ropes biting into her wrist.

She screamed out her terror, high pitched, on and on until a cold wetness came onto her forehead, distracting her. A soft voice began to whisper into her ear, penetrating her mind, and her nightmare.

"There, there luv. I'm 'ere. No one's going to hurt yer now."

"Cynth," sobbed Luna. "Oh, Cynth."

Cynth's eyes grew moist as she hugged the girl to her.

"Whatever was done t' yer," she muttered, "me poor, poor little fish."

Luna sobbed into the comfortable shoulder.

"We need t' get yer a feed, then some help," she said, a smile hiding the concern in her eyes. "I don't know what I can do, but a healer should."

The day passed with Luna hardly noticing the activity on the docks. Groups of men and women were sparring with spears and poles, flashes of steel where others were fighting with sticks and long daggers, cutting and thrusting in deadly earnest.

"I've a mind t' get Luna one of them knives," Cynth said to Woll. "It might help give her confidence in something. Could protect her too if them Sutanites come."

Luna pulled away as Cynth belted a small knife to her waist. At first she seemed too frightened to even look at it but then she slowly pulled it out of its sheath and held it, twisting it to flash in the sun.

"Now gel, put it away. It's just for yer protection. Let's go 'nd find yer some food, eh?' she said brightly, and led her away from the noise of the training.

Cynth pushed Luna down onto a seat in a quiet corner near the accumulated gear piled in the shadowy interior of the large, open kitchen. The room's emanations were almost overpowering, although not unpleasant.

"We kept yer away from here; thought it best," explained Cynth. "Our folk are all here now, since th' blockade."

"Blockade?" Luna's head jerked up. "What blockade?"

"Sorry, luv. Forgot yer didn't know what 'appened. Just wait 'til I get yer some food 'nd then I'll tell yer."

A while later Cynth returned with a plate of savoury stew and a hunk of bread. "Now eat while I tell yer what's been happenin'. This here's th' docks where th' salt's loaded from th' mines 'nd taken by me people down th' river t' Port Saltus; this is all for our mighty rulers, of course."

Cynth stopped and leant forward. "Now, yer know things have been happenin'?"

Luna nodded, gulping down a piece of half-chewed meat.

"Well, it's now happenin' more. Yer rescue, 'nd th' almost rescue of yer friend, th' youngster…which didn't work out, but…"

"Kyel? Is he all right? They didn't hurt him too?" Luna could feel a scream building.

Cynth placed both hands on her shoulders, looking into her wide eyes. "No," she said. "No, he's well. Now where was I?" Cynth's homely face furrowed in a frown as she released her grip and sat back. "Ah, yes, we've gone 'nd stopped th' salt. Caught th' guards here by surprise." She saw Luna flinch. "Keepin' them far from here, in a back storehouse, luv. That Ginrel's a sly one. Got them thinkin' barges were sinking with th' salt, then me folk pushed them all int' th' Salt Way,' she laughed, a short, sharp cough. "They's th' ones gettin' wet."

Luna smiled, distracted by Cynth's humour.

"Good t' see yer eatin'. You've eaten hardly enough t' keep a lizard alive; a small one at that." Cynth laughed again, but it sounded strained. Luna could tell the bargewoman meant well and was even tempted to laugh with her, but the thought quickly died.

"There yer are," came a booming voice. "What yer cooped up inside for? Come out int' th' light. See what we're doin'?"

"Good idea. This little-un has eaten as much as she's goin' t'." Cynth turned back to Luna. "Come luv. Best we go outside, eh?"

Woll looked down nervously as he waited for them to rise.

Luna had no way of knowing how much time had passed. She remembered sleeping and waking, periods of light and dark. The light was punctuated with movement, noise and occasional whispered words. Once she yelled out at the pushing and prodding, gripping her knife hilt until soothing voices relaxed her. With the dark came an unwelcome sleep. Even falling into a doze only lasted until screaming woke her, then a comforting Cynth scent would calm her, slow her breathing and allow her to rest a while longer.

She poked her head out of the hatch, peering through the dim light at the surreal world around her. A vague mist covered the docks, softening the outlines of the barges and buildings and giving the scene a timeless quality. Nothing happened in this world, it was just a colourless image, too vague to allow the imprint of life or meaning.

She climbed over the roof of the barge and down the slight drop to the dock. Pulling Cynth's grey, thick woollen cloak tightly around her, she slipped across the planks towards the buildings. Eyes watched her go, wraith-like, through the gloom of pre-dawn until she disappeared in the dark gap between two buildings. One of the burly bargemen walked quietly after her, listening intently. After a moment he grunted and returned to his post.

Luna, her thin body quivering with the strain, climbed up the rough stony path. It levelled off before winding amongst large boulders, and scrubby trees and bushes; the dry, rocky soil supported little else. She found a quiet place where she could rest and look out east across the buildings below.

Her mind, clearer than it had been for some time, was finally free of the press of people, their thoughts and auras. She shivered, chewed vacantly on a curl of blonde hair and then pushed her cold white hands under her cloak.

It seemed so long ago that she had been living with her aunt in Korla, before being snatched away from her home and friends. Later she had met Kyel and Targ, and then Kyel's sister. She squashed a guilty feeling as she realised just how much those people had come to mean to her over a short time. Kyel was reserved for someone so young, but they had liked each other. He had been brave and helped her; now he was gone, taken by Them. And Targ and Sadir were still out there. Something about Targ gave her confidence, not just because he was large and had those penetrating light eyes, but because he was strong and very, very powerful. "If only he knew it," she sighed. However, it was too late for them to help her. The seekers were surely coming and more of her friends could be going to die.

No, it was too late for help now. But she wouldn't be taken so easily a third time.

She felt better as she saw movement on the docks below. Then the sun broke through the mist, highlighting her face and imbuing the shadowy world with colour and life.

"Luna, luv," wheezed a familiar voice, "yer here?"

Lizards' teeth, she thought as she looked into Cynth's face, red from exertion.

Word had come from the city that a force of the enemy, led by Septus, had left Regulus bound for the Salt Way docks. The resultant activity hardly registered on Luna as she stayed out of the way, while the river people prepared for the coming battle. She heard Ginrel and Cynth speaking near her.

"We'll have t' keep her well out of th' way of it, perhaps with th' children, do yer reckon?"

"Shush, Ginrel," came Cynth's quick whisper. "We can't ignore what she's suffered at th' hands of that Septus. She's been through more than any of us."

"I know that, Cynth," he said. "I don't have t' be reminded that she's a brave young woman, I just think she'd be better out of th' way. It's goin' t' be a hard enough time as it is…because I don't see how our Sanctus scent masters can get here in time." He scratched his weather-lined face while looking at Luna, now wrapped within Cynth's voluminous arms. The people had grown up with scent, used it in their everyday lives and were able to manipulate and defend against odour. However, now they had to fight trained soldiers and expert scent users. He accepted the possibility that many would die, even if their comrades from Sanctus and the mountains could get to them in time.

"Yeah, time's our problem, time," Ginrel muttered.

The sun shone on the river people hiding behind the buildings, in the scrubby gullies at the foothills of the distant mountains, and amongst the higher boulders. Everything seemed to be waiting. The hot midday sun highlighted every tree, bush and rock, making the task of concealment even harder.

Luna, stripped to a brown linen top and grey trousers, felt the heat; her throat was dry, and her head buzzed. Cynth, Zylth and several bargewomen were with her on a slope, hidden behind rocks that were beginning to radiate the sun's heat. She had refused to join the children and other non-combatants, choosing to remain where she could see the battleground. Part of her mind knew that *he* was coming, and she needed to be here, her desire to flee overruled by her loathing of Septus.

If he was destroyed, she wanted to see it. She needed to see him bristling with spears, bleeding on the ground. *Dead!*

"Come, luv, int' th' shade," said Cynth. "They're still a ways off."

Luna shrugged, spat out a loose curl of hair and continued to stare down the path that accompanied the Salt Way to the docks. Thickets of drab, green trees marked the presence of the river.

"At least have some water."

As Luna sucked at the liquid from a leather bottle, a sound drew her attention; something was happening in the river valley.

Scent tendrils rose into the air, accompanied by dust and noise. The shuffle of perac feet, the creaking of gear and other equipment, and the occasional grunt of protest from the animals rode like a wave over the valley.

Luna crouched lower, shuddering as the black of Septus in the centre of the group of riders drew her eye. He had surrounded himself with his seekers, and they in turn were ringed with a wall of solid-looking armed men, spears held high. A number of the perac at the rear were laden with wickerwork cages. The creatures inside had long yellow legs, and black-and-yellow bodies. She quickly bobbed down, her jaw hitting the rock and snapping her teeth together, bringing taste to reinforce the memory.

Septus's force halted in the area between the warehouses and the wharf. In the time it took for the dust to settle, the forty-strong force had formed a square with an outer perimeter of soldiers. Three men, whose dust-coloured clothing didn't immediately place them with the guardsmen or seekers, began pulling the wickerwork cages off the protesting animals.

Luna was grinding her teeth, unable to tear her eyes away.

The river people suddenly swarmed out of hiding and around the sides of the buildings, charging towards the smaller force of the enemy on the docks. Luna got to her feet, before a strong hand pulled her back down.

"No, gel. If things get real bad then maybe. Till then we wait." The tone of Cynth's voice penetrated her mind, forcing her to sink back behind the boulder. "Just wait."

The flash of steel came before the noise of the fighting reached them. Long spears thrust forward into the waiting lines of guardsmen, causing several to stagger and fall to the ground. The response was quick and methodical, weapons slicing like scythes into the browns and greys of Cynth's people. The hand holding Luna down began to grip her so tightly that it hurt.

"We'll get them. They're not as many as us. We'll get them," muttered Cynth. "Oh, yer murderin' haggars!"

Luna heard the gasps of horror as she saw the black knot of Septus and his seekers in action. Long, dark tendrils were snaking past the guardsmen and through the individual odour protection of the river people with little difficulty. When a tendril fastened onto a fighter they stopped fighting, hanging limply on the spike of odour until a spear thrust finished them.

Septus, a smile splitting his pallid face, almost casually flung odour bolts like darts at the rebels. Each hit usually broke through any scent shields and transfixed the fighter.

The river people surged against the wall of soldiers like a wave on rocks. The greater number of the rebels allowed them, initially, to absorb the losses without losing much ground, but the superior skills of the enemy began to show.

Luna focused on Septus's face as if he was standing just before her. A shudder rippled through her body, her hand pulled the knife in and out of its sheath, and her teeth ground on bleeding gums.

"By Ean," Cynth gasped, "he's let them things go. We're done fer."

Luna dragged her eyes from Septus to see several huge insects dropping amongst the rebels, causing panic wherever they went. Thicker clouds mingled with the boil of blood and anger, almost obscuring the fighting. The rebels broke and fled. A knot of them ran towards Luna's hiding place, Woll amongst them.

Septus's gleeful laugh dragged her back. He targeted her friends, thumping massive odour darts at his fleeing victims. Their agonised screams crashed into her skull.

She moved, without thinking, deaf to Cynth's cries, not noticing the rocks that hit her legs. She pushed towards Septus through the fleeing rebels.

Septus's force had spread as the guardsmen pursued the rebels. Only the seekers remained with him, each concentrating on their targets. Luna ran low to the ground, crouching to make herself small.

Septus enjoyed reaching within himself, making huge odour bolts and slamming them down into the backs of his fleeing enemy over increasingly longer and longer distances. He could taste the blood and despair of his victims.

"And so, you're dust!" he screamed, as he aimed at the final few of the group who had almost reached the cover of rocky slopes.

An incandescent pain suddenly ripped through him. He twisted at the excruciating agony and instinctively flung a hand, extending steel bands of odour at the figure hanging leech-like to the knife in his thigh. They cleaved through the attacker like butter.

As the pressure lessened Septus collapsed to the ground, snatching out a small knife embedded in his leg. The pain flared as blood jetted from near his groin.

"Genur! Here!"

The seeker came hurrying towards him.

"Head. You're hurt!"

"Help…fix…it…you fool!" gasped Septus, gripping at his wound. "Stop the bleeding!"

Genur ran to a perac, grabbed cloth and ointment and came scurrying back. The knife had cut down across Septus's stomach before embedding in his upper thigh, and the blood flowed freely. Genur pulled up the robe, pushing a wad of cloth onto the wound and dabbing ointment along the cut. He wrapped a thinner strip of cloth around the bandages and tied it off.

"That will have to hold it for a while, Head. You need an expert healer in Regulus; it's beyond my abilities. At least it's missed your genitals." Blood already seeped through the cloth.

"Who…did…this?" asked Septus through gritted teeth. "Go! See!" He jerked his head towards the body lying nearby.

Genur went to the grey shape on the ground and picked up a small object from the grass.

"Look!" he exclaimed, holding a severed head towards his leader by its dirty blonde curls, "It's a girl!"

Septus peered at it then jerked away, his face ashen.

Genur, not noticing Septus's reaction, touched the small, slack lips. He saw eyes closed in the pale face with the mouth relaxed into a vague smile. Blood oozed from the neck into the dirt at his feet.

Chapter Twenty-Seven

Huge fan-like antennae swivelled and bent in minute movements, detecting even the hint of home scent in the vast aroma sea that filled the night sky. The occasional mote of scent, as diffuse as a drop of water in a pond, reinforced the large creature's direction. Not deterred by the dry wastes softened by the blanket of night beneath, it flew on with a steady beat of its powerful wings, homing in on the familiar odour.

The grey structure in a pale landscape meant nothing compared to the torrent of scent pouring from the black hole in a wall. The tina fluttered in without hesitation, to land next to the cup of nectar, its proboscis probing greedily.

A careful hand on its soft thorax calmed it as the scent pouch was removed.

"Lan," Rasnal called from the doorway of a large room in the captured garrison. The Sanctus inner council, including Targas and Sadir, turned as she entered. "We've received word…but it's not good."

"Whether good or no, Rasnal," responded Lan, "it will help us in our deliberations. Come, tell us what you have learnt."

The short, plump woman, her cropped grey hair visible in the candlelight, bustled over.

"A tina returned with a scent message from the Salt Way docks," she said, sitting next to Quonir.

"From our scout?" asked Brin.

"Yes." Rasnal glanced at him before focusing on Lan. "There are Sutanites at the docks already, scent masters with them. The message says there's been fighting…and now the enemy's preparing to move; that we should get ready."

"But Luna's there," gasped Sadir, looking up at Targas.

"Sorry, Sadir," said Rasnal, reaching over to touch her arm, "nothing about her, or any of the others."

Sadir slumped into Targas.

"Sadir, Targas," said Lan soothingly, "I expect she will have been concealed.

Our friends would not have let her be taken. Do not worry about what we cannot change." His eyes reflected his sympathy. "I know the message has not told us what has happened to our people…but they are sensible enough to have withdrawn when faced with superior fighting power. We must assume that, anyway."

"Rasnal, what numbers are we talking about?" asked Lethnal.

"When are they comin'?" added Brin.

"It's hard to tell except it is a significant number, and we need to prepare now." Even in the dim candlelight Targas could see that Rasnal's round face was flushed, eyes bright with the import of her message. He automatically joined in with a calming odour and kept his arm around Sadir as he tried not to think what might have happened at the docks.

The discussion continued long into the night, until weariness overtook them.

The Sanctus scent masters were not natural fighters or tacticians. While they might have significantly superior numbers with the addition of the reluctant miners, they were not as well-trained or well-equipped as the coming enemy. Tactically, they could be found wanting.

"Please." Targas finally stood up. "Until we know who we're fighting and where we fight, we are just going around in circles. Could I suggest we sleep on it and then get moving first thing?"

"Hmmm," reflected Lan, "I think Targas has the right of it. We will need our sleep and must be ready to leave around dawn. To your beds, my friends."

Targas held a very sleepy Sadir close and made his way to their blankets, trying to calm his active mind.

Perac calling to each other in the pre-dawn roused Targas. He had had a restless night and his mind raced with the implications of the coming fight.

"What's up?" Sadir's tousled head poked up next to him. "Can't you sleep?"

Targas lifted an arm, allowing her to rest her head on his shoulder. "It's not easy, Sadir. I keep thinking that people around us seem too comfortable about the coming fight, despite the fact almost half their number, the miners, have only held pick axes and salt saws. They've no idea of how many they are facing, and the enemy has to be more than capable."

"The Sanctus masters are fairly well prepared, though?"

"Maybe," said Targas, "but back in Tenstria all youth, including myself, are trained in defence because of the history of warfare in the region, and we have a better understanding of conflict and how to prepare for it. Here they appear to be more relaxed."

"Anyway, we'd better get ready to go," he added, as the noise of people and animals grew.

Targas cringed at another cry of protest from his perac as he spurred his mount to catch up with Sadir and Lan. Tel's clawed feet gripped the weave of his coat in response.

"We're going too slowly," he said to Lan.

Lan, Quonir, Brin and Lethnal turned to look at him. Sadir smiled and held out her hand to him, but Quonir frowned.

"We are, Targas, I agree," Lan said, forcefully. He stood in his saddle and looked back over the sea of people. The grey-robed figures of the scent masters on perac led the river and mountain people, some riding, some walking and most holding weapons of a sort. The miners came behind, smaller and more dishevelled, with an air of resignation.

Targas sighed and manoeuvred his perac closer to Sadir, until they touched hands.

He looked at Sadir, breathing her scent, sharing her thoughts. At that moment his skin prickled into thousands of goosebumps; a feeling came over him. He recognised an aura of dread, inevitability and loss, and felt an overwhelming sadness. Before he could stop, Sadir picked up on what he was feeling. Her dark eyes widened, tears erupted and streamed down her face.

Targas's eyes moistened as he fought to hold his emotions. *Something evil's happened.* Letting go of Sadir's hand he reached up and wiped away a tear with a crooked finger. He looked away from her sad face and called to Lan.

"We must be ready to fight the enemy. We must pick where. Let me go on ahead."

"Targas," said Lan, "we have sent scouts out. They will let us know where the enemy is, and report back on the terrain." He hesitated, and nodded slightly. "But I can see you need to do this. Brin, Lethnal," he called, turning to his companions, "go with Targas."

Targas turned and urged his perac to a greater pace, the events ahead soon occupying his mind. Brin and Lethnal joined him, and together they left the main group behind.

Sadir slowed her perac until she was riding alongside Hynal. She smiled at her friend.

"It's all happening, and soon," Hynal said. "It'll be a chance to practice my skills." She paused, looking over at Sadir. "You look scared. It's your brother, isn't it?"

"No," Sadir said, shaking her head, "I don't know. I'm worried, that's all."

"Can you share it?"

"Just a feeling that something bad's happened," Sadir replied.

They rode along the rocky trail for a while, concentrating on the movement of their animals

"Hynal?"

"Hmmm?"

"Can you tell me something? I'm not sure if it's anything, though."

"Go on," Hynal encouraged.

"Well, it's Quonir." Sadir glanced at the man riding alongside Lan just ahead. "He seems to dislike Targas. Do you know why?"

"No," she said, "but he hasn't been the same since his brother, Quon, died. Could be upset about that; Targas turned up as a result of Quon's death." Hynal nodded to herself. "Yes, could be that."

Their shadows were long and misshapen by the rising sun. "Targas," called Brin over the background noise of the perac, "I know we're lookin' for a good place t' take on th' Sutanites but d' yer have any thoughts on what yer after?"

"What?" Targas said. "Sorry. Yes, you're right. We have to find a location that will give us an advantage when facing the enemy, but I think we'll know it when we see it."

Later, they entered a shallow ravine filled with shadows yet to be dissipated by the sun's rays. The ground became slushy underfoot as the area widened out and became flatter. It was a natural basin surrounded by low hills, making it a flat, boggy plain. Marsh grass and fine-tipped reeds abounded. The hum of insects, mainly small, dark flies, filled the air.

The route they had been following led through this wet plain, but the track remained hard under soft topsoil. They rode up a slope, pausing when they could see a well-defined path leading in a southeasterly direction towards steeper hills and mountains in the distance.

"Behind us. That's the place to meet the enemy," Targas said. "What do you both think?"

"We've seen nothing better, and there's little time," commented Lethnal.

"Best yet, I reckon," added Brin as he swung his perac about, "'n Lethnal's right about th' time. Better look it over."

"Be helpful to know what we're facing, though," Targas muttered to himself. "And what, my faithful Tel, do you think?" He continued quietly stroking the lizard's scaly head and felt a moment of comfort as the animal pushed into the caress. "What would you do?"

They moved back to the ridge across the marsh and saw the land from a different perspective. Any attacking force would have to come uphill, have no advantage from the sun's angle and be unable to see over the top of the further ridge. When they entered the natural basin, the boggy ground would make manoeuvring harder and should assist any defending force.

"Yer right, Targas," said Brin. "That marsh'll be useful."

"Yes, the soft ground should help but I don't know if we can pull it off. Perhaps we could hide our people around here, create an ambush—if there's time to set it up—but we'd have to conceal our auras. How do we stop being detected?"

"I think I know a way, Targas," offered Lethnal, "using our ability to amplify and concentrate odour. If we could strengthen the marsh smell, make it more overpowering in the hot sun, we could block off our own scents to a large degree. That will aid our scent masters, who'll find it a strain to conceal all the non-talented for any length of time."

"Yes," interrupted Brin, catching Lethnal's enthusiasm, "'nd if they were distracted by…say, some easy prey, then they'd pay less attention t' what's around them."

"What do you think could be…easy prey?" asked Targas, cautiously.

Brin exchanged a quick glance with Lethnal. "Yer'd need somethin' they wouldn't expect, somethin' that wouldn't make sense, make them sit up, grab their attention, eh?"

Brin raised his eyebrows at Lethnal and looked back at Targas, seeming pleased.

"It'd have to be something unusual." Lethnal rubbed her chin, then raised a finger as if struck by a thought. "Maybe," she said, peering closely at Targas, "maybe it's time to reveal yourself, properly protected, of course." She grinned at him, "Because you're the most unusual thing I've seen in a long while."

Targas remained silent, ignoring the byplay of Brin and Lethnal as their suggestion hit home. "Ah wine's rot, I'll do it," he muttered.

"What did you say?" asked Lethnal innocently.

"I said," Targas said, almost shouting, "that I'll do it. Let's get back." He jerked his perac up, ignoring the prick of the startled lizard's claws in his shoulders. The perac grunted as he spurred it in the direction of Sadir and the others.

Soon they had closed on the large force headed by Lan and Quonir. Targas pulled up, smiled fleetingly at Sadir and started to outline their plan.

He heard a gasp from Sadir, while Lan frowned and Quonir nodded.

"No Targas," said Lan, "you are too valuable to risk." He turned to Quonir, eyebrows raised.

"I'd be for it," Quonir commented tersely. "We've gone to almost incalculable risks to get him," he jerked his head towards Targas, "and with great loss. So let him prove himself. Let's see the mettle of him. See if losing my brother was worth it."

"Quonir," responded Lan, looking at the rigid figure. "I'm sorry that you are so troubled."

"Just do it!" Quonir snapped.

Hynal, who had joined the group, raised an eyebrow at Sadir.

"Lan," intervened Lethnal, "we've considered this carefully. We have limited options and little time."

As if to emphasise her words, two scouts came riding up in a flurry of dust. "Cers," called one, "we've seen the enemy. They're not far; should be with us by midday."

"How many?" asked Lan. "Did you see who they were?"

"Fairly hard to," continued the scout. "Seemed about thirty soldiers, plus eight or nine seekers and no obvious scent master, as far as we could tell. They're moving at pace."

"Well?" asked Targas. "Do we go with the plan?"

Lan and Quonir exchanged glances.

"Look, Lan," Targas said, holding his arms open, palms up, "I don't want to do this either." He looked across at Sadir, whose concern was etched on her face, and gave a tight smile. "Believe me, I don't. But we've come up with the best we could in the time." He paused.

No one spoke. The people behind the leaders became uneasy at the delay, the animals shifting restlessly.

"We need some bait, something to make the enemy come to where we want them. Can you suggest anything better than using me?"

"No, Targas, no!" cried Sadir. She turned to Lan. "You can't let him. There must be a better way," she implored.

He remained impassive; the wait was palpable.

"You have the right of it," announced Lan, so suddenly that Targas started.

Targas glimpsed Sadir slumping in her saddle, but kept his eyes on the leader.

"So…" Lan continued, "we have no time to do anything differently. We must follow this plan and trust in our fate. Brin and Lethnal, join with Quonir and Davd on the positioning of our forces. I will work with the other scent masters." He stood in the stirrups and looked over the people massed behind him.

"My friends," he called, his gaze slowly scanning the miners at the back, then the river and mountain people and finally the scent masters in the foreground. "We go to fight a confident and most capable foe. Although our numbers are superior we must be cautious, and we must fight to a plan. This requires you to remain undetected and to act only when directed. If we keep to this, we will succeed."

Lan's voice rode like a ripple over the crowd. "The ground over the next rise will be where we will fight. All animals and equipment will remain here with those who are not fighting…The time is upon us. Remember, we are fighting for our people and for the future of Ean. Now we move."

Targas walked beside Sadir, his mind flicking through what he should do. The tide of people washed around him as they calmly went to their assigned places.

He could see auras of nervousness and excitement, and wondered whether the scent masters would be able to conceal them from the enemy.

"Here, Sadir, take Tel," said Targas, reaching up to extract the lizard's claws from the shoulders of his coat. Tel was reluctant to go, raising his frill as he was passed across.

"Targas," said Sadir, as she held the squirming animal, "There's something not right about all of this."

"Right or not, my love, I really don't have a choice now. I must do it." He leant over Tel to hug her. "Go now. Make yourself as safe as you can." He looked down into her concerned eyes. "I know this is meant to be," he continued, though in his heart he felt grave concern.

Targas moved away from Sadir, squared his shoulders and walked to where the path began to descend into the basin. He was dimly aware of people moving away, disappearing into the gullies and hiding on the ridges. Time settled, and the normal ambience of the boggy ground resumed.

The smell of the marsh rose until it blocked his nostrils, initially overwhelming his senses until he adjusted to it. He then moved partway down the path to just above the level of the boggy ground, crouched down and waited. He slowly built up his scent memories using non-Ean, foreign aromas. He pushed them out like an expanding balloon of foreign smells.

Targas had set the bait.

Chapter Twenty-Eight

"Regna." Heritis waved a piece of toast in the air. "What's this? It's sharp, but a bit salty."

"The leespread?" asked Regna. Heritis nodded. "Oh, it's new, something to do with the brewers...very popular in Nebleth."

"Popular it may be, but I'd prefer something I'm used to."

"Heritis," she laughed, "you really don't like change, do you?"

"No, I don't." He looked at his attractive consort sitting across from him, and his eyes narrowed. "Speaking of change, we haven't spoken of how you got on when I was in the north; when Jakus came back early."

"Heritis, there is nothing to speak of," she said uneasily.

"I know my cousin, Regna. Did he...take advantage of my absence?"

Regna slumped forward, took a few deep breaths and shook her head, glaring across the table. "What did you expect?" she said quietly. "How could I, a mere consort, go against the wishes of that man? How could I stop him from doing whatever he wanted?" She paused, chest heaving. "I mean, look at how you give in to him," she spat. "You're powerful too, yet you allow him to lie with your partner, without protest?"

She paused, a tear welling in her eye. "Heritis, I'm yours and only want to be with you, but I had no choice." Her voice dropped. "And he laughed when I said you'd be angry."

"Enough!" Heritis's eyes glittered. "Jakus has gone too far. Too far."

He knocked over his chair as he stood. "I must find out what's been happening with our campaign to the Salt Way." He looked down into her eyes, starkly outlined in her white face, and said almost formally, "Thank you for sharing your new foods with me."

"Heritis..." Regna called after him. She remained at the table after Shad Heritis, ruler of the city of Regulus, had left the room.

"Septus!" exclaimed Heritis at the sight of the man lying there, his leg and lower torso bloody and bare, sweat dotting his forehead. Several healers worked on him, bandages around them on the raised bed.

"Blood's stink, what's happened to you?" Heritis was aware Septus had returned, injured, with several escorting guardsmen, but not the extent of that injury.

"That blood-cursed girl," Septus snapped through gritted teeth. "She hit me with a lucky blow, before I killed her. The filth!"

"What?" Heritis's mind raced. "You...you were supposed to recapture her. Get her back. Not kill her! The Shada was clear about that."

"It doesn't...matter," hissed Septus through gritted teeth. "We beat that scum at the docks...and the mines won't be a problem. She wouldn't have been of any value."

Heritis shook his head. *Septus will have to answer to Jakus. What had that young girl, Luna, been put through to end up dying at the hands of this monster?* he thought.

"You fools!" Septus screamed, lashing out with a thick odour dart that smashed into the shoulder of one of the healers. The recipient of Septus's anger crashed into the stone wall. The remaining healer stepped back, eyes wide, arms held out protectively, a bloodied cloth in one hand.

Septus glared at the man through pain-filled eyes. "Where did you learn your butchering? Take care before I kill you," he warned through clenched teeth.

The healer took a hesitant step forward. Septus lay with his arm covering his eyes while the healer administered to the stab wound in his leg.

"I'm finished, Head," the healer murmured as he picked up the remaining bandages and used cloths.

"Just get out," growled Septus. "Get out! Take that...that failure with you." He flung out an arm towards the man on the floor, who sat hunched against the wall holding his shoulder and moaning quietly.

Heritis waited until the healers had left before continuing. "You are a piece of work, Septus. Treat my people with more respect or they may not try so hard next time."

Septus glared up at Heritis, but said nothing.

"So," said Heritis, "Genur is leading the men in your absence. Is there any chance of trouble at the mines?"

Septus grimaced as his leg spasmed. "We intercepted a message from the garrison...saying they were under some scent attack...nothing since. But we beat that rabble at the docks, so the mines won't be any different. Genur's able enough." Septus winced as he tried to make himself more comfortable. "I think he'll reach the mines by sun down... Expect his report the next day. Now I'll try some healing on myself; be better than those fools."

Heritis was happy to shut the door on Septus. Being in the man's company was not pleasant.

Time to make some decisions, he thought. He remembered the head seeker, Jelm, had gone on to Nebleth. Jelm was an astute commander of men and always worth bouncing ideas off. On the other hand, Genur, Jelm's equivalent in Regulus, was in the mould of Septus, ambitious and likely to cause unnecessary distress.

Heritis and Regna sat at opposite ends of a large couch in a corner of the room. Wine and crisp oatcakes with cheese and fruit lay untouched between them. He used a bottle and a plate to weigh down the sides of a large, hand-drawn map of Ean. Their conversation was somewhat stilted.

"From what you say, there's little chance that you'll have any more trouble from those rebels," said Regna. "That man," she shuddered, "seems confident they're controlled." She paused. "Pity the poor girl didn't do more damage. He's evil," she added quietly.

"Be careful, Regna," warned Heritis. He leant over, tapping on the map with a long finger. "Despite what Septus says, I'm loath to place much faith in his opinions. Underestimating your opponent is not a wise course of action." He ran his hand over the stubble on his scalp.

"Well, what are you going to do?" asked Regna.

"Apart from keeping my damn cousin up to date, there's nothing I can do until we hear back from Genur's expedition to the mines. I can only hope he's not as foolish as his master."

Heritis moved his finger along the course of the Great Southern to the northern portion of the map. "But what I can do is prepare for the worst. I have had the normal reports from the administrators in the towns advising little unusual activity. But I've a feeling that all is not as it should be. It's just too quiet." He tapped his teeth with a fingernail. "Again, there's not much I can do. Each town has guardsmen and seekers; there's little value in reinforcing them when any attack would be here or Nebleth, the centres of administration and trade. And there's no value in pulling them back to Regulus. It wouldn't add greatly to our numbers, and would leave the north unguarded. It's a pity the winds for scent communication are mostly useless at this time of the year, almost as if our foe has used this against us."

"But what about *your cousin*," Regna snapped, a slight flush colouring her face. "He'll want to know what you're doing so he can blame you if things go wrong." She toyed with a piece of fruit. "I wonder why he's spent so much time in Nebleth and not up here... Probably found someone new to torture."

"Maybe you're right, but despite what he's done, just watch your opinions. Any scent-talented will know what you think. Meanwhile, I think we should look at our options." Heritis traced the east-west line of mountains separating Regulus from the Great Coastal Plain and Nebleth.

"In the unlikely event the rebels beat Genur and, even more unlikely, try to take on the might of Regulus, we need to be prepared. The strategic value of this city is obvious, and I've asked Jakus to send several hundred men soon, just in case. I doubt even Septus's belief there's no threat would dissuade Jakus from doing that. I think the attack on the Shada himself has made him more cautious."

Heritis sat back and looked through the open door at the clear blue sky. "Then there's this *Targ*. Septus has taken little account of him. I, however, wouldn't be so sure." He rubbed his long aquiline nose, "No, not at all." He touched the map.

"With the extra men, plus what we have on the ground, there should be more than four hundred trained troops, over twenty seekers and scent masters. If any rebels are left over from Septus's battles at the Salt Way docks, and the mines, our forces should easily suffice. And if the Shada finally decides to come north again then…"

A low rumble reverberated through the room, followed by a definite vibration in the stonework around them; a few small pieces of plaster fell from the ceiling, and dust rose.

"What?" gasped Regna as she clutched Heritis's arm.

Heritis laughed, until she hit him on the knee to stop him.

"Oh, you're infuriating," she said. "Obviously that wasn't an earthshake."

"N…no,' he continued to laugh. "No, it wasn't. It's just your friend Septus having some problem with the pain, smashing the wall, no doubt. Hope he hasn't damaged anything."

Regna, relief apparent in her eyes, laughed in return.

Chapter Twenty-Nine

Targas took shallow breaths, shut his eyes and concentrated on the odours around him. Soon he was floating in a sea of scents, drifting through different layers, able to lower or raise his perception at will. But the smells were natural, part of the landscape: the drift of rock, soil and plant essences seeking to override the miasma of the marsh. He could find little sign of his people or their animals. He waited.

Genur halted his mount at the top of the climb, pushed the hood off his head and searched the surroundings for anything out of the ordinary. Thickets of spindly brown bushes and occasional dark green succulents with thorn-tipped leaves grew on the deeply eroded hillside that made up the western side of the trail. To the east the land fell away to a narrow gully with just a hint of water in its depths. To the north the trail led down into a shallow, marsh-filled basin.

Genur loosened the ties on his black cloak to allow cooling air to reach his thin chest. He twisted in the saddle to look over his Sutanite force, a competent-looking group of seekers and guardsmen, just under forty strong.

Hmmm, he thought, *more than enough to take care of any rebels at the mine; without Septus here, too.*

As he prepared to move his force down into the basin, an unfamiliar odour struck him. He peered at the distant, marshy ground, breathing air in through his nose and mouth. His eyes narrowed as he saw a figure move.

"What in Sutan's name is this?"

A cautious, controlled tendril insinuated itself into his space. Targas was not alone. A multitude of scents of unknown perac and men accompanied it.

Targas crouched and used a small stick to poke at a patch of grass on the edge of the boggy ground. He withdrew the stick and made a show of studying the chunk of weed adhering to the end.

He felt an odour tendril of enquiry sipping at his aura, tasting his essence. He did not react. More obvious tendrils followed. Sweat broke out across the back of his neck.

Now! his mind screamed. *Now!*

He looked at a dark mass of men and animals on the southern side of the basin. He could see, and feel, the danger facing him. Targas dropped the stick, stood up and turned to escape back up the path.

One, imperious in his black-and-grey seeker garb, released a dark tendril that snapped across the space and encircled Targas. It began to squeeze, attempting to restrain him. Instinctively, he created a shield to counter the threat. The tendril slipped off. He kept moving up the slope, his back itching as he anticipated another attack.

Out of the corner of his eye he saw the men urge their perac down the path. He kept moving, slowing as if the slope was too steep. Behind, he heard the splash of animals going off the path into the bog and the cursing as the men struggled with their mounts. One stopped to throw a spear. Targas instinctively created a thick odour wall at the point of impact, bending the spear as it hit. The point threatened to break through, but the barrier was strong enough and the spear sprang off, clattering to the stony path.

Targas combined odours with the strength of his anger and pulsed a dark bolt. It crashed into the spear thrower, pushing him off his perac into the side of another before they both fell into the bog. A flurry of spears and odour bolts followed in response.

Targas hunched down, closing his eyes to concentrate and encircle himself with the strongest shield he could create.

The impacts on his shield dazed him, but soon the shocks lessened. His people sprang the trap. The sounds of fighting, the clash of metal, the thud of heavy blows and the squeals of frightened animals came to his ears. He looked up as the hymetta-carrying perac bolted from their keepers and lumbered back up the slope.

Targas could see the opposing forces: professional soldiers and scent users fighting against a superior number of determined, but relatively untrained, Eanites. They had poured from the gullies and ridges, initially catching the enemy by surprise. The guardsmen had lowered their spears at the oncoming force, but were being hampered on animals in the boggy ground. The speed of the attack prevented them from dismounting and preparing a defensive line.

The Sutanite seekers reacted swiftly to the surprise assault by establishing an extended odour shield and driving bolts back at their attackers. Several struck into the flood of people, leaving a number of dead and injured in their wake. Then Lan's scent masters retaliated by extending a blanket of visibly solid scents over the knot of enemy scent users, pushing down on their shields, forcing them to focus on defence.

Their guardsmen, now unsupported by the seekers, were vulnerable to the spears and missiles of the attackers. Many were hit and fell off their perac onto the reddening bog. Others retreated across the marsh to what little protection the surrounding slopes offered. Yet others surrendered. The sheer weight of numbers told and soon only the enemy scent users, protected by their odour shields, remained.

Targas saw that the combined skill of Lan's scent masters was containing the enemy, but he soon realised their leader's power was keeping the scent blanket from coming down and forcing submission.

He joined the attack, coming from an unexpected direction, and pulsed a scent dart into the side of the defensive wall, trying to twist it through. It resisted at first until he applied more pressure, *picking* at the individual bonds that held it together. Once penetrated, the wall started to unravel. The full force of the Eanites' odour blanket pressed down on the enemy, crushing them. Their leader retained his odour shield, shaking with effort as he fought against the attack. Then he slowly turned his head, eyes red with effort, towards Targas. He clambered up the slope, a wall of dark odour moving with him. Targas could taste his scents, and feel his strength of purpose and anger.

"I'm Genur...your destroyer!" he rasped through gritted teeth as he neared.

Targas frantically explored the man's aura. A scent link, small but so recognisable, broke through, almost causing Targas to drop his protection. Its familiarity screamed at him. He gasped, heart pounding. That man had been in contact with Luna, but the linking scents were of spilt blood.

The combined emotions of fear and hatred created a sense of power Targas had never felt before. He stared into Genur's essence, seeking to find a weak linkage before this determined enemy reached him. His head grew cold and clear, and a shiver tightened his skin.

He focused his scent tendrils until they were thin and sharp to try and force his way through Genur's protection. The pressure on his own shield lessened as Genur reacted to the attack by building layers in front of Targas's needles of scent, attempting to sever them. But the tendrils were tough, reinforced by interlocking motes of scent drawn from the battlefield, bound together like a silken steel glove.

Targas could *see* the bonds, the odour fabric of Genur's body and where links were weakest. He plucked at a bond to make it vibrate, change nature and unlock. The consequent reactions only needed his gentle guidance to become unstoppable and make linkages disintegrate.

He pushed through the massed scents of his enemy's skin until they penetrated into his body cavity. Targas made them expand inside the gut, ignoring the widening of the man's blood-shot eyes and panicked gasps.

Genur, his eyes bulging, produced a very powerful bolt in reaction, but it dissipated harmlessly across Targas's shield. Then his body began to break apart as Targas continued the destruction of Genur's very essence.

The unravelling was spectacular to those watching.

Genur's form seemed to waver, skin rippling before expanding and then exploding in a spray of blood and tissue. A light breeze took the finest of the red droplets high, moving them through the air in an insubstantial parody of the man.

The marsh had turned to blood. The midday sun gave the scene a macabre glow, highlighting the odours of the dead and dying.

The fighting had stopped. Those few perac that escaped were huddled against a small cliff face, grunting constantly; the presence of the agitated caged hymetta on several of their number added to their panic. Guardsmen and rebels lay together in death. Groans and screams echoed in that marshy basin as life and death was decided.

Off centre lay the seekers, a small, grey and black mound of bodies crushed by the Sanctus scent masters. The cost had been high for both sides.

Targas felt gutted and empty. He remained crouched high on the path in the baking sun, a clear circle around him where the shield had protected him. Just down the slope a bloodied, crumpled skeleton stretched out, its eyeless skull staring and a bony finger pointing accusingly from a skeletal hand.

Targas stared at the bones, feeling nothing.

"Targas." A familiar voice and a gentle touch jolted him. "Come. Come away from this."

He allowed himself to be pulled to his feet and led from the killing ground, Sadir supporting Targas until they reached the camp. There he sat, too tired to speak, not even reacting as Tel pushed onto his lap and demanded his usual caress. A mug of water placed into his hand broke through his distraction. He saw the dirt-streaked face of Sadir peering up at him, her brow furrowed.

"Oh, Sadir!" he exclaimed, turning away from her as memories flooded into him.

"Targas, look at me." Her hands gently held his head. "Tell me. What have you found out? Is it about the youngsters?"

"Don't know, Sadir," mumbled Targas quickly, "too soon to tell...can't tell. Must wait until we get to the docks...then we'll know."

He clenched his hands into tight, white-knuckled fists, his legs shaking involuntarily. Shock was taking hold of him. He tried to force his mind away from what he knew, what he'd done.

His fight with the enemy leader had extended and changed him. The revelation that he could not only bond scent molecules, but also destroy their linkages, was chilling. Luna's scent, associated with blood, had pushed him through the boundary of humanity. He was scared, for himself and for those around him.

Sadir pushed against his chest, seeking to comfort and be comforted. Tel chirped a protest as he was squeezed between them. They sat silently, an oasis of calm in the noise and activity around them.

"Targas. Sadir. Will you join us?' asked Lan, his face haggard. "We need to go over this day."

They stood reluctantly and followed Lan to a small group of familiar faces in the sparse shade of some slender trees. Targas scanned the group. Lethnal and Brin smiled briefly, Quonir looked up with no welcome in his eyes while Davd stared, lips tight.

"Best we all stay here," said Lethnal, her face strained with the events of the day. "Th' healers are busy, and we'd be in th' way."

"I feel," said Lan, once they had sat on the scattered saddles and blankets, "that despite our victory, our friends here"—he paused, looking at Davd—"will be looking at those of us from Sanctus with a jaundiced eye. We have had many casualties this day and our allies have suffered the worst of it. For that I am sorry."

"Many dead!" interrupted Quonir, staring at Targas, accusation clear in his face. "Why couldn't you have done something, eh? You're our special weapon, after all!" he sneered

"Quonir," said Lan, attempting to quell the man's anger.

But before Targas could respond, Davd broke in. "What's th' cost t' my people, for th' win?" he demanded. "What cost?"

Lan looked from Quonir to Davd pain showing in his face. "We have counted eighteen guardsmen and ten seekers among the dead. Our people, in bravely fighting these *professionals,* paid a heavy price. I am told that over forty were killed or severely wounded. Too many," he sighed. "Strangely, though"—he scratched his chin—"there were no scent masters with the Sutanites. But for that, our losses would have been higher."

Davd frowned at Lan's comments, but nobody spoke further.

A breeze strengthened, rattling the branches, overriding the noise of the activity around them. Targas noticed it was now pushing southwards. A leaf tumbled past towards the bloody marsh, following the downstream course of the Salt Way. The group continued to sit in silence until a scent master brought them some food.

"This is most welcome, Hynal," said Lan, as he accepted some fruit and cheese. Her name dragged Targas's memory back to a time which seemed long ago, a peaceful time in the rooms of Sanctus. Hynal smiled at Sadir and then left them.

"I have an idea," Lethnal announced quietly. Targas, who was merely picking at his food, looked up. "What if we can send a scent message to the enemy; a false message about the battle that will help us, give us more time and keep the Sutanites off our backs?"

"Yer mean send them a message they'll think's been sent by one of their own?" asked Brin. Lethnal nodded. "Yer right. We could do that," agreed Brin.

"Mmmm," nodded Lan. "Yes, it might work. Yes…yes, we will act on it," he nodded decisively. "Thank you, Lethnal."

Lan scanned the camp, seeing groups of people working and others lying exhausted. "I think we will not be travelling on until next day. We need to tend the wounded and respect those who have not…returned. Our scout will have a more detailed report from the docks then and will advise us of what we may expect." He nodded. "With good fortune, many of our people there will be located.

"But tell me, Targas," continued Lan, "the success of this day was as much due to you as anyone. The trap worked and gave us a crucial advantage. But your thorough destruction of the enemy leader was…uh, unexpected." His voice trailed off as Targas's aura darkened.

Targas clenched his jaws and drew in several deep breaths, suddenly ashamed. It was a problem needing to be in the open, amongst those with knowledge.

"I'm sorry, Lan, everyone. I've been trying to work out what I did and how I did it. The *why* I don't have an issue with, but I hope that I'm wrong," explained Targas. "In fact, I hardly want to talk about it…but I must."

Sadir squeezed his hand painfully as he tried to find the words.

Chapter Thirty

If the previous day had been bad, this day promised to be worse.

Clouds of small, winged insects spent their time seeking blood. People with scent talent used it to keep the pests away, but stinging bites rewarded any lapse in concentration. Tel took the opportunity to catch his meal from Targas's shoulders.

The air was still and humid in an already hot day, and both he and Sadir dreaded what they would find ahead. The scout had reported that the docks were silent, rebel bodies lying in and around the warehouses and no sign of survivors. Lan reacted by sending extra scouts out to search for survivors in the surrounding countryside. A further group of healers and their helpers followed more slowly, carrying their wounded and dead on the animals captured from the enemy; the enemy who lay buried behind them.

Targas had insisted that the hymetta be spared, countering the natural reaction of the rebels to destroy them. They horrified, yet intrigued him.

Tel interrupted his thoughts by moving from one shoulder then pushing his rough skin past Targas's ears to peer from the other.

"Tel. Stop it," he growled, but the lizard had frozen, frill spread, mouth gaping.

Sadir frowned at Targas, then followed Tel's line of sight towards the Salt Way River. The path was wider, allowing easy two-abreast travel, opening up where the hills became lower.

"Sadir," said Targas, "I don't like the look of what's ahead."

"No," she agreed, shaking her head. "No." She came alongside. "I don't want to be here. I don't want to find what's there. I just wish we were back home. That none of this was happening."

Their eyes narrowed as they saw a wall of odour, moving as if it had a mind of its own, and numerous dark insects manoeuvring through the substance as though feeding.

A skill that had improved dramatically since his precipitous arrival in Ean was in isolating individual scents within arrays of emanations that almost overwhelmed the senses, but he was challenged this time. The rich and complex mixture of death and decay was a powerful force that could swamp minor scents. It was not hard to recognise the source, even if he had not been forewarned, but he knew that it would take all his new skill and a portion of luck to find what he was searching for.

Then recognition surged through him: Luna's scent intertwined with those of death. He looked briefly at Sadir to catch her staring at him, mouth open expectantly. He shook his head almost imperceptibly, then clenched his jaw and gripped the reins of his perac. He felt Sadir's sadness wash over him.

Targas urged the perac to Lan and Brin.

"It doesn't look good ahead," he commented. "I have a very bad feeling about this. Sadir and I *need* to go first. I don't think there's any danger."

Lan nodded at Targas, sympathy and understanding showing.

Targas urged his animal into a trot. Sadir followed.

One part of his mind could not help registering such an extensive use of solid wood. Their side of the Salt Way River was paved with rows of thick timbers a good three hundred paces in total and extending back another forty. The builders had left a platform projecting over the water where supporting pillars were driven, at intervals, into the muddy bank. The tops of over twenty barges showed, extending two deep along the platform and taking up most of the narrow river.

Back from this structure were a number of warehouse-style wooden buildings, long and low with central double doors. A flatter structure closer to the docks, with normal doors and several windows, seemed to be there to cater for the dock workers.

However, there were no workers. Nothing more than insects and scavenging lizards moved on the docks that hot, windless day. Coils of odour roiled into the air like thick greasy smoke, adding an ominous aspect to an already gruesome scene. Scattered around the area were clumps of what initially looked like rocks, softened by the muted colours of clothing. The telltale stink of death and putrefaction rose from the slain bodies of the rebels.

"Only rebels? Our people?" Sadir's voice quavered.

"Yes. They buried their own. Left ours to rot," Targas growled.

He glanced at Sadir and then dug his heels into his animal's sides. It baulked at his commands, spreading its legs, refusing to move. He swung off the animal, almost upsetting Tel with his motion, the lizard's claws digging through into his skin. Sadir followed suit, dropping the perac's lead to the ground.

They threaded a cautious path through the clouds of death, long thin lizards, large flies and beetles scattering as they went. Targas's nose led them, following an all-too-familiar scent as they avoided the corpses. Ahead, a small, lone mound contained that essence of familiarity Targas dreaded. The knot of his jaw muscles threatened to break through his skin as he reached out a hesitant hand to confirm what his other senses already knew.

A large pool of dried blood spread around the shoulders of the corpse. Luna's body lay abandoned in the hot sun.

Her dusty blonde head was a distance from her body, face already disfigured by scavengers. Targas pulled Sadir in close and squeezed her hard as if the mere action would instantly move them away, out of sight and reality. Sobs racked their bodies and a weird keening erupted from Tel.

"Oh, no, not Luna. She didn't deserve this. Oh Targas...it's just not..." Overwhelmed with pain, Sadir clung to Targas.

"Kyel's not here too, is he? Is he?" Her voice became high and shrill.

"No...by blood's grace." Targas held the shaking woman as an icy shroud covered his heart.

Even the most basic of tasks distracted the mind and allowed the body to work without conscious thought. Tel had shrunk to a shadow, clinging like an elongated collar across Targas's shoulders. He and Sadir had joined a group foraging for wood around the river and surrounding bush, piling it into a heap on the stony ground. The pyre slowly grew to shoulder height, soon covering an area large enough to make even the most stonehearted fighter shake his head. As others placed the bodies of the slain rebels in rows on top of the wood, Targas gently lifted Luna's wrapped corpse and, awkwardly climbing to the centre, placed her amongst her people.

A noise distracted him when he'd rejoined Sadir. He saw river people coming through the alleyways between the buildings, moving towards them and the funeral pyre.

A solid woman, wailing loudly, headed their way. She flung out two massive arms and pulled Targas and Sadir into her chest, exuding a sweaty, faintly salty odour.

"I'm sorry, Sadir and Targ. I'm so, so sorry."

Targas was overwhelmed by the greeting, his brain trying to understand what was happening. She was a river woman and obviously familiar with them, although they'd never met.

"You know us and obviously Luna since she only knew me as Targ, not Targas. What happened? Why did she...?" Targas's voice trailed off.

"Luna was a good girl, brave 'nd good...'n I couldn't stop her. I should've known; should've stopped her."

Bit by bit Cynth told the story, revealing a softness in her that belied her outward, hard appearance. They learnt that Luna had been a hero, distracting Septus from his killing spree and allowing most of the river people to escape.

"I see yer met me woman." A large, heavy-looking man came close, sampling their auras. "Name's Woll, 'nd yer must be Targ 'nd Sadir... She spoke about yer." The man sniffed and put his arm around Cynth. "Yer gel," he continued in a deep voice, "saved our lives, though I don't like what she paid t' do it."

Woll followed the direction of their eyes, seeing the ominous funeral pyre. "We'll ha...have t' give her a decent send-off," he spoke gruffly. "But...she'll be in good company."

Targas and Sadir held each other while learning of what Luna had gone through, and how she had never really recovered from her torture at the hands of the enemy. They quickly bonded with this comfortable couple. They all knew Luna, understood what she had been through and how brave she had been. How the Sanctus *Knowing* had reached its course. Her farewell would be a fitting one.

The wind dropped. Stars sprinkled the sky around the rising crescent moon. People massed together in a mirroring crescent, facing the river and their dead.

Targas and Sadir sat amongst the scent masters of Sanctus. Behind them were almost three hundred river people. Cynth, Woll, cousins Zylth, Janhl, and their leader Ginrel were nearby, while the miners and the mountain folk remained in distinct groups further away. The mood was sombre, overshadowed by the dark bulk of the pyre.

Time had no meaning as they waited. The breeze had stilled, and the moon hung like a sickle, its lower end appearing to penetrate the pyre. Lan stood and turned slowly to face the crowd, grey robes appearing almost luminescent in the dark.

"My...friends," he began, "we have come together on this night to celebrate." He paused as his voice rose. "We are the largest gathering of our peoples for generations. We represent Ean. We represent the future."

A shadow flitted across the moon with a distant thrum that reminded Targas of the tina. A vague vanilla odour caught his nose. He held his breath, waiting for Lan to continue.

"With great triumph comes great tragedy. These last days have brought both triumph and tragedy...the next days will bring more." Lan paused. "My people, for those who have given of themselves so selflessly, we celebrate this night. We celebrate their courage and sacrifice, their giving of life so their families and fellows will have a chance to live a life free from the fears that beset us all. We feel grief and loss, and look to undo what has happened. But to do so would be to deny them their sacrifice, for which they will be remembered...for all time. Yes, we will grieve but they have given us the freedom to do that. We will mourn their loss, but we will also celebrate the loss and the selflessness with which it was made. And we will celebrate their renewal."

Lan slowly turned towards Targas and leant forward, holding out his hand.

"Now I will give you a man, a stranger who has willingly embraced our cause. A man I am honoured to call my friend.

"My people...Targas from Tenstria has given of himself to add strength to us at a time of great need. Without him, this day might have been lost. And we will continue to need his and all our powers, and more if we are to succeed in what we have begun. Targas will aid us to go from dark to light; it is fitting that he joins in our replenishment and renewal; it is appropriate he lights the pyre."

Lan turned and bowed to Targas before resuming his seat.

Targas had no thought of nerves in front of the sea of pale faces. He glanced down at the woman he felt so close to, absorbing her sadness, and then looked around, recognising losses that mirrored his own. There was nothing he could do to change what had happened to Luna, but the opportunity to send her and her companions on their way in a fitting manner was his.

He nodded slowly. It was time. Targas concentrated on the rocky ground, seeking the minute emanations of flint in the background odours, finding, solidifying and binding them into larger and larger balls. A familiar background hum from the crowd didn't distract as he manoeuvred, then pushed paired balls at intervals into the large pile of wood. With a savage twist of his mind, he clashed them together, hard and fast, giving out a satisfying boom. Fire blossomed, racing through the piles of wood as if they were soaked in oil, the flames spreading quickly to cover every part of the pyre.

And the essences rose, initially hidden by the flames until the outpouring of the scent masters made them visible to all. Targas instinctively worked with them to weave scents of sacrifice, courage, loyalty, determination, and love—all those emotions that made the people what they were—into a blanket of soft pinks, blues, oranges and yellows shimmering over the backdrop of the flames. He gradually infused a soft but strong green that came directly from the innocence of the young girl they had lost. It melded into the flickering blanket of scent, making it stronger, more reflective of those it represented. Violet, purple and red came in irregular flashes, reminiscent of the violence and passion of their passing.

The smoke from the pyre rose high into the night sky, spreading mushroom-like as it ascended. The background vibration grew in volume until it blocked the very crackle of the flames. A sweet smell surrounded Targas, pulling him into a trance. He drifted, intrinsically aware of Sadir's presence next to him and others further away. The distant, rational part of his mind was lost as he found himself looking down on the bright flicker of flames, enmeshed in dark, billowing clouds.

Other presences pushed as if seeking to divide his being from Sadir's, but he held close. Her peace and calm covered his concerns and fears.

The sweet smell changed, becoming more acrid, the hissing and crackling coals grew noisier. Targas felt Sadir's hand gripping his and cautiously opened his eyes.

The stars were back with the crescent moon a lopsided smile amongst them. The fire had burnt to embers. Those who had made the ultimate sacrifice were at peace.

Chapter Thirty-One

Odour flowed in solid, pulsating ropes from Jakus's mouth before oozing darkly towards the rigid woman in front of him.

She responded with a burst of scents showing first fear, acceptance and then a sprinkling of desire. Her eyes, dark in her white face widened as the tendrils found, touched and encircled her. Her body stiffened, then relaxed.

Jakus swayed slightly, his tongue withdrawing into his mouth as he focused on moving the odours over her body, splitting off the minutest of tendrils to push into her smell centre and taste her essence. He had control and used it.

Jakus gave a grunt of contentment as he absorbed her scents. *So satisfying after such a disappointing day*, he thought.

When he used her hands to cup her breasts, he sighed and licked his pallid lips.

"Back, Nefaria," he ordered quietly, momentarily releasing his control.

She held his gaze as she slowly backed away across the tiled floor, until a large table pressed against her thighs. She stopped, face expressionless, waiting. He tightened the tendrils, their rich dark colours now interspersed with flashes of yellow and bright red. He remained where he was, using just scent control to force her arms behind her, hands edging out along the surface of the table until her back stretched like a bow.

Jakus paused, inhaling greedily as he absorbed Nefaria's aromas and the gust of her emotions.

"Blood's stink," he swore through gritted teeth; the sensory overflow from her violation was so absorbing that he'd lost control. Jakus swayed as he snapped out of his euphoria. The odour tendrils collapsed and slithered away to nothingness.

"Aaugh," he spat, ripping off and flinging down his soiled robe before striding past her to his washing room.

Nefaria collapsed back onto the table, her legs hanging over the edge. She started to cry as the pain began.

It was nearing noon as Heritis watched his soldiers drilling on the large, cobbled square just outside the castle. The sun beat down on the black-and-grey ranks as they worked to the orders of the master and senior guardsmen. *Should be competent enough to cover any possible rebel reaction after Septus's fiasco at the docks,* he thought. The assurances from Septus that the rebels had been crushed and it was only a matter of time before Genur controlled the salt mines did little to mollify him. His misgivings only served to make him more nervous and determined to anticipate any eventuality.

Three hundred extra troops from Port Saltus, when my cousin decides to send them, would be welcome. He shook his head at the thought of needing them.

Heritis delayed his visit to the scent tower sited on top of the castle until night; nightfall was the time when the breezes usually died down and the day's collection could be best assessed.

The design of the tower was based on efficiency rather than aesthetics, being a square building situated on the highest point, with four large collecting funnels, one each side, siphoning the airs entering. Odours trapped on a sticky, neutral substance could then be analysed. The constantly updated scent map indicated the location, and the vast scent knowledge of the masters identified the source. It was an imperfect way of obtaining knowledge, but usually worked. Details of weather and season, animal and human activity, even specific messages across the country were trapped by the scent tower, and every acolyte spent time there as part of their training.

The building was unlit since this helped to avoid contamination from lamp smoke, so Heritis made his way by memory and smell until he recognised the personal aura of the master on duty.

"Bakis, is it going well?" asked Heritis hopefully. He anticipated there would be something there to help counter his continuing sense of unease. Even though he was a well-trained and experienced scent master he could not pin down what was causing his concern, but he was astute enough to respond to his feelings.

"Yes, Shad," replied Bakis, who was a large, younger man, with a squarish head on wide shoulders, a build more suited to a guardsman than a scent master. "The winds have turned from their regular direction through the Sensory Mountains and Lesslas Hills, and just now we're picking up emanations from the cooling, descending breezes in the Long Ranges and the Salt Way."

"I had hoped that would be the case. No news yet?" asked Heritis.

"No evidence of anything, but I'm in the middle of inspecting the traps and I'll personally let you know."

"Good. Keep at it. If you find anything, anything at all, then I'm to know at once. Keep the other masters working to detect any unusual odours," he emphasised. "It may just be the merest mote but if it is there it is vital you don't miss it. And further, there must be something from Genur this night."

"Yes, Shad," replied Bakis, detecting the unease in Heritis's voice, "as soon as I know anything."

Heritis returned to his rooms tired and impatient, wondering if Regna would have wine and food waiting for him. But he found that she'd retired early, so he helped himself to the wine she had left out while mulling over the events of the last few days. Septus had been sure that Genur would have easily accounted for any rebellion at the mines, so a message should have been intercepted by now.

He looked up in response to Bakis's knock and ordered the scent master to enter.

"Well?" he demanded.

"We have received a message...but I'm not sure about it."

"At last!" exclaimed Heritis, "Let me smell it." He pushed past Bakis in his haste, and hurried towards the stairs leading up to the scent tower.

Soon Heritis was crouching over the scent trap, absorbing the odours. They were complex, even though the message had been separated from the background scents collected with it.

"Genur; strong, but definitely him," he said to himself. "He's made it to the mines. There's been fighting. Is this significant, Bakis?" He leant back to allow the scent master to assess the message.

"Shad, I can detect blood, mainly rebel I think, but maybe our men as well. I believe that Genur didn't have it all his own way."

Heritis nodded. "My thoughts too. I also detect that he's not returning yet, probably to get the operation back in production, I suspect." Heritis rubbed his chin. "A pity he can't report in person. However, at least I'll have something worthwhile to tell the Shada, after what happened with Septus last day."

"Shad," asked Bakis, his square face wrinkled in thought, "do you get a different feel to the message? I mean, I've received messages from Genur before and this one is different somehow."

"Explain what you mean."

"Well," Bakis continued hesitantly, "Genur is usually more...uh...arrogant in his messages. This one is...too polite."

"Hmmm." Heritis squatted back on his heels as he considered the observation. "When the winds change you should send a response asking him to confirm, if it worries you. Keep me informed." Heritis walked down the steps from the scent tower thinking of Bakis's comment. It tied in with the vague disquiet that had been hounding him for some time, in fact ever since Septus had returned. He toyed with the idea of letting his cousin know of his concerns, maybe to get those troops on their way, but Jakus was always keen to blame when things went wrong and loath to give thanks.

He decided to spell out his misgivings in the scent message when the breezes were favourable for Nebleth, including the demand for the promised soldiers.

His concern was for his city and not the vagaries of Jakus's temper; the man was haggars' dung anyway.

"Shada! Shada!" called a voice through the solid wood.

"Wait." responded Jakus, tapping the door with a light scent dart to give emphasis to his command. He looked back at his bed companion. "I think you should go to your room while Akerus delivers his message; your current state of dress might unsettle him."

"Yes, Shada." Nefaria rose, wincing with discomfort, and pulled the translucent wrap around her.

Jakus smiled, assessing her long white limbs and curves as she limped towards the connecting door to her room.

"Enter!" he snapped, sitting on the edge of the bed.

The door opened, and Akerus almost tripped over his long, black robes in his hurry to cross the room.

"What!"

"Sha...Shada," began the scent master, "sorry to disturb you but we've received news from the Shad concerning the campaign."

"It better be good then," thundered Jakus. "I trust that Genur has had more success than Septus."

"Yes, Shada," continued Akerus. "It appears that Genur has the mines operational again and has dealt with the rebels."

"So that will mean the salt will resume?"

"I...I understand so," replied Akerus. "And Heritis—I mean the Shad—has reported that Septus is recovering from his wounds."

"That black k'dorian," snapped Jakus, borrowing a phrase from Kyel, "doesn't deserve to recover since he destroyed my prize captive. The only value he's been is allowing Genur to take over the campaign." He gazed through the open door of the balcony at the grey sky.

"Uh, Shada," interrupted Akerus hesitantly, "Heritis adds that he would appreciate the sending of the soldiers you promised."

"What!" growled Jakus. "What is my faint-hearted cousin complaining about now? Let me think on it."

Jakus rose and walked to the balcony. Despite what he'd said in front of Akerus, he knew that Heritis would not ask for something frivolously. His promise to send soldiers and organising their movement from Port Saltus would be easy enough. He was of a mind to agree since it would not affect the requirements of Nebleth.

"So be it," he murmured. He turned back to Akerus. "Yes, I'll agree to Heritis's request—leave it with me." Jakus waved a hand dismissively in Akerus's direction.

"Oh, Akerus." Jakus's voice brought the man to a halt at the door. "How is my young trainee doing?"

Akerus swung around, gripping his hands together in front of his stomach, bald head showing a slight sheen of sweat. "Ah, Shada...he is going as well as can be expected. I think..." He paused. "If you'll allow my opinion, the magnesa affects him. Too much and he's hard to teach, too little and he has periods where he's hard to control. He seems obsessed with this Targ, his sister and his friend... Luna?"

"Ah yes. Luna," Jakus sighed as he ran his hand down the side of his face, the rasp of stubble audible. "I think it is time I had a talk with our young trainee. Send him in shortly, after I've eaten. You may go."

"**M**y young friend!" exclaimed Jakus with a welcoming smile. "Come here; help me finish some of this fruit." He kept the smile pasted on his face as Kyel slowly walked over and sat without asking permission.

Jakus ignored Kyel's breach of etiquette and watched him eat, while reflecting on the current situation. *Perhaps it was some of my cousin's nervousness rubbing off. I don't think Kyel's Targ has been involved in the business at the Salt Way docks, especially since Septus and Genur reported success...so where is he?* He sighed, shaking his head.

Jakus focused on Kyel, licking his lips as he leant close. He gently released a compulsive scent.

"Kyel?"

"Mmph," Kyel responded, a repugnant noise made through a mouthful of fruit.

"Keep eating,'" said Jakus, trying to keep his face friendly. "I've got something to tell you, but it may distress you."

Kyel looked at him, juice running down his chin, mouth open, eyes slightly glazed.

Jakus repressed a shudder at the sight of half-eaten fruit.

"I'm afraid your Targ has done you a great disservice. It's about Luna." He paused, adding a note of concern to the odour.

Kyel's mouth snapped closed, and his eyes gained focus.

"Targ...Luna," repeated Kyel. "What d'you mean?"

"There is no good way to say this," Jakus replied, reaching across the table and placing a hand on Kyel's bony shoulder, "but Luna is dead." Jakus squeezed the shoulder and frowned with false concern, all the while watching the interplay of emotions in Kyel's face.

"You can't...you can't be serious," cried Kyel, grabbing at Jakus's sleeve with sticky fingers. He looked into Jakus's face as if trying to find evidence of a lie. The slight hint of a smile, a curl of Jakus's lips, wasn't noticed in his panic.

"Targ and Luna..." Jakus shook his head slowly.

"No!" Kyel's head crashed onto the table, knocking the plate to the floor. "No!" Kyel lifted and then deliberately banged his head repeatedly before bursting into tears.

Jakus squashed the smile creeping onto his face, before reinforcing his concern.

"How?" Kyel asked through his tear-stained face.

"You remember Luna was taken from my care and how upset we were?" Jakus reinforced his odours, introducing credibility as he spoke. "We tried desperately to keep track of her, keep her from getting harmed, but we were unable to help her. Only last day did we find her"—his voice lowered, and he moved around the table, stretching his arm along Kyel's shoulder—"where your Targ had left her. We don't know why, but he left her there to die...alone...without anyone."

Kyel's sobs increased while Jakus projected sympathy and friendship, feelings that didn't come easily to him. "She was so young to be left all alone," he murmured, "so young... How could he have done that?"

"But Targ's our friend," sobbed Kyel, tears mingling with his runny nose.

Jakus recoiled at the sight, but managed to keep his arm on the boy's shoulders. "I'm afraid he isn't now."

Jakus forced a powerful compulsion scent at him, then watched as Kyel's expression changed. He stopped weeping, face hardening and eyes growing colder. He smeared the mucus on his face with his sleeve and then nodded briefly.

Jakus doubted whether this simple precaution would ever be needed but he enjoyed making Targ appear to Kyel as the potential enemy.

"Nefaria," he called.

"Yes, Shada?" she inquired, putting her head around the door.

"Take the boy to his room," he ordered. "I think he is in shock."

Chapter Thirty-Two

The early part of the day was fresh and bright, as if the previous night had never happened. Targas walked alone across the docks with no fixed thoughts in mind, hands in the pockets of his Tenstria jacket. He was strangely relaxed and able to consider the future without the bitterness that had dogged him the days before. He wandered over to the line of barges, some with smoke spiralling thinly from the narrow pipes marking the position of their stoves, but even the thought of a cooked meal did not interest him. He acknowledged the odd wave from those stirring on board before he headed back to where Sadir and the others would be preparing for the day.

As he passed a warehouse, a familiar buzz snapped him out of his contemplation and started his heart pounding. He took an involuntary step back, jolted by what he saw. An alien face looked into his, assessing him through the bars of its cage, filling him with a repugnance he found hard to shake. However, the hymetta, head tilted to one side, was looking at him with an air that didn't seem to be assessing its next meal.

Targas froze, mouth half open at the strange attitude of the creature when a thought struck him.

"Where's Rasnal?" Targas asked anyone he saw, until he was directed to the perac holding area at the back of one of the warehouses. He found her energetically combing the side of one of the animals, her solid back to him.

"I was told you'd be here," he said. Rasnal jumped at the sound of his voice.

"Oh, it's you, Targas. Couldn't detect you over the animals," she said, her round face animated by a shy smile. "What can I do for you?" She leant back to the woolly side of the perac and resumed pulling the comb through the fleece.

"Can I raise an idea with you?" asked Targas.

"If you don't mind me doing this as well," was her muffled response as she moved along the animal.

"Okay," he said. "Firstly, you know about the big creatures here, I mean what they are... Sorry, I suppose I mean how they behave."

"What?" asked Rasnal, popping up on the other side of the perac, face flushed. "What're you asking?" She leant a plump arm on top of the perac and looked at him with interest.

"I suppose I'm asking if you know how the tina and the hymetta behave, what their habits are."

"I know as much as anyone, I guess. More about the tina since I work with them, but I'm interested in the hymetta—though not enough to be in the cage with one," she added with an expression of distaste on her face. "Go on," she urged.

"My limited knowledge of wasps back home, which seem to be a much smaller version of hymetta, is that they are generally social creatures and will protect their nests from any intruder, anything that doesn't have the right or familiar smell," he explained as Rasnal nodded. "It intrigued me that the men with the hymetta could control them without being attacked. So, they had to get them to accept their Sutanite odour?"

"I suppose that could be the case," replied Rasnal, "but the tina respond to a general odour and don't really react to a scent they don't know."

"Of course, but tina aren't aggressive and they drink nectar rather than eat meat. I believe that the hymetta will attack anything that doesn't smell *right* if they have the right incentive. But when I saw the hymetta in the cage just now, it seemed to recognise me, and was friendly, if anything. So, if we can make them familiar to our scent, then get them to take that *familiarity* back to their home nest so the whole brood learns our smell, we could possibly remove a very nasty weapon from the enemy."

"That's an almost impossible idea, Targas," said Rasnal, resting her chin in the perac's fleece as she thought it through, "almost impossible. But we've nothing to lose. Yes, that's something we could work on, and soon. I'll follow it up with Lan and the council if you wish."

"Please," replied Targas, "I would be happy to leave it with you." He patted the perac's rump and went to find Sadir. Rasnal resumed combing.

A general feeling of wellbeing remained with him from the previous night. While he could think of all the traumatic things that had happened, he suppressed them to a level that allowed him to function as normal. When he caught up with Sadir she, too, was close to her normal self.

"Targas, I've been lookin' for you." She leant in close, touching him on his chest and hooking her arm through his. Tel warbled a greeting as he precariously bounced from foot to foot on her shoulders. Sadir nudged the enthusiastic lizard to Targas's wider shoulders.

"My love," breathed Targas, patting Tel, "let's get out of here. Go for a walk or something. I need to see over this place, the place that Luna last knew."

They walked away from the river and up between the buildings. The ground gradually rose as they followed a rough track along the top of a ridge, not realising it was the same path Luna had been on days before. They paused to catch their breath, viewing the panorama below them. The ridge they were on was one of a number descending rib-like from the mountains in the north, petering out at the Salt Way River, before resuming as low foothills to the southeast. The buildings had been built on the river's small floodplain, with the dock extending on to the river. The Salt Way was flat and tannin-coloured, blocked with barges spread like a scatter of dark seedpods over the surface. Concentrated wisps of smoke rising slowly in the still air drew their attention to a large black patch of flat ground, near the wooden docks.

Sadir drew in a sharp breath. "Targas"—she squeezed his hand—"let's go back."

"Yes," he readily agreed.

The large accommodation and mess building was packed with people. Over three hundred were settling themselves to get a good vantage point, propped up on a range of benches and bunk beds that lined the walls. The light grey robes and minimal hair of the Sanctus group, the earthy clothing, weathered faces and longer hair of the river and mountain people, and the darker features of the smaller mining folk made a distinctive contrast. Lan, Brin, Lethnal and Quonir were in the centre of the room around a large table holding a roughly-constructed diorama. The high ground of the model was marked by various-sized mounds, while the river was represented as a broad groove leading to one end.

Targas, with Sadir leaning on his knee, sat on some rolled blankets on the floor. Tel was outside sunning.

"My friends," said Lan, "I would give my thanks for your courage, and for undertaking this, the next step. We have already pulled a thread in the enemy's robe, an action which may lead to the fabric of his rule unravelling. We are now ready to take a chance that the enemy is unsure of us, and so relatively unprepared. This has a good likelihood of success, because they will not know our strength and our resolve. And we understand their forces have not been combined as yet. But we, this day, have received a message that time is short and the enemy is moving."

A murmur arose, until Lan raised his hand.

"Please, my friends. I know most of you have had and will continue to play a part in the coming conflict. Some of us may pay the ultimate price, but this time," Lan said, arm poised in the air while he looked slowly around the room, "is the time to make the enemy pay for his complacency. This time he will not feed us to the hymetta. This time we will feed *him* to the haggar!"

A burst of cheering echoed, and Lan waited until it died down.

MICHAEL B FLETCHER

"And this time, if we move quickly," he continued, "we will have the advantage of strength and the benefit of surprise."

After a short discussion on a number of planning issues, people went about their preparations. Lan beckoned Targas and Sadir to the table where Brin, Lethnal, Quonir and Ginrel, the leader of the river people, viewed the diorama.

"Targas," said Lan, "we will go over the layout of the region for your benefit. The Salt Way extends from the docks as you can see, and normally has little water since the Long Ranges are the driest in Ean. However, recent rains have increased river flows and will allow us to move our forces quickly down to the junction with the Great Southern River, then on to Regulus. The Salt Way will have played its part; now we hope the Great Southern will."

Lan ran his finger down the length of the model, stopping where two water courses met. "Once we reach the confluence of the rivers we will float to Regulus in short order. Our goal will be to follow the river into the city." He pointed to a square that denoted Regulus. "You can see that the Great Southern divides the city in two and it is at that place"—he tapped the model, raising a puff of dust—"we make our move."

Leaving the others to discuss tactics, Lan took both Targas and Sadir by the elbow and steered them to a table in a quiet corner. "Rasnal told me of your plan for the hymetta. We are acting on it," he paused. "You never know what may come of that idea, my friend...you never know. Also, the tina message advises enemy troops are moving north from Port Saltus on their way to Regulus, so time is short."

"Nothing about Kyel?" asked Sadir hopefully.

"No, Sadir, but with good fortune," Lan said, "he will be well. Besides, we should have heard if he was not."

Targas had spoken with most of the inner council until he was overtired. He had even spent some time with Quonir to try and help settle the obvious issue between them. Although he was full of misgivings about how he could fulfil the Eanite's expectations of him, Quonir just added to them. He resolved that it would be Quonir's problem from now on. The only bright light was meeting Cynth, with her matter-of-fact way of dealing with life. It reminded him of his mother and the way she had dealt with the occasional crises in their family, a solid rock in the turmoil of life.

"Targas," Lan said, approaching, "we have a plan which, until you, was merely an idea. It is a plan that we believe will help us defeat the enemy at Regulus." He patted Targas's arm and continued.

"We've had success at the garrison and the marsh, because we have not only caught them by surprise, but also bettered the enemy in numbers and scent talent. Regulus is different. The plans that worked before will not apply there."Lan

220

raised his eyebrows, his brown eyes staring intently at Targas.

"Right," Targas sighed. "What do I have to do?"

"Ah, Sadir," said Lan as she came over to their table carrying three steaming mugs, "hot drinks are welcome." He took two from her hands and gave one to Targas. "Sit down and listen to me pushing plans on your man for next day."

"Thank you, Lan," said Sadir, "I'm happy to listen to what you're saying. It's much better than just thinking about things."

"I sympathise with you both," said Lan softly, patting them on their hands before continuing. "You know we can use fog, or mist, to carry an odour." Targas nodded. "Both sides use it against non-talented, although our use is more benign. Then again," Lan added, "any fog is automatically suspicious, so therein is our problem."

"Look," said Targas, "I'm keen to help in any way to get back at those wine-rotted people. Just tell me what you want."

"All right"—Lan's eyes narrowed—"we must get this right. We need you to trap our attack odours within a fog so that there is little chance of them being detected. This we can do on a limited scale, but your skills will allow it to be maintained over a larger area. We must get at the Regulus scent masters before they know we are there, before they realise we are attacking; that is what we need to do." He tapped the table for emphasis.

Targas recalled the strain of holding the odour blanket that suppressed the waves at the river crossing. "I guess I might be able to do it…" he answered uncertainly.

"No," Lan disagreed. "You *have* to be able to do it. Without it we fail. We will be stopped at Regulus and our country, our people, will fall back to a reign of reprisals and fear." He stopped, chest heaving. "Targas"—Lan held his eyes—"you have reason to overcome the Sutanites, and the talent to do so."

"Yes, yes, I know," he responded. "Of course, I'll try. I owe it to you all and"—he looked at Sadir—"those I care about."

"Right," concluded Lan, "now the last thing is to put your idea for the hymetta into action. Then we all need to get some food and rest before we leave late this night. We will strike before dawn."

Targas volunteered to help Rasnal pull the cages of hymetta to an open space on the docks. They had been fed and heavily introduced to a basic Eanite scent, particularly focusing on scent master odour; Targas and Sadir had added their scents to the mix. The creatures were docile and interested in their surroundings, all signs of aggression gone. The cages were moved into open space with their latches tied so they could all be released at the same time. The surrounding people raised their spears, and those with significant scent talent were alert. Then Rasnal, who had remained at the cages, lifted the cord joining the latches.

"Now!" called Lan. The cages snapped open together and the black-and-yellow bodies spilled out. The six large insects moved around like the wasps Targas had known back home, only everything more gross, every movement more exaggerated. They milled around, antennae touching the ground and each other, heads swivelling from side to side.

Targas's stomach lurched. Sadir cringed next to him, and people automatically moved further away from the creatures. However, Targas soon noticed the hymetta's interest was not on them. The creatures were moving, antennae still flicking, as if seeking an elusive scent. Then they took to the air in a clatter of wings, driving the dust outwards. They circled, rising higher until their flight took them over the buildings, the river and across the slopes.

Targas could clearly see the large black eyes and fearsome jaws with the yellow legs hanging basket-like below their bodies as they flew even higher. Then a prevailing breeze seemed to catch their interest and, orientating themselves to the south, they rapidly disappeared into the darkening sky.

Targas released his breath wondering what part they would play, if any. Lan sighed near him. "Should that be a sign, I wonder, for they go the same way we must in but a short while."

Supper that night was a sombre affair as if it was the last they would be sharing. The food was eaten casually by people sitting in small groups on benches and bunks throughout the large mess room. Someone was singing a low, appealing song which had a sombre, blue-green emanation. The words floated through the quiet room.

Targas was in a subdued mood when the singer's voice faded away. Sleep soon came in the peaceful atmosphere.

Chapter Thirty-Three

Heritis gritted his teeth as a familiar odour drifted up the stairs. "Why Septus, I didn't expect you to have recovered so soon."

"Soon?" Septus's voice echoed from the circular stair well. His head appeared from the gloom, a glistening of sweat contributing to his face's unhealthy pallor. "You expect me to stay in the bowels of the castle, while anything worth knowing is up here?" He dragged his wounded leg up the final steps, before sitting to catch breath.

"News…I want." Septus hawked and spat out a glob of phlegm on the flag-stone. "I'm not satisfied with last day's message."

Heritis looked distastefully at the man. "Why? What are you expecting?"

"Genur's report!" he snapped at Heritis, his eyes black holes in his face. "He knows I don't like to be kept waiting."

"Don't we all?" Heritis paused, while casually looking at the stairs leading in the direction of the scent collectors. "No…nothing from Genur. Bakis is up there still checking for me." He slowly turned to look down his aquiline nose at Septus. "And, you may not know that the Shada is sending us the Port Saltus troops as I requested, in spite of your *successful* campaign. Further, he requires your report on Genur's activities. I'm sure you won't want to keep the Shada waiting?"

Septus sat glowering in the dim light. A clatter of footsteps broke the silence.

"Shad!" called Bakis. "Oh, you're here too, Head," he added as he caught sight of Septus. "Nothing further this night…from Genur, I mean." He looked at Heritis. "Do you need to reply to the Shada?"

"No," he said. "Septus has to respond to the Shada, not me." He looked sideways and saw Septus obviously intent on staying. "Anything further, Bakis, any anomalies?"

"I was going on to mention, Shad," answered Bakis, "of something unusual in the limited collections from the north-east, around the Salt Way. The main motes that reached us were of ash, but there are traces of a sweet scent I can't quite determine. That's what I find unusual. Would you care to sample it?"

"Yes!" both Heritis and Septus answered. Heritis glared at Septus before following Bakis up into the scent trap room.

He held the sample to his nose, disregarding the background scents to focus on the ash and what lay beneath it. The sweet smell impinged on his olfactory centre without recognition. Heritis then caught a mote of odour hidden by the sweetness. He recognised the smell of burnt flesh, human flesh.

Septus limped up and pushed past in his haste to get at the sample. Heritis ignored him as he thought through the ramifications of what he had found. It could be merely harmless, or it could signal danger, linked as it was to the unknown odour.

He had a feeling that the arrival of the extra troops would not be soon enough.

The river, bloated with floodwaters, flowed towards the night-shrouded bulk of the city. Large, laden shapes rode the current, hiding beneath the water's misty breath. And the mist had become a fog spreading far beyond the river's banks, rolling gently over everything in its path. The city walls were no obstacle; the mists met, mounted and engulfed the buildings.

The watchers frowned at the fog. Some moved to waken others, concerned at the unusual movement of this *natural* event. But the alarm remained unsounded, concern fell away and the fog was accepted like any other, on any other day.

Heritis, having endured a restless night, moved closer to Regna's comfort and fell into a deeper sleep; his orders that anything out of the ordinary be reported immediately were not followed.

But one was nearly awake, his long nose twitching, a lifetime of paranoia keeping his sleep at a light level. His leg pained, throbbing where the point of the knife had hit bone. His mind twisted at the pain and, at the height of his restlessness, became suspicious of the subtle aroma entering his nostrils and whispering quiet, sleepy thoughts.

A group of seven barges drifted against the interlinked wooden beams designed to bar river traffic from entering the garrison city. The Sanctus scent masters' concentration had not wavered. Targas had stretched his powers to the limit, to provide the constraining link binding the natural odours with the soporific and calming scents controlled by the scent masters. Binding and holding such essences with water vapour and extending it over the bulk of a city was exhausting. He vaguely wondered whether the edges of the fog were already unravelling.

Men jumped off the barges, quickly bound the sleeping guards and then opened the barrier. Once through, the barges drifted to the castle before being secured to the mooring rings set in the carved stones along the bank. Targas saw little of what was happening while he maintained his concentration. He was led onto the river pathway and up wide castle steps in a knot of scent masters. Their target was the castle, making up a considerable part of the western side of the city. Their task was to neutralise any enemy scent masters present.

S eptus sat up, instantly alert, defensive shields automatically in position. He shivered as he quickly dressed in his black robe, belt containing pouch and knife, and pulled on his boots. He stood with difficulty and limped to the window, not noticing the ghostly dribbles of mist oozing through cracks into the dark room. Septus snatched open the shutters allowing the fog to roll in, lightened by the first hints of the rising sun, and sniffed for anything unusual.

He quivered at finding distant smells, strong, insidious scents masked within the fog, seeking to penetrate his shielding. The technique showed powerful scent mastery.

Septus hesitated, uncertain before shuffling to the door, opening it and slipping along the stone wall, dark against dark.

Chink, chink, a noise echoed through the mists ahead and soft footfalls accompanied it. He merged against the corridor wall using masking odour. A group of men hurried past, unknown scent masters with them. Septus breathed out once they had gone, and moved on. He resisted his natural urge to punish the intruders, realising he needed urgent support. He headed towards the room of Heritis, the most powerful scent master in the castle. Septus encountered groups of rebels, but no castle guards or servants. The rebels appeared to have entered the castle without resistance.

He had been sure that Genur had taken care of the rebels left at Salt Way and the mines, but he must have been wrong. Bit by bit, pieces of the puzzle dropped into place. The rebels at the Salt Way docks had no true scent masters amongst them, yet there were scent masters with each group he had seen. He had detected river people and others. He sorted through his olfactory memory and recognised northern scents from his recent patrol there. Disturbingly, these scents were now associated with power.

"Ah," he muttered, "the rebel dung have left their holes."

He tested the gloom as he neared Heritis's rooms. Scents and light came from the open doorway a short distance away. At first he anticipated Heritis was preparing a defence, but then he recognised the same scents that had accompanied the mists, and in greater strength.

His mind almost refused to accept what his senses were saying, that here was a power greater than any of them had encountered. Powerful enough that Heritis, one of the strongest scent masters in Ean, had been captured.

No! He shook his head, *Impossible.*

Septus blanketed himself with his strongest concealing shield and inched forwards.

The force had separated into small units, spreading out through the darkened corridors of the castle. Targas was with the group that was to capture—or kill, if there was no choice—the ruler of Regulus. The bargeman, Woll, was familiar with the castle layout from his many trips through the city, and led them towards Heritis's rooms.

Targas knew that Heritis was one of the enemy elite. He had been involved in the youngsters' capture, and with the sending of the troops that attacked the docks, but he felt no real antagonism towards him. Rumours were that the Shad was strong but fair in his dealings with the native peoples. Nevertheless, this was the domain of the enemy; it was from here that Luna had escaped.

The false fog had done its work and the castle was like a ghost ship. Guards had fallen asleep at their posts; even those with scent talent were taken by surprise and subsequently rendered powerless by scent plugs jammed into their noses. Occasional resistance was quickly overcome.

Their group reached the rooms without difficulty in the gloom of the pre-dawn, with only a few wall torches providing a dim light. They found the Shad and his consort still asleep, with no alarm web in place.

Woll readied his spear to drive through the sleeping man, but Lan held him back while motioning Lethnal and Brin forward. Targas helped them form a strong odour blanket. They manoeuvred it over Heritis and dropped it.

The man's reaction was swift, and violent. The blanket bellied outwards, while Targas winced and held on, pushing down harder and harder, tightening the scent bonds, squeezing them together to stop even the smallest mote from escaping.

"Only able t' do this 'cause he was asleep," gasped Brin. "Hold on, whatever yer do."

And Targas held on, concentrating to maintain the bonds and not be flung off by the struggling forms. He saw Woll drag out the woman next to Heritis and pull her away.

"Quick, Targas," called Lan as the struggles slowed, "make a small gap…near his nose."

"I'll try." Targas found Heritis's head and concentrated on creating a small tear in the bonds.

"Larger," gasped Lan. Then he pushed two scent plugs through the gap and into Heritis's nose. Heritis jerked violently. "That should hold him. Without his smell sense he should be controllable."

A glimpse of movement by the door warned Targas to strengthen his shield moments before an almighty *whumph!* of force crashed into him.

He yelled in agony as he bent in a sharp, backbreaking curve, instinctively firing back a sharp dart of odour as he hit the floor. Targas saw it stopped initially by the attacker's shields, before it began to penetrate. He pushed harder as he struggled to rise and confront his attacker, but the black, crooked figure vanished as quickly as it had appeared.

"Hold Targas," said Lan, grabbing him around the shoulders and helping him to steady against the pain. "He will be taken care of."

"But, don't you see?" he gasped. "That was him…the one who killed Luna. It was Septus."

"Then you are lucky he did not kill you too. You were fortunate," said Lan. "Now we have to take care of our prize here. Septus can wait."

As Targas tried to move, his back spasmed in pain, so he was forced to remain sitting on the side of the bed.

Septus fled down the dark corridor, crashing into a group of rebels in his path, slicing them with strengthened bands of odour in a blood-splattering show of power. As he stumbled down a flight of steep steps leading to the river he was unable to shake the fear that he was being followed. He had seen the stranger all the fuss was about and had had the opportunity to destroy him, but he had failed. He had felt the power of the man, a strange raw power that had stopped his killing blow and had almost penetrated his own shield. No, this Targ was a danger, and no doubt a significant factor in the attack on Regulus.

He had to get back to Nebleth and the Shada, and the power base from which to fight back. Together they would be able to destroy this Targ, and crush the rebellion.

Septus had reached the river at the bottom of the steps before he saw the rebels' shadowy barges, guarded by several dark figures. Despite his fear of the water, and what lived in it, he recognised a means of escape. With a twist of his mind, he formed and flung darts at the men, efficiently and quietly dispatching them. He then used his long, thin dagger to slash through the tether of the nearest barge, before furiously cranking open the giant floating beam that prevented river traffic from moving further down the river. Sweat trickled down his back as he worked, and his thigh wound throbbed in agony. When the gap between the beam and the bank was wide enough, he climbed onto the barge. The current quickly took hold and the huge craft edged through the gap. The speed steadily increased, but Septus took little notice as he focused on the water.

The rising sun revealed a grey and cloudy day with a slight breeze from the west that promised bad weather. He shifted with discomfort, stretching his leg to relieve some of the pain as the river pulled him along at a rapid pace southwards towards the capital.

Near midday, he caught a wash of emanations from a large troop of Sutanite soldiers moving northwards towards the garrison city.

"They'll have a hard time against the rebels and their scent masters," he muttered as he saw the dark mass of men and animals in the distance. He sighed and tried to make himself more comfortable on the hard seat. "But at least it'll give the rebels something to think about until they meet the real power."

Buoyed by his own words and the realisation that Heritis was now out of any calculation in Ean's future, he let the river take him to Nebleth.

Chapter Thirty-Four

Zahnal pushed her fingers hard into Targas's back until something cracked. "Uhh," he yelled, gripping the bedcover with both hands.

"Don't be a baby. It shouldn't be hurtin' a big, strong man like you,' Zahnal said as she continued manipulating the length of his spine.

Targas bit into the cloth to stifle his groans.

"You were very lucky, young man," mused the healer as she worked. "You obviously bent to almost breaking. I'd like to suggest a day or two of rest, but you young folk usually take no notice of us olds." She stopped her pushing and gave Targas an embarrassing whack on his buttocks. "That's all I can do; there's many more who need my help this day. Good fortune to you."

Targas slowly rolled over and sat up with a wince. He was keen to see how the assault had ended. Although it had been successful, he knew there had been a few casualties. Sadir was currently assisting the healers working on the injured; her skills as a healer had been growing with use. The process of securing their position and preparing for expected counterattacks would be in full swing.

He edged his legs over the side of Heritis's bed and stood, stretching carefully to test the results of Zahnal's work before easing his clothes on. Targas realised he had been in no shape to pursue Septus, despite the need driving him; Zahnal's work had shown that. As he shuffled to the door he saw a burly bargeman he vaguely recognised.

"Cer," the man said, a tight smile stretching his grim face, "Yer t' come with me."

"Fine, err…" replied Targas.

"Stakol, Cer, we met at th' mines. Just come this way." Targas followed by keeping his eyes focused on Stakol's back, putting one foot in front of the other, trying to ignore the pain in his back. Zahnal's ministrations had helped, but his spine was still tender from Septus's attack.

He slowly climbed a set of stairs that curled upward, dark and narrow, then along a short, open walkway until he entered a circular room reminding him of a bell tower from back home in Tenstria. Natural light streamed in through four short, brick pipes that pierced the stone wall to end in a series of baffles in the centre of the room; the ceramic pipes were aligned at right angles to each other. As his eyes adjusted, he noticed several people standing by an open door opposite him.

"Cers," said Stakol, "Targas is here."

"Thank you, Stakol," said Lan.

"Cers." The bargeman bent his head towards Lan and then Targas, before disappearing the way he'd come.

"Targas, I think you should see this," continued Lan.

Targas edged past the baffles. "Is this place what I think it is?"

"It is the scent tower," responded Lan. "You have the honour to be standing in the nerve centre of Regulus, where the spider sits in its web sifting the odours of Ean. But enough: I want you to see this."

"What, Lan?" asked Targas as he squeezed next to him, receiving a brief nod of greeting from Brin and the usual stare from Quonir. He looked at Lan. "Where's Lethnal?"

"She's supervising the placement of our people around the city. Now we have the castle, we have to weed out any potential enemies," said Lan. "However, our real concern is outside the city to the south."

Targas looked to where Lan was pointing. The midday sun was a watery presence in an overcast sky. The city and its surrounds lay below their vantage point at the highest part of Regulus. The greys of the sky coloured the landscape and the hills, which stretched into mountains to the west and east. Ahead they could see the Great Southern emerging from the gut of the city like a long, curving drain, the colour of lead, and a mirroring, paved road on the western bank. A strong northeasterly wind added its cold influence.

"There," said Brin urgently jabbing with his arm, "can yer see it?"

Targas's eyes, now accustomed to the monotone of colours, could see a dark line on the horizon that appeared to be flickering and moving as he watched.

"That," emphasised Brin, "is our next challenge."

"Yes," said Lan. "Jakus has given us something else to think about. We must prepare accordingly, once we have sorted out friend from foe within the city."

Most of the citizens of Regulus were neutral, while some few readily aided the rebels. Those scent-tested as loyal to the Sutanite regime were kept in a number of secure areas, while the most dangerous, including Heritis and Regna, had been incarcerated in the castle dungeons. The blocking of the scent talent of such prisoners was done on a temporary basis by pushing powerful odour pads into the nostrils to overwhelm the olfactory centre. A more permanent solution had to wait.

"I must go," Lan sighed, "and see how the organisation is proceeding. You can stay here with Quonir, Targas. Get a better perspective on what faces us, eh?"

Lan and Brin disappeared to help with the organisation of the city's defences. Targas remained with Quonir on the parapet watching the steady advance of the troops. They did not speak.

The cold wind had gained in strength, causing his eyes to water, and making it even harder to see the line of the enemy on the horizon. Suddenly Quonir glanced pointedly up at the scent tower opening facing south towards Nebleth, then turned on his heel and brushed past Targas to head down the stairwell. Though his aura was tight, it was apparent the man still held a grudge.

Targas sighed and squatted down behind a parapet to shelter from the wind. He pushed against the brick wall, trying to relieve his stressed back.

"Ah," groaned Targas as Sadir stooped to put a welcome arm his neck. Lethnal followed and sat on the other side of him.

"Hello Targas," said Sadir, "we were told we'd find you here." She started to massage his neck muscles. "You've been fighting that haggar's dung; did you injure him?"

"No, he got away. Scurrying back to his master, I expect." Targas looked at Lethnal hopefully. "There's no way he'd be with them, is there?"

Lethnal stood and looked at the advancing troops. "It is a sight to make you think, isn't it?" She breathed gustily through her nose and mouth for a few moments. "No, I don't think I can detect him. This wind dissipates the scents and makes it very hard to pick any specific odours at this distance, but they seem to be regular guardsmen, not many scent masters. If I'd hazard a guess, I'd say they were not an assault army but sent as a support for the Regulus forces, since they'd have set out before they knew of our attack. In fact, it seems like they are still unaware of our taking of the city… It's a wonder if they haven't been warned." She turned to Targas. "Didn't we find that Septus had fled towards Nebleth?"

"From what I've heard," answered Targas.

"Then Septus must've met those troops," continued Lethnal, "but it doesn't seem he's told them. That is puzzling."

"Lethnal," said Sadir, interrupting her, "I heard one of the barges is missing so it could be that Septus escaped on the river. Wouldn't my Kyel be at Nebleth too?"

"I'd expect so," she nodded, not noticing her panicked expression, "I'd expect so." She stood. "I must go to Lan with our suspicions on the enemy troops. I'll leave you two here. You can keep watch if you like."

Targas nodded.

After Lethnal had left Sadir squatted next to Targas, watching the thin, dark line in the distance.

"Ow!" she shrieked. "Careful with those claws."

"I'd forgotten about Tel, Sadir," said Targas, "I can see that he wants to come to me."

"You're welcome to have him," said Sadir. "He's heavy and insists on being inside my top."

As Targas helped the lizard go under his coat, he recollected how long he had known Tel and his master, and pondered what might have been happening to Kyel.

"What are we going to do about my brother?" asked Sadir, as if reading his thoughts. "I don't think the Sanctus masters are focussed on him." She squeezed Targas's arm. "So, what are we going to do?"

"I'm worried as well, Sadir. I've a mind to…"

"Yes Targas?"

"I'd like to try ourselves," said Targas. "You know, sneak in and rescue him."

"Do you think we could?" she asked. "What about Lan and the others? They won't let us."

"Yes, Sadir, you're right, but I think we're owed plenty." Targas nodded to himself. "Yes, we're owed."

"**W**hat!" screamed Jakus, veins cording his neck. A darkening aura warned Septus. He threw up a barrier to stop the odour blast, but still tumbled to the floor. Jakus peppered darts at the man, bouncing off his shield, raising dust and rock fragments from the stone floor.

Septus waited for a pause, then sent a thin pulse back at Jakus, shaking the Shada's shield.

"Ah!" exclaimed Jakus. He shook his head and peered at Septus, as if suddenly becoming aware of him. "Blast you, Septus, you blood's spawn; why are you here, leaving my city to those scum?"

From his position on the floor, Septus glared at Jakus. "As if I had a choice," he snarled. "It's your useless cousin you should be blaming. He let them get in. I tried my best, even though I was injured."

"Yes, and we all know which little girl did that to you," sneered Jakus. "Another failure!"

Septus slowly got to his feet. "You're always quick to accuse."

"All right," Jakus said, "let's think. Obviously, the Port Saltus troops wouldn't have reached the city in time, but you've, no doubt, informed them what's happened. They'll be able to hold the rebels at Regulus; don't you agree?" Jakus's eyes narrowed at Septus's blank face. "They do know, don't they?"

"How could I tell them?" Septus retorted. "I was on that haggar-ridden river and only just made it to Nebleth."

"Blood's stink! Yet another excuse," growled Jakus, his face whitening as he pulled his black robes tighter around himself and took a step forward.

"But I met your Targ," said Septus quickly. "Fought him. Hurt him."

Jakus stopped abruptly. "What's he like?" he demanded. "How damaged was he?"

"Not sure, only saw him side on; I was one against many. But he was in the middle of rebel scent masters. And I hurt him."

"Hmmm." Jakus looked hard at Septus. "Come, we've both been upset. Let's go to the meeting room and determine how to deal with this crisis. You go ahead. I'll be there shortly." Jakus strode off towards the guards' rooms in the lower level of the tower.

"Find Rancer!" he demanded of the first guardsman he met.

The man clattered off to find the master guardsman. Jakus followed, descending the steps to the large guard hall.

"Shada?" a large, heavily-built man puffed as he approached, his grey tunic tightly straining against his belly as if the wide black belt was the only thing stopping the seams from bursting.

"Rancer, I want a messenger to head for Regulus on the fastest animal. He's to make contact with our Port Saltus troops. Make sure they know the rebels have taken the city. Tell them to avoid any fighting until our reinforcements arrive."

"Shada?"

"What don't you understand? I...want...to tell them not to try and retake the city from those blood-cursed rebels. To wait for reinforcements!"

"Yes, my Shada." Rancer stiffened.

"Then," he continued, "meet me back in my rooms." Jakus swung on his heels and climbed back up the stairs. He hesitated before walking towards the teaching area. "Akerus," he called, pushing open the door.

A sea of young faces looked up as he entered. "Akerus, cancel the classes. You're needed." Jakus then glanced over at the acolytes. "Kyel. Here. Now."

Kyel scrabbled up from his seat and hurried over to Jakus.

"Come with me." He clapped his arm on Kyel's shoulder and walked him from the room. "I've news," he spoke quietly. Kyel looked up, face blank.

"Your Targ," said Jakus, as he released a compulsion odour, "has been fighting in Regulus and hurting people in the city. Why did you help him? Why?" He squeezed Kyel's shoulder.

"What?" Comprehension suddenly came and tears burst from Kyel's eyes to run down his face. "I don't...know why," he suddenly sobbed, "I really don't."

Jakus gave a grim smile as he rushed Kyel along the corridor.

"I think, by the size of that army, Lan's going to be fairly busy, but we can't stay up here all day. Besides, I don't like the look of the weather." Targas glanced again at the thickening clouds now riding the winds from the Sensory Mountains in the west.

Sadir entered the scent tower, followed closely by Targas, grateful to get out of the wind. They avoided the strong drafts of air pouring through the odour trap openings and descended to the next level, which emerged out of the tower onto a high-walled parapet. A number of rebels were walking along the wide path behind the wall, keeping an eye on all the approaches to the city, especially towards the Sutanite army in the south. Targas saw a Sanctus scent master and struggled to place her.

"Hello Targas, Sadir," she said. "You've been watching as well?"

"Oh, Hynal," replied Targas, recalling the familiar aura of the tall, pleasant-looking woman with short, fair hair. "I'm sorry, but Sanctus seems so long ago."

"We've all been busy," smiled Hynal, "and all had our part to play. Maybe we will have more happier times in the future if this"—she waved her arm at the approaching army—"is soon resolved. I'm pleased to see you both. Oh, and Sadir, good fortune to you." Hynal turned to keep her vigil on the parapet.

A series of stairs led down into a huge internal hall, its roof supported by solid wooden beams sited at regular intervals. Natural light filtering in through slits in the upper walls, together with numerous burning torches, helped relieve the gloom. People, in small groups or on various errands, filled the space.

Targas stopped halfway down the stairs. "I think Lan'll be where the largest group is," nudged Sadir, "over there."

Targas could see the Sanctus leader organising the defence of the city. Excitable people hovered around him, like bees around honey. "Better see if we can help; we've been lucky to keep out of the way until now."

They reached the bottom of the stairs and threaded their way over. Lan looked tired, and was involved in a heated discussion with several scent masters.

People rushed off and others replaced them while Targas and Sadir waited. Lan suddenly caught sight of them.

"Wondered where you'd got to," he said. "Just a moment." He turned and gave instructions to a miner and bargeman, who both immediately hurried off. "Contrary to what you are thinking, we know what we are doing... Planned this for some time, we have," Lan said. "But"—he took a deep breath—"no time to talk, sorry, unless it is vitally important." Targas shook his head. "I will find someone, if that is all right?" Lan looked around. "Ah, Ginrel...take them and tell them what is happening." He smiled apologetically at Targas and turned his attention to Lethnal, who had just arrived, looking worried.

"You didn't have time," whispered Sadir, holding on to Targas's shoulder.

"Don't worry, we'll organise something if we can," said Targas quietly. "He's too busy to be bothered at the moment. Ginrel," he nodded at the bargeman leader.

Ginrel, who was slightly stooped and lean, with a weather-beaten face, grabbed Targas by the sleeve. "Come this way, I think we're better out of th' fuss." He led them to a quieter corner of the hall out of the traffic and sat them down on a convenient wooden bench.

"Well?" asked Targas, "what's happening, and what should we be doing?"

"Reckon there's little yers can do because things, though yer might not believe it, are under some sort of control." Ginrel pushed back against the stone wall, stretched his legs out and looked up at the smoke-stained ceiling. His prominent adam's apple bobbed as he continued. "We was lucky that th' city was taken so easily. We've rooms full of prisoners—Sutanite scent makers 'nd soldiers—'nd th' rest of th' people are for us, or least not against us," he sighed. "No, Regulus is not th' problem, nor them troops out there." He looked back to Targas and Sadir. "They can't stand against our scent masters, yerself too, without any of their own. No, th' problem's that nest of Sutanites t' th' south. It's Nebleth where they are, even though Port Saltus ain't free of them." He said thoughtfully, "Nebleth, that's th' problem."

Chapter Thirty-Five

Jakus had the army assemble in the courtyard of Nebleth tower. It was an elite force designed to travel light and fast to bolster the Port Saltus troops already near the walls of Regulus.

Over one hundred and fifty people filled the courtyard, including all available seekers, acolytes nearing seeker status and twenty full scent masters. The loss or capture of a considerable number of scent-talented people at Regulus was significant but, Jakus believed, not insurmountable. The enemy would fail when faced with a determined opposition and be destroyed. Rancer was to lead his guardsmen, Strona the scent masters and Jelm the seekers, while he oversaw the total force. His scent masters, each a specialist in their own right, gave him considerable back-up. He felt a thrill of anticipation as he prepared to meet this unknown force and the rebel scent masters who were challenging his rule; Targ would be an especially rewarding challenge.

Septus remained behind to supervise the defence preparations of Nebleth. Jakus was slightly annoyed he would not have the benefit of his head seeker's power, but found the excuse of the leg wound almost plausible.

A drizzle was falling when they left the tower. They rode on through the streets, scattering those hardy folk out in the weather, pouring out of the northern gate like a black-and-grey ribbon rolling across a wet landscape. The troops gave the perac their heads and advanced at speed along the roadway.

"We will not stop; we must be at Regulus by nightfall," commanded Jakus, knowing that it might be a difficult task if the rain strengthened.

Septus leant over the balcony of Jakus's room watching the departure of the Shada. He smiled to himself, content to be in charge of the Nebleth defence. Whether Jakus would succeed as easily as anticipated was debatable, since the rebel force that took Regulus seemed competent. How important Targ was also remained an unknown, but Jakus may soon find out, he reflected.

A familiar, feminine scent hit his nostrils as footsteps sounded behind him. He was gratified to feel his manhood harden, proving that the wounding hadn't damaged him.

"Septus?"

He turned to see Nefaria, Jakus's consort, coming onto the balcony.

"What are you doing in the Shada's room?" She looked down and recoiled as she saw the bulge in the front of his robe. "Ugh, you're a detestable man."

Septus reacted by exuding a tendril and winding it around Nefaria's neck. Then he pushed up, causing her to stand on her toes, head tilted back, eyes bulging.

"You"—droplets of spittle flew onto her face—"have no right to speak like that. You're nothing but a piece of ripe flesh to be used...as I see fit!" Septus pushed his face so close that she gagged on his breath. Then he gripped one of her breasts and twisted until she cried out.

"You're just lucky you're too old for me, but"—he released his hold and she crumpled to the floor—"I might just take you here and now." Septus pushed his foot between her legs as he stood glaring down at her, before swinging on his heels and limping from the room.

She lay there crying with the pain.

"Nefaria," said a familiar voice, "are you all right? Did that black k'dorian hurt you?"

"N...no, I'm fine, Kyel." She struggled to get up. "Stay there; don't help."

"He hurt you, didn't he?" accused Kyel. "Just wait till Jakus gets back, he'll fix him."

"Let's just keep this between you and me, please?" she pleaded.

Kyel looked hesitant, as if he did not understand her. "If you're certain..."

"Please. Jakus has enough to worry about, and we'll just keep out of Septus's way, right?"

It was early nightfall when the force met up with the Port Saltus troops some distance from the southern city gates. Jakus called them to a halt, ignoring the effusive welcome of Daltir, the commander of the Port Saltus troops while he studied Regulus.

Animals and men moved around him as he tried to sort through the scent signatures of the city, assessing the general mood of the people, the enemy and the emotions generated. An overall feeling of unease disappointed him. He sighed and dismounted to the task of sorting out the integration of both forces.

Targas and Sadir finally cornered Lan as he took a quick rest with a steaming cup and a platter of food. The merging of the two enemy forces, now camped off to the south of the city, had caused an increase of activity inside Regulus, so it had been hard to catch up with him.

"Hello Targas...Sadir," said Lan. "Come, sit and we'll talk. I am sorry I have been so busy, but we all have our burdens."

They sat each side of Lan at his small table.

"We're very worried about Kyel," began Targas. "He's still in Nebleth as far as we know... Who can tell what's happened to him? We must get him back."

"I'm sorry for the youngster, Targas, Sadir. I appreciate you want to get him back, but my priority has to be making the most of any advantage we have. We are safely in Regulus, a good defensive position, and the enemy is encamped outside, and in the rain too," he nodded. "That is, and must be, our priority."

"I really can't wait, Lan. Kyel is part of the only family I have in Ean and I have to try to get him back. You say I've helped you win this fight and you're now in a position of strength, so I want to do something for Sadir and myself."

"Let me think on it, Targas. I respect your wishes and will do what I can." He began to eat his meal, signalling the end to the discussion.

Targas returned with Sadir to their seat against the wall to discuss the layout of the country, and how best to reach Nebleth, if rescuing Kyel was a possibility. Tel rested on the bench and kept looking between them. Perhaps it was Tel's presence that influenced him. He had let events take him to this point, but now he wanted something.

"We'll go, despite what Lan and the others may say," he said in a quiet voice. "We owe it to ourselves."

Sadir agreed. "It may not be sensible, but we need to, for us and Kyel...and Luna, too."

He sat, elbows on his knees, looking at the rough stone floor at his feet and nodded slowly. Sadir's arm slipped gently across his shoulders. Targas reached up and took her hand.

A short time later they saw an opportunity to put their proposal to the Sanctus inner council.

"Let's go," prompted Sadir, "we'll never get a better chance."

"You're right," agreed Targas, a little reluctantly, "although I don't know how Quonir will react. He still seems to have it in for me."

"Don't worry," she said, taking his hand, "he might be hard to deal with, but I reckon his heart's in the right place."

"Fine," he nodded, "let's do it."

Lan raised his eyebrows as they approached, but allowed them to put their proposal without comment. Targas prepared for some reasoned argument against them but there was little reaction, just an acceptance of what they said. Surprisingly, it was Lan who most supported their case.

"I cannot say I approve of your decision, but I can understand it. If you are going ahead, then you should do it now. We believe that most of the remaining Sutanite forces is concentrated out there, and most likely Jakus himself, although we cannot be sure, given the weather." Lan paused and looked around the small table.

"Come, Lan," interrupted Quonir in an abrupt manner, although his odours were tightly controlled, "tell them why we are supporting their idea. No? Then I will. Your friend there"—he nodded towards Lan—"is a planner, and when you said you wanted to rescue your youngster, he naturally thought how to best use the situation. And unfortunately, we agree, if you do too, of course."

"What do you mean?" asked Targas, puzzled at the lack of opposition to their idea, in particular with Quonir's apparent support.

"It's quite simple really," Quonir continued. "If—and I mean *if*—you succeed in your quest, you could prove to be a distraction, perhaps a significant one, which would help our cause."

"I see," Targas murmured.

"All right, my friend, I was going to tell them, of course I was," said Lan, glancing at Quonir.

"There is no doubt," Lan continued, "we would prefer to have your skills at our disposal, Targas, but it may be that a small group slipping into Nebleth could have value. We have plans in place for this night that, if our river folk carry it off, should cause problems for their army. With a favourable outcome here, Nebleth must be our next target. So, your plan to rescue Kyel has the potential to distract the enemy there. You are powerful for a new scent master. You are unpredictable, which will be to your advantage, that and the size of your group. We all have a final part to play in defeating these tyrants and your part may—and my feeling is strong—be crucial."

"We agree." Targas looked at Sadir's tight face. She nodded. "Then we'll have to leave soon. Who should go with us?"

"I suspect…you need a least two strong men, and another supporting scent master," said Lan, scratching his chin as he thought.

"We can afford no more!" interjected Quonir, his face grim.

Targas glanced at him. "What about Hynal? We met her earlier."

"Ah, yes, Hynal is very competent," said Lan, looking at his fellow scent masters. "What do you think?"

Quonir opened his mouth, then said nothing.

"If she's willing," said Lethnal.

Brin nodded slowly.

"I would say that it is agreed, then, if Hynal is prepared for such a dangerous venture." Lan took Sadir and Targas's hands. "My friends, it will be hazardous, but something deep within me knows the significance of it."

As Targas and Sadir left to find Hynal they didn't notice an animated discussion between Lan and Quonir. Quonir left soon after and climbed the stairs that led towards the parapets and the scent tower.

S adir and Targas saw Hynal in the great hall. "I'll talk to her if you like," Sadir said. "Fine," nodded Targas. "I'll track down Woll, as he'd be useful for us."

Hynal smiled in greeting and took Sadir's arm. "Let's go and get some soup," she suggested, "I can see you've got something to say."

They settled in a quiet corner of the hall while Sadir explained what they were planning. Hynal frowned at the proposal, but soon brightened. "Yes, I can come. I'm familiar with the country and like to think I'd be a match for whatever they can throw at us. Yes," she said, leaning forward and giving Sadir a hug, "together we'll be a match for anything."

T he plan was to take a circuitous route to Nebleth. Going by the river was not possible due to the proximity of the Sutanite army on the west bank, so they were to travel in a small, discrete party on the eastern side. The size of their party and the fact that they were travelling in rugged terrain at night would be to their advantage.

Soon they were standing beside their perac, ready to leave. In addition to themselves and Hynal, their group included Stakol and Woll. Woll had agreed to be the local who accompanied them: as he said, "It were me duty t' look after Luna 'nd what she cared for, 'nd I'm goin' t' see it through."

Targas appreciated having this solid, resolute man and his equally committed fellow bargeman as companions on the journey. Hynal was a full scent master and Sadir was pleased to have her with them. Their group, Tel notwithstanding, was hopefully competent enough to slip through the enemy's defences and into Nebleth.

"The rain may be uncomfortable, but it will also help conceal you," said Lan. "Remember, we will be aware of your venture and once we have fought our own battles, will come to you. Other than that you will be relying on your own resources. May the scent be on your side." Lan moved back to the rest of the inner council. Brin and Lethnal smiled sadly. Quonir remained grim faced.

T hey rode steadily and quietly down the eastern bank of the Great Southern with Targas, Hynal and Sadir maintaining a concealing scent cover over the group. As they moved away from the river and into the dark night, the rain increased, slanting down into their faces and making travel even more uncomfortable.

" D oes this place always have to rain?" asked Targas, after they had been travelling for a time. "Since I've been here I've been regularly rained on, and I'm sick of getting wet."

"It's the season, Targas," said Hynal, her tall figure anonymous under a grey hood. "It'll change to snow soon. At least we're heading downriver, towards the sea. It's not as cold or wet there."

Targas looked around at the others hunched over their perac, vague shadows in the night. He felt the comfort of Tel inside his coat.

They remained off the marked towpath, using the thicker vegetation and more rugged country as cover; the enemy would be keeping a close watch over the land between Regulus and Nebleth.

The prevailing breeze had strengthened, pushing any of their stray scents away and into the mountains, but the growing storm was already showing signs of interrupting the wind pattern, making control of the party's emanations even more important.

Several times they caught strange scents wafting from the western side of the river, revealing enemy movements. It made them even more paranoid over their own scent trail.

"Weather gettin' worse," commented Woll. "We'll be gettin' soaked. Suggest we keep goin' though, as it's th' best time for keepin' hidden."

"Not much choice," responded Targas. "How far from Nebleth are we?"

"A while; just gettin' t' th' foothills for now; keep on till we have t' rest."

They moved on in the half-light, keeping an anxious eye on the thickening clouds overhead. Bursts of lightning flashed over rows of mountains extending across the vast distance to the west, and illuminated the dark ribbon of the river making its way towards Nebleth and the sea.

"That river's th' best way t' go. This walkin's for perac 'nd lizards. Still, we must do what we must," sighed Woll. "We best push on."

The rain increased in intensity as anticipated, aided by a blustery wind that pushed into their faces and made attempts at scent control almost futile. They tried to avoid detection by moving as fast as possible through the foothills of the Main Belt Range and ignoring their discomfort.

With their hooded heads down to allow most of the runoff to fall onto their already wet perac, they became inured to the animals' strong odour; everything squelched and the vague trail became lost in the mists of water. Woll eventually called a halt.

"It'll be dark fer some time," he said. "We've still got some cover from th' trees, so we'll stop 'ere. We'll be wet, we'll be cold, but we should be safe."

They huddled together against their animals. Coats and blankets kept some of the moisture out and the heat in, but it did little to lighten their mood. They ate sparingly of cold meats and dried fruit before falling into an exhausted sleep.

Chapter Thirty-Six

Septus's black form laboured between the lights of the flickering torch flames along the ramparts around the tower. He was filled with nervous energy, and the coming storm added to it.

Storms fascinated Septus, not only for the myriad of odours they bore but also for the sheer power they wielded. It was every scent master's fantasy to be part of such a climatic event, to be able to hold the strings of such majesty and bend it to his will. However, such was the stuff of dreams. The magnesa-heightened euphoria of scents torn from a dying body was as close as he could get, but the desire was a compelling one. Therefore, the scent tower ramparts were the place to be when the storm hit. It brought unexpected odours smashing into the senses, driven by an overwhelming power. Eyes closed, he raised his arms into the tempest and imagined conjuring thick tentacles of odour pouring forth, targeting his enemies, carrying off the largest of armies so all would know his power and bow to his will.

The main body of the storm had passed before a rain-lashed, dishevelled Septus staggered down from the ramparts to Jakus's rooms, breath coming in gasps. Even having been through crackling thunder, arcing electricity and a whirlwind of enticing odours he was unsated by the storm and debated whether to stay and seek out Jakus's woman to relieve his desires. He ran a long pallid tongue along his lips.

Akerus burst into the room.

"What!" snapped Septus at the agitated scent master.

"Head. You'd better come and assess this," Akerus said, his aura signalling high excitement.

Septus followed Akerus back up the stairs and entered the scent tower to sift through and analyse the complex collection of odours. Then he discovered a message, amongst the multitude of scents, the linking bonds making it instantly identifiable as a direct communication from a scent master.

He recognised Regulus as its origin, but there the familiarity ended. A taint of rebel was interwoven with motes, indicating the eastern Main Belt mountains, perac, several people and southerly travel. Then his heart quickened as a scent stood out in the message, like a beacon, a scent moving towards Nebleth. It was Targ, the unknown and powerful scent master. Septus recognised it from when he had attacked him at Regulus, but confirmed it with an aura recognition he had detected in the scent memory of his young victim, Luna.

He concentrated, trying to squeeze the last details from the communication. Indications that the rebels were travelling on the eastern side of the Great Southern made sense since the Sutanite army was on the west, but what he couldn't detect was who had sent the message. There was no clue, other than it had been constructed without the usual Sutanite signature. *Ah,* he thought gleefully, *they have a traitor in their midst.*

"Is that him?" Akerus asked, recognising Septus's excitement. "He's coming, isn't he?"

"Yes!" said Septus. "I don't know who sent the message, or even why"—he jerked his finger towards the collection tray—"but we mustn't ignore it. He'll not be far from the eastern bounds of Nebleth, across the river and in the foothills of the ranges. We must prepare. Now! You come with me!" ordered Septus, as he turned and left the tower, his injury causing him to hobble down the stairs in his haste. "We will prepare a welcome for Targ that he'll never forget."

Septus sent a guardsman to assemble a small force, before returning to find Akerus still descending the scent tower stairs.

"Akerus!" snapped Septus.

"What the..." reacted Akerus, as he almost stumbled. "Sorry, Head. I was just narrowing the location so we'll be able ascertain roughly where they should be. It will aid us in picking up their scents in the dark. Also, the rain's stopped, but I anticipate a fog developing."

"Ah!" replied Septus curtly. "A fog. Good. It'll be just the carrier we need. This time we will take him and maybe"—his face twisted—"destroy this rebel uprising once and for all."

"Ahem," Akerus nervously cleared his throat.

"What!" bellowed Septus.

"P...pardon, Head," he stammered, "but the Shada will want to...ah... question this Targ directly... He won't want him damaged."

"Don't dare question me," Septus glared at the scent master. "I intend to take him alive. And, get another scent master. Manis will do," he ordered. "We have a trap to prepare, and a place to set it."

Septus, together with Akerus, Manis and two guardsmen set off from the eastern side of Nebleth, situated on the far bank of the Great Southern. A light mist hung in the air, infiltrating their clothing as they rode through the night. They had the advantage of clear air, since the rain had cleaned most of the scents from the atmosphere, enabling them to concentrate on the region before them. The bulk of the mountains and the tumble of odours that all things made gave them a clear direction, aided by the additional analysis Akerus had carried out in the tower. They finally reached a wide gully where drifts of scents indicated a small party not far away.

Septus had difficulty remaining calm, determined that this time he would have the advantage and Targ would not avoid him.

"Near enough, I think. Akerus, you and Manis will prepare to use the fog."

Septus walked his perac a few paces before stopping. He looked briefly at the black shapes with him.

"Ready?"

"Yes, Head," both scent masters replied.

Septus took a small portion of the magnesa crystals, and then concentrated on pushing out calming and sleep-inducing scents into the mist; the more they could produce, the greater the effect. Having two helpers sped up the process, making it easier to force the scents on a wide front in combination with the fog around them.

Septus could feel, rather than see, their odour wall ahead of them and held it easily, employing a convenient light breeze to work for them. He started to push the wall into the area where the unsuspecting rebels lay.

They waited as the scents eddied and swirled through the gullies and surrounding slopes.

"Right, enough time I think. We'll take them. I won't tolerate any mistakes," growled Septus as he led them forward.

The emanations of the rebels grew stronger as they approached through the gloom. The sleep odour had now dissipated, so Septus and his party only had to concentrate on their footing.

No alarm system in place? A deadly mistake, he smiled.

The emanations coming from the sleeping people and perac were almost overwhelming. Apart from the background of damp and exhaustion, there were scents that could reveal much if he'd wanted to take the time. But he was interested in one thing only: a dark shape with a distinctly foreign aroma.

"Yesss," he hissed, "I have you now."

They paused at the mound of sleeping people and animals. Septus pulsed stronger sleep scents at the group until he was satisfied they would remain unconscious.

He leant forward to sip at the essences of the body he identified as Targ. Amid the plethora of attached rebel scents, he could detect a feminine aroma, linked to one of the women lying in front of him; also, a tang of lizard and a faint foreign odour that had an uneasy familiarity, similar to a Sutanite smell.

245

"Quick," he hissed to the two guardsmen, "bind him quietly. Tie him to a perac. When you've done that, take her as well." Septus pointed at Sadir's unconscious form. "I think she'll be of value."

"There's another woman," advised Akerus, as the guardsmen carried out Septus's orders.

"Hmmm," murmured Septus, his breath quickening. "Ah, she's a powerful scent master. Let's see what we've got!"

Septus reinforced the soporific scent before he bent down, pulled her over onto her back and gripped the front of her shirt. Hynal grunted, stirred as if wakening, and then relaxed into sleep, exposed and vulnerable. Septus stood above her, drinking in her essence.

"Shouldn't we just leave them?" interrupted Akerus. "They can't do us any harm."

"What? Leave them so they can follow and warn others?" hissed Septus. "No. Not possible."

He squatted across Hynal's hips, knees holding down her arms. She whimpered with the sudden pressure, but did not wake. Septus reached down to his belt and pulled out a long, thin dagger. "Too old for me, but useful," he chortled, drooling from his open mouth. His eyes tightened as he focused on her body. Then, without warning, he drove the dagger into her stomach.

Hynal's body arched upwards, her eyes flew open, saliva and scent gushed from her mouth in reaction. Septus slammed his free hand across her face while pulling down on the dagger. It ripped through her muscles to the pit of her abdomen, releasing a fountain of fluids. Septus bucked with the convulsions of her body, his face stretched in pleasure, laughing.

The swirls of scents gathering in the gloom almost overwhelmed him. As Hynal weakened, Septus fell across her onto the bloody outpourings of her abdomen.

Hynal's eyes bulged above the iron hand covering her mouth, the incandescent pain in her belly pulsing in sheets of fire through her body. The weight of her attacker held her down despite her reactions. She heaved desperately but a lassitude creeping over her limbs did not help. Death was moments away.

In a last convulsive reaction, Hynal pulled her arm from under Septus's knee and wrenched at his unprotected testicles. Septus screamed, clutched himself and fell away from her body.

Hynal sighed a last breath, her essences leaving her body in a gentle rush of soft, mellow colours and dissipating into the covering fog.

The euphoria of the scent master's odours left him. As the agony slowly subsided, he reached over to pull his dagger out of her stomach and punish her further, but she was already dead. Septus sat on his haunches, liquid dripping off his chin, unaware of his companions nearby.

A movement nearby snapped into his awareness; the other rebels were stirring.

"Quick," Septus yelped, "kill them!"

The two guardsmen moved fast, thudding their long spears into the awakening bargemen.

Woll staggered to his feet, pulling at the spear stuck in his side and dragging his surprised attacker to him. He flung an arm around the guardsman's neck and heaved with all the strength of his work-hardened muscles. The crack of the neck bones was loud.

Woll dropped the body in time to meet another spear driving into his midriff. He heaved on the weapon, seeking to trap the second attacker in the same way. However, he tripped over a body lying behind him, his friend Stakol, and fell to the ground. A heavy foot pressed on his chest as the guardsman yanked at his spear in Woll's stomach. Woll crashed a knuckled fist into the kneecap, causing his attacker to stumble across him. A powerful hand crushed the guardsman's throat.

Tears oozed down Woll's face as he lay trapped under the guardsman's body. "Sorry Cynth; don't want t' leave yer," he murmured. "Sorry."

"What now, Head?" Akerus ventured.

"So? We go. Do I have to spell it out?"

"No," replied Akerus, mounting his perac and tying the leads of those carrying Targ and the woman to his own.

"But Head," protested Manis, "what about our men and the other bodies?"

"Those failures?" he queried as they moved away. "No, they'd just slow me down. Leave them."

Chapter Thirty-Seven

The fog used by Septus regularly developed along the river at certain times of the year when conditions were cold and damp. While Septus used fog to ensnare Targas, the rebels had used it as well.

The city of Regulus, perched astride the Great Southern, looked as if a pall of gaseous waste had exited its bowels. The fog roiled out of the river as it passed under the city and joined the thinner mists already creeping from the waters along its length. The mists bellied out, moving across the paved highway and the grasses of the plains, looping over the forms of animals and men enduring the night.

The guards surrounding the large army looked at the fog with some trepidation, and then resignation, as it surrounded them. They knew that their scent masters would protect them, since it had been impossible to have the security of an alarm grid due to the number of people and animals. For their part, the scent masters on duty assessed the damp air, testing it for any rebel sign or any dangers it might pose. However, a long wet night, and the absence of any unusual odour, satisfied them and made them complacent. Jakus slept unaware in his tent.

But the fog coloured everything to shades of grey and made the pink of the haggar pack humping its way through the wet grass off-white, like the huge maggots they resembled. The sound of their movement was hushed by the blanketing mists as they moved unseen amongst the Sutanite army.

The numbing agent in the saliva of the haggars allowed the huge creatures to feed uninterrupted on their prey. As they moved among the sleeping men and animals, they fed undetected. When satiated they left the bodies and returned to the river.

A scream woke Jakus. He flung open his tent flap and saw a flurry of activity before him, the thick fog thinning even as he watched. He forced out a wall of odour to clear the fog from his vicinity, joining in with the efforts of his scent masters.

"Blood's stink!" he gasped as he saw the large forms looping away through the fog. He closed his eyes, doubling his efforts to push the misty covering from the creatures.

Jakus's mind was devoid of emotion as he worked. He couldn't allow himself the luxury of anger.

The rebels were taken too lightly, my scent masters, he thought. *There will be consequences. Be sure of that!*

The sun burning through the mists exposed the bodies littering the damp ground. Jakus considered the small group of nervous men assembled before him, his anger visible as a dull, dark cloud over his head. The noises of the wounded resounded around them.

"Report," he snapped at a guardsman.

"Shada." The man jumped to attention. "Uh, thirty dead and...fifty-seven wounded."

Jakus flung out his arm angrily. "Leave us."

The guardsman turned and hurried to rejoin his fellow soldiers, most of whom were busy attending the wounded and dead.

"You are the keepers and protectors of my army," said Jakus to the tense group of scent masters and seekers. "You are charged with the safety of my troops and with preventing attacks from any source. This is what you are trained to do." His voice was quiet. "We are here, against a formidable foe with unexpected resourcefulness. The mere fact they stand against us—behind the safety of our own city walls—is proof, even to the simplest of my men, let alone those of intelligence, those in command." He paused. "And without even one rebel dead we have effectively lost almost a quarter of our force." Jakus's face darkened. "Why? Because of your complacency, your underestimation of the enemy. That's why!"

Jakus looked towards the now benign river before continuing. "This is unacceptable! Those responsible are accountable. They will be punished!

"Rancer; Daltir," he yelled. "As the master guardsmen of the Nebleth and Port Saltus troops, you are responsible." There was an almost imperceptible movement of the remaining men away from the two singled out. "But they need not stand alone, for they are not scent masters. They were not ultimately responsible for guarding our troops. You!" he shouted, pointing at an older scent master, "Judal, you were in charge of our protection last night!"

Judal, the loose skin of his jowls shaking, fell to his knees with hands upraised, scalp pink against the black of his robes. "It was...wasn't just me Shada, I was..."

"Silence!" Jakus commanded, his gaze sweeping the men before him. "Do any of you accept responsibility?" He paused, his aura visibly thickening. "I thought not!"

Jakus focused on the three men, who hadn't seemed to notice their sudden separation from the remainder. He speared out a thin odour tendril, initially blocked by Judal with his automatic shield. However, Jakus forced it through, driving into the man's open mouth. Rancer and Daltir bent away, white-faced, while the odour tendril manoeuvred within Judal's internal organs, forcing the scent master into a macabre dance as his stomach distended. Jakus stopped his attack and let the body drop to the ground. Rancer and Daltir scuttled back to the group of horrified onlookers.

"Commanders will come to my quarters to consider our options. Now!" growled Jakus, sweat shining on his bald head. "And I want food," he snapped at a nearby acolyte as he walked towards the large tent. "Jelm. Strona. Make sure the army is on alert and then join me." He dropped his voice. "Failure," he hissed, "is intolerable."

Strona and Jelm snapped to attention and then hurried to carry out the Shada's orders.

A fast-moving perac and rider manoeuvring through the troops caught Jelm's attention, so he changed his course and intercepted the panting messenger.

"What news?" Jelm asked, but the messenger just shook his head and pointed towards Jakus's tent. "Come with me, then."

"Shada," he said, pushing open the tent flap, "this messenger's just arrived from Nebleth."

"Ah!" said Jakus, looking up from the map spread before him on a small table, "Your news, man. Spit it out!"

"S...Shada," gasped the man, almost bowing in his haste, "I've come as fast...as I could...as yer ordered...if anything special was happening..."

"What!" Jakus grew impatient.

"It's the Head, Shada," gasped the messenger. "He's caught the Targ."

"You're sure?" Jakus jumped up from the table and grabbed the messenger by the tunic.

The man nodded frantically until Jakus thrust him away.

"Did Septus tell you this?" Jakus barked.

"No, Shada, but I kept watch as you ordered."

"This changes things." Jakus's face tightened and he smacked his closed fist into his palm as he strode back and forth in the tent. "Yes, it changes things."

Jakus's elation at the news overshadowed all other considerations. The shadowy figure that had dogged him, the man who had been involved in the rebel uprising, causing the greatest losses the Sutanites had experienced in a generation, had been captured.

Targ's secrets, his power, his knowledge, will be mine. I'll not only be the most powerful scent master in Ean, but also in Sutan. Maybe, just maybe I could go even further...

"Shada?" A voice broke through his reverie.

"What?" he snapped at Jelm.

"The messenger has asked what you will have him tell the Head. You could leave now," he said, "be in Nebleth by midday, then back after sun down. We'll hold the rebels until your return."

"You're a fool if you think to command the army," growled Jakus. "I already know how well you can manage the rebels." He slumped down at the table and held his head in his hands. "No, not possible," Jakus shook his head.

"So be it, Shada. I'll tell the messenger to ask the Head to hold Targ until your return." Jelm swung around to the waiting man.

"No, blast you!" yelled Jakus, jumping up from his seat, "I must go to Nebleth; I have to. But, before I do we must determine a strategy for engaging the rebels until my return.

"Get Strona and those two useless master guardsmen in here!" He looked down at the map of Regulus, not noticing the glint in Jelm's eye.

"Here!" ordered Jakus when he heard Strona, Rancer and Daltir entering the tent, "I need your views on a strategy for Regulus." He looked up, noting the nervous odours of the two guardsmen before returning his attention to the map on the small camp table. "Well?"

Strona stepped half a pace forward. "Shada, am I to understand that you are returning to Nebleth?" Jakus gave the briefest of nods. "This would mean I'm to lead the attack on the rebels?"

"You, Strona, with Jelm to assist," Jakus snapped. "The other two will be keen to support you." He nodded towards the master guardsmen.

"And," said Jelm, before Strona could continue, "do you wish us to continue the attack immediately or hold the rebels until your return?"

"I intend being away only a brief time, but you may engage the rebels if you feel capable." He looked directly at Jelm and then Strona. "After all, they are not only bottled up in the city, but their chief weapon is now in our hands." He glanced down at the map of Regulus. "Yes, I think it may be a useful idea to show your worth, and your loyalty."

Jelm nodded calmly.

Many eyes watched the small group ride south at a furious pace. Some were apprehensive, some puzzled and one pair was relieved; for now, that his master had gone, Jelm would soon be able to drop the guise he had held for so long. Ever since he had taken the risk to rescue Luna, the pressure on his position had increased, and the Shada wouldn't hesitate to destroy anyone if he thought he had reason. The day's display of fury had been a reminder of the Shada's power.

Jelm felt sorry for Targ's predicament, even though they had never met, but the opportunity to remove the Shada from the field of combat was too good to miss. If he could manipulate the army, work against Strona and the others, he might turn the fate of the country around.

Chapter Thirty-Eight

The city had originally been a trading post sited to intercept the movement of goods between the hinterland of Ean and the coast. The mountains to the west and east acted as barriers, funnelling all traffic to the point where the Great Southern broke through. A wooden palisade had originally enclosed the town and later the city, but when the Sutanites came they established an impressive stone castle, topped by a scent tower, on the western bank of the river. The only southern gate into the city led through the castle. A single northern gate passed through the palisade into Regulus's business district.

The Great Southern River divided the city's homes from the castle and businesses. The river's path was barred by large, inter-linked wooden beams floating on the surface and a continuation of the palisade along its length; two arched bridges connected the city.

Though they had limited intelligence on the number and power of the rebels holding Regulus against them, Jakus had been confident the Sutanite army would be more than a match for the less experienced opposition. They had detected greatly diluted odours, indicating that prisoners were being held in the castle's dungeons while the rebels were concentrated in the castle, the most defensible position in the city. It was there the might of the Sutanite scent users had to be focused. They were battle-trained, unlike their opponents, and would be able to account for a determined opposition. The Shada had been certain that the simple expedient of surrounding the city with a mix of trained scent users and troops would entrap the rebels. Then a co-ordinated battle scent attack on the castle, the location of most defenders, would overwhelm those defences and give easy targets for the efficient slaying. He wanted it quick and brutal.

Jakus, torn between directing the attack and returning to Nebleth, had left once he was certain that his orders were understood. Strona, with Jelm and the two master guardsmen, Rancer and Daltir, were to work out the details and implement the plan.

Strona assumed command even before the Shada's small group had left the encampment, and was determined to precipitate the attack. There would be little subtlety to the assault, simply a matter of using overwhelming scent power to overrun and wipe out the rebels. The principal tactic would be to target the castle with the combined might of the scent masters and their seekers, supported by a force of battle-trained guardsmen. The remainder of the army, comprising acolytes, some seekers and troops would be forming a light cordon around the western half of the city, to the point where it was separated by the Great Southern. They were assuming the speed of their assault would not allow any counterattack from the eastern portion of Regulus, or from the water.

When Jelm tried to qualify Strona's ideas, by finding any way of hindering or altering the plan, the thin-faced woman irritatingly shook her head and refused his advice. Short of having an all-out row with her, Jelm was forced to appear co-operative and work towards implementing the Shada's directive. Jelm's concern was that while the Eanite rebels might be numerically superior in terms of scent masters, they were without the power of Targ and were mere novices in the art of war, particularly when faced with such ruthless opponents. The attackers might be without the power and cunning of Jakus but their strength was formidable. A successful result here could snuff out the rebellion forever.

Jelm had to do something, but he was one man and had no way of communicating with Lan before the attack. *All I can do is be ready to take my chances when and if they come,* he thought.

"Rancer!" shouted Strona, interrupting Jelm's reflections. "Bring the scent masters together. We must move, and soon."

A flurry of activity occurred within the Sutanite encampment. The troops spread out to follow their orders. Groups of seekers, acolytes and guardsmen moved through the low foothills of the Sensory Mountains on the western side of Regulus to cordon off the city up to the river; their role to ensure no one came or left the city while the attack was in progress. The remainder of the force concentrated on the castle from the south.

It was well past noon when a wedge of scent masters led the rows of troops to the castle. Strona was ahead of Jelm, her teeth glistening in her set face; several of the most experienced scent masters were similarly focused by her side. The process of forming the most formidable battle odour that had been generated in living memory began: a scent to batter down the castle gates and overwhelm the opposition.

Jelm knew he had to participate in the assault: he had to support this odour blanket of death and allow it to work; he had to watch when it claimed lives, not reacting but waiting to seize any opportunity; and he would have to act at precisely the right moment to make the attack fail, if he could.

The scent masters encased themselves in a visible bubble of protection, aware that the watchers on the castle walls would be preparing for the imminent attack. Jelm joined his fellow seekers in strengthening the odours into an almost impenetrable shield around the large mass of scent masters. Dark strings of matter, acidic smells of corrosion spewed from the mouths of the masters and fell to the ground, piling up like long coils of wool. As these attack emanations formed, they were manipulated to the front of the line, then shunted away towards the city.

A stray edge of odour brushed an errant foot. The guardsman screamed as his boot and toes dissolved. But nothing distracted the process, and soon a roiling wall of dark odour, filled with flickers of scarlet and deep purple, moved steadily towards the castle walls.

Jelm looked for a rebel reaction, but all was quiet. The sounds of movement, the shuffle of feet, occasional clinks of metal and the creak of leather came as a background to his concentration as he followed the wedge of black scent masters. He was pleased to see the grey, black-cloaked forms of his fellow seekers aligned with him and not ahead with the masters. Even though they were performing an important protective role, there was still a definite hierarchy.

A slight hissing of breath signified the detection of a rebel response. A blanket, formless and misty, began to roll from the castle parapets, down the walls, and across the front of the huge wooden gates. It then eddied outwards and thickened, becoming more rigid until it was a semi-translucent barrier in front of the Sutanite odour attack.

Occasional thuds sounded as rebel odour darts and spears hit. These were deflected by the attacking barrier, which now extended far enough back to allow a degree of protection for the troops massed behind the scent masters. Before long, the opposing barriers clashed at the castle gates. It was like water on fire; a great hissing erupted, flinging large amounts of odour outwards to dissipate in the air.

The corrosive odour wall easily made inroads into the defenders' barrier. Any replenishment of the semi-translucent barrier was quickly eaten away, eventually exposing the bare wooden gate and its stone surrounds. The thud of odour darts and missiles came even more rapidly as the defenders realised the peril of their situation. The attack odour continued, sizzling against the wood and eating through on a broad front. Even stone rotted as Jelm watched. There was little hope of slowing the impetus of the assault.

The remains of the gate fell with a crash and the scent masters, preceded by their noxious brew, rapidly moved into the dark expanses of the entry tunnel.

Their momentum was relentless. A solid caterpillar of attackers moved along the tunnel and up the stone steps towards the great hall. Small sections of troops broke off, to follow narrow corridors and investigate any doorways as they progressed, usually led by a scent master. It was there fierce fighting broke out. Without the protection of the main group's barrier, it became a one-on-one battle. When the attackers won, the slaughter was absolute; the Sutanites took no prisoners.

They entered the great hall, lit by an array of burning wall torches and sunlight filtering though slits in the upper walls. The sight of the massed rebel scent masters at the far end and along the stairs leading to the upper level initially slowed their progress, but the black-clothed attackers soon regrouped. They spread out along the wall, like water running along a gutter, to face the numerous grey and brown forms of the defenders.

Suddenly everything stopped, as if frozen. Jelm could feel the strengthening of will of the Sutanite scent masters as he helped support their barrier shield with his fellow seekers.

"Now!" screamed Strona, her strident voice echoing through the hall.

The corrosive mix of the attack odour snuffed out, to be replaced by the highly recognisable scent snakes—black with yellow bandings oozing from under the barrier in a wriggling mass and targeting the rebels before them. Jelm and other seekers continued to maintain the protective barrier as the snakes met the rebels' defensive shields.

The screaming began.

Odour bolts still hit the attackers' shielding. More powerful now, a few even penetrated the barrier, causing some injury, but the Sutanites generally remained unscathed.

While the grey-robed, rebel scent masters still held strong shields and maintained an aggressive attack on the Sutanites' barrier, their supporters were succumbing to the scent snakes and the battle-trained troops. Bloody emanations rose into the air, highlighted by the occasional spray of bodily fluids. The noise of battle grew.

The entire hall was in motion: rebels falling from the stairways and other higher vantage points, the occasional knot of guardsmen pressing their advantage, and the defenders desperately avoiding the odour snakes. It appeared as though a convulsing, black-and-yellow cobweb covered the floor and shields, pulsing as the attackers poured more of themselves into it to penetrate the defenders' shields. Occasionally one snake would snap back, causing the originator to stagger with the impact, but more frequently an entry point was found and a rebel scent master fell.

Jelm could see Lan at the head of the Eanites, his slight figure rigid in concentration. Near him fought other familiar figures: Brin, Lethnal and Quonir. Though the rebels were numerically superior, the battle-trained strength of the Sutanite scent masters and seekers was beginning to show. More and more of the grey forms began to fall, often transfixed by a banded scent snake. Jelm, frustrated that he could do nothing while firmly part of the Sutanite barrier, saw that the tide of battle was turning against the rebels. He was shocked to see Quonir, one of the most powerful of the scent masters, stagger and fall with an odour snake ripping through his body.

This is it. This is it, he thought hopelessly.

At that moment the rebel shields visibly shuddered as the defending scent masters put an extreme effort into strengthening their own defences, forcing the black-and-yellow cobweb of snakes to slip off. A vibration began above the noise of battle. It grew in intensity until the soles of Jelm's feet could feel the tremor through the floor. The lighting in the hall dimmed perceptibly as the vibration continued to grow. It was enhanced by a vanilla fragrance that even penetrated the Sutanites' barrier. The rebel scent masters were a rock of concentration as they linked to produce a harmonised sound, combined with scent attack. Other rebels, even those with little or no scent ability, joined in to become part of the combined outflow of power. Some died in those brief moments as their attention was distracted, but soon their opponents became uncertain and slowed their attacks.

"No!" screamed Strona in sudden realisation, her neck cording with effort. "Don't give in to it!"

From within the Sutanite barrier, Jelm could feel the pressure of that sound and fragrance. He smiled as he recognised the vibration. He'd only experienced it several times on his rare meetings with the rebel scent masters at Sanctus. It had been a powerful and enlightening experience. He knew his opportunity to work from within had come, so he stepped back from his fellow seekers and joined the rebels' harmonisation. The attackers' barrier still held, with the Sutanites desperately attempting to push forward and disrupt the rebels' concentration. However, like an evaporating cloud, the bonds creating the barrier started to thin and dissipate. With his back to the wall Jelm kept up the harmonisation, working to undermine the barrier by adding to the rebels' powerful attack; the odour of vanilla grew stronger. The Sutanite barrier facing an attack from without, and now within, suddenly snapped out of existence.

The superior numbers of rebels armed with spears and odour bolts took the opportunity to attack and the hall again erupted into a seething mass of conflict. A volley of rebel bolts crashed into the disorientated Sutanite scent masters. Jelm saw Strona, her broken face pouring blood, slump to the floor. Other scent masters and seekers fared little better, trying to cope with a failed barrier and the overwhelming attack. The hated black-clad scent masters bore the brunt of the assault, and many died quickly.

Jelm saw his chance and called in a loud, authoritative voice, "Surrender!"

Those remaining seekers, recognising Jelm's order, immediately moved back to him, ceasing their fight. Other troops followed and the fighting soon died away as the Sutanite forces pulled back.

"Cease fighting and we will respect your surrender," Lan's voice rang into the comparative quiet.

The loss of all the Sutanite scent masters, and capture of the remaining seekers and troops within the castle meant that subsequently the forces ringing the city had no option but to surrender.

In the aftermath of the rebels' victory, Jelm was recognised by Brin in the group of seekers being held prisoner and released. Once freed, he lost little time in trying to find Lan. Eventually he sighted the rebel leader who, together with Zahnal, was tending to a fatally injured Quonir where he had fallen.

"Lan," he said as he reached them.

"Welcome. And thanks, my friend, for doing your task so well," Lan responded, giving Jelm a quick look. "Just allow me a moment, please." He turned back to Quonir, whose head was supported by the old healer. Zahnal shook her head in response to Lan's raised eyebrow.

Quonir raised his arm and grabbed a handful of Lan's robe with surprising strength, bringing him closer.

"My leader," he hissed, face white with strain, "I'm...so...sorry."

"No, Quonir, no. You fought bravely."

"I'm...sorry...Targas!"

Jelm leant forward as he heard Quonir talking about the man he knew as Targ.

"Forgive...me," he gasped, "I..."

"Do not..." admonished Lan, releasing Quonir's handhold and gently pushing him down.

"No! I..." Quonir winced as a sudden spasm of pain ripped through his body. "I betrayed...Targas...told...them."

"What?" Lan spoke sharply.

"I did it...for...my...brother." He slumped back, his eyes closing, before speaking very softly. "He...wasn't...enough...for...Quon's death. Needed...to be...more."

Lan looked over at Jelm, concern in his eyes.

"I'm afraid it's true," Jelm acknowledged. "Targ, I mean Targas has been captured. Septus and Jakus have him even now."

Zahnal gently covered Quonir's face with a blanket.

Chapter Thirty-Nine

The perac collapsed into a graceless heap onto the pavestones. Jakus leapt from the animal as it fell and continued on foot. Without a glance at those of his party striving to catch up, he forced his way through the streets of Nebleth, his powerful shield leaving anyone too slow to get out of his way lying on the ground in his wake. Soon a path automatically cleared, allowing him to reach Nebleth tower without hindrance.

He considered that his ambitious head of seekers was out chasing Targ instead of preparing Nebleth for war. And, instead of informing him of the capture, he'd kept quiet so he could suck out the man's scent memories for himself.

No. This time he has outdone himself. He no longer thinks for the good of the people. He thinks only of his own ambition.

Jakus ran up the steps of the tower to his rooms following the odours of Septus.

He flung open the door with a resounding bang. Septus swung around from the balcony, mouth open to remonstrate before he recognised Jakus. His pallid skin grew whiter and he almost shrank into himself. A nervous stench overcame the perfumes of Nefaria's soap.

"S…Shada, I…I didn't expect you back so soon."

Jakus glared at him while he sought to regain his breath.

"I…I have good news," continued Septus. "I've managed to capture the Targ we've been after for so long…just going to send you a message. Isn't it good news?" he smiled nervously.

"Where is he?"

"I've chained him to the wall, above the killing ground," Septus replied. "Thought the hymetta might help to loosen his tongue."

"I trust Targ's not been damaged," he hissed.

"N…no, not at all. He's not awake yet, just given him magnesa, that's all."

"Then I'll have to go and see, won't I? You can remain," Jakus ordered.

"Uh Shada," Septus began, "there's one other thing. I also caught the woman, the one your cousin let escape." He smiled. "Yes, your young acolyte's sister. Seems that Targ and she are close, very close," he sniggered. "Good tool to use, I'd say? I have her ready in the cavern."

Jakus eyed Septus for a long moment until the man shifted uneasily. "You haven't told the boy?" Septus shook his head. "Right, come with me. But you'll stay in the caverns, with the woman, while I extract this Targ's essences. I don't want any interruptions."

Targ saw a tight mouth overshadowed by a sharp, beaked nose that dominated white skin stretched tightly over a shaven skull. He looked at that face, trying to match it to his memory.

No, he couldn't recall where he'd seen it before, but it was familiar. It seemed important to lock it into a situation, or a place; indeed, the face was almost urging him to do so. He moved laboriously back through his memory, trying to remember.

"Targ," said the face.

"Mmmm, do I know you?" he asked, endeavoring to move his head.

"No, but you will," replied the face in a hard voice, "very soon. How do you feel?"

"Not sure. Need a drink."

The face disappeared and Targas tried hard to clear the fogginess and feeling of wrongness from his mind.

"Drink."

A hand came with the face and put a mug to his lips. The water was strange and slightly salty.

Targas let his head relax back against stone, forgetting what was tantalising his mind, enjoying the soft flood of feeling that came. He was left alone.

His stinging shoulders pulled him into awareness. He flexed them awkwardly and they still hurt. The pain continued down his body, focusing mainly on his ankles and wrists. A thigh muscle cramped and his yell echoed. He usually dealt with cramp by massaging it away, but he could not do it, could not move.

He tried to bend his head, straining to see his leg. The pain was one solid block, and his desperation increased when the other leg threatened to cramp in sympathy. Part of him recognised why he could not move: he was held against a stone wall by metal clamps around his feet, hands and neck. He wore only his shirt, trousers and boots, his jacket and cloak were gone.

He had been caught, but he did not know how. His last memories were of making a wet camp in the hills while travelling to Nebleth to rescue Kyel.

He forced himself to stop yelling and focus. All the fogginess dissipated, blown away by the pain and his strength of mind. He instinctively pulsed a firm scent to the spasms in his leg, pushing, massaging them. The cramp and the pain shifted to the back of his mind.

A light approached. He recognised the scent. "I've met you before?" he asked.

"Ah," exhaled the tall, black figure as he moved into Targas's field of vision. "I'm Jakus, ruler of Ean. How are you?" The smile in his voice did not reach his eyes.

"Let me out of these!" yelled Targas, causing the metal of his shackles to rattle.

"Don't worry about them," Jakus shrugged. "Anyway, I certainly appreciate you coming to me. We've a lot to discuss and I've found that your mind is full of interesting information. I had no idea this Sanctus was so organised. The magnesa has proven very useful, but there's a block there. We've had little time to explore it."

"Magnesa?"

"You've tasted the crystals. It is special, isn't it? It has many uses—I think you'll find it's helped you be most forthcoming. Don't try anything now," he warned as Targas flexed, "for if you do I'll be forced to strip your mind bare and leave you in a permanent imbecilic state. We wouldn't want that, would we?" he laughed.

"Damn you, Jakus!" Targas struggled against the shackles. "Where are my friends?"

"Friends? Yes, you had some friends with you, didn't you?" He smiled. "I'm afraid my impetuous Head, Septus, dealt with them." He paused, watching Targas's face contort. "Now, we have a lot to discuss. I haven't been able to find out where you came from."

Targas gasped out explosively in anger and grief. Jakus stepped back with his shield raised. Waiting. Watching.

A gust of a warm, unpleasant odour, like rancid milk, suddenly wafted over them. He coughed, ignoring the man before him. He had smelt this pong before, but never in such overpowering quantities, and recognised what was down in the dimly lit cavern. He strained to see through a low metal railing into the blackness of a deep hole with a dark floor.

"I can see you don't like it here. That's a pity," mused Jakus. "Still, it should help you to cooperate. I haven't time to be considerate."

A movement in the dimness startled Targas. Behind Jakus's shoulder loomed a dark shape, its thin face ghostly white, eyes staring. It was the blade-nosed shaven skull he'd seen earlier.

Jakus reacted instinctively, thrusting back with his arm and through Septus's hastily erected shield. His odour-enhanced fingers struck the man, knocking him to the ground. "You blood-cursed haggar," screamed Jakus at the sprawled figure, "I told you to stay away. He's mine. Get back to the hymetta; they're more your type." He turned back to Targas.

Septus staggered to his feet and wiped away blood with the sleeve of his robe, his face a twisted mask. His mouth opened impossibly wide and a black odour bolt, fuelled by rage, crashed into Jakus. It smashed through the Shada's reactive shield and crunched into his head. A snap of bone was accompanied by a spray of dark fluid. Jakus collapsed sideways, his legs hitting the low balcony railing before his body toppled into the hole. The thud of his impact with the floor echoed through the cavern.

Targas's mouth dropped open at the sight of the ruler of Ean, a true master of scent power, defeated so easily. Septus limped to the railing and looked down at the crumpled figure.

"Not so powerful now, are you?" His voice was chill as he fired another bolt at the body.

"*Shada,*" he said slowly, as if trying it on for fit. "I like the sound of that title: Shada." His bony head revolved slowly until his gaze fixed on Targas, chained against the wall. "You'll find," he hissed, "that I'm not as nice as the *former* Shada."

Targas could see the dark veins across Septus's shaven skull, the signs of dissipation under the eyes and the small capillaries breaking out across his beak of a nose, a trickle of blood running down to his mouth. Red spittle exploded out as he laughed and a gust of noisome breath caused Targas to gag.

"You have power that I want!" he sprayed. "You have knowledge. And you're mine!" Septus's face seemed to loom even larger as he pushed a compulsion scent at Targas. Targas instinctively put up a barrier deflecting some of that attack, but enough came through and past his magnesa-weakened state, into his head.

Targas felt Septus in his head even as he fought the compulsion to answer the man's questions, but he retained enough awareness to make it difficult. As Septus ranted, Targas saw movement down in the pit where Jakus's body lay. In the dim light two figures in dark brown robes, one a woman and the other a familiar-looking youth, rolled Jakus over and dragged his body out of sight. As Targas continued to fight Septus's assault, part of his mind mulled over what he had seen.

He recognised the youth. It was Kyel, the reason he had come to Nebleth. Then he recalled Jakus talking about the death of his companions. *Were they really dead?* he worried.

"Sadir," he slurred in between Septus's questioning. "I'll give you what you want if I see her."

"What?" spat Septus. "You what? You want the woman?" his high falsetto echoed. "The one that I killed, hmmm"—he thrust his face into Targas's—"or the one I brought with me?"

"You wine-rotted dung heap!" Targas pulled at his restraints. Septus took a step back.

"So, if you want your woman you'll get your woman." He sniggered as he swung around and hurried down the sloping path that led into the depths of the cavern. Targas was left clinging to the hope that Sadir was alive.

"Keeper," screeched Septus, his voice echoing back to Targas, "we have a demonstration to set up!"

Jakus's world was a cocoon of red-tinged pain, blocking out what was around him, even the hardness of the stone floor.

Something tugged at him, pushing lances of agony through his shattered body, so great that he could not even breathe to scream. Then a regular movement began; the pain it brought became absorbed into the whole and he was living the agony, almost welcoming it as it reminded him he was still alive, not dead.

Septus's yell echoed through the dark, bouncing off the rocky walls of the cavern.

"He's gone!" he screamed as he puffed up the slope. When he saw Targas, still securely bound, he swung around and ran back down. "Keeper! Keeper," Septus's voice gradually faded.

Targas knew what Septus was anxious about, for he had seen it happening, Jakus's body being taken by Kyel and the woman. The likelihood that Jakus hadn't died, that somehow he'd survived the high fall onto a solid floor, would give Septus every reason to panic.

Targas focused on trying to escape, ignoring his discomfort and pain, concentrating on breaking his metal bonds and stopping Septus.

He turned his mind inward, locating the drug still circulating in his system. He could see the bonds that gave the foreign element its structure—the scents binding it were clear. He inserted his strength into those links, reversing their bonding and charges of attraction. They soon collapsed, allowing the component elements to dissipate into his bloodstream, safely neutralised. Feeling stronger and clearer of head, he focused on the metal restraints binding his hands, legs and neck to the cold stone. This was not as easy. The iron manacles were old, rusted and thick. Their bonds were in many tight layers, not so easy to feel and infiltrate. Though he had little time, he worked slowly and was soon rewarded by the patter of rust particles on the floor around him. His concentration was such that he failed to notice Septus coming.

A blast of force hit him in the chest and banged him punishingly against the wall.

"Feeling better?" sneered Septus. "Want to co-operate?"

Hate blinded Targas in an instant and he fired a concentrated blast of the foulest smells, hitting Septus's shield and knocking him back several paces.

Septus's reaction was so swift that only the massive swelling of his aura gave Targas pre-warning. Targas fell back on his own response to such an attack, locking an impenetrable shield around him, preventing Septus seeing or reaching him. The Sutanite scent master kept pounding Targas's barrier in fury.

After a time, Targas cautiously relaxed his shield and heard Septus shriek at him from a distance away. The echo dragged his attention to the pit.

Septus stood in that dark hole, drawing Targas's attention to the large wooden cross embedded in the centre of the black floor, and the figure tied to it.

"You see her, don't you?" screeched Septus. "You want her, too. Well, if you had co-operated I might have given her to you."

Targas saw Sadir raise her head and scan the rocky walls until she saw him. She smiled weakly and sagged back down.

Targas's heart pounded as he frantically struggled against his bonds.

"You're too late, Targ, just too late," laughed Septus, shaking his head and moving back against a wall of the pit, still keeping him in sight. He looked at the side where Targas presumed the entrance to be, and then opened his bloody gash of a mouth.

"Keeper!" he screamed. "Release the hymetta."

Chapter Forty

Septus's screech ripped through Targas's mind. He reacted by jerking furiously at his metal bonds as if sheer strength alone could break them. Stabs of pains and a tearing of skin were all that happened; he remained helplessly locked to the wall. He hurled a powerful dart down at Septus, but the man anticipated and easily deflected it with his shield. His laughter infuriated Targas.

Then the creatures he knew moved into the dimly lit chamber. The hymetta bunched together as if suspicious of their surroundings, their wings still, chitinous bodies clattering as they tasted the air around the woman bound on the cross. Sadir did not stir from her slumped position. Septus waited in anticipation.

Targas frantically tried to free himself, knowing he would be too late to save her. He screamed at the hymetta.

Septus chortled. "Watch and enjoy," he called. "Now attack, my creatures," he urged.

However, they hesitated.

Septus, puzzled at their lack of action, moved closer.

Targas suddenly realised what was happening. The hymetta, like the wasps they resembled, would attack creatures that did not have an acceptable smell. It now seemed they regarded Sadir's scent as familiar, in the same way they recognised Septus's. Their ploy at the Salt Way docks in introducing the creatures to their odour appeared to have worked.

With Septus distracted, he knew he had his chance. He dragged a smell from his memory, so foreign that the hymetta would have to be unfamiliar with it. He pushed an infinitely fine tendril of the aroma of unrefined Tenstria malas spirit over the balcony and let it float down onto the man below, like a spider's web drifting on the breeze. It began to stick on Septus's scent shield, creating a cover so light it was undetectable. Then Targas released his control, allowing the aroma to permeate the room.

Septus froze when the huge, expressionless hymetta suddenly focused on him. He instinctively edged towards the entrance with his back to the wall. Their demeanour changed from curiosity to aggression in an instant, wings buzzing as they flew at him.

He instinctively blasted the creatures, blowing off legs and other body parts, green blood spraying out into the air. The remaining hymetta mobbed Septus, probing for weaknesses in his shield. Then the screaming began.

Targas focused on breaking his bonds, urgency lending strength to his efforts. The flecks of iron fell in a steady rain from the metal restraints.

Several hymetta were pulling pieces of their comrades away. Sadir remained slumped on the cross. There was no sign of Septus.

The neck fastening gave way, followed by first one, then the other of the wrist restraints. Targas quickly rubbed his arms and worked on his ankle bindings. When the last bindings broke he took time to stand, the blood rushing to his legs causing him to sag against the wall. He took several moments to pummel and massage his legs before beginning to limp down the ramp.

A last hymetta dragged body pieces down the tunnel entrance as he hurried past to Sadir on the wooden cross. Fortunately, she was unhurt, although still unconscious, so he untied the ropes and pulled her to him.

"Sadir, what have they done?" he asked, gently lowering her to the ground, pushing sweat-darkened hair from her face and touching her cheek. She seemed unhurt, but he could not wake her.

Despite their ordeal, he was not forgetting Septus, being too wary to assume the hymetta had killed him. He left Sadir on the charcoal floor to manoeuvre his way through green puddles of blood to where he had last seen Septus, covered by a heaving mass of large insects. Red blood, contrasting vividly with the green, showed that the hymetta had had some success.

Targas was relieved, until he noticed a splash of red further off and still more leading into the exit tunnel.

"Damn!" he yelled and then gritted his teeth, realising their lives would remain in danger while Septus still lived.

He hurried back to Sadir. "Come, my love," he murmured as he bent and picked her up, "we have to find somewhere safe."

The cavern was quiet. Only the rustle of the hymetta a distance off broke the silence. Targas knew there were other people nearby, including the keepers that managed the large creatures. He could taste their fear.

"Keeper," he called, "I want you here. Now!"

The slow trudge of worn boots on the stone floor alerted him. He steeled his arms to continue holding Sadir's weight, while mentally preparing for any confrontation.

"Cer?" An uncertain voice from the dimness of the cavern preceded a large, unhealthy-looking man in loose grey trousers and jerkin, short hair above a fat, jowly face. He shuffled to a halt some distance away.

"Do you know who I am?" asked Targas.

"Cer, the Head told us you was a powerful master, one who couldn't be let loose," he gulped, looking back the way he'd come.

"Are you looking for Septus? Is he there?"

"Sorry Cer...I don't know where he is, but he's done something terrible to me hymetta... So many hurt." He shook his head. "So many."

"You must have helped bind us, eh?" Targas interrupted him. "Just the both of us, or were there more?"

"N...no Cer, there was no more," continued the keeper. "The Head only had us get you both..."

"And?" asked Targas.

"There were a lizard, one of them scent ones." Seeing Targas's face, the keeper hurried on. "I still got it, Cer, if it's yours, locked up in me room."

Targas felt his spirit lift, knowing Tel had survived all that had happened.

"Take us there at once!" he demanded.

"D'you need help, Cer?" The keeper nodded towards Sadir.

"No, just move," snapped Targas, with an authority he did not feel.

The keeper turned and led the way up the path. Targas stretched out to keep up, feeling his body complain under the double weight. He followed the nervous man out of the cavern and into a corridor. The keeper stopped at the first door he came to, pushed it open and stood back.

"No, after you," Targas said.

Tel's scent wafted out from the room.

"Release the lizard," he ordered, as he put Sadir down on a seat. Tel scurried out of a small cage, stopped briefly to sniff at Sadir before scrabbling up to Targas's shoulder, claws pricking through his shirt. The lizard's rough skin rubbed against Targas's ear.

"Slow down," he murmured. "You'll have my ear off if you keep that up." He turned to face the keeper, who was back against a wall, holding his hands in front of his waist. "Is your room safe? Can it be locked?"

The keeper nodded.

"I want to leave my friend here, in safety." Targas regarded the rumpled corner bed with distaste, and waited for the man to straighten the blankets before lowering Sadir onto it. "If anything should happen to her..." He left the meaning clear.

The keeper shook his head vigorously. "N...no, Cer."

"Ah!" exclaimed Targas, sighting a bundle against a wall. "You have my coat, and what else?"

"I...I was told t...to take it, I was," he stammered. "There's your cloak as well." He hurried to pass the clothing to Targas.

"Now, where did Septus go?"

"The Head, Cer?" The keeper sniffed. "Didn't see him, Cer. Too busy with me hymetta, what's left of them anyways. He must have gone up out of the cavern. Yes, that's what he must have done." His head bobbed rapidly up and down.

"I'll need you to tell me about this place and its layout."

The man's face brightened. "Uh, this is the tower, Cer," he replied, his voice coming thick and slow, "the Nebleth tower. You must know of it?"

Targas looked at him impatiently.

"We're here, Cer, here in the guts of the tower. Me hymetta live down here, out of the way—so do I, and them that helps me."

"What else?"

"The tunnel outside goes to the main entry, the dungeons and the…ah… processing rooms."

"What's above?"

"Next floor's big. It's got learning rooms, places for sleeping and eating. A big hall too. They all meet there sometimes. Then there's the top. The masters live up there, the Shada and Head too." The keeper looked up from his feet and grinned nervously.

"Anything else you can think of?" Targas asked.

"No…ah, yes." The fat man's eyes widened. "There's the scent tower. It's on the top. I don't go there, though."

"Good, good," nodded Targas. "I'll leave my friend here, with the door sealed and the lizard to guard her. We will look for the Head. Yes, I said *we*, keeper."

"Cer," sighed the keeper, gazing at his feet.

Targas carefully put the reluctant lizard on the bed with Sadir and pulled on his cloak. He left his coat as an afterthought, before taking the keeper outside and shutting the door. He scanned the wall and pulled scents from the stone and surrounds, gradually solidifying them over the door to give the appearance of natural stone.

"Best I can do. Right, keeper, take me out of this place. We have work to do."

Targas knew the threat that Septus, and possibly Jakus, posed and that it had to be dealt with. He did not know whether he was the one who could do it, but he had to try. He nudged the keeper in the back to start him moving along the corridor.

He saw two people through a haze of red, concern etched on their faces. In his world of pain, he didn't wonder why people were worried for him, but he responded to it.

He grimaced through the pain, a small stretching of the muscles that allowed his carers to recognise his awareness and react.

"Jakus," came a familiar voice, "my Shada. How badly are you hurt?"

Jakus knew her sound. "Nefaria," he croaked. "Ahh! Don't touch me."

"Oh, I'm sorry, Shada."

"Who is with you?"

"Kyel," replied Nefaria, puzzlement in her voice.

"Kyel?" repeated Jakus slowly, his mind having trouble grasping what had happened. "Does Septus know where I am?"

"No, Shada," said Nefaria. "We thankfully didn't see Septus. Just wanted to get you to where you'd be safer."

"Good...good," he hissed in pain. "You will assist me!"

"Of course, Shada, but you're badly hurt," she replied.

Jakus, overwhelmed by a spasm of agony, gritted his teeth, then yelped as the movement ground bones within his skull. Being helpless was infuriating, for if he was attacked he would be unable to defend himself, unable to even maintain a shield.

That thought pushed the constant pain into the background. He realised he couldn't tell Kyel was in the room, neither could he smell Nefaria; he only knew it was her by her voice. His smell sense was missing, a power he had always lived with. Without it he was helpless.

"I've got to...to get away!" he hissed urgently. "You've got to help me."

"Yes, Shada, of course," said Nefaria.

"No, you don't understand," grimaced Jakus, unable to even move his arm to make his point. "I've got to go. And I've got to...go now!"

"Help me get him to the boat, Kyel," sighed Nefaria, as she knelt beside Jakus. "I have to get him to where he wants to go, to Port Saltus."

"What're we going to do when we get there?" asked Kyel.

"No, Kyel, just me. You're not coming."

"What?" Kyel drew back. "Why are you going with him, then? He doesn't mean anything to you."

"I know he doesn't show much affection and can be thoughtless, but I can't help it. I love him."

Kyel stared at her. "He's got you, hasn't he?" he snapped. "In your head, he's got you."

"Are you going to help?" asked Nefaria, looking up at him, eyes pleading. "I need you to."

The keeper walked slowly, jumping at shadows, constantly looking back to Targas. Whenever someone came, he stood to one side and Targas had no choice but to wait with him, making sure he appeared to be with the keeper. No one stopped and questioned them. They all appeared to be in too much of a hurry, moving along the corridor and disappearing through doors or up stairwells. Most were young and dressed in brown robes. There was the occasional guardsman, seeker and even a black-robed scent master, but not the one they were looking for. Targas could detect Septus against the background odours, so he knew he was on the right track.

"That's the main entry, ahead," whispered the keeper, pulling at Targas's sleeve. "If you go there you'll meet the guards, you will."

"Don't worry," soothed Targas, "we're not going there." He pointed to an age-blackened door set in the stone wall. "We're going here."

"But them's the dungeons," hissed the keeper, "you don't want to go there."

Targas gripped an iron ring and twisted it until the door began to give.

"Now you will wait here. Don't let anyone in, will you?" He reinforced his command with scent.

"Yes, Cer," the keeper replied, jerking to attention.

The door opened to reveal a short series of steps leading down into the darkness. "What I wouldn't give for some decent light," he muttered, as he took the first step.

He could make out a number of iron doors set into the stone walls on both sides at the bottom. Targas could sense Septus was there, somewhere, waiting.

The smell was strong, a mixture of human faeces and general filth that began to overpower the scent trail. Targas bent down to try and locate it.

A slight movement made him reflexively strengthen his shield just as a solid weight crushed against his chest, knocking him onto his back. The staring eyes of Septus were only a hand's breadth away, a jagged tear in the cheek revealing a clenched line of yellowing, bloodstained teeth in the white face.

Targas strengthened his shield, tightening the bonds, blocking all that Septus could throw at him. The power of the assault and his resistance seemed to cancel each other, until they were just wrestling, fighting with all their strength. Targas gradually worked his legs under Septus's straining body, while desperately pushing out with his arms, forcing the grotesque face further away. He manoeuvred his feet until they dented Septus's shield around his thighs, and kicked out hard. Septus went over Targas to land below him at the bottom of the steps.

Targas lay for a moment gasping from the effort until he saw Septus scramble past him and out of the door. Targas staggered to his feet, almost slipping in a large pool of blood, before following.

The corridor was silent and empty. Targas leant against the wall, catching his breath, wondering where Septus, and the keeper, had gone.

The door to the entry hall opened and a slight, brown-robed figure began to walk by.

"Kyel?" Targas asked hesitantly. "Is that you, Kyel?"

"Yes," said the youth, eyes widening, "yes, it's me. Who are... You! You're him. You traitor!" He punched Targas in the stomach before he had time to strengthen his shield. "Targ, you're k'dorian dung!"

Targas hunched over, gasping for breath as he tried to make sense of what had just happened.

Kyel's slight figure disappeared into the gloom of the corridor.

Chapter Forty-One

Targas struggled to sit against the wall, pulling up his feet to rest his head upon his knees. A trickle, and then a flood of brown-robed people came hurrying through the door from the entry hall and past him to move up the stairs. One commented as he went by, "They're gathering in the meeting hall."

Targas tried to make sense of what was happening while the pain in his midriff began to fade. He was tired, hurt and puzzled by how Kyel had reacted.

"No," he shook his head, "Kyel's issues will have to wait." Targas looked both ways, trying to work out which direction Septus had gone but the odour had mixed and spread, promising to make tracking extremely difficult. He could hear the hubbub from the stairwell and people moving, so he scrambled to his feet and followed them up the stairs.

Corridors spread each side at the top, but the noise was coming through open doors in front of him, emanations leaking anxiety and panic. Despite a nagging feeling that he should check on Sadir, Targas moved to the doors and peered into a large, high-roofed hall well lit by burning torches and candles in polished metal holders. A long table stretched down the length of the room where a number of the black-robed people were sitting. Brown-robed, mainly younger, people stood in numerous small groups scattered around the hall.

Targas built up the strong concealing shield, far easier compared to when he had first instinctively used it in Korla some time ago. He slipped silently into the room along a wall at the back of the crowd. An older, plain-looking man with an air of authority stood and raised a hand. Gradually the noise ceased.

"Scent masters and acolytes," he began, "we have some serious matters to consider. Quiet," he shouted as the noise level started to rise, "for unless you hear what I have to say you will not make a considered judgement."

Targas could detect none of the evil aura he associated with the enemy leaders from the man, despite his black robe, and was curious.

"Last night we, Minas and myself, led by the Head, detected and captured the Targ." He held up his arm to forestall any response. "I won't go into any of the unpleasant details, yes," he paused and lowered his voice, "extremely unpleasant. Needless to say, it was a fortuitous capture. And at noon the Shada returned to interrogate this man, this rebel." He paused, looking over his attentive audience, his gaze sweeping across Targas without registering his presence. "The Shada had been leading our army, which is now at Regulus in response to the rebel invasion of the city. Of course, we anticipate the situation to soon return to normal." He glanced at his hands, now spread on the tabletop, before looking over the people around him.

"But several disturbing things have recently occurred. The Shada has gone missing, the prisoner has escaped and the Head is...well...unavailable."

The room broke out in a buzz of conversation. The scent master raised his hands to silence the crowd.

"Now, please allow me to continue before you have private discussions." His face was stern. "We have instituted searches throughout the tower and the city, and apart from some concerns in the hymetta cavern, we have found little. It behoves us not to panic but to help look for the Shada, and also the prisoner. I warn you to stay in groups and not attempt to make heroes of yourselves. Further, we have sent a scent message to Regulus raising our concerns."

One of the scent masters stood.

"Yes, Sinal?" he frowned.

"Akerus, as we all know, the city was taken by the rebels. So, what's happened to Shad Heritis? I mean, he's the Shada's cousin and he'd rule if the Shada was gone..."

"Yes," added another master. "If the Shada's gone missing, and the Shad is captured, then who's in charge? Who will rule?"

"Far too early for that sort of talk," shouted Akerus above the rising noise level, "we don't know all the facts and there's a battle being fought in Regulus, probably as we speak."

"I must say what's on my mind, regardless of consequence," called a young-looking, black-robed woman over the rising din.

"Quiet!" called Akerus. "We'll get nowhere if everyone talks at once." As the noise abated, he signalled the scent master. "Continue, Pamula."

"Thank you, Akerus," she nodded. "I am a woman," said Pamula in a strong voice, "and I am going to say what other women in this room are thinking, but have not dared say." There was a distinct shuffling of the audience. "If I may continue on the issue just raised, the logical direction of your thoughts is that if our rulers are unavailable, then the Head will rule. Is that not so?" She looked around the room, arms outstretched. "And if he is in charge, without the Shada's influence, then none of us will be safe. The Shada has his needs, as we all know and have had to accommodate, but the Head is cruel. Many women...and younger girls, have experienced his...excesses. That's all I have to say!"

Silence filled the room as she sat down. Targas waited, trying to work through what he was hearing. He had come ready to take the fight to the enemy and had found he could not detect the evil here that Jakus and Septus seemed to represent. While the rulers' power was absolute, it seemed paper-thin. Without the rulers, there was a chance for the conflict to be resolved without the horrors of a full civil war.

Targas recognised the time was right to attempt to influence the discussion.

The noise level had risen again. Akerus had sat down, releasing control of the group while talking animatedly with two scent masters. Targas concentrated. Using the natural scents of the room, he strengthened and then bound together a transparent tube which he extended to a group of older brown-robed acolytes some distance away. He maintained it while speaking into it in neutral, clipped tones, his voice sounding as if it came from that group.

"So, we need the Shada to control the Head?" His voice was loud enough to overcome the background noise.

"What?" asked Akerus, his head lifting at the question. He looked at the group. "What do you mean?" When no one responded, Pamula picked up on what Targas had said.

"That's the question, isn't it?" She stood and asked the crowd, "Who controls the Head now the Shada is gone? Can you?" She pointed at Akerus, "Or you, or you?" The other scent masters she pointed at looked away.

Again, Targas waited until the noise level had risen before adding his next comment. "The Head's unbalanced, isn't he?"

This time all the noise dropped away and the group of brown robes split apart, each not wanting to be associated with that comment. However, a rescue came from an unexpected source.

"I don't know," pondered Akerus, standing again, "but I'm forced to agree that he is not himself. I have never seen him so...disorientated."

The murmur of the crowd grew and again Targas, having moved his odour tube to behind a group of seated scent masters, spoke. "Well, who's going to support the Head as the new Shada?"

Akerus looked pointedly at the scent masters, who now appeared horrified. Targas noticed that others further away were nodding.

One of the doors leading out of the hall suddenly slammed into the wall, effectively cutting off all conversation.

A figure appeared in the doorway, black robe highlighting a bloodied, white face. His reddened hand gripped the edge of the door as he dragged something heavy forward. There were audible gasps when Septus pulled an unresisting body through.

"Targ!" The word gurgled through the flapping torn cheek. "I know you're here." His words were indistinct over a thick, bloody phlegm that oozed from the gash in his face. "I have your woman. Alive. Just."

Targas dropped his concealment, attention focused on Sadir. People parted with alarm as Targas started forward. Septus's face lit up.

"You want her," he screamed at Targas, "then you come and get her!" Septus yanked Sadir to him like a rag doll, then stepped backwards and disappeared from sight.

Targas ran through the stunned crowd. He swung around to face them as he reached the door.

"Do you doubt that Septus is mad? Will any of you be safe when he's commanding you? Will your women? Your families?" He turned from the silent room and hurried into the darkness.

Kyel wandered along the gloomy corridor lost in thought, wondering why everyone had let him down. His friend, Jakus had gone, and Nefaria too. *I loved her, really loved her, but she loves Jakus, not me.* And then he'd met Targ. He vaguely knew Targ had pretended to be his friend, but Luna had died because of him. Tears welled as he pushed his back against the stones and slid slowly to the floor, letting his head fall into his hands.

"Chirp."

Kyel straightened.

"Chirp." A creature, pale in the dark, pounced on his leg and scrabbled up onto his chest. He tried to push the wriggly thing away, struggling as he felt claws begin to pierce his clothing. He tried to move away, but the lizard gripped harder. The pain shocked him and he briefly lost consciousness.

"Chirp?" The sound pulled at his senses. A memory came to the surface and he recalled a strange, scared man under a house, a man who followed him. Black-and-grey-clad seekers, attacking them, not once but twice. That man had saved him; Luna, too.

Luna? The man, Targ, didn't hurt her, he saved her. He saved her and helped them get home, to his sister. Kyel stroked Tel's rough, scaly body, the lizard arching into his hand.

Then we left home, all of us. Sadir; Luna; Targ. But we were attacked again. Poor Luna. He recalled her, small and frightened, surrounded by large men. *She smiled at me before we were tied up; then those black k'dorians did terrible things to us, to her. But, haggar's dung, Jakus my friend was there…* His eyes widened at the thought. He needed to know what had happened. *If Tel was here, then Targ must've brought him. Sadir might be here too.*

"Tel," he whispered, "oh, Tel. What'd I do to Targ? We've got to find him."

Targas knew where Septus was heading—the trail was deliberate, purposeful. Above the hall was a floor of rooms occupied by the masters and the Shada, higher up was the scent tower. The trail, punctuated by drops of blood, led upwards.

Targas stopped, listening carefully, sifting the scents. His heaving breath threatening to drown out any noise, his unwashed body now leaving an obvious odour since he was not controlling it.

He edged cautiously up the stairs to the scent tower, thickening his shield as he went.

He sent minute tendrils questing in front of him, seeking what lay ahead, but he could not detect anything. Even though it was early nightfall, he cautiously peered along the dark walkway circling the tower. The odour collection chamber was open, but the scent trail did not lead there. Targas climbed the last of the stairs, before moving along the narrow path between the tower and the parapet. He crept silently, hardly daring to breathe as he edged around a section of wall.

"That's far enough, Targ," came a gurgling voice. Septus leant against the low wall, with an arm clenched around Sadir's throat, an inky blackness behind him.

Targas glimpsed the dim light of the city below and the glimmer of stars in a cloudless sky, but his attention was on Sadir. Her eyes were wide and pleading, face white against the darkness of Septus's arm.

"No further," said Septus, his aura a nimbus of colours silhouetted against the night sky.

The colours of madness, thought Targas.

"Your presence has…injured me, Targ. Ever since I heard your cursed name"—he gulped phlegm—"you've interfered with my plans. Then you had to send a girl—too cowardly to fight me yourself." He chortled wetly. "So, I destroyed her. Now I have your woman and I'll destroy her too." He clenched his arm under Sadir's throat until she whimpered. She struggled for breath, tugging hard at Septus's arm. "Unless you can take her from me?"

Targas edged closer.

"Stop! So, you want to join us, Targ!" An edge had entered Septus's distorted voice, the flap of cheek puffing up to expose a line of stained, clenched teeth.

A black wall of odour erupted from Septus, crashing into Targas's shield, hitting and linking with it.

Targas pulled away, but he couldn't break free; some power of Septus's stuck. Targas was being dragged towards the edge and the long drop into the dark city below. He dug in his heels, trying to halt his slide.

"You can't prevent me, Targ. You'll join us, now!"

Targas felt a sudden shock as the weight of Septus and Sadir falling over the parapet pulled at him, tugging him to the edge. He tried to release the shield but the linkage held. With Sadir's screams echoing in his head and the hard wall grinding into his shins, he began to fall into the abyss.

"No!" screamed a voice next to him. A pair of strong hands grabbed him and helped to halt his progress. At the same moment, the grip on his odour shield weakened and he broke free of the last links. Septus's body fell backwards into the dark, Sadir falling with him, mouth open in a silent scream, eyes locked on Targas.

He reacted instinctively, resorting to something he'd only tried once, in a peaceful valley at Sanctus where he'd captured a lizard with an odour net. Trusting in the grip of the person who held him, he flung a net of scents at the falling bodies, strengthening the bonds as he did so. Almost too late the net hit and twined around Sadir's body, thickening and tightening. Targas felt her momentum nearly tear the link from his mind as Septus held on. Fortunately, Septus's grip broke and he disappeared soundlessly into darkness.

Targas continued to tighten and strengthen the bonds, feeling the pain in his knees, back and shoulders as he held against the incredible pressure. With a supreme effort he pulled with mind and body, joints popping, sinews cracking, desperately keeping the integrity of the scent bonds together. Slowly Sadir rose closer until, yelling with a last effort, he dragged her over the side of the wall and into her brother's arms.

Septus fell into the inky depths, his fingers on fire from the friction as he lost his grip and the scent rope slipped through them, his mind instinctively causing dark tendrils to spew forth. They thickened in an instant, forming an elastic barrier around his body. He smashed into the ground, bounced from the cobbles and crashed into the tower wall. He groaned in agony before edging painfully out of sight into a dark sewer, congealing blood the only evidence of his passage.

Chapter Forty-Two

He moved. Pain pulled at every conceivable muscle, joint and sinew, but sleep was a comfort he did not want to leave. However, the pain, and then a fragrance, feminine and unfamiliar, woke him.

He cautiously opened an eye, wincing at the brightness, the emptiness of his stomach adding to the pain of awakening with a low grumble. An arm moved and came down upon his chest; it wasn't his.

"Targas?"

The soft voice in his ear, the gentle arm on his chest brought him fully awake. He sat up, wincing as every muscle protested.

"Targas," whispered Sadir, "what're you doing?"

"Sadir? Where are we?" asked Targas, stretching back an arm to touch Sadir's shoulder.

"Nefaria's."

"Nefaria?" asked Targas.

"Jakus's consort's room," added Kyel, his tousled head appearing alongside that of Sadir's. "She won't be needing it anymore. Reckon she's left Ean for good."

"Kyel?" Targas screwed up his eyes at Sadir's brother.

"I've got Tel though," continued Kyel cheerfully. "He won't leave me alone; too comfortable. Hey, what did Sadir just call you: *Targas?* And you're a bit friendly with my sister too." He winked at him.

"Yes," he acknowledged, "my name is Targas, not Targ, and I have my memories back, but that's a story for another time." *And, your sister is a very special friend of mine!*

Targas looked around the room, wondering at the quiet in view of the events of the previous night. He remembered limping back from the scent tower with Sadir and Kyel, sneaking to this out-of-the-way room and sealing themselves in with strong odour bonds. It was now past dawn and seemed too quiet.

"Kyel, why is no one after us? Is there any way we can find out what's happening?

After last night, there should be a lot of activity."

"Sure," said Kyel, scrambling out of the bed, "I know me way around and can find out what's happening."

"Can you get us something to eat, too?" asked Targas quickly. "My stomach is sticking to my backbone and I doubt your sister is any better off. Be careful, though. We don't want to lose you again."

Kyel nodded, then pointed to a small door near the head of the bed. "You can use Nefaria's washroom there to clean up. I'll go and see if I can find what's going on. I'll leave Tel with you." He pulled the reluctant lizard off his shoulder, dropped it on the bed and then went over and yanked at the door. "Can't open it. Targas, can you take the bonds off?"

Targas was relieved that the scent linkages he must have placed there were still working. It was hard to believe that they hadn't been disturbed after what had happened. It took a moment before the door could open.

"Be careful," called Sadir.

"Of course," Kyel grinned over his shoulder as he left.

Tel, filled with calm purpose, padded slowly up the bed, eyeing the spot between them.

After re-establishing the odour bonds on the door, Targas and Sadir quickly washed and dressed. They had to work out what to do next, how to survive the coming day in the enemy's home.

A scratching at the door alerted him. He tensed, until he recognised Kyel's aura, then relaxed the bonds on the door. Kyel slipped in, pushing the door closed behind him. He gleefully proffered a full tray of food.

"On the table," Targas gestured while tightening the bonds. "Did you have any difficulty?"

"There's a lot happening," explained Kyel. "I had to go down to the kitchens and saw that the hall was full of people; probably been there all night. And, I talked with the cook—she's used to me. She said that the army's just returned, but that it's different, mainly strangers in it. She reckons the rebels have come. So, I thought I'd let you know; strange that no one was interested in what I was doing."

They quickly ate the meal of bread, fruit and cheese, while discussing how they would get out of the city and to their friends. A gentle knock on the door startled them. Targas pushed Sadir and Kyel into the washroom as he detected the familiar Sutanite scent. He reinforced the bonds on the door.

"Please," called a voice, "we need to speak with you. We followed the boy so are aware you're inside."

"Akerus?" asked Targas, recognising the leader's voice. "Are you alone?"

"There are several of my colleagues with me. We mean no harm. May we enter?"

Targas gestured for Sadir and Kyel to stay where they were, and faced the door.

"Come in," he said firmly, while freeing its bonds.

The handle turned and the door slowly opened. A hand appeared in a cloud of calming odour with minimal shielding. The black form of the master entered, an expression of greeting fixed firmly on his face.

Targas remained motionless, projecting a commanding presence, still dressed in his foreign shirt and trousers. With a few days' growth of dark beard, close-cropped hair and a lined, weary face, he felt he was a figure to be wary of. Three other scent masters followed Akerus, including the outspoken female he had seen before. He let them file in and stand uncertainly while he stared at them.

"Ahem," Akerus cleared his throat, "would you allow me to introduce myself, and my colleagues?"

Targas nodded.

"I'm Akerus, the head teacher. Next to me is Manis, more involved in scent master allocation than teaching." The broad, middle-aged man smiled briefly, his hair a brown fuzz across his wide skull. "Then there's Harkule, supply co-ordinator." The taller, thin-faced man, sandy hair just discernible, nodded. "Finally, Pamula, with…ah, no fixed role really." The thin woman in her late thirties smiled bleakly.

Akerus looked at Targas, glanced at Sadir and Kyel peering from the washroom doorway, and cleared his throat again. "I—rather *we*—have had a harrowing night. We have struggled to deal with many events, and," he added, "you seemed to have had a large part in them."

"I know you from last night, Targ," interrupted Pamula. "It was you that prompted the women and me to speak out." She held up her hand as if to stop the others from interrupting. "The Head has always been hard on the women, especially the trainees, and last night we had to decide how far we could support him, in light of the events that had occurred. You have a way of making a point," she said, looking intently at Targas with a tight smile.

"I'll just add my thoughts, Pamula," said Manis. "I was one of the group that captured you and your partner there"—he gestured at Sadir—"but I had misgivings at the actions of the Head, especially the brutal slaughter of your companions."

Targas grimaced, tears coming to his eyes. Hynal, Woll and Stakol had been honourable companions and had not deserved their fate. He heard a huge sob from Sadir, but remained focused on the scent master.

Manis gulped. "That's brought me to this point."

"The point being," interrupted Akerus, "that our leaders have disappeared, and we are in the process of surrendering, since your people are in the city."

Targas's eyes widened at the news. A lot must have happened in the short time he had been away and now, if they were to be believed, here was an opportunity to limit further conflict.

"Well, I suppose we best meet up with the rebel leaders and see if we can sort something out," he suggested.

He hugged Lan, Brin, then Lethnal. She smiled sadly at him and whispered in his ear, "I'm so sorry, Targas. We found out what had happened to Hynal, Woll and Stakol." As she felt him stiffen she added, "I'm so glad that you've dealt with that creature. He really deserved a harsher death."

Targas gulped and, holding Sadir, stepped away, not wanting to relive the harrowing events of the previous evening.

The large entry hall of the Nebleth tower was full to capacity with groups of rebels, weaponless Sutanite soldiers and guardsmen, and scent masters from both sides. The negotiations between the leaders had resulted in a truce, but it was confusing. From what Targas could discover, the battle for Regulus had been a close thing, but the absence of Jakus enabled the Eanites to win the fight. The remainder of the Sutanite army had capitulated. A forced march through the night had seen them reach Nebleth by dawn.

The subsequent revelation that Septus had fallen to his death, although no body was found, added to the confusion and subsequent surrender of the depleted guard and masters. Targas's role in dispatching Septus had avoided any further bloodshed.

He held his arms around his family, Tel having claimed his usual place on his shoulders. For once he felt a measure of contentment. Until Lan came over, leading a tall man in a seeker's outfit. Targas noticed Kyel smiling at the stranger.

"Targas," said Lan, "you may not have met Jelm, but you will know of him." Targas nodded.

"He has been our contact with the Sutanites," Lan continued. "It was he who rescued Luna at great risk to himself, and it was he who worked from within the enemy army to facilitate its surrender to us. For a long time, he has been in constant fear of exposure. His role has been a significant one in this conflict."

Targas leant forward, holding out his arm. "I am honoured, Jelm, and thank you for all you did for Luna."

Jelm clasped Targas's arm with both of his hands. "It pains me greatly that she didn't survive to be with us now."

Kyel slipped away from Targas and darted off through the crowd. Sadir glanced briefly at Targas with tear-filled eyes and turned to follow her brother.

The rest of the day passed in a round of meetings and discussions on his part in the conflict. Even the revelation of Quonir's role in his capture failed to anger him.

At one stage they caught up with a very stoic Cynth. She sang the praises of Woll, eyes bright with tears, affirming that he had died doing the right thing.

"It's because of th' likes of him we've got a freer world, where children can grow up without fear, 'nd people can live long 'nd fruitful lives."

At a quiet moment, Targas moved away with Sadir to find seats in a less busy corner.

"Targas? What are you going to do now?"

"I don't know," he answered. "I know I want to get out of here with you, but I don't know where I go from here. I seem to have been in Ean for a long time, and so much has happened and changed for me." He hugged Sadir as they sat in silence.

"I wouldn't mind taking you and Kyel"—he kissed Sadir on her head—"back to Tenstria, if not to stay, at least for a visit. I'd like you to see what it's like. Though I don't know how we could get back there."

"Yes, I'd like that," Sadir said into his shoulder.

"The broad green forests, mountain gullies and ferns growing higher than a man… Then there's the wetlands I loved as a boy; if you keep your wits about you, it's great." Targas sighed. "I don't have many relatives, you know. My parents have passed over and I was an only child. I suppose my most recent memories have been of the distillery and the maturation rooms. I love the smells and the tastes. I was good at it, too." He looked down at Sadir. "I wonder if the House of Versent has replaced me; I was their best blender."

"Targas," came a familiar voice.

"Yes, Lan?" Targas looked around to meet the gaze of the man who'd just entered.

"We need to think about what we do next."

"Just what Sadir and I were talking about," he replied. "We will probably be heading back to Lesslas, I suppose."

"No Targas, that is not what I meant," said Lan. "Our problem is this: we have not won control of Ean from the Sutanites yet. All we have done is win several significant battles. We need to ensure that some stability comes to the country, which means stable government without major disruptions. At this time Port Saltus remains unchallenged. There are the towns still controlled by the Sutanites, and the evil spread by Jakus and Septus is there. There are seekers and administrators with the Sutanite taint. They will not relinquish control easily and will have to be dealt with. We still have not found Jakus, or Septus." He held up his hand. "Oh, I know Septus has supposedly fallen to his death, but I will not believe this of an accomplished scent master until we find his body."

"Lan," said Sadir, "Kyel says Jakus was badly hurt and that he helped him get away. Perhaps he'll know more?"

"Good. Can you find him, please?" As Sadir hurried off, he continued. "But what I meant to say is that next day we will need to go to Port Saltus. Although it is a trading town, many people are supporters of the Sutanites and they will need to know there is a new rule…once we've established it, that is," he smiled.

"Sadir, Targas, I've found me friend, Riyar," came Kyel's excited voice. "Do you remember him?"

"Why yes, I think I do," said Sadir, "Wasn't he…"

"From Lesslas? Yep. He was taken last season, but he's here and he's all right," said Kyel.

"Young man," interrupted Lan, "I need to ask you about something… something important. It is about the Shada…Jakus. What can you tell me about the last time you saw him?"

Kyel's face clouded as he remembered. He shook his head. "Nefaria took him away." He saw Lan's puzzlement and added. "Nefaria was—I mean *is*—the Shada's consort. She's the most, ah…" His blush completed the sentence.

"Yes," interrupted Riyar, "we all thought so too, in the class."

Kyel glared at Riyar and continued. "Anyway, when the Shada was so badly hurt we helped him. He made us promise to take him away from Nebleth…in secret. Nefaria and I got him to a boat, but then she stopped me coming with them." He paused, eyes welling with tears. "She said she loved him. Him!" he said bitterly. "Him that used her, hurt her even. And she loved him?"

"Oh Kyel," sympathised Sadir.

"So, they have gone to Port Saltus?" asked Lan.

"Probably," answered Kyel. "I think he's got a ship there."

"Ah…and when was this?"

"Last day…sometime after midday."

"Well," sighed Lan, "I think we may have lost our quarry. He has had too much time and, I expect, will have left the Port by now. Still, this does not change our plans. We must leave here at dawn."

Early next day saw Lan's army moving out of Nebleth, along the road that swung past the docks and then towards Port Saltus. Targas caught up with Cynth, who bore the recent loss of Woll with a fierce strength and a determination to continue the *job* she and Woll had been working towards.

Targas glanced at the number of small craft moored along the docks and wondered whether this was where Jakus had escaped from the city. A sudden movement caused him to react, an odour dart striking his hastily erected shield and knocking him off his perac. A black figure fell on Targas, stabbing down with a long, thin dagger. Targas pushed out, lifting the attacker into the air and throwing him against the wooden pylons separating the road from the jetty.

"Septus!" he gasped as he expanded his shield towards the man lying stunned on the wooden boards. Septus's face contorted as he attempted to twist away, thrusting out with scent power before staggering between the moored boats. He slashed at a boat's tether and fell into it, his momentum pushing the vessel out on the water. The distance rapidly widened as Targas prepared to throw a scent net out to stop him.

"No!" A hand grabbed his arm. "This's mine!"

Targas stepped back as Cynth pushed past him and knelt on the boards of the jetty. She put her hand in the water, remaining in a crouch, and stared fixedly at the receding boat.

The boat had moved out into midstream, Septus cackling hysterically as he drifted away.

Cynth remained in her position, concentrating. Then Targas could see a faint grey emanation flowing down her arm into the water.

The current had taken the boat some distance and Septus was kneeling, his ravaged face lit by his successful escape. But the water bubbled and familiar pink coils looped around the boat. Septus screamed, stabbing at the haggars with his dagger.

His keening, high and shrill, echoed to the shore, as the onlookers saw the first of the haggars wriggle onboard. A seething mass of the worms followed, their sucker mouths covering Septus even as he struggled to free himself. His screams slowly died as if the very sound was being sucked away.

Cynth stood, wiped her hand on her dress and looked straight at Targas, eyes bright with tears. "That's for me Woll, that is. For me Woll, 'nd yer Luna."

Targas took the solid woman in his arms and held her as she sobbed. He felt others join in the outpouring of grief.

Even as he watched the boat, he saw a large cloud of odour rising into the air and floating towards them. He fancied he could see Septus's skeletal face as the fog dissipated above him. A chill ran down his spine and he had the strongest of feelings that the fight was not over. A cold darkness threatened to overwhelm his senses as the evil of the man wafted into his brain, seeking a toehold for itself, sending out tendrils of its own anger, growing within his mind.

He knew he had to get away, leave this place and its memories.

The return of Ean to a wiser, more benevolent rule could be entrusted to others. He, no doubt, had a part to play, but he needed to take Sadir back to her family—take *his* family back to their home—and take Luna's memory back to her village.

He walked over to Sadir, away from Lan and his army.

"Come," he said, holding his hand out to Sadir, "I've decided to go home, with you and Kyel. We've done our part."

Sadir smiled. "I agree. It's time to leave this behind."

Targas took Sadir's hand, trying hard to reject the cackle of laughter echoing faintly in his mind.